HOSTILE OPERATIONS TEAM®
★ STRIKE TEAM 2 ★

HOT Witness

HOT Angel

HOT Secrets

HOT Justice

HOT Storm

HOT Courage

HOT Shadows

HOT Limit

HOT Honor

HOSTILE OPERATIONS TEAM®
★ STRIKE TEAM 1 ★

RECKLESS HEAT, a prequel story to *HOT Pursuit*

HOT Pursuit

HOT Mess

Dangerously HOT

HOT Package

HOT Shot

HOT Rebel

HOT Ice

HOT & Bothered

HOT Protector

"**The perfect mix of action, intrigue, and romance is exactly why I fell in love with Lynn Raye Harris' military romance books** in the first place, and *Seth* definitely delivered."
—U.M.H., Goodreads on *Seth*

"Can I just say … **watching an emotionally unavailable clueless, stoic grump go soft for a woman is probably one of my favorite tropes.**"
—Cassy, Goodreads on *Seth*

"I mean, is anyone shocked that Lynn wrote **another banger of a book**? Because I'm not! I absolutely LOVED Kane's story."
—Katharina, Goodreads on *Kane*

"**If you crave a passionate, emotionally rich romance wrapped in suspense, *Kane* delivers.**"
—Viktoria, Amazon on *Kane*

"I absolutely loved Ethan and Paisley. **Their story and history was so heartbreaking and tragic and my heart hurt so much for them.**"
—Katharine, Goodreads on *Ethan*

"**A gripping, passionate story that burns with love, resilience, and redemption.**"
—BecReadReview, BookBub on *Ethan*

HOT Addiction

HOT Valor

A HOT Christmas Miracle

★ THE HOT SEAL TEAM ★

HOT SEAL

HOT SEAL Lover

HOT SEAL Rescue

HOT SEAL Bride

HOT SEAL Redemption

HOT SEAL Target

HOT SEAL Hero

HOT SEAL Devotion

Check out Lynn Raye Harris' Online Store at

https://shop.lynnrayeharris.com/

for autographed books, HOT themed merch, and more!

Dead to their pasts. Ghosts. No family ties. No connections.

Six men with a top-secret mission move to a small town where they have to navigate local life, protect their secret, and, above all, stay single.

Blaze "Shadow" Connolly
Chance "Wraith" Hughes
Seth "Phantom" King
Kane "Demon" Fox
Ethan "Dragon" Snow
Alex "Ghost" Bishop

ETHAN

Military Protector Hero

Second Chance Romance

Librarian Heroine Running from an Abusive Ex

Secret Baby

Forced Proximity

Found Family

Small Town Setting

ghost ops
book five
ETHAN
NEW YORK TIMES & USA TODAY BESTSELLING AUTHOR
LYNN RAYE HARRIS

FOREWORD

BY ETHAN "DRAGON" SNOW

Hey there, Hotties,

Chatting about books and stuff isn't really my deal. Nothin' against it, it's just more for people who belong to book clubs. Or frequent book stores. Or libraries. Yeah, it'd probably make more sense for a librarian to be handling this, but Ghost tossed the laptop into my hands with orders to "type, dumbass," before pushing me out of his office and—I'm pretty sure—punching his desk. Or maybe he's bouncing his head against it more forcefully these days? I'm really starting to worry about the man's blood pressure and relative skull density.

And ok, sure, maybe he has a right to be wound tight about the rest of the guys. They're my boys, but let's be honest. Blaze, Chance, Seth, and Kane all wandered into Sutton's Creek completely free and easy, and almost immediately fell for the women who entered their lives here. Regardless of orders or mission objectives or the vein on Ghost's forehead that's getting bigger by the day. That's on them. Both those choices and Ghost's steadily increasing eye twitch. But, you see, it's not like that with me. Not at all. I listened to the mission briefing. There was an absolute zero percent chance of me coming here and having my head or heart turned by some new pretty face. It's simply not something that could happen because my head and heart are on lockdown. Have been for about five years now. Been there, done that, never again. In fact, there's exactly one woman on this planet who has a prayer of getting to me, and that's only because she's the one who inspired me to remove myself from the relationship market to begin with. Yeah yeah, unfinished business, whatever. I'm *fine*. More importantly, the mission is fine. No other woman in the world can get to me in any way that's important. And what are the chances the one woman who can get to me would show up in the middle of Nowhere, Alabama, anyhow?

...

...

Apparently pretty damned high considering that she's shown up here, in the middle of Nowhere, Alabama! Waltzing into the Dawg with the other women, like she's part of their crew and it's a completely normal thing to do, knocking the wind out of a man on a random work night without even a hint of warning. Shocked doesn't begin to cover it. I'm tempted to ask Ghost if I can share his desk for head thumping purposes. So what if that's not a rational response? Nothing about me and Paisley has ever been rational. Not that there is a me and Paisley. There's a me, there's a Paisley, but no *and*. We are not an *us*. That ship sailed a long time ago, and she was the one doing the steering. Which is why it makes absolutely no sense that she looked at me like I betrayed her in some way. But it doesn't matter. Sutton's Creek may not be huge, but I'm sure we'll be able to avoid each other. Right? It's not like anything's going to change between us. I have my mission, and she has a kid. A kid who's almost 5...

You know what? I should probably wrap this up. I have some, um, things to think about. If you want to get my full story, keep reading.

I really hope I'm not the source of Ghost's next conniption fit.

Later Hotties,

Ethan

ETHAN

"Hey, you want to join us at the Salty Dawg for a drink?" Emma Grace Sutton asked.

Paisley studied the five expectant faces arrayed around the conference table in the library's meeting room. These women had been open and welcoming since she'd arrived to take over the librarian job in Sutton's Creek. She'd worried at one point that not being a local would be a hindrance, but she'd been wrong. Everyone she'd met was kind, which was something she desperately needed these days.

"It's okay if you're tired," Emma said. "You've only just moved to town and here we are keeping you in the library late for our book club meeting."

It was eight o'clock, and Paisley wasn't tired. Violet would be in bed by now under the watchful eye of Aunt Hettie, who used to be the town librarian until she'd retired recently. Once Violet was asleep, Paisley could carry her through the middle of town with a band playing a John Philip Sousa march and the kid wouldn't wake up.

Aunt Hettie insisted she was a night owl these days so that wasn't a problem either. Hettie had said to stay out as long as she liked when she'd dropped Violet off. Paisley hadn't intended to take her up on it, but maybe a little social time with new friends wouldn't hurt.

"I'd love to go," Paisley said. She wasn't a local, but Hettie really was her great-aunt. She'd moved to Sutton's Creek over sixty years ago when she'd married Horace Woods, God rest his soul. Paisley had been to visit precisely once, when she was five and her grandfather, Hettie's brother, was still alive.

The women gathered the casserole dishes they'd brought, put any leftovers into the fridge for Paisley and her staff, stuffed their books into tote bags, and tidied the room. Nikki Crowell, Callie's teenage sister, picked up the trash and wiped off the counters in the kitchenette.

Paisley's chest ached. These women seemed happy with their lives and comfortable in their friendship. She didn't know what that was like. She'd always been an extroverted introvert, capable of faking her way through parties or gatherings, but she was happiest buried in her books or playing with her daughter.

A current of fear snapped to life as she thought of Violet sleeping soundly across town. But Paisley had a restraining order and the courts knew where she was. She had not snatched Violet away in the dark like a thief. She'd done everything right, and Trey couldn't touch them here, at least not legally. He didn't even know where they were though he could probably figure it out if he wanted to.

That was one of the things about Trey McCann. He knew how to find people. He'd been a soldier in an elite unit before he'd gotten out of the military to start his own business, and he'd maintained ties to people who could get information for him. He'd demonstrated it more than once when she'd still been naive about his nature. She'd chatter excitedly about a new friend at work, or her new hairstylist. Anyone really. He'd dig up dirt on them, and then he'd make her quit seeing them because they were, quote, bad people for her to be around.

That was how he'd systematically cut her off from everyone she knew. How he isolated her and made her dependent on him. He'd kept her scared for the past four plus years until she'd finally had enough.

Until she'd realized that soon enough, it wouldn't be only her he'd abuse. It would be Violet, too.

"We ready?" Rory Harper asked as she stood by the door.

"I'm ready."

"Me too."

"Yup."

"Paisley?" Daphne Bryant asked. "Did we get everything?"

Paisley looked around the room. "Yes. We're good. Thank you all so much for this lovely potluck. I'm going to enjoy those leftovers tomorrow. Everyone will."

The ladies filed over to the library entrance, Paisley checked the locks on the rear and side doors, and then flipped off the lights as she stepped outside to join the women on the sidewalk.

The Sutton's Creek library was small, but the town supported their library. They elected city council members who went to bat for it with the county. There was also a private endowment from the Sutton family that helped buy new materials and fund programs. In short, the library was thriving and she felt lucky to have been selected for the position. It was precisely the new start she and Violet needed.

The walk to the Salty Dawg Tavern, otherwise known as the Dawg to locals, was only a couple of blocks. It wasn't quite dark yet, though the sun had set behind the horizon. Sutton's Creek was quiet, a beautiful Southern town with just enough old buildings and quaint charm to make it a tourist destination in the warmer months.

And the cooler ones too since there was a Christmas tour of homes in the historic district that included carriage rides and warm mulled cider, though people told her it was just as likely to be warm enough for a light jacket in December as it was cold enough for a hot drink. But it wasn't going to be South Alabama or Florida hot, so she couldn't wait to experience the holidays in Sutton's Creek.

The lanterns in the park were adorned with American flags since Independence Day was next week. There was going to be a big festival in town with food and crafts and fireworks at the end of the evening. Violet kept asking if the fireworks were happening today and Paisley had to tell her it was still a few days away. Violet was excited because the children she played with kept talking about it. Paisley had promised to take her downtown for the festivities, and she was looking forward to it almost as much as Violet.

The women laughed and talked about plans for the weekend as they walked. Paisley was quiet, taking it all in. She'd worn a black dress today that she knew looked good on her, to give her a confidence boost for the book club meeting she'd been invited to, and she felt pretty. Her hand snaked to her nape, missing the long hair she'd had until recently. She'd chopped it all off, getting a short style that was more masculine than anything she'd ever had before. She'd cried after she'd done it, but she'd been determined to make a drastic change in the hopes she'd feel different inside.

Violet had blinked at her, patted her head, and told her she looked pretty. That'd only made her want to cry harder, but she'd kept her tears until she was alone so she didn't scare her daughter into thinking anything was wrong. There'd already been so many changes in her kid's life at that point.

Rory led them up the front steps and into the Dawg. Paisley's heart raced at the sight of so many people, but she focused on breathing deep and slow to keep from having a panic attack. Something she'd never had in her life until she'd met Trey.

Townspeople waved at the women. One of the waitresses came over and high-fived Nikki as they called each other sis.

"We call them Big Nikki and Little Nikki," Callie said, leaning toward her. "They've bonded over their shared name."

Paisley smiled and nodded. "Got it. I didn't remember you mentioning another sister."

"Technically, no," Callie said with a smile. Her gaze slid over the other women in the Bookalicious Besties Book Club, a name Paisley officially loved. "But I'm learning that sisters aren't just born. They can also be made."

Paisley didn't know what that was like. She'd been painfully shy growing up and didn't have a big friend group because her mother was constantly moving them around from place to place. Paisley had long ago lost touch with the few girlfriends she'd had as a teenager.

She followed as the women headed toward a table of big, brawny looking men. She knew these men owned One Shot Tactical, the gun range and training facility just outside of town. She'd heard them talked about in the library and the Piggly Wiggly, and she might have seen one or two of them from a distance, but she'd never met them.

Six men looked up as the women approached. Paisley dropped her gaze, her heart beating a little faster. They were former military, like Trey, and that made her more nervous than it should. Not all military men got off on intimidating anyone weaker than they were.

In fact, there'd been a military man once who she'd thought might be The One. Until he left town suddenly for a mission overseas and didn't bother to tell her good-bye. He'd sent Trey to let her down easy. She'd never heard from him again.

"This is Paisley," Emma said after a few moments. "She's the new librarian."

Paisley lifted her head and pasted on a smile. "Hi," she said, waving like she was the friendliest person on the planet.

Six handsome faces stared back at her. She let her gaze slide quickly over them. Her throat squeezed tight, her heart battering her ribs as sudden shock filled her. She forced her gaze past the man staring back at her so intently.

But she wasn't mistaken. It was him.

Ethan Snow. The man she'd thought about almost every day for the past five years.

The room narrowed to just the two of them. She couldn't speak, couldn't breathe.

And then, as if someone had thumped her on the back, her heart kickstarted again. The men said hello, but she could only feel one man's hot stare boring into her. That golden hazel gaze that'd haunted her dreams for so long was the same, though instead of the laughter she remembered filling it before, it was now cold and hard—and stunned.

She'd known him for a month before they spent the weekend together, but she'd thought—

She dug her fingernails into her palms, welcoming the bite of pain. It didn't matter what she'd thought. He'd left. He'd told her she was special, that he wanted to keep seeing her because he felt something for her, but it'd been a lie.

When his orders came down, he'd sent Trey to tell her he'd had fun but it had to be over. Trey, who'd been so kind and sympathetic. Who'd systematically wormed his way into her life and promised to love her forever.

She'd been stupid enough to believe him once it was clear Ethan was never coming back.

Paisley lifted her chin a fraction, watching Ethan in her peripheral vision. He still watched her in shocked silence.

She didn't know what to say, but she knew she couldn't acknowledge him. Not here. Not like this. He'd left her behind, abandoned her after all his talk of wanting to see where the future took them, and her life had changed for the worse.

She wanted to hate him, but her heart refused.

Ethan scraped to his feet, the chair scratching across the wood floor, the sound jarring deep in her soul.

He dropped money on the table. "Gotta get going, guys. I've got a couple of things I need to get done. See you tomorrow."

He strode toward the back of the building, disappearing into the darkened hallway that led to the bathrooms and the back door. She wanted to follow him, to ask him why she hadn't been enough. Why he'd lied.

But she was frozen in place, aching inside, willing him to return and apologize for everything.

He didn't, though. He stayed gone.

Just like before.

Ethan didn't know where he was going when he peeled out of the parking lot. All he knew was that he needed to escape. It'd taken him a second longer to recognize her than it should have because her hair was chopped off, but when she'd finally lifted her head to look at everyone, he'd known that what he'd felt in his gut wasn't wrong.

Paisley Allen was there in the Dawg with Daphne, Callie, Emma, and Rory, waving shyly. Flashing the heart tattoo on her wrist. He wore its twin under his left pec. Nobody really noticed it these days because of all the other ink he wore, but he knew it was there. He reached up to rub the spot, but the ache didn't go away. He knew from hard experience that it wouldn't.

Emma said she was the new librarian, but all Ethan had felt was the rushing in his ears as he stared at the woman in the black dress with the freakishly short hair.

Not that she didn't look amazing with short hair. If anything, she looked even more beautiful than she had five years ago.

He'd needed to escape. Needed to get out of there

before he made an ass of himself by demanding to know what the actual fuck?

He rolled down the driver's window, let the night air fill the truck's cabin as he drove without a destination. He left Sutton's Creek behind, headed down dark roads with thousands of lightning bugs glowing in the trees and fields. It was a sight that never ceased to amaze, and yet his soul remained troubled.

Paisley Rose Allen. The last time he'd seen her, she'd had long hair and the kind of smile that made people stop and look. He'd been on temporary assignment to the Special Forces Group A at Eglin Air Force Base, training with Army Green Berets for guerrilla operations in Afghanistan.

He could remember Paisley walking into the beach bar in Destin where he'd been kicking back with some of his guys, remember the way they'd all stopped talking to watch her. He'd fantasized about her ass, about her legs wrapping around his waist, and then she'd gone behind the bar, put an apron over her shorts, grabbed a tray, and headed their way.

That was the beginning.

For a solid week, he'd gone to that bar to talk to her. Yeah, he'd wanted to fuck her, but he'd wanted to know her even more. There'd been something that drew him to her even more than her spectacular ass and gorgeous eyes.

He'd learned she was from Fairhope, Alabama, that she was twenty-six and working to pay her college loans.

She also worked in a library part-time and hoped to get a full-time librarian job someday.

She was shy, sweet, and she made all his protective instincts flare in ways that surprised him. She was special, and he'd wanted more of her company. More of her. He'd asked her out. She'd said yes. He'd taken her to the beach, to restaurants, to coffee shops, to places where they sat and talked the hours away when they could. He hadn't been in a hurry to get her into his bed. He'd sensed she wasn't the kind of girl to be rushed.

Over the course of a month, he'd fallen for her. And then came the weekend they finally got naked together.

One hot, sexy, amazing weekend where he'd mapped her body's pleasure zones and made her come again and again. He'd been obsessed with her happiness, with having her wrapped around him, moaning her pleasure, begging for more, screaming his name. He'd loved every moment, and he'd known he wanted to be with her forever.

He'd never felt that way about anyone. Ever.

They'd gotten the damned tattoos in a little studio by the beach. He'd wanted something bigger, but she'd loved the heart she picked out and wanted him to have one just like it. So he'd complied, holding her hand and gazing in her eyes while the artist worked.

Like a lovesick fucking fool.

The next week, he was unexpectedly called back to HOT HQ and a mission overseas. It happened so fast he'd had no time to make contact with her, to explain. Instead, he'd asked a work buddy to tell her he had to leave and he'd be in touch as soon as he could. He'd gotten on the plane with an ache in his heart that he hadn't told her he'd fallen in love with her, but that wasn't the kind of thing you had a buddy say for you.

By the time he'd been able to call her a month later, it went to voicemail over and over again. Finally, she'd replied with a text that was still seared into his brain.

I like you, Ethan, but I've met somebody else. Please don't contact me again.

Yeah, that'd fucking hurt. No, it'd *shattered* him.

He'd never felt the things for a woman he'd felt for her, but clearly he'd been the only one.

And now she was here, in his space, in this little Southern town far from the coast.

Fucking hell.

Not that he cared about her anymore. It'd taken time and a lot of painful reflection, but he'd moved on. Didn't give two shits about her now. He'd simply been stunned to see her. Rather than say a bunch of shit nobody needed to hear, he'd chosen to remove himself from the situation. Get his thoughts under control.

Which he had. Paisley Allen wouldn't get under his skin ever again. He was fucking immune.

With that shit sorted, he turned toward home. She lived in Sutton's Creek, and she'd be at the library. Knowing his team's women the way he did, they were going to pull her into the circle because she was new to town and didn't know anyone.

Though maybe she had a husband at home waiting for her. The *somebody else* she'd found.

Ethan's gut twisted hard. He forced the feeling away.

Nah, he didn't fucking care. Whether or not the women brought her into the circle didn't matter. He'd be the politest asshole anybody'd ever seen. And if she didn't bring up the past, he damn sure wasn't going to.

Paisley was nothing to him. Not anymore.

2

"Mommy, can I get an ice cream?"

Paisley looked at her daughter skipping along beside her as they walked toward the town square and the vendor booths. It was July fourth, hotter than the surface of the sun, but that hadn't stopped the Sutton's Creek Independence Day Festival from taking place. For one thing, they'd shifted most of the activities to late afternoon and the humidity wasn't as bad as it'd been just last week. For another, they'd set up water stations along Main Street and around the square to give water to anyone who wanted it. The parade would happen after six, when temps weren't quite fry-an-egg-on-the-pavement hot anymore.

"Sure, Vivi. What kind do you want?"

"I want one of dem rocket things."

"A rocket pop? Red, white, and blue?"

"Yes! Can I have a hotdog, too?"

Paisley managed not to snort, but only barely. "A hot dog, hmm?" She'd tried to feed Violet lunch, but the little girl was vibrating with energy and only managed to eat a few apple slices and a stick of string cheese. Paisley had offered hotdogs at home, but Violet hadn't wanted one.

Now she knew why.

"You can, but not both at the same time. How about the hotdog first and then we'll get the ice cream in a little while. You don't want to be too full to play in the fountain, do you?"

"Noooo," Violet said, shaking her head vigorously.

"Okay, so let's get the hotdog and then we'll go to the park."

Paisley led her daughter over to the food truck selling hotdogs, ordered two with mustard and relish, and got two icy cold bottles of water. Then she ushered Violet over to the shade of a tree and they dug into the juicy hotdogs while sitting on the grass and watching people enjoy the park and the booths.

Her gaze slipped over to the Salty Dawg. Sure enough, Rory, Emma, and Callie were sitting in chairs on the sidewalk in front of the restaurant with their boyfriends. All three women were dating men from One Shot Tactical, though apparently Daphne was now officially dating Kane as of this week. That made four.

And there they were walking toward the group stationed in front of the Dawg, Kane wearing a red, white, and blue cowboy hat and star-shaped sunglasses while Daphne looked beautiful in white shorts with a blue cropped top and a straw hat. They reached the group and took two of the chairs, scooting close to each other and looking like two people in love as they leaned close and laughed about something between them.

Ethan appeared in the doorway of the Dawg and walked down the steps. Paisley's heart skipped. He was wearing cargo shorts and a white T-shirt that had the Salty Dawg's logo on it. He was tanned, muscled, and beautiful. Especially when he smiled, which he did when somebody said something to him. He waved at his shirt with a flourish and Rory got up and hugged him before turning to say something to Chance with her hands on her hips. Then she sat down again and Chance kissed her.

Paisley tried not to be envious, but it was hard. The women were so nice. Rory stopped by the library recently and told her she was officially in the book club, and though Paisley wanted to join them, she was scared too. She didn't say no because the words got stuck as she thought about it so she'd said yes instead. But if it meant spending any time with them as a coed group, she'd have to find a way out. She didn't want to be in the same room with Ethan, wondering why she hadn't been enough for him. Why he'd left without a conversation instead of sending Trey to do his dirty work.

Maybe she'd have taken it better if he'd told her himself. And maybe she wouldn't have been vulnerable to Trey's manipulation if he hadn't been the one giving her news she should have gotten from Ethan.

She couldn't blame him for ending up with Trey. It'd

been her choice to let Trey in, to believe his lies even when there'd been red flags from the start.

"I'm ready, Mama!" Violet said as she jumped to her feet, the hotdog wrapper forgotten on the ground.

"I'm not," Paisley said. "I still have to finish my hotdog. And you need to pick up your trash, young lady."

"Sorry," Violet said, scooping the wrapper up and balling it in her hands with exaggerated motions.

Paisley finished her hotdog and balled her wrapper too. "Okay, can I trust you to walk right over to that can and throw the trash out?"

"Yes!"

Paisley watched her daughter skip to the trash can a short distance away. Out of habit her gaze roved the surrounding area as she looked for a familiar figure. Trey was shorter than Ethan, but he had the body of a man who'd once been a military weapon. Like Ethan. Like the One Shot Tactical men.

She had the restraining order, but that didn't stop her from worrying. It was ultimately just a piece of paper, and she knew what happened to women who thought they were safe because of a court order.

What would happen to her if she wasn't vigilant. The last time she'd been in the same room with Trey, he'd told her she would never be free, that he'd kill her before he let her go.

Paisley shivered despite the heat. What was the alternative though? Stay and let him keep hurting her? Let him hurt Violet? No, she'd done what she had to do. There was no other choice.

Violet tossed the trash and came skipping back as if she hadn't a care in the world. Which was exactly how Paisley wanted it. "Can we play in the fountain now? Peas?"

"Please," Paisley stressed.

"Please," Violet repeated.

Paisley held out her hand and Violet took it. "Yes, we can play in the fountain."

"Yay!"

They walked over to the fountain that gushed with clear, bright water. Kids played in the water, splashing and laughing. People often tossed coins in, but the coins had been gathered up by the city so children and adults could play today and keep cool. The fountain wasn't deep and it was chlorinated. There was also a series of jets that went off at intervals and soaked anyone standing in the fountain.

But that was part of the fun. The town was currently in the process of installing a splash pad nearby, but that wasn't due to be finished for another month.

Paisley had worn a breezy summer dress with a ball cap that said *Reading is my Superpower,* and she'd put Violet in shorts and a tank top that could get wet. She'd also rubbed sunscreen over both of them, and she had the bottle in her bag for reapplication if necessary.

"Okay, Vivi, need you to listen to Mommy."

Her daughter's face was bright and earnest. "Yes, ma'am."

"You can splash in the fountain. You may not lie down and put your head under water. No running or jumping. This isn't like a swimming pool, okay?"

"Yes, ma'am."

"Now kick your sandals off and I'll help you get in."

Paisley held her hand while Violet stepped onto the ledge and then down into the water. "Are you getting in, Mommy?"

Paisley set her bag on the ledge and turned so her feet were in the fountain. Other adults were doing the same. "I'll be right here, baby."

She sat back and watched while Violet found a group of kids to play with. Somebody shouted her name and she turned to find Callie Crowell waving at her. Daphne, Emma, and Rory joined in, waving her over to join them. She let her gaze slide to Ethan. Sunglasses hid his eyes, but she'd swear he was looking right at her. Or maybe it was just her imagination.

She waved back and shook her head apologetically, pointing at her watch as if time was an issue. It wasn't, and she felt like a fool, but there was no way she wanted to gather her child and go join the group. She didn't want Violet and Ethan in the same space if she could help it. It would hurt too much to think about what might have been if he hadn't left.

"Hey there, pretty lady."

Paisley jerked at the sound of the voice beside her. She had to look up, shielding her eyes, to see the man who stood too near for comfort.

"Can I help you?"

He wore a Rocket City Trash Pandas ball cap, a tank top, cargo shorts, and he was holding a plastic cup filled with beer. The downtown area had been designated an entertainment district, and that allowed people to walk around with their alcoholic beverages. This guy had clearly had a few because he swayed the slightest bit as he loomed over her.

"Yeah, you can help me."

She didn't like the way he leered at her. She felt at a distinct disadvantage sitting on the edge of the fountain while he stood over her, but she wasn't going to give him the satisfaction of standing up and moving away. Yet.

"I'm sorry, but I'm here with my daughter. My—" She couldn't say husband because it felt icky when she was in the process of divorcing him, so she went with the next best thing she could think of. "My boyfriend went to get us some ice cream. He'll be back any minute."

The man frowned. "Been watching you since you walked into the park. Didn't see a boyfriend."

Paisley's heart squeezed. This time she got to her feet because she felt the need for escape. Why did men think it was flattering to say they'd been watching her? Or to get up in her space and expect her to be happy about it? She wanted to tell him to back the fuck off, but Violet was nearby. Not to mention she was still new in town and she didn't know if he was a local or one of the tourists that had come for the day's festivities.

"Just because you didn't see him doesn't mean he isn't coming," she grated. She hated that she felt obligated to explain, but the alternative was angering him when she told him it was none of his business. If she'd learned anything in the past few years, it was not to make men angry.

The man took another step closer, until her face was practically in his chest. With the ledge behind her, she had nowhere to go. Panic unfurled in her sternum as she started thinking of how to defuse the situation.

"Aw, come on, honey. You don't have to lie. I'm not gonna hurt you. Just want to get to know you."

Paisley lifted her hands to push him away. He was gone before she could make contact. Just simply not there anymore.

She stared at the space he'd occupied, and then at the big man who had her tormenter by the back of his T-shirt and the waistband of his shorts, hustling him in the other direction. She didn't hear what Ethan said, but he let go with a shove. The man stumbled and fell onto the grass, his beer flying from the cup. Then he scrambled up and stumbled away without a backward glance.

Paisley was frozen in place as Ethan stalked over to her, tall and lethal and so gorgeous he made her throat ache with unshed tears. Still handsome. Still magnetic. Still the man who'd broken her heart.

"You okay?"

"I...um...yes. Thank you."

"You're shaking."

Well, damn. She'd thought it was only on the inside. "Am I? It'll stop soon. I-I didn't want to make a scene in front of Violet."

She glanced at her daughter who'd stopped splashing to watch her mother warily. If she'd seen the altercation with the man, Paisley didn't know. But she saw Ethan now and the look on his face was thunderous. Paisley smiled at Violet to let her know it was okay.

"To hell with a scene. Man gets up in your face like that, you need to make him back the fuck up."

"And how should I do that, huh? Look at me. I'm a lot smaller than he is. And we're in public. He wasn't going to do anything."

She didn't know that, not really, but she hoped it was true. Being in public hadn't always protected her from Trey's rages. He might not slap her around in a restaurant, but he could dig his fingers into her arms or thighs until she wanted to cry out in pain. And then he could slap her when they got home.

Or worse.

Paisley wrapped her arms around herself, instinctively trying to make herself smaller. Ethan's gaze narrowed.

"First, you don't know that he wouldn't have escalated. He's drunk and horny and you're pretty and convenient. Second, you have the ability to take down any man you want if you know where to aim. And no, I'm not just talking about a knee to the groin."

"Mommy?" Violet called, a note of fear in her voice.

Paisley forced the smile back onto her face as she turned to her child. "It's okay, baby. Mr. Snow is a friend. Could you please smile?" she said to Ethan, her voice pitched too low for Violet to hear. "And maybe take off the sunglasses for a sec."

She didn't know if he would do as she asked, but a moment later he slid his glasses up his face to perch on his head. Stormy hazel eyes met hers. Then he smiled, and her heart legit skipped a beat. That smile had once meant everything to her. When she'd been young and stupid and convinced you could fall in love in an instant.

She had a memory of hot skin, kisses so deep they stole your soul, and happiness that she'd thought would never end. She'd been wrong.

"So you do know me," he growled through his teeth.

Her skin grew hot. "Never said I didn't. I was surprised to see you before. And you didn't say anything, so I didn't either."

He scratched the back of his neck. "Honestly, I'd prefer you hadn't shown up in Sutton's Creek, but you're here and I'm here and we gotta deal with it. Though maybe we don't tell anyone we met before, huh?"

"If that's what you want." It stung to hear him say what she'd been thinking.

"Up to you, but I think it'd be easier, don't you?"

"Probably. I'd rather people didn't know how dumb I was or that you dumped me almost immediately after you got what you wanted."

Well, crap. She hadn't ever wanted to let him know how much he'd hurt her, but she'd held onto the pain for so long that it slipped out the first chance she got.

Brilliant move, Paisley.

His eyes widened. "Seriously? That's what you're going with? I dumped you?"

Her heart throbbed. "Smile, please." Because he suddenly looked furious. It confused her and rattled her at the same time.

"I am fucking smiling. I called you, Paisley. Repeatedly. You never answered. Then you sent me a text and said you'd found someone else."

Her insides turned to ice. "I didn't." She had to work to force the words out. "That's not true."

But it was the sort of thing Trey would have done. Assuming Ethan was telling the truth. She didn't know why he wouldn't, but she'd given up trying to figure out other people's motives.

He snorted. "Okay, fine. Rewrite the situation to suit yourself. Doesn't matter fuck all to me." He jerked his head toward the group on the sidewalk. "I know they've added you to their book club. They like you. If you're staying away because of me, don't bother. I'll be polite, and I won't bring up the past. Far as I'm concerned, you're a stranger I just met."

Her heart bled likc it'd been ripped out and stomped on all over again. Either Trey had lied from the beginning or Ethan was just as big a liar as he was, revising their history for his own reasons and making her feel like crap in the process. Maybe he didn't trust her not to tell his friends they had a history and he wanted to get in front of it with an alternative that didn't make him into an asshole.

"Mommy?"

Paisley sucked in a breath and turned to her daughter. Violet stood by the ledge just inside the fountain. She was wet, her hair dripping, and she looked concerned despite Paisley's best efforts to smile and make Ethan do so too.

"What is it, honey?"

Violet cut her gaze toward Ethan. He looked back at the little girl, and Paisley's heart thumped hard. She'd always wondered if Ethan was Violet's father rather than Trey. She'd been with Ethan first.

Trey had been a drunken mistake when she was grieving losing Ethan. After that first time, she hadn't slept with him again for weeks. By then she'd known she was pregnant, but not whose baby she was carrying. Trey had sworn it didn't matter, that he'd take care of them both.

She studied her daughter and the man looking back at her. Violet had blonde hair, which neither Trey or Ethan had, and hazel eyes that were remarkably like Ethan's now that she was seeing them again. But Trey had brown eyes and she had blue which meant they could produce a hazel-eyed child. Eye color wasn't enough to determine paternity.

And right now, she didn't want Ethan to be Violet's father. She'd been through hell to get temporary custody from Trey, and she didn't want to have to fight another man if he decided to cause trouble.

"Um..." Violet's eyes were big as she stared up at Ethan. She rolled her lips in and pulled at the bottom of her shirt. Paisley's heart ached. Trey hadn't always hidden his violence. There were times when he yelled and stomped and hit, and Paisley knew that Violet could hear it from her room. She'd always told her daughter she was fine, but it wasn't always true.

Ethan dropped to a knee and held out a hand. "Hi, I'm Ethan."

"It's okay, baby. Mr. Ethan is a friend of Mommy's new friends at the library, so that makes him a friend of ours too."

Violet put her little hand into Ethan's, and Paisley had to bite her lip not to whimper at her daughter's sweet bravery.

"You looked mad. My daddy looked mad sometimes and then he was mean."

Ethan shook his head and kept the smile on his face, though she saw the way he stiffened at that little bit of oversharing. "I'm not mad. And I'm never mean, promise."

Violet stared warily. "You won't hit Mommy, will you?"

"Vivi!" Paisley cried. "Don't say things like that." Heat crawled over her skin. If the ground cracked and swallowed her up, it'd be a relief. Ethan didn't look at her, thank God.

"I would never do that, Violet. No matter how mad I was, I wouldn't hit her. Or you."

"Okay," Violet said, dropping her gaze.

Paisley's heart hammered. "Baby, go play for a little bit longer and we'll get that ice cream, okay? Mr. Ethan and Mommy are talking about library books."

"You should read *Where The Wild Things Are*," Violet said very seriously. "Five stars." Then she grinned and went to join a game of catch with other children who were throwing a beachball around.

"Sorry about that," Paisley said past the tightness in her throat. A glance at the people nearby told her that nobody was side-eyeing them, so maybe they hadn't been listening. She hoped not. And she really needed to talk to Violet about the things she said to random people she'd just met.

Ethan was on his feet, towering over her. He made sure not to stand too close, not to loom, and he somehow managed to look relaxed when she knew he was anything but.

"What the fuck, Paisley? You aren't still with this guy, are you?"

"No, I'm not. He's in Destin. We're getting a divorce."

It seemed surreal that he didn't know she'd married Trey. But then, according to Trey, they weren't close. They'd worked together in DC and then hung out when Ethan was at Eglin on temporary duty, but that was it.

He huffed a breath. "How long were you married?"

She didn't want to answer him but she couldn't think of a good reason not to. "Four and a half years. And before you say anything, I didn't know he was like that when I married him. The violence came after."

He was frowning again. "Is he still a threat? Are you safe here?"

"He doesn't know where we are. The court does, but he doesn't. You know, I really don't want to discuss this with you." She waved a hand around. "I was in a bad marriage, I left, I'm here and he's not. Violet and I are healing, or trying to. And no, he never hit her, though I'm sure it was coming soon. She's four and she's getting sassy, like kids do. But she clearly has some trauma, much to my shame, and I'll never forgive myself for it. There, I'm done," she said, folding her arms around herself. "Thank you for getting rid of that guy. I appreciate it."

He was studying her in that way he had. The way that said he could strip back all the layers and get her to tell him anything if he tried hard enough. She knew because she'd done it before. When she was still naïve and hopeful.

Well, not again. She was older, wiser, and life had taught her a few things. "Don't let me keep you from your friends."

"You aren't keeping me. Shit," he muttered so low she almost didn't hear it. "Look, there are a lot of tourists in town today, a lot of guys, and they're drinking. Come over and sit with us in front of the Dawg. It's prime real estate for the parade and the fireworks later. The women will be happy and y'all can talk books. And I won't have to rip some guy's head off for bothering you."

She stared at the mountain of a man in front of her. "Did you just say *y'all?* I thought you were from Brooklyn."

He looked adorably sheepish in that moment. "Yeah, they're corrupting me in the south. Besides, I like y'all better than youse."

She wanted to accept, but that desire was reason enough not to. She didn't need to be near Ethan Snow any more than necessary. "Thanks, really, but it's not your responsibility to watch out for me. I'll be okay."

"You willing to take that chance with your daughter here?"

She ground her teeth. She wanted to tell him she'd been taking care of her and Violet for the last couple of months, but she hadn't been equipped to deal with a drunk, aggressive man and she knew it. She could have kicked him in the balls, but Violet would have had to witness her fighting with a strange man and that wasn't going to work for either of their long-term mental health.

Accepting a safe place to take Violet for the festivities was the wise thing to do. If she'd known how crowded the town square would be, she might have chosen another activity. But Violet had wanted to go so badly, and Paisley wasn't yet comfortable letting her go with anyone else. The neighbor had offered to take her along with her kids, but Paisley's gut feeling wouldn't allow it.

"Fine, I'll join you. But first Violet is going to play in the fountain. Then I'm getting her a rocket pop because I promised."

"Fair enough. I'll wait with you."

"No," she said in a rush. "I don't want you to do that. Just go back to your friends and we'll be along soon."

Because hanging out with Ethan and trying to make small talk—or, worse, ignoring each other awkwardly—was too uncomfortable to imagine.

He plopped down on the edge of the fountain and took out his phone. "Nope, staying here, Payz. We don't have to talk, but I'm not leaving until you're done."

Dammit.

She stared down at him with his head bent to his phone, scrolling and ignoring her, and wanted to ask him where the fuck he'd been when she really needed him. He said he'd called her, but she'd never gotten a single call. Never had any missed calls or messages either. How could Trey have intercepted them all? Surely one would have got through.

Paisley couldn't sit with him, not with her emotions boiling like this. She moved a few feet away and thumped down to watch Violet, her mind whirling with too many thoughts about what might have been. *If only* wasn't in her vocabulary anymore.

Because it didn't help a thing. Worse, it hurt.

That was the thing about dwelling on the past. All it did was create chaos and regret. It didn't fix anything about her life and how far off the rails it'd gone.

That task was up to her. She was an island, solely responsible for her own happiness and that of her child's.

Nobody else mattered. Nobody else cared. It was her and Violet against the world.

She wouldn't forget that ever again.

3

Ethan pretended to look at his phone, but nothing was as interesting as Paisley. She sat a few feet away, laughing at something her kid did, and he tried not to let that voice dig deep into his soul and excavate memories he'd rather forget.

He hadn't known she had a kid until Emma said something about it at the Dawg a few nights ago when Paisley was at the bar picking up food. He'd been more stunned by the news than he'd liked.

Paisley had a kid. A four year old kid. Which meant she'd met and married her husband shortly after he'd left Florida. She said she hadn't sent him that text message, but she'd sure as fuck married somebody and had a kid with him. And pretty damn quickly, too.

Except she'd seemed genuinely shocked when he mentioned the text. Her eyes had gotten big, her mouth falling open like she hadn't expected him to say it.

He ground his teeth and looked away, keeping an eye on the crowd in the square. Paisley had been naïve in many ways when he met her, but no way she hadn't changed since then. Especially with a husband who'd hit her.

Jesus.

He'd been trying to process that since the instant her kid let the cat out of the bag. That sweet child had looked up at him with wide eyes, fear written on her face, and asked if he was going to hit her mommy. In that moment, it was him who felt like he'd been punched in the gut. He wanted to hunt the motherfucker down and give him a thousand times worse than what he'd done to Paisley.

Not that Ethan knew what the man had done, but if the kid was scared of her own father, then it hadn't been pretty.

He'd been torturing himself with thoughts about it since the moment he'd sat down to wait. She'd been married, the fucker abused her, badly enough that she'd been allowed to take their kid and leave the state without him knowing where they were.

Ethan wasn't stupid. He'd been in the business of dealing with evil people long enough that he knew the abuse had to be life-threatening. There was probably a restraining order too.

Yeah, he'd been pissed that Paisley hadn't waited for him to return from his mission, that she hadn't answered his calls, but if he'd had any idea she'd met a man who abused her, he'd have charged down to Florida and ripped the guy's head off for daring to harm her.

He closed his eyes and willed his temper to cool down. He was jumpy, pissed, his skin tight with anger. He felt like all it would take was a pinprick and he'd explode like an overfilled balloon.

He wasn't used to being this angry. He was methodical, cool, a planner to his core. He was the practical one on his team, the one who cut through all the distraction and saw the way to the goal. His guys knew they could name the objective, talk about the obstacles, and leave the details about how to get there to him.

He couldn't see how to get back to the calm center of his being in this moment. Not with Paisley so near, and not with this knowledge about her boiling inside him.

Out of the corner of his eye, he saw her hold out a hand to help her daughter onto the ledge. She produced a towel from her oversized bag and wrapped it around the little girl, rubbing her briskly before taking her hand and letting her jump down with the towel still wrapped around her. The kid slipped into her sandals and Paisley led her over to where he sat. He looked up like he hadn't noticed her presence until that moment. But the truth was he could feel an invisible line pulling between them with every breath he took. Anchoring him to her.

"We're going for ice cream if you want to come with us. Or we'll join you when we're done."

He unfolded himself and got to his feet as casually as possible. "Ice cream sounds good."

Paisley's mouth tightened as if she wanted to argue, but she turned on her heel and walked away with her daughter bouncing along beside her. Paisley's dress was loose, a floaty flowery thing that went to mid-thigh. Her legs were slender and long for someone so short, and he remembered what it'd felt like to run his palm along her calf, up her thigh, cupping her ass as he sank into her. Her skin was soft, smooth, her body welcoming and wet.

He shook the memory away like peeling off a layer of old paint from a wall before he coated it with something fresh and new. One of his hobbies since moving to Sutton's Creek was restoring old homes in his spare time. Diego Hernandez had let him work with his crew whenever Ethan had the time, and now he was helping out at a renovation in the historic district whenever he could.

It kept his mind occupied, kept him from thinking about the kinds of things that cropped up in his head more often of late. Leaving active ops to move to Sutton's Creek with his team had been a big change in his life, one he hadn't anticipated giving him so much down time. So much of a *regular* life to fill compared to the tempo of frequent missions.

The mission in Alabama might be the most important one of his career, but the pace was a lot slower. As the Athena Project lumbered toward completion, and enemy agents lay in wait to sabotage progress, maybe the pace would ramp up. Until then, he needed to be busy. Hence the construction projects.

The ice cream tent was in front of the town hall. The

entire square had been blocked off from traffic so that people could walk through the streets adjacent to the park, and vendors had set up their tents along the streets where the parade wasn't going to pass. Wendy Cochran's Kiss My Grits Café had a tent with pastries and ice cream, and that's where Paisley led Violet.

Paisley ordered a scoop of ice cream in a cup and a rocket pop, which Violet attacked like a hungry lion that'd just been thrown a steak. After she paid, she stepped to the side to wait for her ice cream while Ethan ordered his own rocket pop. Not technically ice cream, but delicious and refreshing on a hot day.

"You like the rocket pop too?" Violet asked, staring at him with wide eyes.

He peeled off the paper and licked it. "Yup. Pretty much my favorite cold treat on a hot day."

"Me too. Mommy says it's too sweet."

Paisley accepted her ice cream and turned a frown on him. "It's very sweet," she acknowledged. "But I prefer vanilla."

"Ours is better," Ethan said. "Right, kiddo?"

"Yep!"

Paisley looked like she wanted to say something, but she didn't. They continued to walk down the street, eating their ice cream and ambling toward the Dawg.

"How did you end up in Sutton's Creek?" he asked.

She slanted a look at him. Violet was in front of them, humming to herself as she ate her treat. "I might ask the same of you. Seems an odd place for a special operator."

She knew what he was because he'd been at Eglin to train, but she didn't know about the Hostile Operations Team. She'd thought he was a Green Beret, and he'd let her believe it because he had to.

"Not really. There's a Green Beret platoon in Birmingham. National Guard soldiers, but important for South American operations. There's also Redstone Arsenal. But I'm no longer active duty. Moved here with my buddies to start the range and training facility."

"You aren't old enough to be retired."

Of course she knew enough about the military to know that twenty years was the magic number.

"That's true, but sometimes the military offers early retirement as an incentive. I took it when it came down from command." He sucked on the syrupy goodness of the cold ice. "Now what about you? How did you get from Destin to Sutton's Creek?"

She spooned ice cream into her mouth and kept her eyes on her child. "My grandfather was Miss Hettie's brother. She moved here when she got married, and she became the town librarian. When she decided to retire, she told me to apply for the job. It took a few weeks, but the committee selected me. And here I am."

It was crazy how they'd both ended up in the same small town in a tiny corner of Alabama, but that was life for you. It was random and unpredictable. He knew it better than most. Not only because of what he did, but because of the childhood he'd had. When you didn't have a place to call home, when your bed could be on the streets or in a shelter, when you never knew where you'd lay your head each night—well, that was about as random and unpredictable as you could get. Especially when you were eight and didn't understand why other kids had homes and you didn't.

"You cut all your hair off." He didn't know why he said it except he needed to get his mind on something else.

She didn't speak for a long moment. "Yes. It's cooler and easier to manage. And I like it. I don't care what anyone else thinks."

"Looks good on you."

"Thank you."

Emma and Callie spotted them and waved. Ethan tamped down on the disappointment that their walk was nearly over. He looked for an empty chair away from where Paisley and Violet would be, but of course the women had put three chairs together. Now that Daphne and Kane were paired up, that left Ethan and Alex as the only singles in the group. Nobody would dare try to fix Ghost up with a woman, but they had no such qualms about him. He was fair game.

"Hey, Violet," Emma said as Violet ran the rest of the way. "How are you, kiddo?"

"I'm great! Mommy let me have a hot dog and a rocket pop!"

"Oh, she did? That's awesome!"

Daphne had disentangled herself from Kane's side. She came over now, looking concerned. "You okay?" she asked quietly.

For a moment Ethan thought the secret was out, but Paisley nodded and he realized Daphne meant the man who'd gotten too close and looked belligerent. Daphne had excellent instincts about people. Turned out that she had to considering the family she'd come from.

"I'm fine. It was just a drunk who thought he was making a smooth move. Ethan took care of it."

Daphne turned her gaze on him. There was something in it he didn't recognize. A smirk? A gleam?

"That's our Ethan. Always riding to the rescue."

He glared daggers at her because he knew what she was doing. Trying to push him and Paisley together, thinking they'd start dating, maybe fall in love the way she and Kane had. And not just them, but everyone else on this damned team except for Ghost.

Fuck.

He tipped his head toward the guys. "Any of us would have done the same. I just happened to see it first because the rest of them were distracted. Not that I'm pointing fingers or anything."

Daphne arched an eyebrow and laughed. "That's certainly a fair point. I take full responsibility for distracting Kane. Though he's rather distracting himself if I'm honest."

"He sure is today," Ethan said, eyeing his teammate who sprawled in his chair with a colorful cowboy hat and star sunglasses like he was Elton-frigging-John.

Kane raised his glass and took a swig with a big grin.

Daphne rolled her eyes. "Oh lord." She hooked an arm

in Paisley's. "Come on, Paisley. Let's get you a beverage and you can tell me what you think about the next book we've selected for the Bookalicious Babes. I started reading but things have been a bit, uh, busy and I need to get back to it."

Ethan watched them walk over to the cooler and dragged in a deep breath. How the fuck was he going to spend time in Paisley's company, watch her become a part of his friend group, and not think about everything that might have been if she'd only cared enough to wait instead of moving on to the next guy?

He didn't know, but it was clear he had to figure it out.

4

Violet loved the parade. But by the time the fireworks happened, she was fast asleep on Paisley's lap.

"Baby, you want to see the fireworks?" Paisley asked, bending to speak in her daughter's ear.

Violet slumbered on, as expected, and Paisley sighed. She was going to be so disappointed tomorrow.

But the booms didn't wake her. The light shaking of her body when Paisley jiggled her didn't either. When Violet was out, she was out.

Ethan sat beside them in his lawn chair, gazing at the fireworks as they cracked and boomed. He flinched from time to time. She didn't need to ask why. She'd watched Trey do the same thing when loud noises startled him. He'd said it was nothing when she asked. She'd stopped asking the first time he backhanded her for it.

The other men sometimes flinched too, but none of them seemed angry about it. If anything, they hugged their women a little tighter. The only one who never seemed to react was Alex Bishop. He leaned back in his chair, watching it all as if bored somehow.

A woman had walked over to talk to them earlier. She'd been tall, blond, and she'd been holding hands with a guy who'd looked even more bored than Alex. Her name was Diana and her arrival was the only time Alex had looked anything other than perfectly cool. If anything, he'd seemed a touch angry.

Paisley recognized it because anger was something she was finely attuned to. She'd had to be to survive. Not that every man who seemed angry was also violent, but she had to act as though they were. Because survival and protecting her child were paramount.

When the fireworks ended, people were busy everywhere packing up their chairs and blankets, their coolers, their kids. Getting back to her car was going to take time. Driving home would take even longer. She sighed as she levered herself out of the chair with Violet's body limp in her arms.

"We're going into the Dawg while the crowds disperse," Rory said. "It'll be easier to get to your car then if you want to go with us."

Paisley hesitated. It was already well after nine and she had to be at the library by eight in the morning to prepare for the day.

"I'll take you to your car."

It was Ethan's voice coming from behind her. She turned. He had his hands shoved in his pockets as he looked at her and Violet. "I can carry her for you, if you want me to."

Her mind rebelled. The last thing she wanted was Ethan carrying her child—but Violet was heavy and there was no way Paisley would make it the three blocks to her car without stopping several times to rest. Whether she did it now or when the crowds were thinner made no difference. She supposed she could leave Violet here, go get her car, and return. But if Violet *did* wake up, she'd be scared to find herself in a strange place without her mother.

"I need to get her home, so that would be great." She turned to Rory. "Thank you for asking me to stay. But it's been a long day and I have to be at work early."

Rory's gaze slid to Ethan. Her lips curled in a big smile. "No problem at all. I'm just glad you could join us today. Stop by any time if you want to chat or need anything. You can text or call, too. Hey, y'all, Paisley's leaving."

The guys waved and called out their goodbyes, but the women came over to basically echo Rory about stopping for a chat or giving them a call. Paisley could honestly say she really liked these women. They made her feel like Sutton's Creek was a good choice, and not just because she'd needed to get far away from Trey.

Paisley hesitated when Ethan stood before her. "I can carry her if you get my bag," she said.

"I'm not going to drop her, Payz."

Her gaze darted to the others but nobody heard him shorten her name like they were old friends. "Okay, fine."

He hefted Violet easily, laying her head on his shoulder and supporting her with an arm beneath her bottom. She sleepily wrapped her arms around his neck, and Paisley's heart squeezed. He looked natural holding her—and she looked safe in his arms. Tiny, too.

Ethan was a big man. Tall. His arms bulged, but not from the task of holding Violet. They bulged because he was well-muscled and fit. He wore a Yankees baseball cap pulled down over his forehead and a Salty Dawg Tavern T-shirt that stretched across his chest. His hair curled against his neck where it hung below the ball cap. She wasn't used to seeing him with longer hair. He'd always had a close-cropped military cut before.

She called goodbye to everyone one more time, waving. A frown creased Dr. Emma Sutton's face as she looked at Ethan holding Violet. Paisley's heart skipped. *It doesn't mean anything. There's nothing to see.*

Emma's gaze slid to Paisley for a second, but then Blaze wrapped his arms around her. He bent his mouth to her ear and the moment was over. Didn't slow Paisley's pulse though.

"Which way we going?"

Paisley jerked her gaze to Ethan. "Toward the library. I'm parked behind it."

They started walking with the crowds filtering out of the square. Paisley kept her eyes on people as they made their way down the street. It was habit to anticipate trouble. She thought it might always be, and that made her sad in a way. She'd been trusting once. Convinced that people would be nice to her because she was nice to everyone else.

Didn't work that way, though.

"Where are you staying?" Ethan asked when the crowd had thinned a little bit and they could hear each other.

"Aunt Hettie has a rental property in town. We're staying there."

Hettie wouldn't let her pay for it, though. She insisted the house had been paid off for years and she didn't need the money since her last tenant had moved out a few months ago. Plus it needed updating. Paisley couldn't deny that it was helpful not to have to pay rent, but she hoped she'd be able to once she was divorced and her lawyer bills were paid off. Hettie might not need the money, but Paisley didn't expect to live free forever.

"She lives in that Queen Anne house on the corner of Oak and Line in the historic district. Beautiful house," Ethan said.

"It is. But how do you know that?"

"She had Diego Hernandez out for some work recently. I moonlight with his crew sometimes."

Not what she'd expected. "You do?"

"Yeah. I like construction work. It's a hobby when I'm not too busy at the range."

"That's cool."

"Keeps me busy."

They walked in silence for a few minutes. "So where's this rental property of Miss Hettie's?" he asked.

"It's in the historic district a couple streets over from her house. It's a small Craftsman on Chestnut Street." The houses on Chestnut were technically in the district, but they weren't as grand as the homes just a couple of streets over. Small houses, cozy, in need of renovation. But she liked the district because there were old oak trees and sidewalks, children for Violet to play with, and a sense of community she hadn't had anywhere else.

"You're close to work, then."

"Yes. It's less than two miles, but it's too hot to try and walk it."

"Probably best not to."

She shot him a look. "What do you mean by that?"

He glanced down at Violet's head. She hadn't moved a muscle. "I mean don't make yourself a target."

"I don't intend to." A chill slipped down her spine. Intended or not, she already was.

"Not saying you do, but protection is my specialty. Sometimes people forget to be careful when they think they're safe. You said he doesn't know where you are, but in my experience that's only as good as the people keeping the secret. If you told anyone other than the court, those people are potential leaks. But there's also the fact you're here, in Sutton's Creek, working in a public space. People see you. Know your name. And you never know how people are connected to others."

She shivered. She'd told no one where she was going, and she'd asked Hettie not to share it with the Fairhope family either. Hettie knew she was getting a divorce, but not how bad it'd been. But that didn't mean the news wouldn't leak at some point. Aunt Hettie was eighty-three years old. She was mostly sharp as a tack, but she had moments when she was somewhat forgetful of what she'd said to whom. She would tell Uncle John, her son, if she hadn't already. And he might talk to Paisley's mother at some point.

If she resurfaced long enough to ask the question. Paisley often didn't hear from her for months at a time while she went nomad. Then she'd be back, wanting to tell Paisley all about whatever scheme she'd gotten involved in or new boyfriend she'd met, etcetera.

Not that she would tell Trey anything on purpose, but Bree Allen was the kind of person who sailed through life a day at a time and didn't think about the past or the future much at all. She acted in the moment, which had always been frustrating to Paisley as a kid. There'd been no permanence, no stability, with her mother. She was just as likely to sell everything one day and move the next when Paisley'd been little, which meant a school change —if she got enrolled at all.

"I'm doing the best I can. I keep an eye over my shoulder at all times, watching for him. I'm exhausted from all the vigilance, but I won't stop doing it. I can't."

Her voice was close to cracking.

"I'm sorry you ended up with someone who hurt you."

"Me too. Can't change the past, though."

There were so many things she wanted to say, questions she wanted to ask, but what was the point? Ethan had left, and she'd ended up with Trey. It didn't matter why anymore.

"There's my car," she said as they walked around the back of the library to the parking lot. She hit the remote to unlock it and opened the rear passenger door. Ethan stooped to place Violet gently into her carseat, then clipped the seatbelt. Paisley's eyes pricked with tears at how gentle he was with her daughter. Not only that, but the fact he'd belted her in so carefully.

She reminded herself not to read too much into it. It was only a seatbelt. Didn't make him into a hero or anything.

He straightened, towering over her again, and she took a step back instinctively. A frown marred his handsome face. "Not going to hurt you, Paisley."

She sucked in a breath. "You already have. But I know what you mean. I can't help it though. It's instinct, and I doubt I'll ever get over it."

He nodded. "Understood. For the record, the deployment was short notice and we went radio silent immediately. It happens in special ops. As soon as I could, I called you. You never answered, never texted. Except once."

Her heart hammered. Sweat beaded on her skin. She didn't want to have this conversation and yet she needed to. Maybe getting it out there in the open would heal at least a tiny corner of her heart. She would never be the same person she was before, but every step forward was a good one.

"It wasn't me, Ethan. You sent Trey to tell me you were gone. Well, he did that. And then he was there to pick up the pieces. If you called me like you say you did, then I expect it was Trey who made sure I never got the calls. And I expect he's the one who texted you—because it damned sure wasn't me."

The murmur of voices, the closing of car doors, the starting of engines as people got into their cars became a hum in the background as she watched the expression on Ethan's face morph from denial to confusion to understanding before landing on hot, blazing anger. She wasn't scared of the anger. Not this time. She knew where it was directed, and it wasn't at her.

"Wait a fucking minute," he growled. "What did he tell you?"

"That you'd had fun but you were moving on. That you were sorry you had to leave earlier than you'd anticipated, but it was best to make a clean break."

His expression was a study in shock. Eyes wide, jaw hanging open. That only lasted a few seconds before fury returned in full force. "Jesus fucking Christ. That's *not* what I told him to tell you."

She believed him. His reaction was too raw not to. All these years she'd wondered why she hadn't been good enough for him, why he'd left her without a word, and how she'd had it so wrong. He'd gotten a tattoo with her, for heaven's sake. Yet he'd dumped her like yesterday's trash and sent Trey to do his dirty work.

But of course he hadn't. It was Trey who'd lied. Trey who'd orchestrated everything. She didn't have the energy for anger after all these years of hell. Instead, weariness wrapped itself around her heart. She just wanted to go home and hide beneath the covers. Maybe she'd cry, or maybe she was too numb.

"Then I guess you didn't know Trey as well as you thought you did, huh? Because that's what he said. And when I cried, he was there to comfort me. Such a helpful guy, that Trey."

She couldn't help the bitterness coating her words.

"I'm sorry, Payz. I thought—shit, I thought he was a decent guy. I don't know why he lied to you."

"You can't figure it out?"

He stared. She continued on, recklessness spurring her forward. It was too big to carry alone anymore.

"Trey McCann only cares about himself and what he wants. I'm sorry you didn't know that. Might have saved me four and a half years in hell if you had. Not that I blame you for my own lack of judgement."

He'd gone utterly still. "Are you saying...? Is he the guy...?"

She closed the door gently on her sleeping child before she faced him again, her pulse tattooing despair with every beat. "That I married him? That he's the man who beat me black and blue and threatened to kill me if I ever left him? That I'm terrified he'll come after me? That he'll hurt Violet? That our lives are in danger every second of every day for the rest of our lives?"

She dragged in a magnolia-scented breath and steadied herself.

"Yes, that's exactly what I'm saying. Welcome to the hell that's my life."

5

He couldn't sleep. Ethan lay on the bed and stared up at the ceiling, his body strung tight with the kind of energy that would consume him if he didn't do something about it. Paisley had married Trey McCann.

Trey, his fucking buddy who'd been supposed to tell her he'd be in touch as soon as he could. Trey, who'd transferred out of HOT and stayed in Florida before separating from the military. They hadn't been best buds or anything, but they'd both been HOT at one time. Ethan had always thought that meant something.

Apparently not.

He swung his legs off the bed, shoved a hand through his hair, and made a noise somewhere between anger and pain.

Then he shot to his feet and started to pace. It was two in the morning and there was nowhere to go.

Or was there?

He dragged on his shorts, T-shirt, and shoved his feet into his hiking boots. He had to get out, had to move before he exploded. He prowled toward the back door, but came up short when Ghost looked up from where he stood at the kitchen counter with his laptop open.

"Going somewhere?" Ghost asked, arching one eyebrow.

"Can't sleep. Thought I'd go for a drive." He'd been so focused on escape that he hadn't noticed the flickering light from the computer screen. If Ghost had been an enemy combatant lying in wait for him, he'd be dead.

Ghost shook his head. "Yeah, welcome to the club. I was hoping a beer and something mindless on the computer would help. So far, no dice."

Ethan studied his boss. Since Kane and Daphne had hooked up and were living together in the smaller of the two farmhouses on the property where the One Shot Tactical Range and Training Facility was located, Ethan had moved in with Ghost. Chance and Seth used to live there, but both of them had found love and moved in with their women.

Blaze was the only one who'd never lived on the property, but he was also the first to shack up.

With the town doctor, which was helpful in some ways. Like when Chance had gotten winged by a bullet on a stealth incursion one night.

Or the time Ethan had fallen off the porch and hit his head because a spider dropped on him out of fucking nowhere. He hated those little bastards. For something so small, they creeped him the fuck out. The last time there'd been one inside the break room at the range, Daphne had calmly scooped it up with a bug catcher and took it outside before lecturing him on why spiders were good for the environment.

He knew they were good, dammit. He just didn't want one on him.

Fortunately, he hadn't hit his head hard and Emma had confirmed he didn't have a concussion. Not that he'd have asked, but she'd been there when it happened—they all had because it had been at one of the group's regular cookouts—and she'd insisted. She hadn't laughed at him, but the others did.

Stupid spiders.

And why the fuck was he thinking about spiders when everything he'd thought he'd known about Paisley was a lie?

Because spiders are easier to think about than emotional trauma.

"You okay, Dragon?" Ghost asked, eyebrow arching.

His gut was ice. "Yeah, fine. Just thinking about some shit I'd rather not think about. Everything okay with the mission?"

"No changes, nobody breathing down my neck at the moment."

"That's good."

"I'd say so. Waiting on the other shoe to drop though."

Ethan sighed and rubbed his forehead. "We've been

here nearly eight months. I thought it'd be different than this, gotta admit."

"I didn't know what to expect. Still don't, if I'm honest."

Daphne's brother had been planning to sell Stinger missiles to disciples of the Russian oligarch Viktor Dashevsky, but the team had put a stop to that before it'd happened. Jackson O'Malley was in jail and the Stingers were in the FBI's possession. They hadn't been able to tie it to Dashevsky's people though, and that was a damned shame because those fuckers were still plotting something.

Until the Athena Project reached completion and went live, Ghost Ops had to cool their heels in Sutton's Creek. How long that might be at this point was anybody's guess. The president and her team said it would be soon, but Ethan no longer believed they were right. Neither, he thought, did Ghost.

Ethan took his leave and headed for his truck. He'd told Ghost he was going for a drive like it was a random thing, but he knew precisely where he was going. He drove the short distance to downtown, weaving through the streets until he reached Chestnut Street. He knew which house to look for because a quick internet search revealed which one belonged to Esther Woods, otherwise known as Miss Hettie. He drove by the brick Craftsman, studying the house and yard.

Paisley's Kia sat in front of the house because there was no driveway or garage. Not unusual for historic homes of the era. The blinds were closed and the porch light was on. He parked down the street and watched the house, feeling the need to be vigilant. She'd been terrified and it made him sick to know it was Trey who'd hurt her.

He thought back to that night when the orders had come down. He'd been on a training run with a group of Green Berets. There'd been no time for anything except grabbing his duffel and getting on the transport. Trey had promised to tell Paisley that he'd be back. He was supposed to say that Ethan would call when he could, but it might be some time. And he was supposed to tell her that Ethan was sorry he had to miss her birthday, but he'd make it up to her when he returned.

Instead, Trey had lied to her. Told her Ethan was done with her.

Then he'd inserted himself into her life and stolen the woman Ethan loved.

Trey had married her, made a child with her.

Ethan's gut twisted. Somehow, that was the worst of all. Because Trey was clearly a monster who'd hit Paisley in front of their kid. A monster who would have hit Violet too if Paisley hadn't left.

Jesus.

Anger, cold and dark and yet somehow hotter than the sun, filled Ethan's soul. He wanted to scream, and he wanted to destroy.

The master planner in his brain kicked into gear. Because he needed to make plans or he'd lose his ever-loving mind. It was what he did, how he coped. It'd always been so.

What would he do first?

He'd go to Seth for information, because Seth would find everything Ethan wanted to know.

Seth would learn Trey's routines, his habits, find out where he worked, what he ate for breakfast, when he took a piss, and how much he owed to whom.

Ethan would study all of it carefully. Then he'd find a reason to take a few days off. He'd head to Florida, shadow his prey. When he'd had enough of waiting and watching, he'd strike.

He wanted to kill the motherfucker. Destroy him so utterly there was nothing left.

He enjoyed the fantasy for all of a minute before he let reality sink in.

He couldn't kill Trey. Not only was he not particularly fond of going to jail for the rest of his life, he was on a mission where the stakes were no less than life or death for millions. Those millions included his friends, the good people of Sutton's Creek, and Paisley and Violet.

Revenge wasn't worth the risk to any of the people he cared about.

Ethan leaned his head back on the seat and blew out a slow breath. He could at least beat the hell out of Trey, warn him what would happen if he so much as breathed in Paisley's direction. He wanted to. So fucking bad.

Except he hadn't gotten where he was in life by going off half-cocked, even with an elaborate plan. Beating the fuck out of Trey McCann would definitely be satisfying—at least for a few hours—but it wouldn't change what'd already happened. It might also make Trey more determined to hurt Paisley.

Ethan closed his eyes, shoved a hand through his hair. He wasn't supposed to get involved. Period. He couldn't risk what it would do to his team if he let himself sink into this morass of rage and pain, which he would do if he spent any time with Paisley and Violet. He needed his mind clear, needed to focus on why he was part of this team and what they were in Alabama for.

But how could he sit back and watch Paisley flinch every time a man got too close? How could he watch her look over her shoulder with fear in her eyes when he knew what she was running from? When he felt at least partly responsible because he'd trusted the wrong person?

Sure, Paisley could have said no. She could have walked way. She should have. But who was he to say she'd done the wrong thing when he hadn't been there? Trey had fooled him, made him think he was an honorable man who had a fellow soldier's back.

Ethan didn't have to ask himself why Trey did it. Paisley was the kind of woman who turned heads. When she'd walked over to their table in the bar that day, every man there had been tripping over his tongue. Every man had wanted her. Ethan had staked his claim first. Yeah, it'd been pure attraction then. He'd wanted to fuck her.

But then he got to know her, and he fell for her. He'd imagined a future with her, and he hadn't hidden those thoughts from his buddies. He may not have said the L-word, but he'd definitely talked about being with her beyond his temporary assignment to Florida. Trey had known Paisley was important to him.

Known, and deliberately sabotaged the relationship.

He couldn't change the past, but he could make sure that Paisley and her daughter were safe in Sutton's Creek. He didn't have to get involved with her to do it. He'd make inquiries, find out how bad it'd been, get her some security cameras and an alarm system if she didn't have one.

Once he was sure she had resources, he'd be content to see her around town or with the Ghost Ops women. Wouldn't be a problem at all.

Plan made, he started the truck and headed for home.

6

Paisley woke at six, like always, feeling more wrecked than she should have considering she'd been in bed by eleven.

But she hadn't slept well. All she could see was Ethan's face when the realization hit him that Trey was the one who'd betrayed him. And when he'd figured out that Trey was the abusive husband she'd run from?

His anger in that moment had threatened to blot all the stars in the sky. It'd taken everything she had not to jump into her car and lock the doors.

There hadn't been much else to say after that, not really. He hadn't asked questions, and she'd been grateful for it. If she'd had to explain how she'd fallen for Trey's lies or, worse, why she'd stayed after the first time he hit her, she'd have cracked into a million pieces that would never be whole again.

Maybe she already had. Because she was trying every

damned day to hold herself together and she'd thought she was doing a pretty good job of it. Seeing Ethan again in the Dawg, and then again yesterday, had made the illusion shimmer.

They'd said their goodbyes and she'd gotten into the car, asked him if he wanted a ride back to the Dawg because it was the decent thing to do after he'd carried Violet three blocks. She'd been relieved when he said he didn't.

She'd left him standing in the parking lot, hands shoved in his pockets, watching her until she couldn't see him in the mirrors anymore.

Then she'd cried angry tears, smearing them away with her palm, willing them to stop before she got home. If Violet woke up, she didn't want her daughter to see her crying.

When Paisley cried, Violet got anxious. Because she was accustomed to bad things making her mommy cry. To seeing Paisley with black eyes and split lips, to having her yelp in pain because her ribs were bruised when Violet hugged her.

Usually, Paisley could redirect Trey's anger, defuse it. But not always. That was when he lashed out, and when Paisley thought about her daughter in her room, her fingers in her ears and her eyes squeezed shut. In those moments, Paisley prayed that Violet would stay, that she wouldn't come running.

So long as Trey didn't touch Violet, Paisley could endure.

She'd shuddered, sniffling softly as she turned onto her street and then parked in front of the house. It was small, only twelve-hundred square feet, but it felt like more of a home than any she'd had before. Her home with Trey had been grand, because his business had made a lot of money, but everything in it was the way *he* wanted it. She hadn't been allowed to put any of her personality into it. It was decorated, but only because he'd hired someone. He'd wanted it to look like rich people lived there. Everything was stale and modern and empty of soul.

Not like the bungalow. She didn't have many possessions yet, but the rich wood accents inside the house made her happy. Maybe if she lived there long enough, she'd fill the house with beautiful things. She hoped so, anyway.

She'd left all the lights on because she didn't want to enter a dark house. She always looked up and down the street before she parked. Her neighbors had been outside, setting off sparklers and bottle rockets in the street, and that had made her feel better. If she screamed, they would hear.

After getting Violet to bed, she'd poured a big glass of white wine and taken a book to bed. She'd fallen asleep quickly enough, but she'd kept gasping awake, straining to hear the noises she'd heard in her dreams, afraid they were real.

Shattering glass. Creaking wood. The sound of a pistol being cocked.

Fortunately, it was only her imagination.

Paisley got out of bed and went to the bathroom down the hall. There was an ensuite bath in the main bedroom, but she'd had to shut the water off to the toilet because it kept running and she hadn't gotten around to figuring out how to fix it yet. She could mention it to Aunt Hettie, but she wasn't going to because then her aunt would very likely send a plumber and insist on paying for it.

If the problem required a plumber, she'd call one. But first she needed to Google running toilets and see if it was simple. She added that to her mental checklist for the day, then took care of business and had a quick shower before returning to her room to get dressed. When she walked into the kitchen to fix breakfast for her and Violet, the sunlight streaming though the windows helped chase away the lingering effects of fear from last night.

Everything looked better with sunshine to burn away the shadows. She went through the motions of making oatmeal, adding apples and cinnamon and butter, her mind constantly replaying the look on Ethan's face when he'd learned the truth.

For a moment, he'd looked as shattered as she felt. As broken. It was probably her imagination, because while she'd endured Trey and his systematic dismantling of her self-worth, Ethan had moved on. He'd had other women, other lovers. His life had changed and grew. Hers changed too, became smaller and harder.

"Dammit," she muttered as her eyes stung.

She washed the dishes and let the oatmeal simmer.

Violet trudged in a few minutes later, looking grumpy in her pink kitty cat pajamas. Paisley's heart squeezed with love. Her child had never been a morning person. She didn't let Violet have coffee at four years old, but she was positive Vivi would be the sort of person who didn't function without it when she was older.

"Good morning, honeybun," Paisley said brightly. "You want some oatmeal?"

Violet propped her elbow on the table and put her chin in her hand before nodding. "Uh-huh."

"And the magic word is?"

"Peas."

"Please," Paisley repeated, emphasizing the L and long E sound.

"Please," Violet said.

Paisley scooped oatmeal into a bowl and set it in front of her daughter. "Blow on it before you take a bite."

Violet dug in and lifted the spoon, blowing hard. Paisley bit back a smile. Nothing like a kid's exaggerated interpretation to make you laugh. She was grateful she still could.

"Did I miss the fireworks, Mommy?"

Paisley got her own bowl of oatmeal and sat at the table. "I'm sorry, honey, but you fell asleep. I tried to wake you."

Violet let out a long-suffering sigh. "Okay. Can we go again tonight? I really wanna see dem."

Paisley reached over and squeezed her daughter's

hand. "I'm sorry, Vivi, but the fireworks aren't happening tonight. It was last night."

Violet's eyes grew big and liquid. "You can't make it happen tonight?"

"No, honey. I'm sorry. Independence Day is over."

Violet's lip quivered. "I wanna see," she whispered, her little voice tortured and painful to hear.

"I know, sweetie. There will be other chances to see fireworks. Just not tonight."

Violet's chin and cheeks reddened. She dropped her spoon and bowed her head, her shoulders shaking as she cried.

Paisley's heart broke. "Aw, honey, come to Mommy." She opened her arms and Violet came into them, burying her face against Paisley's white blouse. She'd probably have to change before going to the library, but that was the price of taking care of her baby. "It's okay, sweetie."

Violet cried far harder over missed fireworks than she probably should have, but Paisley knew some of it was a reaction to everything that'd happened in her life. She'd been afraid of Trey, but she also looked up to him because he was a manipulative son of a bitch who'd doled out his affection whenever Violet needed it most. He'd lied to her constantly, and she'd believed because she was a child.

Which meant that Paisley held her sobbing baby, whose reaction to missing fireworks was over the top but quite possibly wasn't about fireworks at all.

Paisley stroked Violet's hair until she quieted. With a last hiccup, she pushed away and returned to her chair, moving her spoon around her oatmeal without enthusiasm.

"Eat, Vivi. You get to go to Lily's house today and play. Her mom's going to fix lunch and everything. You can play with Barbies, watch movies, whatever you like."

"Okay."

She didn't sound enthused but Paisley knew, when she dropped Violet at the Parks' house later, she would be bursting with excitement to spend the day with Lily Park. Mrs. Park made Korean food for lunch, and Violet was learning to love pickled vegetables and bulgogi. The Parks had lived in Sutton's Creek for the past three years when Mr. Park took a job at LG Electronics in Huntsville. They were frequent library visitors, and an absolute godsend when Paisley needed someone to watch Violet for a few hours. Not that Aunt Hettie wouldn't, because she would and did, but Paisley couldn't expect her aunt to become a babysitter in her retirement.

There was a knock on the door. Paisley's stomach dropped. But Trey wouldn't knock that way. He'd pound on the door and yell. God, would she ever respond normally to random knocks or unexpected arrivals ever again? This was the South. People dropped by, sometimes with tomatoes from the garden or with an extra loaf of zucchini bread or some other goody, simply because that's how life was here.

Paisley smiled for Violet's benefit as she stood. "Eat your breakfast, baby. I'll see who it is."

She laid her napkin on the table, smoothed her skirt,

and made her way to the front door, her heart pounding. It could be a neighbor. A church lady. A kid selling something for band. Didn't matter that it was July. They started early sometimes.

The knock sounded again. "Coming," Paisley called. Still, she stood on tiptoe to look out the peephole. The top of the wood door was decorative glass, but she couldn't see through it even if she tried.

The man standing on her front porch in a baseball cap and shorts wasn't who she'd expected to see. She fumbled with the chain on the door, sliding it free.

Then she pasted on a smile and opened the door to face the only man she'd ever loved.

7

The door swung open to reveal a smiling Paisley in a cropped white blouse with wet spots in one area and a long maxi-skirt in shades of black and white. She wore white sandals on her feet and a pair of small gold hoops in her ears. Her hair was shorter than his, but it really worked on her.

She blinked at him with her pretty blue eyes, her smile clearly pasted on as she waited for him to speak. Ethan asked himself again what the fuck he was doing here. This hadn't been the plan when he'd gotten up this morning. He was doing some work with Diego's crew on the next street over for a few hours this morning, but they weren't starting for another hour because the homeowner had a personal emergency to take care of first.

Instead of going back to the range or, hell, over to Miss Mary's Diner for coffee, he'd found himself here. Standing on Paisley's front porch, feeling his heart constrict in his chest the instant he saw her.

"Hi," she said, standing in the opening with her hand still firmly on the door. Not opening it all the way. Not inviting him in. Not that he needed to go inside. He didn't.

"Morning. I was in the neighborhood." *Lame.* He cleared his throat, hooked his thumb over his shoulder. "Working on a house on Maple. I, uh, was thinking about the situation."

A line formed on her forehead. "What about it?"

He looked past her, into the small living room. It was a neat house, sparsely furnished. She'd had a small apartment in Florida when he'd met her, and she'd had stuff everywhere. Maximalism, she'd called it. This was more minimal than anything. Then again, she'd probably left Trey with only what she could carry. Yet another thing to twist him into knots when he thought about it.

"You need protection. Do you have security cameras? An alarm system? That kind of thing."

She shook her head. "No. I just moved here and started my job. I don't have hundreds—or thousands—of dollars to spend on a security system right now."

"It doesn't have to be expensive."

She sighed and rubbed her forehead. "I hear you, and I understand where you're coming from. But, respectfully, I don't have money to spare. What I need first is my toilet fixed. More furniture. A mattress without lumps to sleep on. Then maybe I can consider it."

He could hear the frustration in her voice, the over-whelm. "What's wrong with the toilet?"

She seemed surprised. "It's running all the time. I had to turn off the water until I can figure out what the problem is and get it fixed. I have no idea how much it'll cost."

"I can fix it. Probably just the flapper not sealing all the way."

"You can? How much is that?"

For the first time since she'd opened the door, she almost looked happy to see him. Almost.

"Few dollars for the part. Nothing much."

He didn't tell her he wouldn't take her money because he knew she'd insist. So he'd fix the toilet and then refuse when she tried to pay him. If things were that tight, she needed everything she had.

"Oh wow. That's good."

"Yep." He tipped his chin toward the interior of the house. "If you want me to look now, I can take care of it today."

She hesitated a second, then pulled the door wide. "Sure, come on in."

"Hi, Mr. Ethan!" Violet called out when he walked into the living room. She was standing in the opening to the kitchen, her blonde hair messy with sleep, her kitty pajamas shockingly pink. But she was smiling and waving at him, and he waved back. Her eyes were red though. Like she'd been crying.

The wet spots on Paisley's blouse?

"Hi, Miss Violet. How you doing this morning?"

She shrugged. "Mommy says the fireworks are gone and I missed them because I didn't wake up. I'm sad."

"I'm sorry to hear that. But I'm sure you'll get to see them next time."

Her little shoulders sagged. "Yeah, I know. But what if I sleep then too?"

Ethan wanted to move mountains for this kid. Wasn't his place, though. "I'm sure your mom will figure something out."

"Mr. Ethan's going to fix the toilet in Mommy's bathroom, Vivi," Paisley said. "Can you go and brush your hair for me? And get your Wednesday clothes out of the drawer and put them on, please. Close the door behind you."

"Yes, ma'am," Violet said before trudging down the hallway.

Paisley waited until her bedroom door was shut before giving him a small smile. "She's a little drama queen sometimes. Thank you for being nice to her about the fireworks."

His chest tightened. What kind of asshole couldn't be nice to a kid over a disappointment? He locked that thought behind iron bars before it could expand. Still, Trey McCann's face appeared in his head and his chest grew tighter.

"No reason not to be nice. She's a kid. Everything's dramatic at that age."

"I suppose it is. I hate that she's disappointed, but if I'd forced her to wake up last night, you'd have thought somebody'd replaced my kid with a tyrannosaurus rex."

"Grumpy, huh?"

"Beyond grumpy. Rampaging, more like."

He laughed. "That was me until I joined the military. They kinda take that shit out of you and force you to adapt. Plus coffee. That helps."

She blinked suddenly, her lips rolling in. Her voice was softer when she spoke, like she was holding down an emotional response. "I've thought of giving her coffee, but I think it's a little premature."

"Probably. But you know, we can make fireworks happen if it's important to her. The range is outside town limits, on farmland, and we can shoot some off there. Nothing too big so we don't scare the cattle a couple miles down the road, but a few wouldn't hurt."

"You would do that?"

"Why not?" He wished somebody had cared enough to make his wishes come true when he'd been a kid. "It's not hard. The stands are still open for a few days."

"How much do you think it'll cost?"

"Nothing. I can afford a few fireworks, and the guys will pitch in too. We'll all enjoy it, so no reason to think you need to pay for anything."

She seemed to consider it. "I want to contribute though. It's only fair. And I don't want you to do it if it's inconvenient. Your friends were all there last night. They might be fireworked out."

There was no way he wasn't doing this. He knew what it was like to have your life torn apart as a kid, and if he could make one little girl smile for a few minutes when her life had been turned upside down so recently, he was doing it. But he wasn't telling Paisley that was the reason.

"I'll talk to the guys. Let you know. But I'm thinking maybe Friday or Saturday."

Her eyes shimmered before she turned away. "Thanks. Let me show you the bathroom."

He followed her, deliberately keeping his gaze on the back of her head and not letting it slide to her ass. A part of him was busy asking what the hell he thought he was doing. He ignored it. Paisley had meant something to him once, and she was in a bad spot in life. Least he could do was help her out.

Even if it killed him to think of her with Trey. She must have fallen for Trey pretty quickly, or she'd never have married him. Made a kid with him.

He ground his teeth together and forced down the anger blooming hot inside. It wasn't just that Trey had deliberately sabotaged his relationship with Paisley, but also that he'd had nearly five years and a child with her while Ethan had spent that time moving from one empty encounter to the other whenever he needed release.

He felt *cheated.* And that wasn't even the worst of it. The worst was how Trey had treated the woman and child he should have loved most. If they'd been Ethan's, he'd never want to see a moment's fear or sadness on their faces. And he damned sure wouldn't be the one putting it there on purpose.

"In here."

Her bedroom was sparsely furnished, like the rest of the house. There was a bed, a nightstand, and a mirror. Her bed was made, though she didn't have a bunch of pillows on it like she used to have. Everything about this room was simple, uncomplicated.

It smelled like her, though. Like roses and vanilla with a hint of citrus. A sweet, floral scent that was hers alone. He'd smelled that combination on other women, but it wasn't the same at all. He'd wondered if it was his memory playing tricks on him over the years.

It wasn't. Paisley's scent was uniquely hers.

The attached bathroom was bigger than he'd expected, with an old iron tub/shower combo, white subway tiles, and a bright floral wallpaper. The sink was a single, but the vanity ran a good forty inches. Plenty of room for knickknacks and toiletries. The floor had white octagonal tiles with black rosette inlays. A typical old-style bathroom that still had the original features.

Except maybe the wallpaper. That was garish and probably stuck to the wall with industrial strength ancient glue.

The single window was tall and surrounded by a stained wood casing. No whitewash here. Ethan went over to the toilet and took the lid off. The water had drained out of it so he bent down to turn it back on at the rear of the toilet. The tank started to fill immediately. The water reached the top of the overflow tube and the float stopped moving. But it was still trickling into the toilet, which meant the water would start to run again when the level dropped. He turned the water off and looked up to find Paisley in the doorway, arms crossed, nibbling her lip worriedly.

"Relax. It's the flapper. I'll pick up a new mechanism and replace the whole thing. It's less than twenty bucks."

"Thank God for that. And thank *you* for looking. I really thought it was something more complicated."

"Nah, toilets aren't that difficult. Even if it was the wax seal between the toilet and the floor, it's not a lot of money and I can fix it."

"It'll be nice to have my own bathroom again. I really appreciate it."

"You're welcome."

Her gaze traveled over the wallpaper. "Would you happen to know how to take that stuff down?"

"Yeah, but it's probably not going to be easy. I'm betting there's a lot of glue under there. Still, it's doable. What do you want to do after you get it down?"

"I was thinking something less busy. Paint, probably." She sighed. "But it's not a priority. I just think about these things whenever I'm in here."

"Got anything else you need repaired?"

She laughed softly. "Probably? I don't know what though. Unless you can look at the drip in the kitchen sink? It's very minor, but annoying in the middle of the night."

"I'll take a look."

They went into the kitchen and he had the sink pulled apart and figured out in under a minute. "Washer's old. Needs replaced."

Paisley smiled and an electric current zapped over him, leaving the hairs on his arms standing. "Well, that's not so bad."

"Nope."

Violet came into the kitchen then. She'd changed from pajamas to shorts and a T-shirt, and her hair was mostly combed. She had a coloring book and a box of crayons.

"Can I color, Mommy?"

"Yes, you may," Paisley said. Her eyes softened as she looked at her daughter. He could remember when she'd looked at him that way. Long ago.

"Do you want to color, Mr. Ethan?" Violet asked, gazing up at him with golden-green eyes. Pretty eyes. The color was similar to his own, but that didn't mean anything. He found himself wishing it did, though. He tried to see any hint of Trey in her features, but all he saw was Paisley. Her little chin, her serious expression, the shape of her lips. Those were Paisley's for certain.

"Thanks, Miss Violet, but I can't today. Another time?"

"Sure. I might have this book all colored in, but Mommy will get us another one."

"Sounds good."

She went into the living room and sat on the floor, spreading the book onto the worn coffee table in front of her. Then she selected a crayon from her box and started on the page.

"You're pretty good with kids, you know that?" Paisley said quietly.

He followed her cue and lowered his voice so Violet didn't hear them. "Never thought about it. I just talk to them like they can think for themselves."

She grinned. "They can, but some of them will talk your ears off if you give them an opening. Trust me, I have experience."

He must have looked puzzled because she continued. "Children's story hour at the library. You wouldn't believe what some of them say." Her gaze slipped past him to Violet in the other room. "She's always been more inwardly focused. Like me. She loves to play with other kids, but then she also likes her alone time. Sometimes she tells me she's done peopling for the day."

Ethan couldn't help but snort a laugh. "That sounds like you all right."

Her cheeks glowed. "It's my fault she learned that phrase. I have to admit I find it amusing when she says it the way she does."

His mind turned back to the original reason he'd found himself on her porch. "She's a sweet kid. I'm sorry if she has trauma from what you both went through."

Paisley's gaze dropped. "Thank you."

"I can get you a security system, Paisley. Nothing expensive. Just something to give you alerts so you can see who it is before you walk across that floor. The creaking boards from your footsteps are a dead giveaway that someone's home. If it's someone you don't want to talk to, you'll know it before you creep to the door to peer out the peephole. The system will also let you know if anyone suspicious is hanging around, or if anyone breaks in. I know you have a restraining order, but think of this as another layer of protection."

Her mouth dropped open. Closed. "Why would you want to help me? I married your friend. And though I didn't dump you, you have every reason to think it was me who sent that text and told you I'd moved on. It's only my word that I didn't."

"Trey wasn't my friend. We were work buddies. I thought I could trust him to do what I asked. I was wrong, and I'm sorry."

"He fooled us both. I can't blame you for not seeing what he was when I didn't either." Her voice was soft, troubled.

He dragged a breath into his tight chest. "I know you aren't lying to me about the text. You forget I knew you pretty well, Payz."

"People change, Ethan."

Fresh guilt sliced into him. "Know that too. But I can more easily believe he blocked my calls and hid it from you. Then he sent a text to make me go away."

He hadn't considered it at the time because why would he? Trey hadn't done anything in the short time Ethan was at Eglin to make him think he'd steal Paisley away and then hurt her. It had never occurred to him that Trey was capable of such a thing.

Trey's deception had succeeded so fucking easily, and Ethan would never get over that. But what had he been supposed to do? Find time between missions to go to Florida and confront a woman who told him she was done with him? What kind of creepy stalker behavior was that?

Still, he wished he had. Maybe both their lives would have turned out differently.

"You must have been so angry when you got that text. And confused."

He nodded. He'd left town excited for a future with her, and it was in pieces at his feet when he returned.

"I thought we had something, and I wanted to come back from the mission and see where we went together. But you'd moved on, and there was nothing I could do about it. I spent a lot of time asking myself how I got it so wrong. And then I moved on too."

Or so he'd thought. Until seeing her again knocked the breath out of him and left him questioning everything he thought he knew. Maybe doing this for her, helping her, was the way to finally close the door on that chapter of his life.

She folded her arms around her middle. Protecting herself. "I was so shocked when I saw you in the Dawg. It was like seeing a ghost come back to life." She shook her head. "We aren't the same people anymore. Even if Trey lied to us both, that time is gone. So I guess I just wonder why you'd want to help me when all it does is drag up the past for both of us?"

He chose his words carefully. "Nobody knows about our history but us. But more than that, I know Trey McCann. Not as well as you do, but I know how he was trained, what he's capable of. Because I have the same training. So do my guys. You said he threatened to kill you and you're scared he'll come for you, that you'll have to live in fear for the rest of your life. I can't stand by and do nothing, Paisley. Not when I share some of the responsibility for you ever meeting him in the first place."

"You don't. He was in the bar that day, same as you. If you hadn't been there, he still could have been. Maybe I'd have gone out with him and still found myself in the same place."

He closed his eyes for a second. "Maybe you would've dated him, but that doesn't mean you'd have ended up with him. You were upset because you thought I'd dumped you, and he took advantage of your feelings. Let me have my guilt, okay?"

She huffed a breath. "It's not your fault, but I can't stop you from feeling what you feel. Even if I disagree."

"Now that we've got that out of the way, let me at least have a look around, see what you might need. I'll work up a quote for you. You can make payments if you have to. Or, hell, cook me some of those Cajun dishes you learned from your mama and don't worry about the money. Just let me do this, Payz. For you and Violet."

She stared at him, her blue eyes brimming with

emotion. Then she sighed, her shoulders slumping. "Fine, give me a quote. I want to know how much it is and then we can talk about how to proceed."

"Great. You got time now for me to check things out or should I come back later?"

She looked at her smart watch. "I have to take Violet to the Parks' house before I head to the library, but I don't have to leave for another thirty minutes."

"That's enough time. I'll need to go into all the rooms, and I'll need to see the basement and attic. That okay with you?"

"Have at it."

"Thanks. Need to go out to my truck and get a tape measure, unless you have one handy."

"I don't. Sorry."

"Then I'll get mine."

She caught his arm as he turned away, then dropped her hand like he'd burned her. He understood the feeling because his skin stung where she'd touched him.

"Sorry," she sputtered. "I-I just wanted to say that I appreciate this. So much. I don't know that I'll be able to afford it, but the fact you want to help us—it means a lot, Ethan. Thank you."

"You're welcome, Payz. And don't go thinking you know the answer before I tell you the price, okay? We'll make this work because you and your daughter deserve to live in peace and safety."

She dropped her gaze to the floor. He didn't wait for her to say another word. To stop him or place restrictions on him. He went outside to his truck, grabbed his tape measure, and returned to the cute Craftsman bungalow determined to make sure Trey McCann never laid a hand on Paisley again.

Because if he tried, Ethan didn't think anything on this earth could stop him from making Trey suffer for what he'd done to the woman Ethan had once loved.

The woman he wasn't sure he'd ever stopped loving.

8

The next couple of days passed quietly. Violet went to play with Lily Park during the day, and Paisley worked at the library. She loved the job of being Sutton's Creek's librarian and she threw herself into designing educational programs and services for the community. So far they'd added a scrapbooking work-shop, a reading challenge for children, and hosted a mystery book club open to newcomers as well as the private Bookalicious Besties club. She was even planning a romance novel book club that was open to everyone, and she hoped they might get a thriller club started too.

There were other duties to perform, including helping patrons find what they were looking for, answering emails, and updating the collections. The staff, comprised of two library techs and a handful of volunteers, wasn't a big one, but she liked them all. Well, almost all.

One tech in particular, Fern Carter, made no bones of

the fact she thought Paisley had stolen the job that'd right-fully been hers. She also had her library science degree, she'd been employed at the library for the past five years when she'd moved back to town after a decade away, and she had ordained herself to be Aunt Hettie's designated successor because of those things.

The problem was that Fern had pissed off too many people to ever get the job. She held grudges over minor disagreements, she made snide comments, and it was even rumored that she'd harassed a former volunteer she didn't like with anonymous emails to the point they quit.

Paisley didn't know how true that was since Fern was still employed, but nobody wanted her in charge. The library staff had apparently threatened to quit en masse if she was promoted.

When Paisley arrived, Fern had given her the full silent treatment, complete with a superior stare down her nose, for a solid week.

Now she'd progressed to grunts, disapproving silences, and passive-aggressive suggestions, anonymous of course, peppered at random throughout the day. Paisley sighed as she took the latest suggestion from the box and read it.

Outside groups should not be allowed to bring food into the library. The book club meeting last week, and the resultant casserole crowding of the refrigerator, forced people to leave their lunches at home. Suggest people eat before or after their book club meetings.

The refrigerator had hardly been overcrowded, and everyone had enjoyed the leftovers. Except Fern, of course. She'd brought her lunch, as always, but she'd had to put the bag into the crisper drawer.

Where it had been the *only* item in the drawer for pity's sake.

Paisley folded the paper very carefully and tucked it into the book she'd checked out. When she took it home tonight, she was going to toss this suggestion in the trash where it deserved to be. Or maybe she'd take it to the gun range and ask Ethan to set it on fire when they lit the fireworks.

A little shiver traveled across her skin. Ethan had poked around her house day before yesterday, making notes, and then said he'd get back with her. They had exchanged phone numbers, her heart pounding the whole time she'd typed his in so she could send a text back to him.

He'd gotten her text, added her to his contacts, and then he was gone before she had to take Violet to the Parks' house. She hadn't heard from him since, other than a brief text to tell her the fireworks were Friday night at nine and he had the parts for her toilet and sink. He said he was sorry that he'd been too busy to swing by, but he could install them this weekend if that was fine. She'd said it was.

A few minutes later, Daphne had texted to tell her all the details about Friday, which was tonight. There would be food at hers and Kane's place. There would be drinks. Fireworks would commence the moment it was dark, and they would all take turns keeping Violet awake if necessary. There was also a goat and a pony, which they thought would help with keeping Violet interested enough to stay awake.

Both animals were on loan from a farmer, and he'd assured them neither cared about fireworks. The goat was deaf and the pony was a badass. There was a saddle and a bridle, and Violet could ride the pony if she wanted.

Paisley teared up thinking about it, same as she had when she'd gotten the text. She'd debated texting Ethan to ask if it was his idea, but she'd refrained. If he wasn't texting her, then she didn't need to start a conversation with him.

Problem was, she wanted to. So badly. Because he was the only person in this town who'd known her before—well, other than Aunt Hettie, but that was different—and he knew Trey. Not only knew him, but had worked with him at one time. Trey hadn't been openly monstrous, but Ethan hadn't suggested she was making it up. He'd said it himself. He knew how Trey was trained, knew what he was capable of. Having someone understand made her feel less alone.

Not that it fixed anything between her and Ethan. Nothing ever would. Too much time, too much heartache, too much distance to ever breach again.

Megan, the other library tech besides Fern, appeared in the door to the tiny office where Paisley had her desk. She looked harried. "Fern's out there haranguing Mr. Watson about his T-shirt again."

Paisley got to her feet. "What's it say today?"

Fern had a thing about sayings on clothing. She managed to take the most offense possible, no matter the circumstance. And Mr. Watson had a variety of T-shirts that she *really* hated. Paisley was pretty sure he delighted in lighting her fuse and did it on purpose. Still, she had to shut that shit down ASAP.

"Well, it's pink for one thing. And it has a unicorn on it."

"Okay. How is that offensive?"

"It's probably the slogan. *Not Today, Sparkletits.*"

Paisley snickered. "Oh lord."

"To be fair, there's an asterisk in place of the I."

Mr. Watson was a small man, wiry, approximately seventy, and he was a regular. He stood with his hands on his hips, chest puffed out, in the mystery section. Agatha Christie and Louise Penny were his current favorites, though he also went for the serial killer stuff sometimes. Fern ought to take note of that, but of course she didn't. Her face was mottled with crimson and she had a finger pointed at his chest.

"Can I help?" Paisley said, stepping into the fray.

Mr. Watson spoke first. "Yes, dear. Please tell this harpy I can wear a pink unicorn shirt if I want to. It's none of her business."

Fern's eyes bulged. "Mr. Watson, it's not the color. It's the...the word. Specifically the word at the end."

"Sparkletasterisks?" Mr. Watson said, purposefully misunderstanding. "I grant you it's not a real word, but you never know what they'll add to the OED, do you?"

Paisley rather doubted sparkletasterisks was going to catch on and wind up in the Oxford English Dictionary, but she supposed one never knew. "Please don't call Ms. Carter a harpy, Mr. Watson. And Fern, Mr. Watson's shirt isn't violating any rules about library attire. He has a shirt, and we aren't in the business of policing what people wear unless the language is obviously obscene or abusive. I don't think you can make the argument in favor of this being so."

Fern was practically frothing at the mouth. She glared at Paisley. "Yes, well, you would side with him."

"I'm not siding—"

"You're not from around here and you only got this job because your aunt forced the committee to hire you." Fern's furious gaze raked over her. "Or maybe you used your assets to get in good with the city council. I hear that Councilman Armstrong will do anything for the promise of a good time. Yes indeed, the only harpy around here is *you*."

Paisley took a step back, too shocked at the woman's vitriol to respond right away. Mr. Watson puffed up even more.

"You foul old turnip," he growled at Fern. "You're just a jealous, spiteful hag and you know it! Miss Paisley is a breath of fresh air in this musty old library and you can't stand that. Not to mention she wouldn't waste a microsecond of her time on Chuckles Armstrong. You might, though..."

Fern whirled on her heel and marched off. "I'm going

to the mayor," she yelled over her shoulder. "This is harassment and a hostile work environment!"

Megan's eyes were wide. Debbie Rich, the volunteer on duty, peeked from behind the circulation desk. If there were any other patrons in the library, they hadn't shown themselves. Paisley sighed. Mr. Watson turned to Megan and Debbie. "You two are delightful," he said. "I'm sorry about the musty library comment."

"It's fine, Mr. Watson," Megan said.

"You aren't wrong about Fern," Debbie added. "She's jealous. And mean. Did she quit? Because I really hope so. Life would be so much nicer around here if she did."

Paisley took a deep breath. Her heart raced and her skin was hot, despite the coolness of the AC. She hated being yelled at. She'd never liked it, because who would, but Trey had turned it into a blood sport. Because of him her fight or flight response was coded to flight, and it flared whenever anyone was actively unpleasant to her.

"I doubt she quit," Paisley said, focusing on her breathing. *In, out. In, out.* "But she's bound to be extra unpleasant for a while."

"The mayor isn't going to do a damned thing," Mr. Watson said. "She likes you, and she doesn't like Fern. You're safe."

"Maybe so, but do you think maybe you like to bait her with these shirts, Mr. Watson?"

He grinned at her. "I guess I enjoy it a might bit, yes ma'am. But I'll be more careful with my choices on library day. Or I'll put something over it before I walk in."

"Thank you," Paisley said. "I appreciate it."

Mr. Watson patted her shoulder. "You're a good kid, Miss Paisley. Just like your Aunt Hettie. Not that she's a kid, but she used to babysit me when I was knee high to a grasshopper. Always liked her. Like you, too."

"Thank you. Are you here for the new Louise Penny? I think Debbie has it behind the desk for you."

"Yes, ma'am. Grabbing some Michael Connolly too. Always love a good Bosch novel. Though I gotta admit, Mickey Haller is a close second for me these days."

"What happened to Jack Reacher?"

"Jack's in a class by himself."

"True." They walked to the circulation desk where Debbie pulled out Louise Penny. "Would you be interested in leading a thriller discussion group sometime?"

"I'd love to, dear girl. Just let me know."

"You got it. I'm going to leave you in Debbie's capable hands while I go call the mayor and give her a heads up."

Paisley said her goodbyes and returned to her office. She placed a call to Susie Green's office. Susie had once been an actress in daytime soaps. She'd lived in New York for years, playing a hyper-sexed diva turned matriarch (as time went on), but then she'd retired and come home to Sutton's Creek. She'd promptly gotten involved in politics and found herself sitting in the mayor's seat in the town hall. Fortunately, Susie Green didn't put up with a lot of crap. But Paisley still owed her a call now that Fern had kicked up a cloud of dust.

Mayor Green took her call right away, sighed a lot,

then promised to take care of Fern. Paisley set her phone down and put her head in her hands. Her heart still beat faster than normal, and a shiver rolled down her spine. Anxiety did that to her, and the aftermath of confrontation always left her anxious. Being a librarian wasn't all books and reading, no matter what people thought. It was a lot of tasks, many of them managing other people's emotions as well as her own. Like retail work, only without the selling.

Her phone pinged with a text. She didn't intend to pick it up, not until she was calmer, but her eyes were drawn to the screen. When she saw Ethan's name, all thoughts of Fern Carter fled.

> **Ethan:**
> I've got some free time now if you'd like
> me to take care of the toilet and sink.

Paisley sighed. Just her luck.

> **Paisley:**
> I'm at work. I don't get off for another
> two hours.

> **Ethan:**
> I can swing by and pick up your key, get
> the work done, and bring it back to you.

Her stomach tightened. She knew Ethan wasn't the bad guy. Knew he wasn't going to do anything to hurt her and Violet. And yet she couldn't help but think of Trey and how innocently he'd behaved at first. Wanting to help her. Comfort her. Get food for her, pick up her prescriptions, grab things at the grocery store.

Three dots flashed across the screen before she could formulate a reply.

Ethan:
Something just came up. I'll be there later, after you're home. Does that work for you?

Paisley:
Yes. Sorry, I was answering a question for a patron.

Ethan:
It's fine. See you around six.

Paisley:
See you.

Paisley put her phone down, her heart pounding. She hated—absolutely hated—how paranoid she was now. How she overanalyzed everything and couldn't make up her mind because she wasn't sure if her instincts about a person were right or if she was missing something.

Trey had done that to her. Changed her. Made her mistrustful and suspicious. She wanted the old Paisley back—but she would never come back. That Paisley was dead and buried.

The reason for the new Paisley was so she didn't wind up dead and buried for real.

When her phone buzzed again, she picked it up automatically, thinking it must be Ethan.

But the number was unknown. Her throat constricted. Black spots crawled into the edges of her vision.

> **Unknown:**
> You'll get what's coming to you. Wait
> for it.

9

than parked in front of Paisley's house and grabbed the plastic bag with the parts before strolling to her door.

He'd spooked her earlier, asking for a key. He hadn't thought about why that might not work for her until she didn't answer right away. Once he thought about it, he'd given her an out. When she'd responded immediately, he knew he'd gone beyond her comfort zone in asking for a key.

It bothered him, and yet he understood. If she gave him a key and he went inside her house without her there, he could do things to violate her privacy. Go through her belongings, plant listening devices or cameras, make a copy of the key and return when she wasn't expecting him. It wasn't something he would ever do, but he didn't blame her for being cautious.

He knocked on the door, studying the perimeter of the

porch ceiling for any signs someone may have planted cameras to spy on her. There was nothing. It was possible Trey wouldn't do anything, but Ethan couldn't help but remember the man's intensity when they'd been stationed together at HOT and then later when Ethan was TDY at Eglin AFB.

He'd thought little of it at the time because a man had to be intense to do what they did. To face fear and death on a regular basis, and to stay coolheaded while it was happening. Ethan had thought nothing of Trey's story about his decision to leave HOT and go to Eglin full-time, but now he wondered. Especially since it'd happened before either of them met Paisley.

The door opened to reveal her in a jean vest and long white skirt. She was beautiful, like always. Even with her hair much shorter than he was used to seeing on her, she took his breath away. Her smile wasn't quite genuine though.

"Hi. Come on in."

He didn't move, studying her instead. "Everything okay?"

"Why wouldn't it be?"

"Bad day at work. Something from your lawyer. Any number of things might ruin your day."

Her fingers gripped the door harder, the skin whitening. "My day isn't ruined. But yes, it was a bit of a bad day at the library. Could you come in please so I can shut the door and not pay to cool the outside air? Which, I might add, is a futile effort."

He stepped inside and she moved away so he could shut the door. "What happened at work?"

She shrugged and gave him more of that fake smile. "Fern Carter and Hiram Watson."

"Huh. Is that one of those romance novels the women are reading in their book club?"

She stared like he'd spoken another language. Then she snorted, slapping her hand over her mouth like she was afraid once she started laughing, she wouldn't stop. "Lord no," she finally said. "Fern is one of the library techs. She thinks I stole her job. Oh, and slept with a city councilman to get it in the first place."

"What?"

"I didn't, of course. I've sworn off men for a while. Maybe forever, if I'm honest."

Now why did that little piece of information make his gut tighten? "I didn't think you did. Why'd she say it?"

"Because she's a bitter cow who thinks she's entitled to the job and can't figure out that she's made life so difficult for people there was no way they'd promote her. Would you like something to drink?"

"I'm good. Keep telling me about Fern while I replace the washer in the sink."

They went into the kitchen and he got to work, bending over to turn off the valve beneath the sink. Paisley leaned against the counter and watched him work.

"Fern?" he prodded when she propped her chin in her hand and didn't say anything.

"What? Oh, yes." She straightened. "Hiram Watson is a library regular. He reads a lot, and he's always in there getting new books. He has, shall we say, interesting taste in clothing. Today's shirt was pink. There was a unicorn, and the slogan was *Not today, Sparkletits.* Except sparkletits had an asterisk where the I is, just to make it less obvious. Fern took exception, like she always does, and argued with him about the obscenity. I stepped in, pointing out—quite reasonably I thought—that sparklet-asterisk-ts isn't really considered an obscenity and we couldn't ask him to leave. That's when she unloaded on me and said she was going to the mayor. She stormed out and marched straight over to Mayor Green's office. I called to warn her. Not sure what she said, but Fern *really* wasn't happy once it was over. She didn't come back to work."

"Damn, sounds like a reality TV episode."

She laughed. "Oh yes, *The Unhinged Librarians of Sutton's Creek.* A real ratings hog, that one. I hear there's going to be a Season Two."

Ethan grinned. "It's nice to hear you laugh."

She dropped her gaze and folded her arms across her chest. Protecting herself. He hated that she felt the need.

"Yes, well, sometimes you have to laugh or you'll just cry. How was your day?"

"Fine. Busy. We've been getting more women signing up for self-defense training lately. Between that and the security consulting we're doing for defense contractors in Huntsville, some days are non-stop."

"But not all days or you wouldn't be working with Diego."

He finished tightening the faucet. "True. I like to be busy, and I like working on house projects."

Because he didn't like it when he had too much time to think. The older he got, the more he thought about where he'd come from and where he'd been. And he wondered where the fuck he was going, because he didn't have some of the things he'd thought he would by this age.

A wife. A kid or two. A house.

Stability.

The guys would laugh if they knew he wanted those things. Or maybe they wouldn't since they were all trending that way themselves. Six of them had moved to Alabama with the intention of sacrificing all for the mission and then getting the hell out if they were alive and able. Now four of them were staying forever.

Then there were the thoughts about Paisley that had returned in full force since she'd dropped back into his life. He didn't see those going away anytime soon, especially now.

He turned the water on and ran the sink, then shut it off and waited. Nothing dripped.

"I had no idea it was that easy," Paisley said. "And I should have. I'm a librarian. All I needed to do was look it up."

He gathered up the bag. "Don't be hard on yourself.

You have more important things to worry about. Let's get the toilet now."

She led him to the bathroom. "That's nice of you to say. But I could have at least looked."

"Turns out you didn't have to. You just had to ask me." He got to work on the toilet. "Where's Violet?"

"She's next door. The neighbor's cat had kittens and she went to see them. She really wants a kitten," Paisley added with a sigh.

"Why not? A pet's a good thing for a kid to have. Teaches empathy and responsibility."

Her eyebrows lifted. "Easy for you to say when you don't have to be the one to take care of it when she forgets to do something. I can't handle one more living thing in this house right now."

"Understood. There's always next month or next year. Kittens happen all the time, unfortunately."

"Unfortunately?"

"Relax. I like cats. I said *unfortunately* because people don't spay or neuter their pets."

"You're right. Breaks my heart to see all the strays without homes."

He knew all about being a homeless stray. Living in shelters at night, on the streets during the day. Wondering where the next meal would come from. It was a part of his life he didn't share with anyone—but he would never forget how it'd shaped him into the man he was. How it still drove him.

"A fact of life, I'm afraid." His voice was gruff. "Until

people do the responsible thing, there'll always be more animals than people who care about them."

More kids, too.

He turned the water on again. The toilet filled and then stopped where it was supposed to. He flushed to make sure the flapper seated itself properly. When it did, he put the lid back on. "There you go. Good as new."

"Bless you. How much do I owe you for the parts?"

He wadded up the bag with the empty packaging. "Nothing. Consider it a gift."

Her forehead creased. "You don't have to do that. I can afford to pay for parts. I'm just not sure about an entire security system right now."

"It's no big deal, Payz. It was like thirteen bucks and some change. Buy me a coffee and a muffin at Kiss My Grits one of these days. Or a beer at the Dawg. As for the security system, it's not as bad as you think. I wanted to talk to you in person, show you where things would go."

She'd folded her arms over her chest again. "First give me the bad news."

"This house is old and the walls are plaster, so wiring it would be a lot of work. But we can do a wireless system, cellular, with motion lights on the house and cameras mounted in hidden locations. All for under five-hundred dollars. Professional monitoring adds roughly fifty bucks a month, but you don't have to go with a company if you want to let us do the monitoring for you."

"Us? You mean One Shot Tactical?"

"And security, yes. We'll respond to alerts faster than a company will, but it's up to you."

"How much is that?"

"Nothing. It's not something we do for everyone so there's no price structure. It's me and the guys. We'll get alerts on our phones, and we'll respond."

"What if you're asleep?"

"Not an issue. The alerts are loud. Or you can go with a monitoring company if it makes you feel more comfortable. They'll call the police if they get an alert and you don't respond when they call you to confirm it's not a mistake."

She rubbed her forehead. "I honestly don't have five-hundred to spare. I have to put Violet in daycare once school starts since she's not old enough for school yet. That isn't going to be cheap."

"How about this? I'll put it in and you pay what you can, when you can. We'll do the monitoring. If Trey so much as shows his face on the property, we'll know. And you can share the evidence with the court. How long is the protective order for?"

"Six months to start. The judge can renew it though."

"A system could be invaluable then. You said you feel like you and Violet will be in danger every day for the rest of your lives. This could give you some peace of mind."

"I know, but—"

"No buts, Payz. Listen to me when I tell you that I know how Trey operates. If he were to come after you, he wouldn't just break in and kill you in your sleep. He'd watch you, trail you, and he'd break in when you weren't home so he could case the place, make a plan, figure out how to murder you and make it an accident. He's violent, but he's not the kind of man who intends to do jail time for it. If he wants to kill you, it won't be in any way that implicates him. It also won't be an impulse. So your best shot of stopping him is catching him early, when he's still making the plan."

Her eyes had gone wide. She hugged herself tighter, and his throat knotted. He wanted to kill the sonofabitch himself and put an end to her fear.

"I'm sorry for being so blunt," he said. "I'm not trying to make it worse for you. I want to help, and I want you to realize why you need that help."

She dragged in a breath. Then she nodded. "I know. Okay, let's do it. I'll give you some money when I get paid, and I'll keep giving you something every couple of weeks. As long as you're sure that's okay."

He didn't want to take her money at all, but he would if it's what she wanted. Hell, maybe he'd donate it to a shelter. He didn't need it and she did, but she wasn't going to let him do this if he didn't accept payment.

"It's okay. I got you, Payz."

"Why?" Her voice was soft, whispery. "After everything?"

"Because it's the right thing to do."

10

Joy filled Paisley's heart at the sight of Violet perched on the little black pony, laughing in sheer delight and having the time of her life.

Callie led Merrylegs—named after the pony in the classic tale *Black Beauty*—around the yard, telling Violet how to sit and hold the reins, and the little girl brimmed with happiness.

Paisley's heart was full. It was a tenuous joy, though. The text she'd gotten at work today kept intruding on her thoughts. She'd planned to tell Ethan, but she hadn't found the right moment before Violet had returned home, full of excited chatter about the mama cat and her kittens.

She should have told him when he first asked what was wrong, but the words wouldn't come out. She was used to relying on herself these days, being careful who she trusted, and not making the mistake of thinking anyone else could fix what was wrong with her life.

Of course she'd panicked when the text came in. But then she'd made herself think about it, and she had to admit she wasn't certain if she was being overly paranoid or if the text could be explained by the fight with Fern. The timing was too convenient, and though Fern had supposedly only sent harassing emails to the volunteer who'd quit, nothing stopped her from leveling up to texts. Anyone could buy a burner phone.

Fern was angry with her, and Fern had her number. Trey did not. She'd gotten a new phone when she'd arrived in Alabama, and the only people from her old life who had the number were her lawyer and the court.

She wasn't stupid enough to think Trey couldn't discover her new number eventually, but she also thought it more likely he'd track her down and show up suddenly if he did. He wouldn't warn her with a text. Like Ethan had said, he would have a plan. And that plan wasn't going to involve reckless texts that could be attributed to him.

She needed to be smart and she needed to tell Ethan. It was ninety-percent likely to be Fern, but just in case. Plus, did she really know what Fern was capable of? What if the woman had a violent streak? All Paisley needed was two violent assholes angry with her.

Emma sauntered over to where Paisley stood, a bottle of water in her hand, a big smile on her face. "Isn't that pony the cutest darn thing?"

"She really is," Paisley said.

"So is Violet. Though I think you may want to kill

Ethan after this. It was his idea to get the pony, but I don't think he thought about how much Violet would love riding. She'll want a pony now."

Paisley laughed. "I'll kill him later. Right now, she's having fun."

Really, life was good. That's what she had to focus on. Life in Sutton's Creek was promising and bright. Despite Fern. Despite the distant threat of Trey. This moment with these people was lovely.

"Thank you all for doing this. It means a lot to Violet to get to see the fireworks she missed."

"It was Ethan's idea, but we're all happy to participate. We have frequent cookouts together anyway. Adding some fireworks and barnyard animals wasn't a big stretch." Emma put a hand on her very small belly. "Besides, there will be children at our get togethers next year, so why not start now? Though I think the pony will have to wait a few years for this little one."

"Not as long as you think," Callie said as she strolled by with Merrylegs and Violet. "My mother had me on a horse when I was eight months old. Of course she held me up there while somebody else led, but you can start them early."

Emma shuddered. "This kid's not going to be a horse kid. Seth cringes every time Nikki gallops toward a fence, so I know Blaze won't handle it well."

Callie laughed. "He's a big old baby about it, but he doesn't let Nikki see. He melts down in private."

"Nikki's a teenager," Paisley said to Emma as Callie got out of earshot. "What's the big deal?"

"Fences," Emma said. "Nikki jumps them. When Seth fell for Callie, he fell for Nikki too. He loves that kid, and watching her hurl a twelve-hundred pound animal over a fence kind of freaks him out."

Paisley imagined Violet galloping toward a fence and shuddered. "I get it. Poor guy."

"Just don't get her a pony and you'll be okay. Probably."

Since she couldn't afford a pony, that wasn't going to be a problem. Maybe a kitten wasn't such a bad idea after all. Might distract Violet from the pony idea if she got started on it.

Emma took a sip of water. "I think Ethan likes you and Violet."

Paisley's stomach clenched. "He's a nice guy."

"Mmm-hmm. The way he looked at you in the Dawg before he took off that night made me wonder if maybe you'd met before."

Paisley's throat was a desert. She hastily took a sip of her Coke. She didn't want to lie, and yet she didn't want to share her entire sad history. She also didn't want these women to think she and Ethan were a possibility.

"I, um, don't think so. But I met a lot of people at the library in the first few days."

"I guess that could be it. Or he had a sudden bout of indigestion. I did think of that. It happens."

Rory wandered over, saving Paisley from a reply about the state of Ethan's digestion. Thank heavens.

"Isn't that the cutest?" Rory exclaimed.

"So cute," Emma agreed. "The goat's adorable too."

The goat was currently standing on the bench beneath one of the big oak trees. They'd had to chase him off the table earlier, and he'd been eyeing Daphne's car before that. She'd threatened to make stew out of him while Kane laughed his head off. Which had not amused Daphne. She'd threatened to open the doors to his Tahoe and let the goat have his way with the interior.

That'd shut Kane up quick.

Paisley couldn't help but be amazed at how much these men seemed to love their women. They were all former soldiers, like Trey, but they were nothing like Trey. They didn't posture, didn't scowl at their women, and didn't look like they were on the edge of an explosion over the slightest thing. Like threatening to let a goat into a vehicle.

If Paisley had said that to Trey, he'd have pinched her side or her arm and twisted hard while pretending to smile and telling her what he'd do if she tried it. She'd learned very quickly not to joke around with him.

"Did you ask her?" Rory said to Emma.

"I was working up to it."

Paisley blinked, her gaze sliding between them. "Ask me what?"

The two women shared a look before turning their

gazes back to her. Paisley's heart dropped as she frantically tried to imagine what they wanted to know. She'd seen Emma studying Violet, but that didn't mean anything. Yes, Paisley did sometimes think that Violet's eyes were remarkably like Ethan's—but hazel eyes weren't unique.

Emma cleared her throat. "I somehow got roped into serving on the committee planning the Christmas tour this year. It's still a few months away, but we need hosts and hostesses for the homes and businesses on tour. You basically take a shift, usually an hour or so. You stand in a particular room and tell people about it when they enter —the history, anything the owner wants you to tell people, etcetera. Many owners get their friends to help, but I thought it'd be nice if we had a pool of volunteers this year. Make it less stressful on the people getting their homes ready."

Paisley's knees wobbled. "You want me to be a hostess?"

"Well, yes. It would only be for an hour or two on a Saturday in December. But you don't have to if you're too busy. And it doesn't change anything. We didn't invite you into the Besties just to ask for favors."

Relief made her giddy. "Yes, of course. I'd be happy to help."

Rory lightly slapped Emma's shoulder. "Told you she'd do it. And you were afraid to ask."

"Why?" Paisley asked.

"You haven't been in town very long, and I didn't want to overwhelm you with yet another task. The people of this town are going to ask the librarian to participate in a lot of events, and I didn't want you to feel obligated to say yes or to think we've invited you to hang out with us so you'd be a volunteer."

Paisley laughed. "Honestly, if an hour or two of my time is all you wanted and you went to all this trouble to get it, then I'd say I'm still getting the better end of the bargain. I'm happy to help in any way I can. I want to be part of this community. I want Violet to grow up here. Aside from one coworker, life has been good since we arrived."

Emma rolled her eyes. "Fern Carter. Lord love a duck. That woman has the sourest disposition of anyone I've ever met. She's mean as a snake."

Paisley tried not to let her surprise show, but she must have failed because Rory patted her arm. "It's okay. Everyone knows Fern. Though she doesn't frequent the Dawg, thank heavens."

"Speaking of the Dawg, how are Theo and the gang holding up without you tonight?" Callie said as she joined them. Paisley's gaze shot to Violet and Merrylegs, but Ethan had the lead rope. He was talking to Violet and she had a big smile on her face. Paisley wished she could hear what he was saying. Instead, she dragged her attention back to the conversation.

Rory spread her hands. "They swear they've got it. Whenever I check the receipts, business is brisk. I have to think if they were failing to get the job done, business would fall off. It's not, though. We've hired more shift workers, and both Nikki and Amber are handling the bar just fine. I'm working days most of the time, and I have to be honest and say it's best. I get more tired than I used to. Plus I'm enjoying my reading, some gardening and decorating. Chance and I are discussing the renovations we want to make to the house, too. And a wedding. Eventually. I'm in no rush for that."

Everyone agreed it was a good thing that Rory was taking time for herself, and that she and Chance were making plans. Paisley got the impression that Rory had been a bit of a workaholic before she got pregnant.

"So I heard Fern got into a fist fight with Mr. Watson today," Callie said. "Nikki heard it from a friend who heard it from her cousin who got it from somewhere else. Honestly, I figured it was exaggerated."

"It was a verbal altercation," Paisley said. "In the library. Over a T-shirt."

She relayed the story. The women snort-laughed at the slogan. Of course they did, because they were awesome that way.

"Unfortunately, she's just one of those people who hates everything and everyone," Emma said. "She's always been that way. When she left town, nobody thought she'd come back. But she did. And she didn't improve while she was gone either. Her husband is a decent guy. Not a local, but people like him. Can't figure out why he puts up with her, really."

"I haven't met him yet," Paisley said. "I honestly don't

know if Fern quit today or not. She didn't return to the library after she left the mayor's office."

She didn't tell them about the text and her suspicions.

"She'll be back on Monday," Rory said. "Sitting at her desk like nothing happened. I don't think she ever gave Miss Hettie that kind of grief, but I've heard of her acting like a first class bitch. And then acting like it didn't happen."

"Great," Paisley said. "And here I was hoping she'd had enough."

"I mean she could, but I doubt it."

Daphne emerged from the house with a platter containing burgers ready for the grill. Kane followed with chicken on another platter. They both sported goofy grins like they'd just had the quickest of quickies in the fifteen minutes they were gone. The women smirked knowingly at each other. They included Paisley in it, but she felt out of place anyway. She'd never felt that kind of happiness in a relationship—other than the short few weeks she'd spent with Ethan.

"Food will be ready soon," Daphne said.

"I hope so," Chance called. "I'm starving over here. What the hell—heck have y'all been doing in there anyway?"

"Getting the food ready," Kane said. "What do you think?"

Chance opened his mouth to reply. Then closed it when he and Rory exchanged a look. She turned back to the women, grinning.

"We're working on language. Both of us are fond of a curse word, but we're trying to clean it up with the little one on the way. I'm sorry that one slipped out with Violet here."

Paisley smiled. "It's okay. Violet's too enamored of Merrylegs to notice."

"And of Ethan," Callie said.

They all turned to watch the man lead the child around on the pony. He laughed as much as Violet did, throwing his head back, the laughter coming from deep inside. Paisley's heart squeezed to hear it. If only. Those were the words she thought of in the moment.

If only.

If only Ethan hadn't been sent away. If only she hadn't fallen for Trey's lies. If only she'd waited.

Ethan would have called, and maybe she'd have been pregnant anyway. Maybe Violet was his instead of Trey's. If only she hadn't been weak and vulnerable, she would still have Violet and the three of them would have been a family this whole time.

Her throat tightened as tears gathered in the corners of her eyes. She couldn't cry, not now. Not in front of these women and not over something so simple as a man leading a child around on a pony and laughing. They would all think she was nuts.

"It's okay," Emma said, putting an arm around her shoulders and squeezing. "You don't have to tell us anything you don't want to."

"W-what do you mean?"

Rory handed over a tissue. Paisley took it and dabbed the corners of her eyes.

"You're a single mom. We don't know anything about Violet's father or your relationship with him. And we don't need to know. But you seem a little emotional seeing her enjoying a man's company, so maybe you're missing him or wishing things were different. You don't have to explain, but you can also ask for a tissue or a moment alone."

Paisley squeezed the tissue into a ball. "You're scary good," she said with a laugh. It was that or cry harder.

Emma shrugged and smiled. "I'm a doctor. I'm used to listening, and I see a lot of emotional responses. I don't mean to call you out, but you're with friends. Just wanted you to know it."

"She's right," Rory said. "We're all hot messes in our own way. But we've adopted you, so you can be a hot mess too. No explanations necessary."

"Thank you," Paisley replied. "I..."

She was planning to make an excuse, but then she thought, why not? Why not share some of the burden?

"We're getting a divorce," she said simply. "It wasn't a good situation, and Violet and I are here to start over."

"Oh, honey," Emma said. "I'm sorry. Anything we can do to help, we will."

The other women agreed.

"When I needed help," Callie said. "These ladies were here for me. The men too. This is a really, really great group of people. If we don't know how to help, we'll figure it out."

"Yep," Rory said. "We gotchu. Daphne would agree if she weren't over there making googly eyes at Kane. The Bookalicious Besties have to stay together. We're a sisterhood."

Paisley shook her head. "You're so nice to me. You don't even know me, not really, but you've asked me to be a part of your book club and now you're telling me I'm one of your sisterhood. I...I just don't know what to say. I've never really had that before, and I don't know why it's happening now, but I *am* grateful for it."

The three women exchanged a look. Rory seemed to be the one chosen to speak. "Emma Grace and I are from Sutton's Creek, but we both know how it feels when you think you don't belong. I've been something of an outcast my whole life. Honestly, I think most people feel that way to some extent. We never feel like we belong, do we? Anyway, Daphne and Callie aren't from Sutton's Creek— and neither are the guys, by the way. But we've all felt something, that pull of friendship or whatever you want to call it, when we met each other. I knew the night we had our book club that you belonged. I think all of us did."

"Yep," Callie said. Emma echoed it.

"You don't have to say anything," Rory continued. "Just know that you can call us if you need to talk, or you need somebody to watch Violet for a few hours, or whatever. We'll make it happen. And if you need somebody to go and kick Fern in the lady balls, then I'm your girl."

Paisley couldn't help but snort. The other women laughed too. The tension that lived between her shoulder blades eased a fraction. Maybe it was all going to be okay. Maybe the bad parts were behind her and only good stuff lay in front of her.

She fervently hoped so. Even if experience had taught her that hope was a fragile flower, easily crushed.

fter the fireworks and goodbyes, Ethan loaded Violet into the back of his truck while Paisley hovered. Then she climbed into the front of the cab and belted herself in while he went around to the driver's side. He glanced back at Violet as he started the engine.

She was, of course, completely passed out. The fireworks had been a huge hit with her. The pony, the goat, the food. All of it. But the fireworks were what she'd most wanted to see. He'd bought some big ones, maybe bigger than he should have, but it was worth it when he'd looked at Violet. The wonder and joy on her face made his heart happy.

He still couldn't wrap his head around the fact she was Trey McCann's kid. Or that Trey could be so monstrous that he could ever consider hurting her. The man Ethan had known had been complex, like most people, and he'd had a quietness to him that hadn't always made sense. Like he was thinking about something.

But what if it wasn't quietness at all? What if it was darkness?

Darkness. Sickness. Evil.

"Thanks for driving us," Paisley said. "You really didn't have to, though."

She'd argued with him when he'd suggested giving them a ride to the range and back again. But he'd pointed out it would be dark and late when the fireworks were done and asked if she wouldn't feel better having him there to help her get Violet inside. She'd frowned for a second before admitting she would.

Now he wheeled the truck around and headed for the road. "Happy to help, Payz."

"I feel badly that you have to take us back to Sutton's Creek and then drive home again."

"We're a couple miles outside town limits. It's not like I'm driving you to the other side of Huntsville."

"True." She was quiet a moment, her hands fiddling around in her lap. He remembered her doing that when they were dating. It was a tell that she was nervous or uncertain. "I like your friends. They're good people."

"They are. And they like you too."

They didn't have a reason not to. The women had made her part of their group, and the men accepted her because the women did.

Ethan hadn't told his team about his past with Paisley yet. He needed to. Needed to explain about his time in

Florida and the relationship he'd once had with her. He'd hesitated because it hadn't seemed necessary to drag up the past that way. He'd hadn't wanted the questions or contemplative looks when they thought he didn't know he was being watched. He certainly hadn't wanted any pity at the way it'd gone down.

But if he wanted to protect her, he needed to let his guys know about Trey. They'd help him look out for her.

"I think the ladies want to set us up," she said.

"Yeah, not surprised about that. I don't think they'll push it though, especially if we indicate we just want to be friends."

She looked down at her clasped hands. "I told them I was getting a divorce and that it wasn't a good situation. I didn't tell them how bad it was, but I think they know I'm not ready to leap into anything."

"I'm glad you told them about the divorce. You'll need friends to talk to sometimes. You can always talk to me, but I figure you may not want to about some things. Hell, maybe you don't want to talk to me about anything. And that's fine. I get it. Our situation is pretty, uh, effed up." He'd just barely managed to correct the word on his tongue to a milder version, but he'd remembered Violet at the last second. Not that she was awake, but he needed to get into the habit of policing his language around her anyway.

"I just mean," he continued, "that we were a couple once, with feelings for each other, and it ended suddenly and without explanation for both of us. So I guess talking to me about the guy you did marry might be difficult at times. Though you can. I want you to know that."

"Thank you." She sighed and tilted her head back on the seat. "I don't want to talk about him at all, but I know I have to. There's a lot to process there. Especially when Violet asks about him, which she sometimes does. He scared her with his temper, but he also made grandiose promises to change that she believed."

Ethan gripped the wheel tight. He was having his own issues with temper whenever Paisley talked about Trey, but he wouldn't let it show. Wouldn't ever want her to feel scared of him or his emotions. Those were his problem, and he intended to keep them in check.

"To be honest," she said, "You're the only person I feel comfortable talking to about what Trey was like. Because you knew him."

"Not well enough, apparently." His voice was sand-paper over stone.

"He fooled everyone. You couldn't have known. That's what abusers do. They lie and pretend and act like the perfect partner when they're laying their trap for you. They continue to act perfect in front of others so nobody will believe you if you dare talk. Trey was a master at deception. There are people in Florida right now who think he's the victim here, that I've lied and manipulated and stolen his child away. Honestly, I don't care what he says about me so long as I never have to see him again."

His throat was tight. "I wish I'd been there, Payz. I wish I'd gotten on a plane and went looking for you when you didn't answer me. Hell, even when I got that text, I wish I'd gone after you to demand an explanation."

"It's not your fault. It's Trey's fault. He was jealous of you. Not that I realized it at first."

She turned to look out the window and he wanted to stop the truck and drag her into his arms. She was breaking his heart here.

"What aren't you telling me, baby?"

She sniffled and swiped her hand over her face. Wiping away tears. It killed him that she was crying. Because he couldn't fix it.

She swiveled to face him. "He couldn't let it go that you and I were together. And that's not your fault either, by the way. He was *always* going to be triggered by that. It was an excuse. Jesus," she hissed, wiping her face again. "I hate him, Ethan. So much. He would lose his shit and then he'd apologize and cry and swear it would never happen again. I should have left, but Violet was a baby and I had nowhere to go. No medical insurance if I left. No way to pay for the things she needed. I was also terrified he'd take her away from me even though I knew he didn't want her."

It was strange to feel the way he did in that moment. Both murderously angry and numb at the same time. His anger wouldn't help, and the numbness was a coping mechanism. Because he felt helpless in the face of all she'd suffered.

"I'll never get over the things I should have done, but I'm not letting him hurt you ever again."

She looked away. "I feel like I should tell you that you can't control that—but instead I'm gonna say thank you."

"You're welcome."

Silence filled the space between them for a few seconds before she spoke again, her voice barely more than a whisper. "I need to tell you I got an anonymous text today. I think it was from Fern."

A squeeze of fear tightened inside him. "What did it say?"

"It said I'd get what was coming to me and to wait for it. I didn't tell you earlier because Violet came home before I could. There was never really a good time until now."

He hated that she felt like she had to justify herself. Even if he wished she'd told him earlier. "You told me now. Thank you for trusting me."

He meant that. He knew trust was hard for her, but if she trusted him with her safety, that was a huge win to him. The text could be from the library tech. She was spiteful enough to do it. But he wouldn't rule out Trey McCann. He couldn't. Too dangerous to ignore him.

"I got a new phone when I got here. My lawyer and the court has the number. I had to provide it since I have Violet and we're in the middle of proceedings. Trey doesn't know it, though."

"What did you do with your old phone?"

"It's turned off and sitting inside an empty cookie tin. I wrapped it in foam and then I wrapped the tin in foam and taped it."

Ethan threw her a look. "You learned that from Trey?"

"Not all of it. He was paranoid with his business so he had Faraday cages—boxes, really—in the house. He kept his laptop and a couple of phones in them. He didn't tell me why, but I researched the boxes and found out that a cookie tin wasn't completely reliable as a Faraday cage. You need a tight seal. I used the foam to help with the seal, and I taped it all around."

"Good thinking, Payz."

"I *am* a librarian," she said with a smile. "Research is my jam."

"Can I ask you to give me the cookie tin? I'll store it at the range. Just in case."

"I suppose so. I don't need the phone, but I didn't want to throw it away. I couldn't sell it either because I couldn't guarantee that Trey wouldn't track the new owner down."

"I'll take it off your hands and keep it safe. As for the text, we can't assume it was Fern. Not saying it's not possible, but I can't dismiss it that easily. Gonna need to take some precautions."

They reached the town limits. He hooked a U-turn at the first cross street and started back the way they'd come.

"Where are we going?"

He heard the anxiety. Hated it. But he knew what he had to do. "I need to grab a few things. Won't take more than fifteen minutes."

"I don't understand."

He lifted his gaze to the rearview so he could see Violet. Her eyes were closed, her little body slack in her car seat. He shot a look at Paisley before turning his attention to the road again.

"I said I was going to keep you safe, Payz. Can't do that from a distance, can I? I need to grab some clothes and my toothbrush. And a sleeping bag since you've only got two bedrooms."

Her mouth dropped open. "You can't stay with me! People will see your truck. They'll talk about the new librarian shacking up with a guy. And it's not necessary anyway. I'm sure it was just Fern being a bitch because she didn't get her way. I'll confront her about that on Monday—"

"And if she confesses, great—though I wouldn't expect it. Most people don't admit to shit like that. Until I get the security system installed, not leaving you and Violet alone in the house. Once that's in, we'll talk about safety and how best to proceed."

Paisley folded her arms over her chest and stared straight ahead. She heaved a breath. Then she heaved another. When her shoulders collapsed, he knew he had her. She was scared enough about the possibility of Trey not to argue with him, and that was all he needed. Not that he wanted her scared. He fucking hated that she was. But scared was good if it made her unwilling to take risks. He understood that she wanted to believe it was Fern. But he wasn't willing to accept it so easily.

"How am I going to explain it to Violet?"

"She's four. I'll be in a sleeping bag in the living room,

or on the couch. Do you really think she's going to question it?"

"You're a man in our space. She doesn't have the greatest experience with that."

It was like she'd punched him in the gut. Fucking Trey. "I know, honey. I'll make sure she's comfortable with the situation, okay? I won't yell or swear, and I'll ask her about her feelings when I'm there. I just—I need to make sure the two of you are safe. It's important and you know it."

She dropped her head. He wasn't sure she planned to answer him. But then she did, her voice small and soft.

"You can stay."

12

Trey McCann hated three things in this world. People who thought they were better than him. People who underestimated him. And people who tried to get one over on him.

Paisley fell into the last group. She'd thought she was clever when she'd packed her bags and left him the last time he was working a job out of the country.

He'd started his own security firm when he'd left the military. Some people thought he'd never amount to anything, but he'd proven them wrong. The work he did had made him rich enough to tell all his former commanders to fuck off, if he cared enough to find them and do it. Stupid assholes. He got shit done, and now he got paid for it by people who didn't care how he did it so long as he delivered results.

But the things he provided—a big home, expensive

cars and clothes, the best of everything she could want—weren't enough for Paisley.

Nothing was enough for her. Since the kid had been born, Paisley paid more attention to the baby than she did him.

He should have done something about it long ago, but making a kid disappear was a lot of work. People tended to get their underwear in a twist when kids were involved.

And he'd been too busy building his empire to take care of the problem. Besides, he'd gotten a lot of satisfaction out of knowing he'd taken something far more valuable from Ethan Snow than the man would ever realize.

Raising Ethan's kid as his own had given him such a charge. Until it didn't. Until the kid started to resemble Ethan and not him. Paisley hadn't known when she'd gotten pregnant whose kid she was carrying, but Trey did. He couldn't have kids. He'd had a vasectomy years ago because the last thing he wanted was some bitch coming after him for child support.

He didn't even like kids, had no intention of having any until he couldn't quite pass up the idea of stealing more from Ethan than just the woman he loved. He'd figured he could handle the kid for a few years and then he'd make her disappear. Should have gotten rid of her before now, though.

Trey sat in the rental he'd picked up when he got to Huntsville and watched the house where his fucking wife was staying. She thought he didn't know where she was, but she was so fucking wrong it was laughable. He knew she had an aunt in this two-bit town in northern Alabama, and he knew the aunt's name. Not hard to track down any property she owned.

After that, he'd made subtle searches until he found that, yes, Paisley Rose Allen—she'd dared to start using her maiden name again—was living at 223 Chestnut Street. Once he'd discovered that, he decided to take a trip.

Not that he intended to do anything about it. Yet. He wasn't a fool.

He had business in Huntsville from time to time, but nobody knew he was here right now. He'd flown out of Destin yesterday, headed for an overseas trip. Instead of leaving the US immediately, he'd used a different identity in Charlotte to board a new flight and landed in Huntsville this afternoon. He'd head back to Charlotte on Monday and fly out as scheduled.

Fucking child's play for a former HOT operator like him.

This trip was a fact finding mission. See where Paisley and the kid were staying, learn their routine over the next couple of days, pick out the vulnerable points, and then leave. He planned to let her think she was safe. Planned to let everyone think he didn't give two shits that she'd sued for divorce and convinced the judge to issue a protective order.

She'd taken his kid—legally his—from him, but even that was okay with the judge. Because Paisley had gone and opened her mouth, told them the things he'd had to do to keep her ass in line. Suggested he'd do the same to Violet if he wasn't stopped.

As if he'd waste his time on that brat. He knew how to make her a non-issue, had it planned for years. Once he'd started making money, he'd figured boarding school would get her out of the way. Killing her would be more fun, of course, but it wasn't always the optimal plan.

He ground his teeth back and forth as he thought. Paisley was the one who brought punishment on herself, disrespecting him the way she did. Judging him. Comparing him to the man whose name she still sometimes said in her sleep. He could have killed her when she did that, but he'd shown restraint.

And this was the thanks he got.

He'd loved her once, but now he fucking hated her. He was going to break her for her insolence. Her ingratitude.

He sucked down the Dr. Pepper he'd picked up at the convenience store, shoved a handful of potato chips in his mouth, and waited. It was late, after ten, but his intent was to put a tracker on her car when the neighborhood went completely quiet in a couple of hours. It was Friday night and people were still randomly shooting off fireworks and laughing in their back yards.

He wouldn't take the risk of being seen.

He was just settling in with a true crime podcast—amazing what you could learn from those—when a truck slowed and pulled into a spot in front of the Craftsman. There were no designated parking spots on the street.

Could be somebody headed to one of the other houses, but he watched anyway.

The driver's side door opened and a man got out. Tall, muscular, shadowed so that Trey couldn't see his face.

He watched with half-hearted interest as the man grabbed a duffel bag and slung it over his shoulders. Then the passenger door opened and Paisley emerged.

Trey's heartbeat quickened and then slowed. She'd cut all her goddamn hair off. That was the first thing he noticed when the streetlight hit her. He might not have known it was her if not for the light on her face.

How dare she cut her hair when he'd told her never to do that? He liked it long, liked to wrap his hands in it and expose her pretty neck while he thought about how easy it'd be to slice clean through it when she made him angry.

But who was the fucking man? Had she been seeing somebody behind his back? Is that why she'd left him?

He'd kill them both if that was the case.

The man strode around the back of the truck so that Trey couldn't see him. He fooled around on the passenger side, then emerged with a little girl in his arms.

Rage boiled to life inside Trey's veins. It was a fire in his soul, scouring him from inside out. Because the light shone on the man's face as he gazed down at Paisley and cradled the kid in his arms.

Fucking Ethan Snow. What the ever loving *fuck* was he doing here?

Rage, hot and sharp, twisted in Trey's gut. He hated Ethan Snow. Ethan, who'd thought he was such a fucking god that he deserved Paisley. Who'd never even considered that every man at that table in the bar had seen her at the same time. There'd been no debate about who got the shot with her. He'd simply taken it.

It was more than that, though. It was the way he'd swaggered into the unit at Eglin like he was some kind of god, the way he took control and had everyone eating out of his hands. Ethan never said anything about it, but Trey was convinced the man knew that Trey had been reassigned, kicked out of the Hostile Operations Team because his own team and the commanders were a bunch of pussies who would have let soldiers die if he hadn't taken care of the situation.

If he hadn't made the hard call and did the necessary thing. His men didn't back him up, and he'd never forgive them for it. He hated everyone in fucking HOT because of the way they'd treated him. He couldn't make them all pay, but fucking up Ethan's life had been a good diversion.

Trey ground his teeth together, pulled in deep breaths so he didn't do something stupid like grab his Walther and double tap the bastard on the sidewalk where he stood.

Paisley started up the path to her door. She stepped up on the porch, Ethan behind her. The light illuminated the three of them as she inserted the key in the lock and opened the door.

Trey fantasized about the room exploding in a fireball the second the door swung inward, incinerating Ethan, Paisley, and Violet all at once. He loved a good fire more than anything, especially when it took the people he hated with it.

He could do that. Wire the room to explode the next time. He considered it.

But that wasn't satisfying enough, not really. What good was it to put people out of their misery before they'd experienced any? They needed to suffer first. They needed to think they were safe, that they had everything they wanted, when in reality time was ticking away before they lost it all.

No, he had to do much more than wire the room to explode. He had to plan it so they suffered the most emotional damage possible before they died.

That was going to be the fun part.

13

Paisley woke with a start, gasping for air as the hands around her throat squeezed tighter. Panic flared bright—and then settled when she took in her surroundings.

It was morning. Her room. The sun peeked through the blinds. And Violet was curled up beside her, arms around Paisley's neck.

Paisley took a moment to breathe and settle her racing heart. *In for a count of eight, out on a count of eight. In, out. In, out.*

Violet murmured in her sleep and then turned over. She must have crept into the room at some point during the night. It still happened a lot, though not as often as it had in the days when they'd first left Trey. One thing he would never allow was for Violet to get into bed with them. Or for Paisley to go and sleep in her daughter's room.

When they'd gotten free of him, Paisley didn't say no when Violet was scared and needed her. Maybe it was the start of a bad habit, but she'd deal with that bridge when she had to cross it. For now her baby needed her and Paisley wasn't saying no.

She waited to make sure Violet didn't wake before easing herself from the bed and tucking the covers around her child.

She went into the bathroom, brushed her teeth, and threw on a bra beneath her pajamas since Ethan was asleep on the couch. She still couldn't believe she'd let him talk her into staying over, but she had to admit she'd slept better than she did when it was just her and Violet.

Other than the rude awakening she'd had when she'd been dreaming that someone was strangling her, it'd been a restful night. Usually she woke up a few times, her heart racing.

But not last night.

That in itself was worth the awkwardness of having the man she'd once loved—the man who had a fifty-fifty shot of being Violet's father—only a few feet away in her living room.

Her stomach fell at the thought of Ethan being Violet's father. Not because she didn't want him to be, but because of how painful it would be to think about all they'd lost. Hell, it was already painful. But if Violet was truly his?

She squeezed her eyes shut. *God.*

Should she tell him there was a chance? Or should she

let him continue thinking Violet was Trey's because it was easier? She'd thought he would ask at some point once he thought about the fact Violet was barely four, but he hadn't. Either he wasn't doing the math or he didn't care that she could be his because he didn't intend to let it change anything about his life.

But was he acting like a man who didn't care?

No, he wasn't. He made sure Violet got to see fireworks, ride a pony, and pet a goat. He'd personally led her around on the pony, and he'd made her laugh.

And now he was here, in Paisley's home, because he'd promised to keep her and Violet safe. Those weren't the actions of a man who didn't care.

Which meant he wasn't really thinking about Violet's age and the implications. He thought she was Trey's, and he still treated her better than Trey ever had. With more kindness, understanding, and patience, which was something Trey lacked.

Violet might go through life without a father, but no father was better than a terrible one. Paisley hadn't known her own father because Bree hadn't been married to him. Whenever Paisley had asked questions, she'd been shut down. Bree had told her it was just the two of them, and they would be fine.

And they had been.

To this day, Paisley didn't know if her father had been a good man or a bad one. She certainly didn't want a nomadic life for her child like she'd had, but she also knew Violet didn't have to have a father to grow into a healthy and well-adjusted human being.

No father was better than the man who legally filled that role. That was a fact.

Paisley decided to go fix coffee and then sit on the back porch where it was shaded before it grew too hot. It was early enough to still be tolerable, but she always woke early. Even on weekends.

The second she opened her bedroom door, the scent of roasted coffee filled the air. Ethan had beat her to it. She remembered mornings with him years ago when he'd make coffee and then carry it to her in bed. He'd kiss her forehead, murmur sweet words, and wait for her to prop herself on the pillows before he handed her the steaming mug.

"Morning," she said as she walked into the sunny kitchen.

Ethan looked up from his study of the refrigerator's contents. His gaze skimmed her body, and she found herself warming beneath it. "Morning. You sleep okay?"

"Yes, thanks. You?"

She'd been worried about how the couch would work out for him, but he'd told her last night that even the lumpiest couch beat some of the places he'd had to bed down on missions.

"Slept fine."

"The couch wasn't too bad?"

"I put the sleeping bag on the floor. Couch is too short."

Well of course it was. But the floor? "Wasn't it hard?"

"Nah, got a pad for the bag. It's good."

Paisley sighed. "I'm sorry."

"Don't be." He nodded at the fridge. "Want me to scramble some eggs with cheese? We could make some toast to go with it. I'll pick up more eggs and bread at the Piggly Wiggly later, a few other things too."

"You don't have to get any groceries. The least I can do is feed you."

"You told me money's tight, Payz. It's not tight for me, and I want to get some groceries since I'll be here for a couple of nights. Now you want those eggs or what?"

"I feel like I should tell you to sit down so I can cook, but I won't say no. It's nice to have somebody cook for me for a change."

He took out the carton of eggs and set them on the counter. Then he grabbed a bag of shredded cheese and the butter. "Consider it done."

She retrieved a bowl for the eggs, found a whisk, and took out plates and flatware. Ethan cracked the eggs and whisked them into the bowl.

"Should I make enough for Violet? Or wait until later when she's awake?"

Paisley's heart squeezed at the care he showed her daughter. "She'll sleep for another hour at least. Best to wait."

"Gotcha." He turned on the gas and then whipped the eggs with a little milk, salt, and pepper. Paisley put bread in the toaster. A few minutes later, they were sitting down in the breakfast nook with plates of cheesy eggs, buttered toast, and coffee. It was companionable and strange at the same time.

"Thanks again for last night. I know Violet's going to chatter nonstop about it when she wakes up."

He grinned as he saluted her with his toast. "You're welcome. It was easy to make her smile, so why not?"

"Still, you didn't have to. It would be easier to avoid us, I imagine."

"It would be, but that's not how I operate." He frowned as he chewed. "I've lived through a lot, seen a lot, and done things I'd like to forget. But life is messy and complicated, and I believe that helping people is the right thing to do. Even if I didn't know you, didn't know Trey, I'd have shown up on your doorstep to talk you into a security system once I knew you were being threatened by your ex."

"I believe you would have."

Because Ethan was a good man. She'd wondered, after she'd been with Trey for a while and discovered what kind of man he was, if her instincts had always been so wrong. If Ethan wouldn't have been any better, even if he'd only made her feel butterflies and giddiness when she'd known him.

She'd never had giddiness with Trey. She'd never even thought she had. What she'd had with Trey, she saw now, was a shared grievance—Ethan.

Her grievance had been about being discarded like yesterday's trash and then finding out she was pregnant.

She hadn't been certain who the father was, but she'd nursed her grudge against Ethan for abandoning her and the baby anyway. Trey's grievance had seemed to be Ethan himself. He'd certainly said all the right things, coddled her and told her she deserved better. He'd fed her grudge for months, until she'd married him, and then he'd changed. Became angry and distant. Mean.

Sitting across the breakfast table from Ethan nearly five years later, she knew she hadn't been wrong about him. Trey had been kind to her, but not really. She'd mistaken his attention and shoulder to cry on for kindness when it wasn't.

"My plan, if you were wondering, is to get started adding the window and door sensors today," Ethan said. "I've got some other equipment to pick up, but I can start the project. Since I'm not cutting holes in walls to feed line, I'll have to get creative. Everything should be up and running by Monday so you can have your house back."

"Thank you. Though I think it'd be better to say you can get your bed back and not have to sleep on the floor."

"That, too. But the sleeping bag and pad are comfortable. Like camping, but without bugs."

Paisley smiled. Then she fiddled with her coffee cup as silence descended. Once, she'd have known what to say to this man. She'd never tired of talking to him back then. She took a bite of eggs as he picked up his phone to look at something. When he put it down again, she said the first thing that popped to mind.

"You never got married?"

"No, I never did."

"I'm sorry. It's none of my business. I shouldn't have asked."

"It's fine. Truth is I never met anyone I wanted to marry. Came close once, but it didn't work out."

Her heart pinched tight. It was jealousy and relief and probably a million other things she had no right to feel.

"I really shouldn't have asked."

He leveled a look at her. "I'd be asking the same thing if the situation was reversed. It's understandable. But I lead the kind of life that's always been difficult on relationships. Nobody ever stuck."

"You said it almost happened once..."

"I did, didn't I?" He sipped the coffee and studied something across the room. Then his gaze slid back to hers. "You can't figure it out, Payz?"

Her stomach dropped. Her fingers suddenly shook where she held her cup. "You mean me. Us."

Gold-green eyes held hers steadily. "Yeah."

There were so many things she wanted to say. But none of them would fix the heartache. For either of them.

Her gaze dropped to her coffee. She hated that she didn't know the right thing to say sometimes. She'd always been like this, always retreated into herself when she didn't know how to respond. Some people thought she was conceited, but no, she just didn't want to open her mouth and prove that she was an idiot.

The doorbell buzzed and she jumped, nearly spilling hot coffee on her pajamas. Her heart pounded as she jumped to her feet. Ethan put a hand out, caught her wrist before she could walk past him. It was a gentle touch, but she reacted instinctively, shrinking away. He let her go as he stood.

"It's okay. Just let me get it." He held up both hands as if to show her where they were. "I'm sorry I touched you."

She didn't want him to be sorry. It felt wrong. "You surprised me. That's all. I know you aren't going to hurt me."

The doorbell buzzed again but their gazes remained locked. Then, very gently, Ethan skimmed the back of a finger over her cheek. "Good, because I never would. I'd hurt myself first."

He dropped his hand and strode away. She drifted after him, arms folded over her chest protectively, skin tingling where he'd touched her. Tears stung in the corners of her eyes but she didn't let them fall. Being here now, with him, felt like an alternative universe. And it was torture.

Ethan peered out the window. Then he opened the door just enough to reveal her visitor. Not enough to invite her in, though. Colleen Wright was clad in a black caftan, her gray hair thick and loose as it fell to her shoulders in a stylish bob.

"Oh my," she said, her gaze drifting up Ethan's big form taking up all the space in the entry before moving past him to land on Paisley.

Her skin heated at the certainty in that look. She

wanted to explain, but didn't. "Hi, Mrs. Wright. What can I do for you today?"

Colleen glanced at Ethan again before fixing her gaze on Paisley. "My dear, I have come prepared." She held up a thick wad of leaves that resembled a fat cigar. A closer look revealed the leaves were bound together with string. Not a cigar then.

"I beg your pardon, but prepared for what?"

"To smudge your house, of course. The spirits are angry at the abomination visited upon your front door."

Colleen's gaze slid sideways and then back. With a muttered curse, Ethan yanked the door completely open.

Dark red streaks coated the wood from top to bottom. Spatters of it stained the rug she'd bought at the hardware store. It said *Welcome* and featured a bouquet of sunflowers. She'd loved it immediately and spent fifteen dollars even though she probably should have spent it elsewhere.

Ethan swore as Paisley stared, her mind not wanting to process the damage. Fixating on the rug and how much she loved it instead.

Until a wave of nausea threatened as she continued to stare at the red streaking her door and splattering across her rug.

"Oh my God—is that blood?"

14

"Wait a minute—you're telling me somebody smeared red paint on Paisley's front door? And you just so happened to be staying overnight at her house because you have history with her?"

It was Ghost who'd spoken. It was Monday morning and the guys lounged around the conference table in the SCIF—the specially compartmented information facility where they usually discussed the top-secret Athena Project being built in nearby Huntsville and made plans for how to protect it.

They'd been sent to Huntsville on a secret mission—so secret they'd had to leave the military and take cover as a group of friends who owned a shooting range and training facility—and they were supposed to keep themselves to themselves.

That hadn't exactly worked out so far. Blaze and

Chance were engaged to local women and expecting their first children. Seth was living with Callie Crowell at her place, and no doubt staring down an engagement of his own. Kane had just admitted his feelings about Daphne Bryant, their capable assistant who was so much more than she'd seemed, and now they were living together too.

Ethan and Ghost—Alex—were the only two left who hadn't technically broken one of the prime directives of the mission. It wasn't that having a girlfriend was bad. It was that relationships—love—made them vulnerable if the wrong people came looking for them. A man unwilling to talk about national security and top secret projects was presumably a lot more willing if somebody had a weapon pointed at the person he loved most in the world.

They all knew the risks, and yet his friends had been picked off one by one by Cupid's arrow. They weren't making their relationships official yet, but they would just as soon as Athena was operational and safe from the foreign agents trying to sabotage or steal the technology. In the meantime, they worked as security consultants and instructors both in the range and for defense contractors in Huntsville. It was a far more rewarding job than any of them had thought possible when they'd arrived.

Ghost looked intense. The other men's faces were carefully blank.

"Yes, sir. Paisley and Fern Carter had a run in at the library. Not the first time Fern has given Paisley grief, but this time was especially bad. Fern went to the mayor, who basically told her to pound sand, and she got pissed. Paisley got a text later from an unknown number telling her that she'd get what was coming to her. Then the paint got smeared on her front door during the night or early morning hours between Friday and Saturday. Colleen Wright is a neighbor and she came over to smudge the house. That's, uh, with sage apparently. She lights it and walks around with the smoke coming from the sage while she chants and waves it around."

He knew that because Paisley had told the woman to go ahead and do what she needed to do. This was after Ethan had ascertained it was paint and not blood before Paisley fainted. Colleen had looked slightly disappointed but she'd lit her sage and started waving it around while chanting something too low for him to make out.

Ethan had urged Paisley to call the local PD just to get it on record that someone had vandalized her door. She did, and an officer came over to take pictures and a report. After that, Ethan got to work cleaning the paint from the door. It had taken hours because he hadn't wanted to damage the wood. Then he'd started installing the sensors and cameras for the security system. It wasn't the most state of the art system possible, but it was enough for what Paisley needed right now.

Violet had accepted his presence easily enough. She'd asked questions—a million questions—about his life, his job, what he was doing, if he liked chocolate or vanilla, could she go ride his pony again soon, did he like cats, and so many other things he'd lost count. Then she'd wanted to camp out with him in the living room when it was time for bed on Saturday night.

Paisley had said no, and Violet had started to cry. Ethan somehow ended up promising to take her and her mom for a real camping trip one of these days. He wasn't specific but Paisley had glared daggers at him. He'd forgotten that she wasn't an outdoorsy girl. She'd once told him she didn't want to camp because it was dark and buggy—not to mention the potential for wild animals. Oops.

Ghost pinched the bridge of his nose. "Yep, got that. I'm specifically talking about that part you sped over—the one where you know Paisley Allen from a TDY assignment to Eglin five years ago. Details, soldier."

Ethan rubbed the back of his neck. "Yes, sir. It's a fucked up situation in so many ways."

He launched into the story of his assignment to Eglin for training with the Green Beret detachment. He talked about meeting Paisley. Dating Paisley. And then the last minute mission when he'd had to deploy suddenly. When he mentioned Trey's name, Ghost's frown intensified.

"Trey McCann?"

"Yes, sir."

Ghost's brows arrowed down as a frown creased his face. "That dude is bad news." He scanned the room, fixing each of them with a hard look. "You may have heard rumors at the time. McCann didn't leave HOT of his own volition. None of you were on his team back then or you'd know he wasn't quite...right. Only way to say it.

He has a sadistic streak, and he was accused of willfully killing civilians on a mission to Qu'rim. Barricaded them in a house and burned it down."

The shock roiling inside Ethan was reflected on the faces of his friends. Joining HOT was a privilege. Being the best of the best, called on to rescue people from danger, helping those poor souls caught in conflict-torn areas, was an honor. It was the best of what they did. The reason for all the training and hardship.

To help. To protect.

Ghost looked angry. "There was no proof. We had nothing to try him with because everything burned up with the house. He'd been sent to find an alternate route, and he'd been alone when he came across a refugee family hiding out. Nobody saw him do it, but more than one of his teammates told us in depositions they believed he'd killed those people. He had a habit of playing with fire and saying things that weren't right—but that's not enough to convict someone, nor should it be. Though I wish it had been in his case." Ghost swore. "We still thought we had enough to get him thrown out of the military. But McCann got a good JAG attorney who fought to get him reassigned so he could finish his enlistment. That's how he ended up in Florida. Last I heard, he'd left the Army and started his own security operation. He takes shit jobs for douchebags bigger than he is, or so I've heard."

Ethan's gut twisted. It would have been fucking nice to know those things five years ago, but even douchebags had rights. And Trey's JAG officer had done a damned good job of making sure he kept all of his. But what about the people who'd suffered at his hands? Not just the civilians in Qu'rim, but Paisley and Violet as well?

Made him sick, and made him more determined than ever to make sure Trey never got close to her again. How the fuck hadn't he known what an evil prick the man was? If he'd had an inkling, maybe none of this would have happened.

"Trey is Paisley's husband," he said, his throat a knot of despair and fury. "She's divorcing him. Has a protective order and the court allowed her to take Violet out of state."

"Jesus," Ghost said. "How bad was it?"

"He hit her, but Paisley says he didn't hit Violet. Yet. She found the courage to leave when she thought he was about to cross that line. Violet is four, and getting sassy."

"Four?" Ghost said.

"Yeah."

Ghost stared at him for a long moment. Ethan was starting to wonder what the fuck the boss was thinking when Seth started tapping his keyboard at lightning speed. "I'll see what I can find on Trey McCann. Movements, business, any arrests or convictions. And I'll dig through the divorce proceedings if I can get access. We'll find out where he is and we won't let him near Paisley."

"Amen, brother," Kane said as the others nodded sternly.

A weight that'd been pressing down on Ethan since he'd learned Paisley's violent ex was someone he'd trusted started to lift. It wouldn't go away entirely, not until he knew Trey wasn't a danger to her and Violet, but sharing the burden with his team gave him breathing room.

It occurred to him that she might be upset he'd shared their history, but he had no choice. Not after the threats she'd gotten.

He looked at the faces of his friends and told them what he knew. "The blood on her door was only red paint, and the threatening text she got was from an unknown number. Fern Carter seems likely because of the incident, but I don't think Trey can be ruled out. Paisley says he doesn't know where they are, but we all know we could find someone if we wanted to. Unless they've had our training, people don't know enough to erase their trail."

The guys all nodded. They knew how easy it was to track people down. It took a well-trained person not to leave a trail. Most did. It was simply the way modern life worked. Cameras in stores, gas stations, restaurants, banks. Neighbor's door cams. Online tracking through receipts and phone records. Most people went about their daily lives in predictable ways, using grocery delivery apps, ordering a shit ton of crap from online retailers like Amazon or Walmart, getting packages delivered to their homes, asking Alexa or Siri for information and directions, and never thought about how easily they could be found. Not to mention the mobile phone in their hands, pockets, purses. Those digital leashes that went everywhere they went.

Trey would know how to find her. He probably already had, even if he'd done nothing with the knowledge. He wasn't the kind of guy to accept that he didn't have the right to know her whereabouts.

Ethan pulled in a breath. "She's scared of him, scared he'll track her down. She said he told her he'd kill her if she left him. And while it could just be the shit thing you say when you're pissed, seems as if Trey's the kind of guy who'll take it to the next level if he's motivated enough."

"Not if we've got anything to say about it," Blaze growled. The others backed him up, and the hard knot that'd formed in Ethan's gut as he'd talked loosened a fraction.

Kane reached over and put a hand on Ethan's shoulder. "You aren't alone and you know it, you stupid asshole. Can't believe you didn't ask for help installing that security for her. Or tell us this days ago."

Ethan grinned at his friend. "You've been a bit preoccupied yourself, asswipe. Until this shit happened over the weekend, I just thought I was helping keep her safe with a warning system. Didn't know some asshole was gonna start threatening her."

Chance looked thoughtful. "Rory says that Fern's a bitter, jealous woman and always has been. And while I could see her sending the text because it's pretty hands off, do we really think she'd sneak over to Paisley's house in the middle of the night to smear red paint on the door?"

Ethan frowned. "I get what you're saying, but I'd think Trey more likely to use real blood. And string up the animal he killed while he was at it."

"Sick fuck," Seth muttered.

"So how do we find out if this Fern woman has red paint stashed in her garage?" Kane asked.

"We break in when she's gone or asleep," Chance said.

Ghost shook his head. "No breaking into her house. We've got enough to worry about without that kind of incursion. Figure out if she bought red paint recently. Figure out if she picked up a burner phone. But no trespassing on her property, you got me?"

A chorus of *yessirs* sounded around the table.

"All right. If I can have your attention, we've got other fish to fry right now. Lemme make it clear, though: Paisley Allen and her kid are under our protection. Don't get your panties in a twist about it, Dragon. You aren't alone on this one. Understood?"

"Yes, sir. Thank you, sir."

Ghost shook his head. "Now we got that out of the way, let's knock it off with the sir crap. All of you. Time to get down to business."

Ghost dragged his keyboard toward him and typed in his password. The overhead screen blazed to life. "Colonel Brent Gannon, USAF Retired. Works at the Missile Defense Agency on Redstone Arsenal. He's still a person of interest."

"Was he Jackson O'Malley's contact for the Stingers?" Ethan asked, wondering if Ghost had gotten confirmation from the FBI.

Daphne Bryant, whose real name was Josephine Daphne O'Malley, had turned out to be a mafia princess whose father and brother were involved in all kinds of disgusting shit until they were arrested recently. But it was her brother, Jackson, who'd been in Huntsville with a stolen shipment of Stinger missiles he'd been intending to sell to an unknown contact.

But since Jackson had taken Warren Trigg hostage in an effort to smoke Daphne out, and since Daphne had gone to save Warren, the Ghost Ops team had to intervene before the buyer arrived. It was that or let Jackson torture Warren and then kill him and Daphne both—and that hadn't been about to happen. Kane would have torn that warehouse down around their heads if anything happened to Daphne.

Diana Corbin, the FBI agent who'd ended up sticking her nose into their mission—because she had friends in high places and found out who they really were—had been pissed about losing the buyer. Too fucking bad. Daphne was alive, and Warren was back to managing the Piggly Wiggly and dating the nurse who'd taken care of him when he'd spent a few days in the hospital after the incident.

"The FBI thinks it likely. I don't disagree, but I also don't think he's the only possibility. There are a couple of militia groups in the area, and while none of them have openly embraced the Dashevsky Group, it's a safe bet those groups are more likely to get involved with Dashevsky's brand of authoritarianism than your average person. Since we don't know the identities of all the members of those groups, any one of them could also work for a defense contractor involved in the project."

Viktor Dashevsky was a Russian oligarch who espoused humanitarian causes, but his organization was really just a front to supply more weapons to war zones and recruit disgruntled and desperate people for his own ambitions. According to Agent Corbin, Dashevsky was recruiting his own private army. Not just at home, but globally.

And Huntsville was in his crosshairs.

The Athena Project, a military shield intended to protect the United States from nuclear threat, could be a weapon in the wrong hands. If Dashevsky wanted control of Athena, then he'd need contacts involved in the project. A former colonel working for the Missile Defense Agency was a good possibility.

"Is Gannon working on the project?" Blaze asked, clearly thinking the same thing.

"Officially he works on GMD, but Athena is closely tied into GMD and its concepts."

The Ground-based Midcourse Defense system was intended to fire upon missiles in space once they'd been launched at the US, but it only had about a fifty percent success rate in tests. Athena was a step up, meant to cast a net over a geographic location that stopped any nuclear attacks, period. It was ground-breaking and revolutionary —and terrifying at the same time when you considered what it could do in the wrong hands.

No doubt this was one of the things that kept the president and her staff up at night.

"What are we supposed to do about Gannon?" Seth asked.

"I'm glad you asked, Phantom. Not that she'll admit it, but Diana has trouble getting people in the Huntsville office to do what she wants. Kinda like when she brought us that Glock so we could research the trigger mechanism because she couldn't get anyone over there to take her seriously."

Ethan exchanged a look with Blaze, who was closest to him. He knew what Blaze was thinking because he was thinking it. Since when did the boss call Agent Corbin by her first name? He didn't even like the woman, and she certainly didn't like him. But they'd reached a truce of sorts when it came to information. Mostly because Diana used the sledgehammer of her connections in Washington to make sure Ghost assisted her inquiries.

"Can't she just call her uncle in the CIA? Or the FBI director who's such a close personal friend of the family?" Chance drawled.

"You'd think so," Ghost said. "But apparently her superiors in Huntsville get a bit put out when she goes over their heads."

"Over their heads?" Kane said with a snort. "More like

she springboards into the stratosphere to ask God for help squashing a bug."

"Probably why they don't like her much," Ghost replied. "Anyway, since she can't get her superiors to see the light and approve her plan, we're going to shadow Gannon and learn his secrets for ourselves."

"And for her?" Seth grumbled. Seth wasn't inclined to like Diana after the way she'd seemed to ignore the danger to Callie and Nikki when she'd been chasing after the Russian spy Dima Smirnov and trying to connect him to Viktor Dashevsky. Smirnov took Nikki hostage, and though it was resolved quickly and without harm to the girl, the fact that the US government gave Smirnov back to the Russians in a prisoner swap still had Seth spitting fire whenever it came up.

"I've agreed to share information, yes. She kept Daphne out of the public eye when the O'Malleys were arrested, and she's kept her end of the bargain to make Daphne's current identity her official one. I know she didn't handle the Smirnov situation well, but she went the extra mile this time."

"For which I am profoundly grateful," Kane said.

Seth was still grumbling. "I'm not a fan, but I can acknowledge she's learned from her mistakes."

"We need to figure this out," Ghost said. "See if Gannon has any connection to the Dashevsky Group, or to Jackson O'Malley. Official information on him is light. He was offered early retirement in lieu of charges when he was accused of sexually harassing a female airman under his command. Then he transferred to Huntsville to work at MDA as a contractor. He's been here for about a year now. Divorced. Ex-wife stayed in Virginia. Kids are grown, in their twenties, and on their own. Gannon's potentially lonely and probably has a grudge against the government. Doesn't mean he's looking to join a cause, but we can't rule it out."

"We should find out where he lives first," Ethan said, turning it over. He could always see a plan come together like a big map in his head. It was one of the things he loved to do. "That'll give us a range of where he likely shops, eats, drinks, and hangs out. Then we can watch him, see if he makes contact with anyone on Agent Corbin's list."

"Got it," Seth said, studying his computer. "Research Park. He's renting an apartment near Bridge Street."

"Dude," Chance said. "That was lightning fast even for you."

Seth grinned. "Maybe I've worked with Ethan long enough to know where that brain of his is headed. I started searching while Ghost was talking."

"Work your digital magic," Ghost told him. "Get me a report by end of day and we'll decide our next move." He looked at his watch and sighed. "Meanwhile, I have to teach a ladies beginning shooting course in an hour."

Blaze laughed. "The testimonials Daphne's been getting from these women are gold. What did she offer them?"

"Nothing," Kane said. "It's our magnetic personalities making it happen."

"You mean our washboard abs," Chance snickered. "I heard Daphne telling Mrs. Blodgett that she was sure to get a peek at some abs during the class if she praised us in her review. Said it swelled our heads and made us want to preen."

Ghost barked a laugh. "That girl is a marketing genius. Hell, I may just let her start that events side hustle she wants to run on the property. Bet she'd increase profits astronomically. We could be men of leisure once this is over."

They looked at each other. Then they burst out laughing.

Leisure? Them? No, they'd be warriors until the day they died.

15

Paisley was sitting in a circle of children, reading a story about a bear and his best friend—a fish, of all things—when a large, muscular man strolled into the library. Her pulse ticked higher at the sight.

Dear God, he was still a beautiful man. He wore faded jeans, boots, and the navy blue One Shot Tactical polo shirt that clung to his chest like a lover. His tattooed arms bulged with muscle, and she caught herself staring as he took off the mirrored aviators he wore and tucked them into the neck of his polo.

He jerked his chin in acknowledgment when their eyes met, but he didn't head her way. Instead, he went to the circulation desk where Fern sat, looking sour as she logged returned books into the computer. Her expression changed when Ethan approached. She actually smiled. Her gaze slid over him the same way most of the women's in the library had, cataloguing all the gorgeous parts of him.

The parts that made panties melt and hearts pound.

Paisley couldn't see if he smiled back or not. She finished the story and excused herself as Megan took over with questions and another book. Children's story hour was popular, and Paisley loved participating when she had the time to do it. Often, she didn't. And right now, she thought she might be needed at the circulation desk.

Fern wasn't smiling anymore as Ethan leaned casually on the counter in front of her. In fact, her face was paler than usual. Alarm flared, prickling the skin on Paisley's arms.

"Ethan," she said as she approached.

He turned to her, grinning huge, and her heart skipped a beat. Did he have to be so damned handsome? And not only handsome, but good with Violet? That was the biggest turn on of all. The way he'd been patient and kind when Violet peppered him with questions over the weekend, how he involved her when he was working— letting her hold screws for him, explaining what the cameras were for in a way that didn't frighten her—and how he thought about what she wanted when he bought groceries or fixed a meal.

He was nothing like Trey. *Nothing.*

Not that she'd expected him to be, but being married to Trey had twisted everything she'd believed about men. To be around one who regulated his emotions and handled a child's exuberance with ease was almost surreal.

"Hiya, Payz. Just talking to our friend Fern."

Fern's eyes were big. For once, she appeared at a loss for anything to say. Ethan turned back to her.

"I was explaining that burner phone numbers aren't as untraceable as someone might believe, at least not for people like me who know where to look. Oh, and how most stores have cameras now and you can actually see people buy groceries or phones or, you know, cans of paint. Then again, when someone's house has a red door, you don't even need to find when and where they bought the paint. Especially if you can tell the shade is the same as the paint used on another door. Remarkable, right?"

Paisley blinked. Then she looked at Fern. The woman's face was red.

"I have no idea what you're talking about," she spat. "None."

Ethan scratched his chin. "That's okay, ma'am. Just be assured that if it happens again, it won't be me coming for a friendly chat. It'll be the police with an arrest warrant."

Fern shoved her chair back and stood. Her face was mottled now. "How dare you threaten me? Who do you think you are?"

"Just a concerned citizen, ma'am. And I'm not threatening you. But you go ahead and call the PD. Chief Vance would love to speak to you, I'm sure."

Fern spun on her heel and fled toward the back offices. Ethan straightened from his slouch against the counter. He towered over Paisley, but he didn't make her feel unsafe or afraid.

"Was it her? How did you find out that fast?"

Ethan shrugged. "Don't know if it was or not. Though she does have a red door, and she lives two streets over from you."

Paisley stared. "You mean you said all that to her and you don't even know? Ethan, are you sure that was wise?"

"Trust me, babe. I've spent years doing what I do, and I've got pretty good instincts about people. She might not have sent the text message, but she definitely painted the door."

"How do you know that?"

"She has red paint under her fingernails. Didn't scrub good enough, apparently."

Paisley was surprised at the anger that boiled low in her belly. "That absolute bitch," she muttered. "She swanned in here this morning like nothing had happened, said good morning to Megan but not to me, then plopped her ass down here to take care of the tasks I'd assigned her last week. And you think she's responsible for the paint on my door?"

Paisley tried not to hate people, because it was unproductive and there was a price to carrying it, but Fern was quickly joining Trey on the list of people she actively despised.

"Yeah, I do. Based on her reaction, I think the text was her too. She didn't buy a phone, though. Probably used

Google Voice and thinks it's anonymous. Seth's digging for info there. If she did it, we'll know."

"Why did you say all that to her then?"

"Because I think she's a bitter woman who thinks she can get away with tormenting you, that maybe it'll make you want to leave or something. But she's a bully and I hate fucking bullies. You and Violet don't need any more negativity in your lives right now. If she didn't do it, then fine, she can be self-righteous and indignant, and she can call Chief Vance and report me for harassing her. Bet you a dollar she won't though."

Paisley sighed. She thought he was probably right, but she wasn't sure that making Fern angrier was the answer.

"Babe," Ethan said, his voice softer than before. She tipped her chin up to meet his gaze. He was so tall. So much bigger than her. He could break her in two if he wanted. But she didn't fear him. It was a nice feeling.

"Yes?"

He gave her a cocky grin. "I explained to her that absolutely any overt hostility toward you that made you uncomfortable would result in consequences. She may not be a ray of sunshine going forward, but she's not going to yell at you and say shitty things in a library full of patrons. And she's not going to send you messages or vandalize your property. I told her we're watching her. Six full grown former special forces soldiers who know how to find things people prefer to hide."

Paisley's jaw dropped a fraction before she remembered to shut it. "You're crazy, you know that? But thank you. I appreciate that you want to help me."

"Help you? Honey, I've got your back. We all do. Speaking of which, I had to tell the guys. About Trey, about us, about everything you're going through. I'm sorry, but after this weekend you need more than just me looking out for you."

The heat of shame rolled over her. It was a ridiculous reaction, but all she could think was if his friends knew, their women would know too. And then they'd look at her with something like pity and horror. She pressed a hand to her chest as if she could stop her heart from racing.

"Hey, you okay?"

She sucked in a breath. Counted to eight. Let it out again. How could she explain when he was only trying to help?

"I will be. I just..." She closed her eyes. "The book club. They've been so kind, and now they'll know. And they'll think I was dishonest for not telling them." Her eyes bugged. "Oh my God, I actively denied having met you before moving to Sutton's Creek!"

What would they think of her? They were so easygoing with each other, and they'd accepted her. And she hadn't been honest.

Ethan took her hand and led her away from the desk and into the stacks. He took her all the way down one of the aisles to where it met the wall and turned her until her back was against the shelves. He didn't crowd her, but he didn't back away either. He tipped her chin up, studying her face.

She could drown in those golden green eyes of his. The pupil was ringed in a starburst of brown, but the rest of the iris was green. A darker green ring surrounded the exterior of the iris. Gold flecks dotted the green. Beautiful eyes. Distinctive.

The same eyes that stared back at her from Violet's face.

A chill shuddered through her. He mistook it for a reaction to what they'd been discussing, which meant she didn't have to explain. But he'd told his friends. They knew the truth now.

Somebody was going to ask questions about Violet eventually.

Those eyes.

Once you saw it, you couldn't unsee it. But was she right or imagining things she wanted to be true?

"They won't judge you, Payz. Those women are some of the strongest, kindest, fiercest people I know. You'll be surprised if you let yourself believe in them."

There was nothing she could say. The cat was out of the bag. Elvis had left the building. And maybe it was a good thing. Instead of shouldering her fear by herself, she'd have people who knew. Even if she didn't want to talk about it, having people who understood why she was afraid would help her feel like she wasn't alone.

His hands slipped to her shoulders, held her. "You good?"

She nodded. "I'll be fine. It's just a bit of a shock. And Fern." She flung her hand vaguely in the direction of the library. "I know it made sense that it was her, but I didn't want to believe it really could be. Which is stupid because the alternative is so much worse."

"Seth is working on finding Trey's location. Once we know, we'll keep tabs on him."

The tightness in her chest eased. "Thank you."

"You're welcome. Where's Violet today?"

"She's with Aunt Hettie this morning, and then she'll go over to Lily Park's house this afternoon. I'll pick her up after work."

"Sounds like she'll have a good day then."

"I hope so. She likes Aunt Hettie's big house with the secret hiding places, and she loves Lily and her family."

She was babbling now. It had to be his proximity. The fact they were in a secluded area of the stacks. His overwhelming size. His scent—a mix of steel, leather, and the tang of gunpowder. Heady stuff.

And then there were his hands on her shoulders. His hands were smooth, but not in a soft way. Smooth and strong and firm.

It took her a moment to realize what that thing in her core was. A thing that uncoiled and slid through her limbs, softening them. Her body grew pliant and she knew without doubt her panties were damp.

Holy shit, Ethan Snow had done the impossible. He'd revived her sex drive. Not that she intended to tell him. No way.

"What's that look of surprise, babe?"

"Uh, what? Nothing. Just remembered something I need to do."

He grinned. It was sexy, masculine, and completely knowing. He leaned forward until she thought he might kiss her. Panic unfurled in her brain and her hands went up to his chest—but to push or pull? She didn't know.

His lips brushed her forehead. Then he straightened.

"I'll let you get back to work. I've got some things to do. But I'll see you later."

"Later?" she said stupidly.

"When I pick you and Violet up and take you to dinner."

He stepped back, still grinning, and then pivoted on his heel and strode down the middle of the stacks like he owned the damn library.

Sexy. Self-assured.

And so very dangerous to her heart.

16

than's phone rang as he was swinging onto the road and heading back to the range. He hit the button on his steering wheel to put the call through.

"Yeah?"

"Trey McCann left Destin early Friday," Seth said. "He's in Charlotte right now, stayed for the weekend at the airport Hilton, flying overseas tonight. Looks like his destination is Dubai, though it's probably not the final stop."

"That's good. Means he's not here."

"Still working on tracing the phone number that sent the text. That's taking more time."

Ethan tapped his fingers on the wheel and frowned. Nothing to do about it though. Seth was the best. If there was anything to find, he'd find it. "Thanks, man. Appreciate it."

"You got it. Sorry I don't have more. I'll keep looking though."

The call ended and Ethan thought back to the moment he'd pulled Paisley into the stacks. He hadn't intended to do anything like that, but she'd seemed upset that he'd had to tell his guys about their past and he'd wanted to talk to her away from prying eyes and ears. Not that the library was jammed with people, but he'd wanted to get her alone. He fully admitted it.

Paisley Allen had always done things to his body and brain that no other woman had ever accomplished. From the moment he'd seen her in that beach bar, he'd been willing to do whatever it took to get his hands on her ass and his cock buried deep in her pussy.

He'd thought that was all it was in that moment. Attraction. Chemistry. Animal instincts.

He'd wanted to fuck her, badly, and he wasn't going to let any of the men he'd been hanging out with get to her first. His belly twisted into a knot. The idea that Trey had been with her, created a kid with her, made him want to unload about a thousand rounds on a target with Trey's face plastered on top.

He didn't blame Paisley. How could he? She thought he'd dumped her. And he wasn't such an arrogant fuck that he believed she should have resisted Trey and pined for him. Yeah, he'd been in love with her, but he hadn't told her. Had she felt the same? He thought maybe she had.

But it was five years later, and the past was the past.

Still, he'd recognized her reaction to him today. It was the same reaction he'd had to her. He'd been dangerously close to claiming that sweet mouth right there in the stacks. Backing her into the shelves, his hands gripping that ass, pulling her into his erection so she understood what she did to him.

And then she'd looked up at him, such an expression of surprise on her face, and he'd known. He'd just fucking known because he could feel the electricity popping between them.

Paisley was aroused and shocked by it. Like maybe she hadn't felt desire in a long time and she'd thought she never would again.

Until they'd stood in the stacks, their bodies closer than normal, silence surrounding them, and he'd put his hands on her shoulders. To steady her, reassure her. Her eyes had glazed, her mouth dropping open, her chest rising and falling a little faster.

Then the shock on her face. The realization that she wanted him, at least in that moment. He'd almost kissed her then, but he'd shifted at the last second to brush his lips across her forehead. And then he'd stepped back, because it was that or claim her, and told her he was picking her and Violet up for dinner.

He'd thought she might refuse, but she hadn't. She'd accepted, and triumph had surged through him.

He'd taken his time with her five years ago.

He could do it again.

Decision made, he headed for the range feeling lighter inside than he had in years.

At five-forty-five, Ethan parked on the street near Paisley's house. It was mid-July in Alabama, hotter than blazes, but the big oak trees lining the streets of the historic district helped to keep things marginally cooler. He studied the neighborhood, wanting to get a feel for what was normal there.

The yards were neat, though not all were manicured. There were no cars on blocks, no cars parked in yards, but the houses varied greatly from the Craftsman style that Paisley and Violet lived in to Queen Annes, Cape Cods, bungalows, colonial revivals, Victorian cottages, ranch homes, Tudors, and one salt box at the end of the street. In other words, the district featured variety. Chestnut Street with its smaller homes was no exception.

One of the nice things about this neighborhood was how many houses there were, which meant plenty of neighbors. Obviously that hadn't stopped Fern Carter from her late night painting spree, but it meant the neighborhood was generally safe.

There were no cars out of place, no out of state plates, and nobody sitting in a car, studying the neighborhood. Other than him.

Ethan swung open his door and stepped onto the asphalt.

He hit the key fob to lock the vehicle—too much New Yorker left in him not to—and made his way up the sidewalk toward Paisley's place. There were pink hydrangea bushes on one side of the porch, and a big tree in the middle of the front yard. A child's bicycle with training wheels and a little helmet in the basket sat on the porch near the front door. There was a porch swing with a pillow that said *Welcome* and a couple of potted plants. It was homey and inviting.

A glance told him the camera he'd installed on the ceiling near the door was still there. It was small, and hidden as well as he could hide it without punching holes into the siding. The front door still had traces of red paint, but most of it was gone. He'd attacked it as soon as he could once the police took their report, and he'd managed to get it off without ruining the wood.

Probably ought to send fucking Fern a bill for the labor. She'd huff and puff and deny it, but they both knew it was her.

He took his phone out. The camera was functioning properly. He was displayed on the screen, looking down at his device.

The doorbell camera was obvious, perched as it was beside the door. If Trey showed up, he'd rip the camera off the wall and smash it. Anyone could, but the plan was if they went for that one, they wouldn't look for the one overhead. The doorbell cam was feeding to the cloud, but that wouldn't stop Trey. He'd scope the place out before he approached, know where the cam was, and take it out while keeping his face hidden.

Ethan ground his teeth. He really wanted to install something more robust, but this was a good stopgap measure for now. This system and Ghost Ops. If he had to move in with Paisley and Violet, he would. Whether she liked it or not.

Since Sutton's Creek wasn't a hotbed of criminal activity, the kind of system he had in mind was overkill. Expensive overkill. Not that he would've minded paying for it. But Paisley wasn't stupid, and she'd have known what he was doing when she got a good look at the system. You didn't fool a librarian. If they didn't know the answer, they knew where to find it.

Besides, he knew where Trey was and where he was headed for the next few days. Gave Ethan time to establish a safety protocol with Paisley.

Seth had unearthed more information this afternoon. Basically, Trey was a rich man these days. He'd started his own security company, McCann Solutions, and he fielded teams of mercenaries into conflict zones around the world. He used his HOT background to sell himself. Without saying Hostile Operations Team, of course. Not many people outside the halls of government knew of HOT's existence.

That was deliberate. Let the SEALs get the glory. Let Delta Force have their day. Let the Green Berets take care of business wherever and whenever they were needed.

But HOT was silent, secret, and somewhat mythical, at least so far as the general public went. There were no television shows, no books, no speeches and appearances by former members.

Oh, sure, there were groups online that discussed their existence. Threads on Reddit, Facebook, and in the darker corners of the internet. That was part of what contributed to the myth.

Trey had used the mystique for his own ends, and people paid him handsomely for it. Whether or not he deserved it.

"What are you doing, Ethan?" a disembodied voice said over the doorbell cam.

He grinned. "Testing your system. Guess it works, huh?"

"It does."

"Can I come in? Or are you ready to come out?"

"We're almost ready. Violet is going to come let you in. She really wants to be the one to open the door."

"Gotcha."

Another second and the door opened up to reveal Violet standing there in a sundress with daisies, daisy sandals, and a daisy headband in her hair.

"Mr. Ethan, peas come in."

Jeezus, the cute. It was overwhelming. A hot, sharp feeling pierced him. How the fuck could Trey ever want to harm a hair on this kid's head? If Ethan had married Paisley and had a child with her, he'd never do a thing to make them want to leave him.

"Pleeeeze," Paisley called out from inside the house.

"PLEEZE," Violet nearly shouted.

Ethan suppressed a chuckle. "Thank you, Miss Violet."

He stepped into the living room and waited for Violet to close the door behind him. She did, but she didn't engage the locks. Ethan did it for her as she skipped over to the coffee table and picked up her drawing.

"Look, Mr. Ethan. I drew a kitten!"

He took the drawing when she handed it to him. It was a black blob with yellow eyes and yellow teeth. He wouldn't have known it was a cat if not for her telling him.

"How pretty is this? Good job, Violet."

"Thank you," she said, her chin dipping modestly as she did a half twirl with her body, hands clasped in front of her. She gazed up at him, her eyes wide and innocent.

He stared back at her, cataloguing her face. The eyes that weren't brown or green but something in between. The long lashes framing those eyes. The shape of her nose, her mouth. The way she peered up at him.

She was Paisley in miniature. Where was Trey? He didn't see it.

"Hey," Paisley said, and he jerked his gaze from Violet to her. She was standing in the entrance to the small living room, smiling at him, her short hair and red lips striking. She had on a pair of white cotton shorts and a black sleeveless button up that she'd left untucked. Her toes were cherry red, and she wore a pair of white sandals with a small heel.

"Hey. You ready to go?"

"Yep. Vivi, can you put your drawing away so we can go?"

"No, it's for Mr. Ethan."

His gut clenched. "This is for me?"

She nodded enthusiastically.

"Thank you," he said, hugging the drawing to his chest. "This is the best present ever. I'll hang it up at home."

"You're welcome. Are we having pizza?" Violet asked, switching gears like she was a Formula One driver on a course. "I really like pizza."

"Vivi," Paisley said. "Mr. Ethan might have a different idea, and he invited us."

Violet's expression fell a little. "Oh."

"I like pizza too," Ethan said, and her little face brightened. His teammates were always giving him shit about how picky he was when it came to pizza. But hey, when you were raised in New York, you knew what real pizza was. And it was *not* any of those delivery chains. "I hear there's a new place in town. You want to try it?"

It might turn out to be the worst pizza ever, but what the hell?

Violet nodded. "Yes, please!"

Ethan looked at Paisley. "They've got lasagna and stuff too. That okay with you?"

"Sounds good to me."

"Then let's get moving."

"I should drive," Paisley said, adding, "The car seat."

"Well aware, babe. But I can move it."

"You shouldn't have to. Besides, it wasn't easy the last time."

It was true he'd had to wrestle it, but he didn't expect he'd have to do that again. Everything had a learning curve, and he was confident he knew enough to make it happen quicker tonight. "Not a problem. Besides, your car is too small for me."

She didn't have an argument for that because she knew it was true. The three of them made their way outside after Ethan watched Paisley set the alarm. He took the key from her and locked the front door. "Sorry," he said when he realized he'd done it. "Habit."

"It's okay," she said with a smile. "I don't mind you hovering over us when it's this important."

He would have them back before dark, but he'd told her to turn on the outside lights anyway. The lamps inside weren't smart bulbs, but he was about to fix that. That way she could have them come on at dusk and stay on all night if she wanted.

Colleen Wright was in her front yard as they strolled to Ethan's truck after he'd retrieved the car seat. She seemed to be staring, but didn't she always? Usually before making some wild pronouncement about the spirts or her spirit guide. Sometimes it was aliens she communicated with. She was sweet, but a little strange.

It'd taken him a while to get used to her. In New York, the psychics were a bit more abrupt. Colleen was like a Southern grandma. Except she talked to ghosts, communed with aliens, and usually dressed like a stereotypical psychic in a movie. She also drank kombucha rather than sweet tea.

"Hi, Mrs. Wright!" Violet yelled. "We're going to get pizza!"

"Hi, Violet. Isn't that just lovely? I hope you have a good time."

"I will! I gave Mr. Ethan a kitty cat and he said it was pretty!"

Colleen drifted over. Instead of a caftan, she was wearing baggy overalls, rubber garden boots, and gloves. "A kitty cat, hmm?"

"A drawing," Paisley said.

Ethan held up the hand holding the drawing. "Here we are. A real masterpiece."

Colleen smiled. "I see. And what is the kitty cat's name, Violet?"

"Ethan," she said, sounding somewhat shy.

"Oh my, that's a nice name." Her gaze lifted to Paisley's. Then she looked at Ethan before meeting Paisley's gaze again. "Children know things, don't they? They feel them, deep inside. Or perhaps one soul recognizes another. Recognizes where it belongs. This is a good thing."

Ethan could feel rather than see Paisley's tension. "You're the expert, Mrs. Wright," she said.

"My dear, there are some things that are obvious to anyone paying attention. Namaste, sweet people. I must return to my garden. Reba and I are having a seance tonight, and I need a few herbs."

They reached the truck and Ethan secured Violet's car seat in the back before lifting her into it. He stepped back to let Paisley belt her in. It was only a short ride to the pizza place located on the square. Ethan found a parking spot and the three of them made their way to Luigi's. The restaurant was new, but the building it was in was old. The awning was red, white, and green and there was a neon sign that said *Pizza* in red letters in one window.

It reminded Ethan of pizza joints in New York, but he didn't hold out hope it'd be any good. It was hopping, though, and they had to wait twenty minutes for a table. He found himself talking to people as they greeted him like he'd lived in Sutton's Creek for years rather than months. The warm feeling in his chest was a good one, he decided.

Not quite belonging. Never that, because he didn't trust it, but happiness in the moment. Sutton's Creek was a good place with good people.

"Hi, Ethan! Rob, come meet my shooting instructor!" A middle-aged woman with long black hair waved at him as she arrowed in his direction.

Ethan stood. "Mrs. Harney. How are you, ma'am?"

"Oh please, call me Michelle." She hooked her arm into his as she turned, her black hair whipping around, and urged a short, pudgy man forward. The man was sweating and looked about as happy as a sweaty man inside a crowded restaurant could look. "Rob, you need to meet Ethan. He's the reason why my grip is so much better. He doesn't let me cheat or quit."

Paisley smirked. Or Ethan thought she did before she turned her head so he couldn't see her face. Violet was playing with her tablet and not paying any attention to anything but the screen.

"Sir," Ethan said as the man stopped and tipped his head back to gaze upward like he was contemplating the high jump at the Olympics. "Pleased to meet you."

They shook hands and talked about Michelle's shooting and her improved grip. She finally let his arm go, gave him a little wave, and then looped her arm into her husband's as their name was called for a table.

Ethan sank down next to Paisley and pulled in a breath. She arched an eyebrow at him.

"Not a word. That was uncomfortable."

She snorted. "Why? She's an extrovert. An effusive one who likes to be the center of attention, I'm guessing. Her husband is probably going to start coming to lessons with her."

"Why would he do that?"

"Because you're six-foot-three inches of hard muscle and he's not? Because she latched onto you like a lifeline and sang your praises while he got a crick in his neck looking up at you?"

"Oh."

"Yeah, oh." She giggled, and he loved the sound every bit as much as he once did.

Fuck.

"It's not my fault I'm tall," he grumbled.

Paisley's laugh was sudden. "Tall," she said on a wheeze. "That's the problem. You're just too tall."

Ethan grinned because her laugh was infectious. "Glad I amuse you."

"You do. Thank you. I didn't know how much I needed to laugh."

"Happy to help, Payz. I like making you laugh."

Her smile hadn't dimmed. "I like laughing. Been too long, really." She glanced down at Violet, then put a hand on her daughter's head and stroked her blond hair. Violet didn't look up from what she was doing.

A good thing because Ethan was busy feeling too much as Paisley's gaze tangled with his. They stared at each other, cataloguing faces, studying lips, remembering. At least he was remembering.

He wanted to kiss her. Wanted to lean forward, hook a hand behind her neck, and claim her mouth the way he once had. *Mine.*

Then he wanted to take her home, strip her naked, and kiss every inch of exposed skin before he slid his tongue into her pussy and made her moan his name the way she used to.

"Thank you, Ethan," she said softly.

His voice was rough. "You're welcome, Payz."

Her lashes dropped. Before she could look at him again, before he knew what was in that gaze of hers, if she wanted more too, his name was called.

They followed the waitress to a booth where Ethan took the seat with a view of the door. It was a booth in the back, near the emergency exit, and he had clear access if he needed to get Paisley and Violet out. Not that he truly expected Trey to come through the front door with guns blazing, but it was second nature to look for escape routes. He'd been too long in special ops not to plot an escape from every building he entered.

They ordered a large pizza with cheese and sausage, a basket of mozzarella sticks, and waters all around. Violet got busy coloring the placemat the waitress had given her, humming to herself as she worked. Occasionally she'd show them her work, but mostly she concentrated on what she was doing.

He and Paisley talked. Not about anything deep or meaningful. Small talk about her job, his job, the weather, and the upcoming holiday season where she'd been asked to participate in hosting a house in the historic district.

It was regular stuff, nothing exciting—and he loved every moment of it. This could have been his life if Trey McCann hadn't interfered. Him, Paisley, and a child. But that child wouldn't be Violet, and he couldn't wish for her not to exist. She was a sweet kid, a little shy, but she seemed to like him. That wasn't anything to scoff at considering the way Trey had behaved.

The pizza arrived, and Ethan served slices on plates before he took one for himself.

"Moment of truth," he said with a grin.

Paisley cut Violet's into bite-sized pieces and the little girl practically bounced up and down on the seat as she waited. He felt her excitement in his soul. He just hoped the pizza was decent.

"Go ahead," Paisley told him. "You don't have to wait for us."

"I'm waiting."

He might have been raised on the streets, but he had manners. When everyone was ready, Ethan picked up his slice and bit into it. He expected disappointment, but that wasn't what happened. The pizza was about as right as it could be for not being made in New York.

"It's good," Paisley said. "What do you think, Vivi?"

Violet nodded her head exaggeratedly. "I love it! I want to eat all of it!"

"Maybe not all of it," Paisley told her. "You'd have a pretty serious tummy ache."

Violet shrugged, and Ethan chuckled. Smart kid. Good pizza was worth a little discomfort.

"Okay, pizza snob, what about you?" Paisley turned to him and arched an eyebrow.

She was so damn pretty. Even with her hair cropped close to her head. How did it suit her so well? He'd loved her long hair, but he might just like this better. Then again, maybe it was just her he liked. Didn't matter what her hair looked like.

"Hello?" Paisley snapped her fingers. "Earth to Ethan."

He laughed. "Sorry, I was in heaven for a moment there. Yeah, it's good. Best pizza in Alabama so far. Somebody in the kitchen must be from New York."

"Oh, of course. It couldn't be that somebody did their research and figured out a great pizza recipe."

He shook his head. "Nope, can't be that. Research only gets you so far. Pizza's in the blood in New York."

"I'll get there one day," she said. "See for myself."

His heart hitched. They'd talked about New York when they were together before. He'd wanted to take her there someday, take her to all his favorite haunts. Show her Broadway and Times Square, too.

"When can we go camping?" Violet asked.

Ethan didn't miss the shiver that rolled over Paisley. "Uh, not until it's cooler, kiddo. Fewer bugs. Besides, you want to go when the leaves are turning and everything's pretty. Now's too hot."

"Then you just turn on the air conditioning, silly."

"Honey, there is no AC in a tent," Paisley said. "That's only in buildings."

Violet looked disappointed. "Oh."

"Promise I'll take you, Miss Violet. But it's gotta get cooler out. You can't have a campfire in this heat, and you definitely want one of those."

She tilted her head. "Why?"

"For toasting marshmallows and making s'mores."

Her eyes got big. "Ohhhhhh."

Paisley smiled at him before she ran her hand over her daughter's hair. "Sometimes we have to wait for the good things, baby. Mr. Ethan will let us know when it's time. Can you wait?"

She laughed and nodded again, then picked up her

placemat and showed it to them both. It was a pizza with a section to color, a slice to draw toppings on, and a puzzle. Violet had drawn all over the placemat with her crayons, ignoring lines entirely, but Ethan and Paisley both praised it for the Picasso it was. Violet preened. Then she dived into her pizza again, eating it with gusto and asking for more.

Ethan ate four slices, listened to Violet chatter about a stunning variety of topics, talked with Paisley, and enjoyed every moment.

It was the best pizza date he'd ever had.

17

All the way home, Paisley told herself she shouldn't invite Ethan inside. She should say goodbye outside, thank him for the pizza and the lovely evening—and it *had* been lovely, because they'd talked about so many things that weren't painful—and then go inside and put Violet to bed. After, she could have a glass of wine and read her book. The perfect end to a perfect day.

Ethan turned onto Chestnut Street and parked in front of her Kia. It wasn't dark yet, but dusk was fast approaching and she was glad he'd told her to leave the lights on. Her house was lit up and welcoming.

"Don't move," he said when Paisley reached for the truck's door.

She waited with a hot feeling in her chest as he walked around and opened it for her. Then he opened Violet's and helped her down from the car seat. In less time than she expected, he had it unbuckled from his truck and slung across one arm. Paisley closed the truck door and took Violet's hand in hers as Ethan put Violet's seat into the back of her Kia and secured it. When he closed the door, she hit the fob to lock it again.

Now was the moment of truth. Tell him goodnight and thank you. Let him walk away.

"Thank you for dinner. We enjoyed it very much."

"You're welcome. I enjoyed it too." He nodded at the house. "I'll wait until you get inside."

The words tumbled out before she could stop them. "Would you like to come in? Unless you need to get back. I completely understand."

He smiled, and her chest squeezed tight. "I can come in."

Her heart took off, careening wildly against her ribs. "Okay, great. And now I'm nervous about doing everything right to get inside."

He grinned. "You've been doing it right, haven't you? I haven't gotten any alarms."

"Yes, but you weren't standing over me."

"Was when we practiced it this weekend."

That was certainly true.

"Hey, Miss V, want to stand with me while your mama opens the door?"

He held out his hand to her daughter and Violet went to him without hesitation. It made Paisley's breath catch, and it worried her too. Was it wise to let her child form an attachment to him? Then again, it was a little late to worry about it. Violet already liked him, and he'd promised to take her camping.

Was it truly so bad to let her have a positive experience with an adult male instead of the confused and terrifying experience she'd had with Trey?

Paisley swallowed her reservations and got to work disarming the system and opening the door. She wasn't afraid anyone waited for her inside. There'd been no alerts while they were out. The camera had picked up neighbor kids riding bikes on the sidewalk as well as a couple of neighbors walking dogs, but nobody had approached the house.

It was a peace of mind she hadn't thought she'd get so soon after leaving Destin. And she owed it all to the man she'd never thought to see again. He let Violet go in front of him and then followed her inside and shut the door. Naturally, he locked it.

Paisley fixed her gaze on Violet. "Need you to get ready for bed, Vivi. It's after eight."

As if on cue, her child yawned. "Don't wanna go to bed, Mommy. I want to talk to Mr. Ethan."

"You've been talking to Mr. Ethan, honey. It's time to get ready for bed." Violet had a bath before dinner, so another wasn't necessary. A good thing since Violet wasn't a fan of baths. "Go put on your jammies and brush your teeth. I'll come read you a bed time story when you're ready."

"Want Mr. Ethan to read one."

Paisley met Ethan's gaze. He shrugged. "Sure, I can do

that. Best get ready like your mama said or we can't have story time."

Violet ran down the hall to her bedroom and slammed the door behind her. "Well," Paisley said with a laugh. "She moved a lot faster than I thought she would. She likes you, Ethan. Thank you for being gentle with her."

He'd shoved his hands into his pockets. She wasn't accustomed to a tall, broody, gorgeous man in her small living room, but she liked it. Even though he sucked all the oxygen away just by being there. He'd worn a black short-sleeved henley with cargo shorts and flip-flops and she couldn't stop thinking about what he'd look like out of them.

Which was *not* what she needed to be thinking. Her life was too complicated. Trey wasn't the distant memory she wanted him to be. He was an ever-present threat. Plus there was Violet to consider. Her daughter liked Ethan, but if Paisley did what she wanted to do and let the physical side take control, what would happen then? Ethan wasn't going to fall in love with her after she'd been with Trey. He wasn't going to marry her and raise a child that he believed to be Trey's.

"Gentle is the only way to be," he said, his voice a soft rumble that stroked her senses with remembered tenderness. "I'm sorry Trey was a dick, Paisley. He had the best things in life with you and that kid. He should have treasured you both."

She needed a glass of wine. Now. "You want

anything?" she asked as she moved toward the kitchen. "A beer? Wine? Tea?"

"Beer's good."

She didn't turn on the light. It was dark in the kitchen, but the light from the living room spilled in and illuminated the space. She got a glass out of the cabinet, took the wine from the fridge and poured it nearly to the top. Then she got a beer and went searching for the bottle opener. When she couldn't find the opener in the drawer, she slammed it harder than she should have.

Silent tears coursed hotly down her cheeks. She gulped them back and told herself to get a grip.

Strong arms wrapped around her from behind, tugged her against a hard chest. His mouth was at her ear.

"It's okay, Payz. I've got you. Cry if you need to."

"I hate him, Ethan. I hate what he did to us. He ruined everything. Because he wanted to. No other reason."

Ethan squeezed her a little tighter. She put a hand on his arm. Warm. Firm. Strong. The kind of arm that took care of you, held you, supported you.

"I know, baby. He took you away from me, but he also gave you Violet. You can't regret that."

Oh God.

"No, of course not." Her throat felt like she'd swallowed razor blades.

"She's a sweet kid."

God, it hurt. "She is."

Ethan lay his cheek on top of her head and held her while she got herself back together. The pain subsided. It didn't go away, because it never would, but it lay dormant inside, waiting for the trigger.

"You good?" he asked after a few minutes.

"Yes. Thank you." She sniffed and wiped away the tears. "I couldn't find the bottle opener. I guess I sound unhinged if that's all it took to make me cry."

He let her go and picked up the bottle, twisted the cap like it was nothing. "Don't need one, babe. Besides, we both know it's about more than a bottle opener. And that's okay. You're allowed to be angry about what he did. You can hate him and wish him dead if you want. God knows I do."

"I definitely wish him dead. I fantasize about him not coming back from one of those overseas jobs of his. I know it's wrong, but I honestly don't care. I'd finally feel safe again."

"When did he get out of the military?"

"About a year after you left. His enlistment was up, and he wanted to start his own protection business. He said that military commanders tied the hands of operators, and that he could do more good if he recruited guys he knew and did the jobs the military couldn't or wouldn't." She took a big drink of her wine, let it scald her throat on the way down. "He didn't hit me until after he left the military. I thought maybe it was the pressure of starting a business. I made all kinds of excuses for him, but I had Violet by then and I didn't think I had anywhere to go. The one time I got the courage to leave, he locked me in a dark closet for hours and told me what would happen if I ever did. He made me so terrified that I wouldn't even leave when he was gone for weeks." She snorted. "God, I loved it when he was gone."

Ethan's throat moved. He turned his head and focused on a point on the wall. His expression was hard and angry, but she thought maybe his eyes were a little glassy. Like he was fighting tears of his own.

"I shouldn't be saying these things. It does no good, and it makes you mad."

His gaze whipped to hers again. "It makes me fucking insane, Payz. I want to find him and put a bullet in his head. I won't, because I can't see a way to do it without putting the people I care about in a difficult position, but if he ever shows up here and threatens you, all bets are off. I'll drop him like the rabid dog he is—and I won't care who knows it."

Paisley shivered. "I don't want you to do that. I don't want him on your conscience."

"He already is."

They stared at each other without speaking for a long moment. She wanted to go to him, fling herself into his arms, and beg him to hold her. And then she wanted to get naked with him, feel the way she used to feel when he was inside her. She wanted nothing between them, just skin and heat, her slick channel surrounding his thick cock as they moved together, lightning sparking inside her.

She wanted to forget everything that made her sad,

lose herself in him, remember what it was like to feel pleasure and happiness, even if it was only temporary.

"Ethan," she began.

"Mommy! Mr. Ethan! I'm ready for a story!" Violet yelled from the hallway.

"It's okay," Ethan said softly. "Let's go read that story and make her happy. You can tell me later."

But she wasn't sure she could. The moment was gone.

And maybe that was best.

18

Ethan decided after he left Paisley's house that maybe he needed some distance. She had the alarm system, he got alerts along with his guys, and Trey was on a flight heading to Dubai. She was safe for now, and that gave him breathing room.

But, holy Jesus, when she'd told him about Trey locking her in the closet and threatening her, he'd wanted to break down. His throat had been tight, his eyes stung, and rage twisted like angry snakes beneath his skin. It was a fine thread holding him together at that point.

He'd killed in the line of duty. He hadn't enjoyed it, but he'd done it. In that moment, he'd wanted to kill for sport. He'd wanted to pin Trey to a wall with knives, carve pieces of him away, and make him endure every agonizing moment of it while he was forced to look at a picture of Paisley and Violet.

Strike that because they were too good for Trey. No, a

bag over the head so he couldn't see what was coming next. And a gag so he couldn't scream.

But his ears—now those Ethan would leave alone so Trey could hear everything Ethan intended to say to him. So he could tell the man precisely what a fucking loser he was and how he should have never laid a hand on Paisley. Never should have stolen what was *his*.

Except, fuck it all to hell, that was a pretty sick fantasy to have. Not to mention the danger to his team and mission if he actually went through with it.

Which was why he needed distance. If he had to watch Paisley cry again, he'd lose his shit.

He drove home, parked, and went inside. Ghost's car was gone and the house was quiet. He needed the quiet.

He thought about taking a six pack to his room and drinking them one after another, but that wasn't who he was either. His family had ended up on the streets because his old man loved the bottle more than he did his wife and kids. His mother worked hard, scrimped and saved, and every time she'd get enough for them to stay somewhere safe, maybe have a home for longer than a week, his old man would take the money and drink it down.

One day, he'd stopped coming back. He moved to Jersey, found somebody else to shack up with, and left Ethan, his mom, and his brother without a home. Maybe his mother wouldn't have gotten addicted to heroin if she'd had a chance in life instead of getting kicked in the teeth every damned time, but the slow wearing down of her defenses had made her vulnerable.

Ethan's dad leaving them with nothing only cemented it. Dani Snow started turning tricks to make ends meet, and her kids lived on the streets with the other people who didn't have homes to go to. There was an entire community of them out there, living on the edge of society.

Homeless. Unhoused. People experiencing homelessness. Whatever the correct term was these days, it didn't change the fact there were people who didn't have enough money to afford a roof over their heads even though many of them worked full time jobs. Debating what to call it didn't fix the problem, and it damned sure didn't make those without homes feel any better. Hadn't for him or his little brother.

By the time child services took them in and sent them to live with a cousin of a cousin, Eric was also experimenting with drugs. Except he'd found meth, and that was even worse.

Ethan swore as he raked a hand through his hair. This wasn't the memory trip he'd planned to take tonight. He'd been thinking about Paisley and about killing Trey, and now he was brooding about his fucked up childhood and how he couldn't save the people who'd mattered the most back then.

He wasn't that helpless kid anymore, though. He'd make sure Paisley and Violet had a future, even if he wasn't part of it.

Ethan went to his room, shucked everything but his boxers, and flopped onto his bed. He turned on the TV, but nothing appealed.

He could still see Paisley in her kitchen, looking at him with longing in her eyes after all she'd told him. Before Violet had interrupted, he'd have sworn Paisley was going to ask him to stay the night with her.

He wanted to, but he also wasn't sure it was the right thing to do. At least not yet. He wanted to stay, so fucking bad, but he didn't want it because she was upset and wanted comfort, or because she was grateful for his help or even for fucking pizza. He wanted her to have a clear mind about what she was choosing, because the next time he got naked with her, got so deep inside her he could feel her heartbeat, he wasn't giving her up again.

Didn't know how he'd explain that to Ghost, but maybe he didn't need to. The man had already accepted that everyone else on the team was in a relationship, so why not one more?

Did he love her? Still? Or was it lust and anger and the urge to claim what had been taken from him?

He wasn't sure yet, but he felt something strong. For her and Violet both.

That kid. She had every reason to be leery of him, yet she looked at him with those hazel eyes and he wanted to melt. Her eyes were like his. He'd wondered at first if he was imagining it, because he wanted a connection that wasn't there, but he'd realized tonight while reading to her that, no, her eyes really were the same color as his.

Her hair was blond like his mother's, but that didn't mean anything. He knew it didn't, and yet...

He shook his head. Mother Nature was a cruel bitch sometimes. Showing him what he might have had with Paisley if Trey hadn't lied. What he could still have. It wasn't too late.

He was finally starting to doze off when his phone buzzed. He snatched it up, his heart pounding because the tone indicated an alert from Paisley's surveillance system.

Everything inside him went cold as he peered at the screen.

A man with a ball cap pulled low stood in her back-yard, staring at the house.

19

aisley's hands shook as she rushed for Violet's room. She fumbled her phone twice before she got a good grip on it. Then she speed dialed Ethan, thankful he'd put himself into her favorites. He picked up before it even rang.

"I'm on the way. Don't go outside. Don't open the blinds or look out where he can see you. Stay calm and I'll be there in ten minutes."

Paisley dragged in a breath. Her heart fluttered like a trapped butterfly. Violet was sound asleep in her bed and her room was undisturbed. "Please hurry," she whispered.

"I'm hurrying, baby. Stay on the line with me, okay?"

"Okay."

"Just because somebody tripped the camera in your backyard, doesn't mean it's Trey. My sources tell me he's overseas on a job right now."

She was seeing spots. Fear had its claws wrapped around her throat. *Breathe.* "How can you be sure?"

"Plane tickets, itineraries."

"What if he faked it so he could have an alibi?"

It's exactly the kind of thing he'd do if he wanted to kill her. Fake a trip, give himself an alibi, show up and murder her and Violet in their sleep. It was nearly one a.m. Nobody had any business being in her yard at that time of the morning. So who else could it be? It was definitely a man, not Fern. Her husband? Was he part of her nasty scheme to harass people she didn't like?

Ethan was silent. "He could do that. Not gonna lie to you. Doesn't mean he did, though. Where is the man now?"

Paisley's fingers shook as she swiped to the app she needed. "He's not there."

"Play it back."

She swiped the screen until she got to the beginning of the video. The man wore a ball cap and what looked like a thin jacket that covered his arms and torso. It was big, shapeless, and she couldn't tell if the man was muscular like Trey or not. He appeared to hop the back fence. He walked into her yard and stared at the house before poking around the back patio. Then he disappeared.

"He went around the side. Where the bedrooms are." She was still standing in the door to Violet's room so she knew he hadn't come through the window.

"Go to that camera."

She did as he told her. "He climbed over the fence. I-I think he's gone."

Her relief wasn't complete though. The man might be gone, but he could return. If it was Trey, he had a plan. He always had a plan. She wasn't safe yet. She would never be safe so long as Trey was out there, biding his time. Why had she thought she could leave him and get away with it?

No.

She'd had to leave. For herself, for her child. Staying would have meant giving up, consigning Violet to a life of abuse and terror. No fucking way.

"That's good, baby. Just stay where you are and don't look outside. I'll be there soon."

Paisley went into the living room and sank onto the couch before her legs buckled. She drew her legs up, her chin on her knees while she rocked back and forth and told herself Ethan was nearly there. Any minute now. He talked to her about the things he saw on the drive. A herd of deer beside the road, munching grass. A coyote scooting across the pavement in front of him. The town limits. The American flags that still hung from the light poles after the Independence Day Festival last week.

"I'm turning on Chestnut now. I'm going to park down the street and have a look around. I'll text you when I'm at the door, okay? Don't open until then."

"Okay."

"I'm gonna hang up now, Payz. Need to concentrate

on what I'm doing. But I'm here. You aren't alone. You understand me?"

"Yes."

"Good girl. See you soon."

The call went dead and she swiped open the security app again. Her alarm was on, and there was no movement on the outdoor cameras. Still, she couldn't look away until she saw a figure appear in the field of view. He wasn't wearing a ball cap, and she recognized the swagger. He walked past her house, crossed the street and disappeared. When he walked into view again, she let out the breath she'd been holding.

Her phone pinged with a text and she leaped up and went to the door, looking out the peephole as instructed. The porch light illuminated the big man on her stoop.

"I've disabled your alarm," he said through the door. "You can open it now."

She fumbled with the locks until she had them free, then yanked the door open and nearly burst into tears. Ethan stepped inside, looped an arm around her, and closed the door. He locked everything again and reset the alarm from his phone.

Then he had both arms around her, dragging her in close. She wrapped hers around his waist and held on tight.

"You're shaking, honey. It's okay. I've got you."

The second time tonight he'd said that to her. Well, not tonight, but it might as well be since she hadn't actually gotten any sleep between the time he'd left and now. She'd been reading in bed, hoping she'd get tired, but still juiced from the evening spent with him and Violet.

"I'm sorry," she said. "Maybe I'm being too paranoid. If this had happened last week, I wouldn't have known. And it doesn't mean it was Trey. I know that too."

He bent and hooked an arm under her knees, swinging her up as if she were a little girl and not a full grown woman. Paisley wrapped her arms around his neck and pressed her face into the hollow there. He smelled so good. Like pine and leather tonight. The gunpowder wasn't there this time, but it was never far. Not considering what he did for a living.

He carried her over to the couch and settled down on it with her in his lap. Her insides began to melt like simmering wax. Being this near to him, smelling him, feeling his arms around her—it called up memories of safety and belonging that she hadn't had in years.

"I didn't see anyone." His voice rumbled in her ear. "I checked the yard and I went down the street, crossed to the next, but the only thing out right now are cats and coyotes. And one barky bastard of a dog. I'm sure the neighbors are thrilled about that little nutcase."

Paisley couldn't help but laugh a little. "Oh, you mean the dog behind us, at the end of the street. They never walk him, just let him out to do his business and then forget him. He barks his head off until they let him in again."

"Why have a dog if you don't want to do anything with it?"

"No idea."

She plucked at the collar of his henley, smoothed it again. She told herself to get off his lap, put some distance between them. Her heart didn't need the confusion. Or the temptation.

But she didn't want to go. Ethan was shelter. He was safe and beautiful, the kind of lethal predator who offered safety and security. She didn't know why she trusted him not to turn into a Trey, but she did.

She wasn't sure she trusted him with her heart, not after everything she'd been through, but trust he wouldn't do anything to harm her? Absolutely. Not a doubt in this world. Not after watching him with Violet over the weekend and tonight. He wasn't faking that kind of patience and gentleness. She knew enough about abusers to understand how they wormed their way into your life. She'd experienced it first hand.

They were good, so good, at manipulation. But with Trey, there'd always been something unsettling. The way he'd maneuver her back to her hurt and anger over Ethan dumping her. He never let her forget it. He kept it fresh in her mind while soothing and promising he wasn't that way, that he'd take care of her and her child. That he didn't care whose child she was carrying and he didn't want or need a paternity test to love the baby as his own.

Such a liar.

Ethan's hand skimmed over her hip, rubbing softly. "Did you get any sleep?"

"Not really. I was reading a book."

"Mm."

"I'm sorry if I woke you."

"Wasn't you, Payz. It was the surveillance alert."

She yawned. "Thank you for coming. I was scared he'd try to break in."

"I'd have called the police if he did. There was no way I wasn't gonna be here though."

"Do you think it was Trey?"

"I honestly don't know. Seems unlikely since he didn't try the doors or windows. Could have been a teenager taking a shortcut. A neighbor's kids sneaking out, maybe. The clothing was shapeless enough I can't tell how big the guy was."

"There are some teens on Pine, right behind Chestnut. They can be a little rowdy sometimes. Their parents work shifts, so sometimes they're alone in the evenings. One of them plays on the football team and I've seen him in baggy athletic gear. It seems to be the cool thing to wear."

Why hadn't she thought of that before? It was a weeknight, but it was summer. Some kids ran wild during the summer. Then again, did a teenager need a summer vacation to run wild? Not necessarily. But they didn't have to be at school right now, which meant they could stay out all night and sleep all day. And their parents wouldn't notice it as easily as they would an absent kid from school.

"I'll have a thorough look around in the morning. Might see something more than I did tonight. For now, though, maybe you should head to bed and get some sleep. I'll stay out here."

Her heart dropped. "I want to stay. With you."

"Honey." His voice was soft. "You'll sleep better in bed."

"I won't. Not unless you go with me."

The silence between them was heavy.

"Payz," he finally said, all deep and rumbly. "I can't do that. I can't lie in a bed with you and not touch you. Not *be* with you."

"Maybe I want you to touch me." She tipped her head back to meet his gaze. There was heat in those eyes. Heat and regret. Her heart sank again.

"I want to. Badly. But maybe it's not the right thing to do now. You just got out of a bad relationship, and we just started getting to know each other again. I don't want to rush into something and have you regret it."

"The only thing I regret is that we lost almost five years together. And maybe it won't be the same, but it could be." She closed her eyes, thought of everything that'd happened during those years. The pieces of her life she'd lost and would never get back.

Maybe she wasn't ready for this. Maybe she'd never be ready again. The only way to know was to try.

"Listen to me," he said. "I want you. I want everything you have to give me. I want you naked. I want to watch my cock disappear inside your luscious body. I want to make you come, and I want you to beg me for more. I want it more than I want my next breath. But this is fucking *fast*, Payz. Too fast with everything that's going on in your life. So let's slow it down, okay? I'll stay here tonight, watch over you and Violet. Hell, I'll stay every night if you need me to. But we aren't gonna fuck yet. We're gonna talk, spend time together, and I'm spending time with Violet. You need to know if you trust me with her after what she's been through."

"I know you would never—"

He put a finger over her mouth. "Of course I wouldn't. But what if she decides she doesn't like me after all? Or she gets scared of me because I remind her of Trey? I'm bigger than he is, and I can't promise I'll never get angry. Not that I intend to do it in front of her, but what if it happens? What if Fern says something to you and I get pissed about it? Or what if some guy thinks he can demand your attention again, and I get in his fucking face? Can't guarantee she won't see that, won't be scared by it. And I think, if I carry you to bed now and we get naked, it'll be more difficult because she'll know we're together somehow and yet she won't really *know* me. You see where I'm coming from?"

Oh, God. She was completely in love with this man. Again. Still. He cared about her daughter enough to put her needs before his own desire.

Guilt pricked her. She really, really needed to tell him that Violet could possibly be his child. But how did you tell someone they might be a father, but you didn't actually know it for sure—so maybe they weren't? How?

And then what? Would he demand paternity tests? Demand partial custody?

She couldn't face it right now. Simply could not.

"Yes." The knot in her throat made her hoarse. "Thank you, Ethan. For caring."

His smile was wistful. "Can't believe I just talked myself out of sex with a hot babe. What kind of idiot am I?"

She lay against his chest again, snuggled her face into his neck. She wanted to lick him, but she refrained. "A wonderful one."

He looped his arms around her and pressed his back deeper into the couch. "You going to bed or what?"

"I'm already where I want to be."

"Me too."

20

leeping with Paisley in his arms was totally worth the stiffness in his back.

Ethan stretched from side to side as he stood in the shower—her shower—and hoped the soreness would work itself out. He'd thought she would eventually get up and return to her bed, when she got uncomfortable enough sleeping against him, but she never did. He'd shifted them onto the couch, even though his legs were too long, and dozed fitfully through the night.

She'd lain curled against him, her head resting on his chest, her arms folded against her body once she'd let him go. She'd slept better than he had because he'd heard her snore from time to time. Not a big snore, but a tiny one. Cute, like her.

Maybe he should have taken them both to her bed. What would the difference have been at that point? She was asleep, and he wasn't a beast. He wasn't going to be all over her simply because they were in a bed.

But, truth be told, he'd thought if he took her to her room, she'd roll away from him when he still wanted to hold her. And there was always the danger Violet might wander in during the night. Paisley had told him once before that while Violet was a sound sleeper most of the time, sometimes she had nightmares and came to her mother's bed in the middle of the night.

He hadn't wanted to scare her if that happened, so he'd stayed on the couch. And, yeah, it was murder on his lower back, but fuck it. Totally worth it to hold Paisley all night.

Like old times. He hadn't forgotten how good it felt to be with her, though he'd believed he had. He'd tried to excise her memory from his life, but it'd never worked. She'd always been there, the hole in his life he'd never managed to fill. He'd spent years believing he'd fallen for a woman who'd discarded him as soon as being with him became inconvenient.

She'd found somebody else, moved on, while he'd been stuck, wondering how he'd been so wrong about her.

Except she hadn't found somebody else, and she hadn't moved on. Not without lies. Not without a whole lot of manipulation.

Fucking Trey McCann.

Ethan didn't know if the person on her camera feed last night had been Trey or not. No, he hadn't tried the doors or windows, but he didn't necessarily need to.

Ethan hadn't told Paisley, but it was possible that Trey was watching for a response. Not that he would have known she had Ethan in her life again, but he might have expected something. Test everything and make a plan. It's what Ethan would do.

That's why he planned to treat the situation as though it'd been Trey, because that was the only logical response, but he also planned to see what he could learn from any neighborhood doorbell cams or trail cams in yards. People these days put cameras everywhere because they were inexpensive and effective, and he knew how to hack them. Or knew who to ask, more to the point.

Not that he couldn't do it himself, but Seth would do it faster and cleaner.

Ethan finished showering, put on the clean shirt and boxers he kept in a duffel in his truck, and dragged on his cargo shorts. Paisley had an extra toothbrush and a disposable razor, though he'd decided not to shave. What was a day's scruff? He remembered that she used to love it when he didn't shave for a couple of days. Maybe not the feel of his beard between her legs, but she'd liked how he'd looked with a couple of days worth of stubble.

Paisley was in the kitchen, making toast and coffee, and he strode over and kissed the back of her pretty neck while she bit off a moan.

His dick responded to that sound, swelling swiftly to life. "Morning, gorgeous," he said roughly. "Thanks for the shower."

He dragged his gaze from the place where her neck

made a graceful curve into her shoulder and told himself to think unsexy thoughts. Hard to do when Paisley wore a pretty summer dress that fell to just above her knees. He could imagine lifting that skirt, sliding his hands up to cup her ass before dragging her panties down and sliding two fingers into her. His other hand would make the trip around her hip and into her cleft where he'd stroke her clit until she shattered around his fingers.

Then he'd get down on his knees, put his head under that skirt, and—

Jesus. Stop.

Paisley turned then, her blue eyes dropping over his chest before lifting to his. "I could hardly tell you not to use my shower after you raced over here last night. Thank you again."

"You're welcome. Coffee ready?"

She had one of those coffee makers with a stainless steel carafe and he couldn't see if it was done brewing or not.

"Yes. Want me to pour a cup for you?"

"You finish the toast. I'm gonna grab a cup and go outside, look around the yard a bit."

"I can fix eggs or oatmeal if you like."

"Toast is fine."

It wasn't enough to fill him up, not really, but he'd grab a breakfast sandwich at Kiss My Grits before heading to the range. Wasn't going to tell her that, though. And he wasn't going to ask her to fix breakfast either. She had to feed her kid and she had to go to work. That was enough to worry about without cooking for him.

"Okay. Let me know if you change your mind."

"You look pretty, babe."

Her lashes dropped. "Thank you."

He put a finger under her chin and lifted it until she had to look at him. "I mean it, Payz. Don't know what kind of mind fuck games Trey played on you, but you're beautiful. Sexy as fuck. I'm hard just looking at you."

She blinked. "You don't have to say that. But thank you."

"I'd guide your hand to my dick to prove it, but I don't think that's the solution I'm looking for. Better if I think about Rob Harney glaring at me during his wife's shooting lesson or something."

Paisley laughed. "Oh, I doubt he'll glare unless it's behind your back. You're twice as tall and three times as big."

"Maybe not three times."

"Maybe not, but you've got more muscle on your arms than he has on his whole body."

"You're cute." He poured coffee into a cup and lifted it in salute. "Thanks for making coffee."

He left Paisley at the counter and went outside to poke around the yard. It was summer so no leaves in the yard to disturb. There was a wood privacy fence surrounding the yard, but it was old and could use repair in places. He went over to where the trespasser had climbed the fence and looked around.

The house behind Paisley's was a shotgun style. It was in good shape with a pretty yard filled with flowering bushes and mature trees. There was only a picket fence between the shotgun house and the one next door, so somebody could have come from that direction and hopped the fence there before climbing over Paisley's fence.

Ethan walked the perimeter, carefully checking the ground for anything that might have fallen from the trespasser's pockets or for a wet patch of ground and a footprint. He also checked the fence for fibers from the man's clothing. There was nothing.

Whoever it was, they hadn't left a trace. Could be Trey, or could be that football playing teen sneaking out. It could even be Fern Carter's husband, if he was the kind of guy who'd do her dirty work for her. Man better pray he wasn't, though. If Ethan found out it was Fern and her bullshit, sending her husband over to harass Paisley, shit was hitting the fan.

He set his coffee on the picnic table in the backyard and sent a message to Seth.

Seth responded with a thumbs up. If there was anything to find on the neighbors' cameras, he'd find it.

The screen door creaked. He turned to find Paisley walking toward him, coffee cup in hand. He liked watching her move, the way the skirt caressed her bare legs, revealing and hiding creamy skin as she glided across the grass in her white Keds.

"Find anything?"

"Nope."

"Well, damn."

"It's okay. Seth will check the neighborhood cameras for movement, see where our guy came from."

"How do you know there are cameras?"

"I walked the block last night. Several of your neighbors have doorbell cams. And I've spotted at least two trail cams in back yards since I walked out here."

She looked up at the trees in the neighbor's yard. "Oh."

"People like to watch squirrels or chipmunks or whatever. Cameras are cheap, and you can view the wildlife in your own backyard." He shrugged. "Not the only thing they catch, though. And all that video is stored in the cloud. Seth will find it."

"Holy cow." She shook her head. "I guess I should have known. Trey was always scoffing at people's doorbell cams and the security risks of using the cloud."

"For most people, it's not an issue. But it's helpful when we want to find out who was in your yard."

"I guess so." She tilted her head back as a ray of sunshine filtered through the trees and caressed her face. "It all seems surreal in the light of day. Like a bad dream, or an overreaction to someone cutting through the yard. I hate that I'm so suspicious and fearful. I was never that way until I married Trey."

It twisted him up inside to hear her talk about her life with Trey, but he had to listen. He was the only one who could. His friends' women could, and would, but Paisley wouldn't be as open with them. Yet. He had hopes that she'd find true friends in Emma, Rory, Callie, and Daphne, but trust took time.

"I hate that he did that to you." Birds chirped in the trees and a soft breeze blew, though it'd be hot and humid in a couple of hours. "I think I've always been suspicious. Always wondering what people were up to, thinking about how to neutralize threats. Guess that's why I made a good operator once I joined the military."

"Trey said you'd gotten into some trouble. That you were accused of using excessive force on civilians. It was something he said early on, when he was convincing me what a lucky escape I'd had. He made it sound like you had an explosive temper."

Ethan shook his head and sipped his coffee. It was that or punch a tree. "Yeah, no, that was him. That's how he ended up with the Green Beret unit at Eglin. He was kicked out of the unit we were both in. I didn't know that at the time or I wouldn't have trusted him anywhere near you. Jesus," he growled as emotion boiled in his gut. "He really is a fucking waste of space."

"Not going to get an argument from me."

He reached over and took her hand, twined his fingers with hers. The electricity arcing through his body was no surprise. Neither was the need. But he could wait. Just being here, with her, when he'd thought she was nothing but a hurtful memory, was enough.

"The only explosive temper I have is when somebody

threatens those I care about. Can't promise I wouldn't tear him limb from limb if I got my hands on him."

She sighed and squeezed his hand. "As much as I think he deserves that, I also wouldn't want you to do anything that could get you into trouble. Honestly, if he'd just get blown up overseas, I'd be a happy woman. I know that sounds awful, but I can't forgive and forget, even if he never comes after me. He wrecked my life for no reason other than he wanted to hurt you. And probably me for choosing you in the first place."

Ethan tugged her against his side and slipped an arm around her. Then he dropped a kiss on her sun-warmed hair and breathed in her floral scent. Everything about this woman triggered his protective instincts. He didn't know how he was going to do it yet, but Trey McCann's days were numbered.

He didn't get to hurt Paisley and Violet and keep breathing. He didn't get to live a life without consequences.

One way or the other, Ethan was taking him down. Permanently.

21

"s she being nice to you?" Megan sounded surprised. They were standing in Paisley's office and Fern had just left after coming to ask about one of the reading group sessions they were starting to host in the library.

"I don't know that I'd call it nice," Paisley said. "But she spoke to me and didn't glare, so I guess that's an improvement."

Maybe Ethan's not so subtle threats had worked. Fern had been angry and denied she'd painted the door or sent the text, but she might have realized she had no ground to stand on. At least when it came to the paint. She didn't want the police poking around her basement or garage, looking for a can of paint that matched her door. Even if it hadn't been her who'd done the vandalism, it looked bad that the shade was the same as her front door.

"I'd say she was almost respectful," Megan said with a

grin. "Guess it doesn't suck to have a hot, muscled hunk of a man willing to call her out on her bullshit."

Warmth spiraled through her. "I'm sure that didn't hurt."

"Sooo," Megan said. "Are you dating him?"

"We're friends." Damn, it was hot. Maybe they needed to dial the AC down a couple of degrees. And why didn't she just say that, yes, they *were* kind of seeing each other?

"Ah, okay. Well if you don't want him, send him my way. I'd like to see what's under that snug-fitting shirt of his."

Paisley arched an eyebrow. "Oh, is that all? No interest in what's under the rest of the clothing?"

Megan snorted. "*All* the interest. It's been months since Dan and I broke up. Mama's feeling a little neglected, if you know what I mean. Wouldn't mind taking one of those One Shot Tactical hotties for a spin. But there's only two of them left now, alas. I'm always a day late and a dollar short."

Paisley laughed. "Hey, that's still two chances to score."

Megan shook her head. "Not really. I think Ethan's more interested in you than he ever would be in me, so maybe climb on and ride that thang while the riding is good."

"You're ridiculous. But fun."

"Heh, I am, aren't I? Okay, lemme go make sure that Fern is behaving herself. Mr. Watson usually shows up about this time. He may have promised to dial it down, but I'm not sure he's capable of it."

"Oh lord, please let him be capable," Paisley muttered.

"Amen, sister. Oh, don't forget that the librarian from Angels Cove called. She wanted to discuss a joint book festival with you."

"Got it. Is this something we've done with them before?"

Megan shook her head. "No, and I'm honestly not sure how she expects it to go. Angels Cove is on the other side of the river. The car ferry is the connection point between our towns, unless you drive to the Tennessee River bridge on I-65, which is even farther. Not that it can't be done, but we're both small towns so what's the idea and all that?"

"I guess I'll find out when I talk to her."

"Don't get me wrong, I love Angels Cove. It's peaceful and quiet, not that Sutton's Creek isn't, but we get more traffic from Huntsville because we're on the same side of the river. The ferry isn't reliable since it doesn't always run as scheduled, though you can drive to I-65 or the 231 bridge if you miss it or don't want to wait. Just takes longer."

"I've been meaning to take Violet over there on a day off and explore, but I haven't done it yet."

She'd been busy, and she'd been wary. It'd felt like leaving the confines of Sutton's Creek meant exposing herself, though last night had proven she didn't have to go anywhere to feel unsafe.

"It's really pretty. There's a protected cove where you can swim. It's shallow because there's a sandbar, so it's great for kids. The town is a lot like this one, with quirky shops and restaurants, and there's also has a thriving art community. Worth a trip when you get time."

Maybe it was something Ethan would want to do with them. Paisley imagined the three of them crossing the river for a day out and felt nothing but quiet joy at the idea.

After Megan left, Paisley got to work calling the librarian, getting the details about the book event she wanted to do, and then turning her attention to emails and other things that had to get done. People sometimes thought that librarians just got to read books all day, but that was so far from the truth it wasn't funny. She might have gotten into the profession because she loved to read and thought she'd be surrounded by books, but libraries were actually community centers.

And, unfortunately, when people needed help and nobody had an answer, they often sent those people to the library, as if the librarians could find the answers. Need your taxes filed? Go the library. Need a place to sit inside the air conditioning because it was hot and you didn't have AC or maybe a home at all? Go to the library.

Librarians didn't file taxes and didn't fill out the forms for you, but they could give you forms. And though she was happy to have people shelter from the heat in the library, what happened to them when it was closing time and they still had nowhere to go or no AC?

By the time Paisley felt caught up enough for a lunch break, it was after one o'clock. She headed for the small break room to retrieve her sandwich from the fridge and carry it back to the office when her phone rang. She kept it on her at all times, in case her aunt or Mrs. Park called about Violet, but it was Ethan's number that flashed on her screen.

Her heart skipped for a different reason as she answered the call.

"Hi, Ethan," she said.

"Hey, Payz. You free?"

She glanced around the library. Everything seemed under control. Fern was calmly assisting a patron. Megan was on the computer. "I could be. I was just about to eat lunch at my desk. Why?"

"Nah, don't do that. I picked up a Reuben for you. I know how much you like those."

Her belly growled. She hadn't indulged in a Reuben in too long. Mostly because it was cheaper to fix her own lunch and bring it to work. She had to watch every penny. Even though she lived in Aunt Hettie's house for free, she still had lawyer bills. And taking care of Violet, which was a delight but also cost money.

"I do like Reubens. But you didn't have to do that."

"I know. Did it anyway. I'll be there in five minutes."

In precisely five minutes, Ethan strode into the library, looking ridiculously handsome in jeans and the One Shot Tactical polo. He'd left her house early this morning, after they'd stood in the yard and drank coffee, because he needed to go home and change for work. Violet hadn't been awake yet, which meant no explanations had been necessary.

He carried a bag from the Kiss My Grits Cafe that smelled divine and gave her a grin that made her belly clench.

"Hey, babe. Got time to eat with me? Or should I drop yours off and see you later?"

Every female in the library had stopped what they were doing to look at Ethan. Even Fern, though maybe she was looking for a different reason.

Paisley swallowed. "We can eat in my office."

She led the way, conscious of the stares and grateful for the moment they passed into the small hallway that hid them from view. Ethan didn't close her office door behind them, for which she was grateful. She'd have asked him to open it if he had. Didn't need the staff wondering what she was up to in her office with the handsome shooting instructor.

She'd surfed over to the One Shot Tactical web page a few days ago. The testimonials from women who'd taken instruction from the men were often laughably obvious in their appreciation for the masculinity on display. Just like Michelle Harney had been last night.

Paisley's favorite review on the site was an anonymous one about Ethan.

Very thorough instruction! Ethan can show me anything and I just can't look away! That's how good an instructor he is! Also, his chest and arms are swoon-worthy!

Aside from the copious exclamation points, the woman—person?—had a point.

Ethan took the sandwiches from the sack along with two bags of potato chips. "Figured you had drinks here."

"Yes. We have water and Coke products. What do you want?"

"Water's good. It's hot out there today."

Paisley went to the break room to grab a water for him since she already had a half-finished bottle on her desk. When she returned, he had everything laid out for her. The paper was unwrapped and the chips were open. He'd pulled a chair to the side of her desk and was currently sitting in it, waiting for her.

"This is really sweet of you," she said when she was sitting at her desk with the wonderful smell of corned beef, sauerkraut, and Thousand Island dressing invading her senses.

"You gotta eat, I gotta eat, and I wanted to see you."

"You just saw me a few hours ago."

He grinned. "Yeah, but I wanted to see you again."

Paisley bit into her sandwich, moaning as the flavors filled her tastebuds. "So good. I saw these on the menu at Kiss My Grits but hadn't managed to try one yet."

"Wendy makes a pretty good Reuben. For a Southern lady." He winked with that last bit, and Paisley shook her head though she was smiling.

"One of these days, I want to go to New York and try all this food you keep insisting is the best."

"Maybe we can go next year. You, me, and Violet."

Hope was a fragile flame inside her. "Next year. That might work."

"You sound a little doubtful."

"Sorry. It's just that I've been so focused on the day to day, getting through the divorce proceedings and staying safe, that I haven't thought a lot about what happens next year. I haven't even thought about next month more than I have to, if I'm honest."

He ate a potato chip. "How long will the proceedings take? Do you know?"

"Three to six months is the average, and that's if Trey doesn't decide to be an asshole. All I want is full custody of Violet. My attorney doesn't think that's a problem because of the abuse, but if Trey wants to fight, he can. He doesn't care about Violet, but he might do it to hurt me. On the other hand, the publicity that would come with a fight probably wouldn't be good for business. He has a couple of high profile clients around Destin, and though most of his business is focused on jobs overseas, those people are easy money he won't want to lose. Plus it just doesn't look professional to be a wife beater."

Trey had always been concerned about his reputation. He chose the right house, the right decor, a pretty wife, and he made everyone think they lived a charmed life. He wanted to be seen a certain way, and he'd tolerated no deviations from that image. That she'd left him and taken Violet had surely shaken that image to its foundations.

"He doesn't want anyone to know he's an abusive asshole."

"Definitely not. I tried to make this very easy for him. I didn't ask for child support, and I didn't ask for assets. I just want out."

He looked pissed and troubled at the same time. "I understand. I think he ought to have to pay you for what he did, but I also know why you wanna make it easy for him to walk away."

Not everyone understood why she didn't demand anything. "Thank you. My attorney wants to go for the jugular. I think she's disappointed in me."

"It's your life, Payz. Nobody gets to tell you how to handle this. You know what you and Violet need."

"It'll be harder without child support, but my mom managed. It's not that I think a man shouldn't pay, or that a woman shouldn't fight for her child, but this situation isn't typical."

"You don't have to explain it to me. I'm on your side. You and Violet need anything, you can ask me."

Her heart squeezed. "I appreciate that. I don't want to ask, and I won't unless it's important."

"You need to know something, babe. I understand that if I want a relationship with you, it's not just you. It's Violet too. If we do this—date, sleep together, *be* together—I want to be a part of her life as much as yours. I don't know shit about kids, not really, but she's yours and that means I want her to be happy and I want her to feel like I'm someone she can trust. I'm gonna be here for her just like I'm here for you. Even if all we do is end up friends,

I'm her cool uncle she can count on to be in her life. That work for you?"

There was a knot in her throat. "Yes," she whispered as tears swam in her eyes.

"Good. Now eat that sandwich before it gets cold."

"I'm trying. I didn't expect you to make me cry."

"Wasn't trying to, but you needed to hear it. I won't abandon you again, Paisley. And I won't abandon her."

Her heart beat erratically in her chest. "You're a good man, Ethan."

"Not always. But I am when I'm with you."

She didn't know what to make of that statement, and she didn't ask. She knew in her bones he was a good man, no matter what he said. Actions revealed character, and Ethan's actions were always honorable and considerate. She didn't doubt he'd had to do things in the line of duty that might make him question himself, but she didn't.

"You want me to stay at your place tonight?" he asked after they'd finished lunch and he'd cleaned up the mess, putting everything back into the bag from the cafe.

She should tell him no, that they'd be fine. The alerts had worked the way they were supposed to and she'd known there was someone in her yard. She could have called the police if she'd needed to, and she could if it happened again.

But having Ethan there, ready to defend her and Violet, made the fear recede. Plus she liked him being there. Liked having another adult to talk to, someone who'd known her before her life turned into a survival drama.

"Do you mind?"

"Wouldn't offer if I did."

"Then yes, I'd like it if you'd stay with us."

"Saw you had a gas grill. Does it work?"

"It does. The previous tenant left it, but I cleaned it up and filled the gas bottle. I used it to make hamburgers once."

"Excellent. I'll get something to throw on the grill and fix dinner for us."

Paisley touched his arm. It was like touching a live wire in some ways. Always had been. The way her body reacted to a simple touch was ridiculous, but she'd known the instant he'd put his hand against her back to help her into his truck five years ago that she'd end up in bed with him. How could she not?

That same feeling was there now, sparking and snapping to life in the deepest parts of her. He must have felt something too because he stepped closer, crowding her against her desk, and let his gaze drop to her breasts before lifting to her eyes again.

"I, um, I just wanted to say you don't have to keep feeding me. I'll give you some cash for the groceries."

"You won't," he growled. "You're a single mom going through a divorce from a shit husband and you aren't asking for child support. I've been on my own for years, I've accumulated a lot of combat pay, and I have a lot more money in my bank account than I spend in a month. Maybe if I liked designer clothes, expensive vacations, and fancy sports cars, I'd have to watch it more than I do. So let me spend money on groceries for you and Violet, okay?"

"I don't want you to feel like you have to."

He bent and kissed her, a quick peck on the lips that left her mouth tingling. The first time in nearly five years that she'd felt his mouth on hers, and it was every bit as intoxicating as it'd been then. Even if it was a chaste kiss.

"I don't feel like I have to, Payz. I feel like I want to. I want to take care of you and Violet because I care about you. Never stopped if I'm honest. Seeing you again knocked me on my ass, not gonna lie, but knowing what really happened to us? It set something in me free again."

Her heart hammered in her chest. It was everything she wanted, and everything she feared losing once more.

"Me too," she whispered.

"Good." He dropped his mouth to hers again, lingered a moment longer. No tongue, but that didn't stop her panties from growing damp. She wanted him as much as she ever had, and it scared her.

"You tempt me too much," he growled. "I'd love to shut this door, slide your panties off, and bend you over this desk. Gonna save that for another time, though. First time we're together again, I want it to be more than a frantic fuck with witnesses only a few steps away."

He reached around and cupped her ass, squeezed just enough to make her moan. "Gotta get back to work, babe. Think about me when I'm gone."

"I doubt I'll think about anything else."

He grinned as he stepped away, and her heart skipped. So hot. This man was so damned hot, and he wanted her. It'd amazed her back then and it amazed her now. Especially after all that'd happened.

"Later, babe."

She sat against the edge of her desk for a good five minutes after he was gone. Things were moving fast, like he'd said. Two weeks ago, she'd have never thought she'd be in a position where Ethan was sleeping at her house, kissing her, and where she was dreaming about the moment they finally made love again.

But the thing that kept popping up in her head when she thought about the future was that she had to tell him the truth. She had to tell him everything about what'd happened after he'd left and she'd thought he'd abandoned her.

He needed to know he could be Violet's father. Anything less was wrong.

His erection was gone by the time he got back to the range. Just thinking about bending Paisley over that desk, cupping her ass, and burying himself to the hilt inside her had kept him in a state of agitation for almost the entire drive. Thankfully he'd gotten a grip on himself.

Not a literal grip, though that was happening later since he needed to release some of this tension. But at least Paisley was feeling the tension, too. The way she'd moaned when he'd squeezed her ass told him all he needed to know.

It hit him deep inside to know she could still respond to him that way after all she'd been through. If he thought about Trey touching her, it made him want to howl. Worse was the thought of Trey hurting her, though.

Motherfucker was going down. Somehow.

"Hey," Seth said when Ethan walked into the office. "I was just gonna call you."

Ethan dropped his backpack on a chair. "You got something?"

"Fern Carter has a burner. Picked it up at Walmart about a month ago. The number matches."

Ethan's gut twisted with anger. "That absolute bitch." He hadn't felt in the least bit guilty about chewing her ass out in the library before he had the facts, but now that he did, she was due another talking to. If she *ever* made Paisley scared again, he'd make sure everybody knew what a cunt she was. Hell, he might do it anyway if Paisley agreed.

"Yeah, she's a piece of work. She returned to Sutton's Creek because there was some controversy at her old library. She and her husband were living in Mississippi where she worked as a substitute teacher and part-time library volunteer. She outed one of the librarians for being gay. It was apparently an open secret, but somebody calling attention to it, well, people got up in arms and the man ended up resigning. Fern didn't get his job, though. She left because there was a lot of anger toward her after that."

"How spiteful do you have to be to do that to someone? To think that what you want is more important than someone else's reputation and livelihood?"

And that right there earned her a special visit. He hated a bully. Erik had turned to drugs because of the shittiness of their lives, but it was the bullying that kept him there even after they had a home. He'd been too small and too shy to fight back, and Ethan wasn't always there to do it for him.

"You got me. People like that could do the world a lot of good if they'd fuck right off the edge of it."

"No kidding."

"I also got a hit on the doorbell cams in Paisley's neighborhood. I can't pinpoint a house, but the guy first appears at zero-forty-eight, walking down Cherry Street. He keeps that ball cap pulled low, so no face shots, and the clothes are too baggy to get a real indication of size. Sharper cams and daylight? Maybe, but not at night. Could be a big guy or a regular guy in big clothes. Anyway, he cuts across yards to get to the next street instead of sticking to the sidewalk. He hops the fence at Paisley's at around one. After he left there, he kept going down the block, then cut across another couple of yards. About an hour or so later, he reappears in the first place I clocked him."

"So he made a circle."

"Yep, seems that way."

Ethan scratched his chin. "Could be a teen sneaking off for some kid bullshit, I suppose."

"Could be. Hard to say. If I coulda got a look at a car, or the house he came from, that would've helped a lot. I hacked Fern Carter's doorbell cam too. He didn't come from her house, so not her husband looking to get revenge for slights to Fern. She seems to be handling that job all by herself."

"That's good about the hubby. I didn't really want to have to whip his ass. Figured Ghost wouldn't approve."

"No, I really wouldn't," the man himself said, walking in the opposite door. "No beating up the citizens of Sutton's Creek, even if they deserve it."

"Party pooper," Ethan said.

"Sorry not sorry." Ghost grinned, then got serious again. "So the trespasser might have been a teenager, or it could be Trey McCann reconnoitering the neighborhood and making plans."

"Yeah," Ethan said with a frown. "I'm staying over there tonight in case he comes back."

Ghost sighed. "You're gonna be the final nail in my coffin, aren't you? Four down, one left to fall. Contravening direct orders not to get romantically involved with anyone for the duration of the mission."

"Sorry not sorry?" Ethan offered.

"Asshole," Ghost said, but there was no malice to it. Blaze had been the first to fall. Then Chance got Rory pregnant and fell in love. Seth had thought Callie was their target, the person responsible for trying to take the Athena Project down, but that didn't stop him from falling at her feet. Then there was Kane and Daphne. Kane had tiptoed around Daphne for months, claiming to think of her as a little sister. And now they couldn't keep their hands off each other.

Along came Ethan and Paisley. "In all fairness, I fell for Paisley five years ago. Didn't expect I'd ever see her again. We're getting reacquainted at the moment."

"Is that what they're calling it these days?" Ghost sighed and shook his head. "Not sure Washington gives a flying fuck though. Their interest in what we're doing seems to have waned a bit."

The three of them were silent. They'd arrived in Sutton's Creek almost eight months ago, filled with noble purpose and in regular contact with the president and her team. As the months passed and the mission dragged on, the president seemed to have turned her eye toward other matters. Like keeping her poll numbers up and trying to broker peace deals between historic enemies. Athena lurched toward completion and Washington checked in periodically, like a distracted parent making sure the kids were still on the playground but not really checking to see if they were actually okay.

Typical politicians. They were always more distracted by the issue of the moment, whatever it might be. Or manufacturing issues to keep you from focusing on the real problem.

"What about you, boss?" Seth winked at Ethan. "Surely there's some lucky lady that's caught your eye."

"Nope," Ghost said, shoving his hands in his pockets. "Not in the least."

"Agent Corbin's pretty hot," Ethan said.

Ghost's head snapped up. "No. No fucking way. That woman makes my head hurt."

Ethan and Seth exchanged a look. Ghost saw it and shook his head vigorously. "Don't get any fucking ideas in your heads. I have to deal with her because she's shoved her way into our business. I don't have to like her."

"Don't have to like who?" Blaze wandered in with Chance close behind.

"Diana Corbin," Seth said. "He doesn't like her."

"What's new about that?" Chance asked, blinking like an owl.

"Nothing's new," Ghost said. "These two clowns were suggesting that since all of you are hung up on women despite orders, I might want to join the club."

"With Diana Corbin?" Chance laughed. "No fucking way. She's a nightmare."

"She is," Ghost said. "I'd rather date a wolverine."

"I'm sorry, what?" Daphne stood in the doorway, a folder in her hand.

"Well, hell, why doesn't everyone just come on in," Ghost grumbled.

"Don't blame me," Daphne said. "I was coming for a signature on this paperwork. Ordering those folding tables and tablecloths you told me I could get for the future events business. I'm innocent here. But why are you dating a wolverine? Aren't there any eligible—and less angry—women in this town? I hear Wendy Cochran is single. And let's not forget the widowed Mrs. Wright. She'd be fun."

The guys snorted. Ghost glared.

"You want those tables or what?" he growled.

"Yes, I most definitely do."

"Then don't suggest Colleen Wright as a potential date. That'd be like kissing my grandma."

"There's still Wendy."

"No. Another word, Daph, and no events business. Which, considering I only told you to start small yesterday, you haven't wasted any time, have you?"

"Meanie. And no, I never waste time."

"You forgot one," Blaze said dramatically, leaning in.

"I did?" Daphne tilted her head.

"FBI."

"Ohhhhhh. Yeah, no. Not her. She's a bit too intense. So's Alex. Put all that intensity together, and it wouldn't be pretty."

"Precisely. Thank you, Daph. You're back in my good graces." He held out his hand and she gave him the folder. "And now if you're all done harassing me, I'm going back to my office for some peace and quiet."

Once Ghost was gone, Daphne eyed them. "I didn't want to mention this in front of him since he's so grumpy today, but what would y'all think about posing shirtless for an ad?"

They all looked at each other. Chance shrugged. "I mean I'd do it. Why not?"

"No," Seth said. "Not happening."

"Aw, come on, Sethie. Don't make me get Callie involved."

"Yeah, not feeling it either," Ethan said. "This is a shooting range and training facility, not a Chippendales show."

Daphne grinned. "You wouldn't know it to read some of these testimonials. Big men, tight abs, hard muscles, chests to swoon over. It reads like a Chippendales show."

"Still not doing it," Ethan said.

"Count me out," Blaze added. "That's three against one. Alex won't go for it, so that's four. What's Kane think?"

"Kane will do whatever I ask him to do. Just have to ask him the right way. But, fine, I see the point. What if we broaden this idea—there are six of you and we'd need twelve photos for a calendar. We could get some kittens and puppies, and y'all could pose shirtless with them. Two photos each. How hard could it be?"

"Still no," Seth said. "But I'll happily contribute to an animal shelter you pick."

Daphne sighed dramatically. "For a bunch of badasses, y'all are certainly the biggest prudes I've ever met. Fine, I'll think of something else. Babies," she added as she flounced back the way she'd come.

"You'd really pose for a shirtless photo so she could plaster it on the wall at the Dawg and blast it out to the whole town by advertising in the Bee?" Blaze said to Chance.

"Why not? Women pose in bikinis to sell shit, so why not use what we've got and do the same?"

"Good point. But still no," Seth said as he tapped away on his computer. "This body is for my woman to ogle, not for every woman in Sutton's Creek to gawk at in a picture. Or tuck it away in her spank bank."

"News flash, friend. They already do that," Chance said. "They just do it from memory."

"Things I don't want to think about for a thousand," Seth grated.

Chance rolled his eyes. "Denial ain't just a river in Egypt, friend. And on that note, I've got a class to teach."

Blaze went over to his desk and sat down. "You going with me on that security consult tomorrow, Phantom?"

"Planning on it," Seth said.

Seth had discovered that while Brent Gannon worked on the Arsenal three days a week, he also went to an office in Research Park for two days. Bugging Eagle Defense System's office was a lot easier than bugging the Missile Defense Agency. If Gannon was meeting with Dashevsky's people, maybe it was there. Which was the real reason why Blaze and Seth were going tomorrow.

The plan was to surveil through electronic means as well as some in-person surveillance. Later this week, Kane and Daphne were headed to the brewery in Huntsville where Gannon seemed to spend a lot of time, according to his credit card receipts. They would watch him for a few nights and report back.

Seemed odd to have Daphne involved, but then again she'd been instrumental in helping them take down her brother before he could sell those Stingers, so why not? She was smart and capable, and she took no prisoners when she set her mind to something.

Ethan looked at his watch. "Better go relieve Kane as RSO."

He'd spend the entire hour thinking about the way Paisley had looked at him when he'd told her what he wanted to do to her. And trying not to get hard. He couldn't wait to get off work, pick up some groceries, and spend the rest of the evening hanging out with her and Violet.

"It's not busy today," Blaze said. "I had two people the whole time."

"Wait a minute," Seth called as Ethan headed for the door. "Just got this. Looks like McCann didn't leave the country as scheduled. Ticket canceled."

Ethan stared at his friend. "Do you know where he is now?"

Seth typed and stared at his screen. Then he looked up and Ethan's stomach tightened.

"No. He didn't board any planes in Charlotte. He isn't at the hotel anymore. I'll search for a rental car, but when I tell you I've hit more roadblocks looking for this asshole than I expected, I'm not kidding."

Ethan's temples were starting to throb. "He was in HOT, like us. He knows how to fly under the radar."

"Doesn't mean he's on the way here," Blaze said calmly. "If he's working covert ops, he might have used another ID to obscure his trail before he headed out on a job. We would."

"Yeah, and he could have used it to head straight for Sutton's Creek."

"He could," Blaze said, standing. "And maybe he did.

Not gonna say he didn't. Go check on your woman and her kid. I'll take your shift."

"Thanks, man. I appreciate it."

Blaze shrugged. "You'd do it for me."

"I'll keep searching," Seth said. "I've got nothing going on right now. I was gonna head out early and surprise Callie with dinner on the table, but I'll just take her out instead."

Ethan thanked them both again and sprinted for the parking lot. He didn't know what he was going to say to Paisley since he didn't want to scare her, but until he got eyes on her and Violet both, he wasn't going to feel in the least bit calm.

23

Paisley opened the door to the Sutton Building, her heart hammering. She stared at her phone and the text she'd sent to Emma.

> **Paisley:**
> I need to talk to you about something. Is there a time when I could come see you in your office?

Emma had texted back about ten minutes later.

> **Emma:**
> I've got half an hour before my next patient. Do you want to come now?

Paisley had responded that she did. Before she could change her mind, she'd slung her purse diagonally across her body, told Megan she needed to run out, and headed for Emma's office.

A woman looked up from the front desk and smiled. "Hi, can I help you?"

"Um, yes. I'm here to see Dr. Emma Sutton. I'm Paisley."

The woman flipped through some papers. "I'm sorry but I don't see you. Is there another name?"

"Oh, no. It's not an appointment. I'm a fr-friend."

So embarrassing to stumble on that word but she wasn't used to having friends. The woman smiled. "Oh, I'm so sorry. Of course! I'll tell her you're here."

"Thanks."

A moment later, Emma walked through the door separating the reception area from the offices. "Paisley, I'm so happy to see you. This is Greta. She's our receptionist."

The willowy blond woman was sinking into her chair again after going back to get Emma.

"Pleased to meet you," Greta said, holding out her hand. "And I'm sorry again."

Paisley clasped her hand and shook her head. "No, no. I should have said I was a friend. It's my fault."

"Come on back," Emma said, holding the door for her.

Paisley waited inside the door so Emma could lead. She went into an office with a big wooden desk and photos on the wall that Paisley assumed were her parents. Emma followed Paisley's gaze.

"It's my dad's office. Mine is being painted." Emma looked businesslike in her lab coat and glasses. She had a stethoscope around her neck and her face radiated confidence and friendliness. "What can I help you with today?"

Paisley's heart beat harder than ever. Heat flooded her until her palms were damp. "I...um...oh shit."

Emma was on her feet, pressing a bottle of cool water she'd magically produced into Paisley's hand. "Breathe, Paisley. Sip that. It's okay. You can tell me what's going on. You aren't technically my patient, but we're in my dad's office and this space is sacred to me. You can rely on me not to share anything you say."

Paisley took a sip of water and closed her eyes. Then she worked on breathing for a couple of moments. "Sorry," she said.

"It's okay."

There was nowhere to start but at the beginning. "You asked if Ethan and I had met before. I said no, but that's not true. I'm sorry I lied."

"Paisley," Emma said with a serenity Paisley envied, "you don't owe me any explanations. Your private life is yours. I should apologize for prying."

"What? No." Paisley shook her head. "You were right. When I saw him in the Dawg—well, it'd been five years and I thought he'd dumped me. A man he thought was a friend told me he had, and I believed it. Ethan was sent on a mission and couldn't call me until he returned. By then, Trey—that's the man he thought was a friend—had managed to hack my phone and intercept all calls and texts from Ethan. Then he sent a message from my phone telling Ethan I'd met someone else."

"Oh no."

Paisley sucked in a breath. "It gets worse."

She closed her eyes and told Emma the rest of it. How she'd been drunk and slept with Trey. How she'd learned she was pregnant later and married him. How he'd been abusive and she'd finally found the courage to leave. And then she said the words she'd never said aloud to anyone except Trey. The words she'd skipped over because it hurt to say them. "I don't actually know who Violet's father is. Trey or Ethan. And I-I need to tell Ethan but I don't know how. And what about Violet? What do I tell her?"

Tears slid down her cheeks. She took a tissue from the box on the desk to wipe them away. "Sorry."

Emma slid her chair around the desk and took Paisley's hand. "Oh, honey. Don't apologize. What a terrible, terrible thing you've had to endure. I don't know if this will help or not, but I know what it's like to think you've found a decent man and then he winds up abusing you. Before I met Blaze, I was with someone like that. Nothing like what you endured, but the first time they hit you—well, it's shocking. You don't know what to think, and you wonder if it's your fault. It's not, of course. But they make you believe it is."

"Yes," Paisley said, her chin quivering.

Emma sucked in a breath and squeezed her hand. "I saw the way Ethan reacted that night in the Dawg. And I see him with you and Violet now. He was dealing with shock and pain that night. But the way he treats you both now, well, I see caring there. He already knows you married the man he thought was a friend, and that didn't make him run away, did it?"

Paisley shook her head and wiped her nose.

"Okay. Then I think the way you tell him is that you sit him down and say what you said to me. If either of you want to find out for sure, we can do that. A couple of cheek swabs and we'll get an answer in a few days. You can offer him that, but I'll tell you what I see. This is the friend talking now, not the doctor. She favors him. Her eyes, the shape of her nose, her smile. She has your chin, your cheekbones, your forehead. But she so clearly belongs to you both from what I can see. Again, not a formal diagnosis, just your book club bestie telling you what she's observed."

Paisley drew in a breath. It shook on the way out. "I think so too. I wasn't certain at the time, and then when he came back into our lives—" She shredded the tissue in her fingers. "Well, I thought I was seeing what I wanted to see. That it was hope and not reality. But if it's true, if Ethan is her father—well, I don't know if it helps my divorce situation or hurts."

Emma frowned. "I don't know either. But your husband's name is on the birth certificate, and he's her legal father. I don't know what the process is in Florida, but I would imagine you'd have to petition the courts with the information. They might also order another test of their own, though I don't know for certain. I think you need to talk to Ethan. Tell him the truth, give him a chance to react. You don't have to tell Violet anything until you and Ethan establish what you want to happen."

Paisley nodded. "You're right. I know that. I just—I

needed someone to talk to. And you're a doctor, so I figured you were used to hearing people's problems." She bit back a bubble of hysterical laughter. "Maybe not these kinds of problems, though. I'm sorry if I presumed too much."

Emma laughed softly, and Paisley felt a little better. It was a warm laugh. Friendly. "You'd be surprised what people talk about sometimes. I've heard a lot of things I wasn't expecting. But I can't say I wasn't expecting something about Ethan and Violet at some point. Like I said, there's a resemblance. Not that any of the others have said anything to me about it, but I think I'm more in tune with the human body than the rest of them. Do you feel any better?"

Paisley sat quietly for a moment, feeling the chaos in her soul. It wasn't the whirlwind it'd been, but it wasn't gone either. "I do. I'm still scared to tell him, but I know I have to. I just have to find time to do it when Violet isn't there. I don't want us to have to tiptoe around her."

"Can I help? Blaze and I can take her to Rory and Chance's place. They have chickens and goats, but no ponies. There might even be a cow out there somewhere."

"I...I think that would be amazing, yes. She loved those animals, didn't stop talking about them all weekend. She still talks about them, but she's also kind of hung up on the kittens next door."

Emma pulled her phone from her pocket and started typing something. "How's tonight? I'll text Rory, make sure it's okay."

Paisley swallowed her apprehension. Was she ready to do this? To tell Ethan he might be a father, and then endure the inevitable emotional fallout of that conversation? No, but there was never going to be a good time and sooner was better than later at this point.

"That would be great. Are you sure it's not a problem?"

"Positive." She sent the text. A moment later, an answer pinged in. "And there's Rory saying yes, come on out."

"I have to pick her up at five. I can bring her by if that's okay. I think she'll be excited."

"That works. We'll stay at the farm until you text me. And don't worry, I won't tell anyone what it's about. They'll just think you and Ethan want some alone time."

She got to her feet. "Thank you, Emma. For listening. For not judging. For being supportive."

Emma stood and pulled her in for a hug. And Paisley, who wasn't effusive with anyone, hugged her right back.

"That's what friends are for, honey. Told you you were in the club."

"Best club ever," Paisley whispered, and meant it.

24

"She stepped out for a few minutes."

Ethan's pulse zipped. He'd arrived at the library and gone straight inside to find Paisley, but Megan was telling him that Paisley wasn't there. She also wasn't answering her texts. Dread swirled in his gut but he forced it down. It was a bright, sunny day out. If Trey was in Sutton's Creek, and that was a big if, he wasn't going to grab Paisley in the middle of the day. He'd wait until dark to act.

Darkness was a special operator's friend. They could operate during the day, and did so when necessary, but night was preferable.

"Did she say where she was going?"

"No. She just said she needed to run out but she'd be back."

Frustration hammered him. Why wasn't she

answering her phone? "Any idea which direction she went?"

"No, I'm sorry. Is everything okay?" Megan's eyes widened suddenly. "Did something happen to Violet?"

"No, nothing like that. Violet's fine." He'd driven past the Park house without stopping. They didn't know him, and he wasn't going to scare Mrs. Park by knocking on her door, but he'd seen the girls in the backyard. They'd been playing on a swing set and yelling happily.

It wasn't lost on him that Trey would also be able to see them if he knew where to look. But, again, he was unlikely to act during the day with witnesses who could identify him to law enforcement. If Trey wanted revenge, he'd do it silently and secretly.

Ethan thanked Megan and went outside to think it through. Paisley's car was in the parking lot, which meant she'd gone on foot. Wherever she'd gone, it had to be close. Maybe she wanted a coffee. He started in the direction of the town square because he couldn't stand around and do nothing. He'd look around there first. If he didn't see her, he'd swing back to the library and hope she'd returned.

He punched the screen to call her and lifted the phone to his ear. It rang four times. He was just about to end the call when her voice came across the line.

"Hey, what's up?"

Relief coursed through his veins. "Hey, babe. Where are you?"

She seemed to hesitate before she answered. "I had to

run out for a few minutes. I'm just seeing your texts. Sorry I missed them. I'm on my way back to the library. I had to do something."

He wanted to ask what, but didn't. This thing with them was fragile and new and he wasn't going to make demands. Unless it was about her safety. That was an area in which he planned to make demands.

"I'm at the library. Need to talk to you. Which direction are you coming from? I'll meet you."

"The square. Is everything okay? Did something happen?"

"Stay on the line and I'll tell you in a minute." He covered ground quick, finally seeing her as she crossed the street from the park. She looked worried as he approached. He tucked his phone away and she slid hers into her bag. A moment later, they were standing in front of each other, and Ethan was so fucking grateful he wanted to drop to his knees and thank the Lord.

"What's happened?" She looked fearful. "I'm going to assume Violet is okay since Mrs. Park hasn't called me—and since you don't seem panicked."

"Violet's fine. I drove by there and she was playing in the back yard. I'd like you to call Mrs. Park, though. Make sure everything's good."

"You're scaring me."

He huffed a breath. "Trey didn't go overseas as planned. We lost track of him in Charlotte. Doesn't mean he's here, but since you had a trespasser last night that we haven't yet identified, I think caution is wise."

Paisley stepped closer to him and darted a glance around the area as if expecting a sniper to fire at any second. "He could be watching us now."

"He could be. But he's not going to act in daylight. Too many potential witnesses." He looped an arm around her shoulders, dragged her in close. "Let's get back to the library. Call Mrs. Park."

"I should go pick her up." She looked at her watch. "I can leave early. It's only an hour, and Megan and Debbie can cover it. Fern was gone at three, but it's Tuesday and we aren't too busy." She glanced up at him. "Do we need to find somewhere else to stay for a while?"

"I'll be with you, Payz. And we've got surveillance. You can stay in your house."

"Okay, that's good. Violet's had so many upheavals lately. If I drag her somewhere else, well, it'll just be another one. I'm not unwilling, but if I don't have to, I'd rather not."

"I don't think you have to. I'll tell you when I think it's necessary, okay?"

She nodded. "I trust you."

He kissed the top of her head. "I'm glad for that. By the way, your anonymous text was Fern. She has a burner phone."

"Wow. How sick do you have to be to send texts like that to people? She doesn't know my history, but that doesn't give her a pass."

"No, it really doesn't. You could probably take it to the police. Or the library board."

She was silent as they made their way down the street. "I'll think about it."

They made it to the library and she went to tell Megan and Debbie she needed to leave for the day. They assured her they had it covered. The library was open until seven and they had another volunteer coming in at five to run that evening's book discussion about fantasy novels.

Ethan followed Paisley to her office where she shut things down and gathered up her tote bag. She called Mrs. Park while she put books in the tote.

"Hello, Mrs. Park. Yes, it's Paisley Allen. I wanted to pick up Violet in a few minutes if that's convenient. Okay, yes, thank you. See you soon."

"Sounds like everything's normal," she said when the call ended. "I'm not panicking because there's no reason yet. And I have you and your friends to watch over us."

"You do."

She nibbled her lip. "Emma and Blaze were going to take Violet tonight for a couple of hours so you and I could spend time together and talk. They were going to Rory and Chance's so she could see the animals. I should call Emma and cancel."

Surprise stopped him in his tracks. "You arranged for us to be alone?"

She faced him. "Yes. I-I wanted to talk about things. Without worrying that she could hear us or that she might need me when we were discussing something important."

He didn't know what that could be since they'd

already talked about a lot of things, but he knew Paisley probably had more to say about her time with Trey. He wasn't going to discourage her if it helped her feel better. Even though it was hard to hear it.

"I don't think you need to cancel. She'll be with Chance and Blaze, and they already know Trey isn't in Charlotte. She'll be safe with two soldiers to guard her. Unless you'd feel better having her near you."

"I need to think about that," she said. "On the other hand, I don't want to stop living our lives just because Trey didn't stick to his own itinerary. He could be coming for us, but he might simply be adapting to the client's needs for the job."

All of that was true, and he didn't want to tell her to barricade herself inside her home and never come out. He'd be there to protect her and Violet. No way was he letting some fucking loser who'd gotten kicked out of the best special ops group on the planet beat him at his own profession. Trey might be willing to play dirty, but so was Ethan. When it involved this woman and her child, Ethan would do whatever it took to keep them safe.

"I'll follow you to the Parks' house," he said, pushing aside thoughts of fighting dirty.

Paisley sucked in a breath and let it out with a smile that shook at the corners. "I don't know what we'd do without you. If you weren't here, I wouldn't know there'd been anyone in my yard last night. I wouldn't know where Trey was, though I'd be scared he was just out of sight, watching me. Until you showed up and made me get a security system, that's what I did. I looked over my shoulder and prayed. This is better, even if I'm scared right now, so thank you."

He tipped her chin up and pressed his mouth to hers. He wanted to linger, but now wasn't the time. He lifted his head, watched her lashes flutter upward to reveal pretty blue eyes.

"You're welcome, Payz. Let's go and get your little girl."

25

Paisley had worried that Violet would sense something was wrong, but Ethan had gone to the door with her so she could introduce him to Mrs. Park and explain that he might sometimes pick Violet up when she couldn't.

Violet had been too excited by Ethan's presence, and his promise of dinner, to notice they were early picking her up. After she said her goodbyes to Lily, and Paisley thanked Mrs. Park, they went to the Salty Dawg for dinner since Emma and Blaze were taking Violet to the farm in an hour.

Paisley watched Ethan pointing to the pictures on Violet's placemat. She was busy coloring them in and Ethan was asking her about it. She thought about what she had to tell him later and her stomach tightened into a knot.

Would he be angry? Hurt? Shocked? He wouldn't walk

out on her, she was certain of that. Not while Trey was quite possibly in the area. But he might withdraw. He might want to put distance between them while he processed the news.

"Here we go," Amber said as she arrived with a tray. "One kid's cheeseburger, one shrimp pasta, and one meatloaf with mashed potatoes, green beans, and turnip greens. Can I get you anything else?"

"Think we're good, Amber," Ethan said. She winked at him, and Paisley told herself she had no right to feel the twinge of jealousy flaring inside. He wasn't hers yet. He might not be hers ever again, but she hoped he would. Someday, if her life ever got normal again.

If Trey decided he'd rather get on with his life, run his business, make money, and find a trophy wife, maybe he'd give up the idea of revenge. Surely he'd see they were better off going their separate ways. He didn't really want her, and he certainly didn't want Violet. He'd never shown any interest in her even when she was a baby. He made promises to her and then broke them, but he never hugged her or held her or read her any bedtime stories.

He'd always treated her like she was someone else's kid, not his. Maybe she really was. He'd known there was a chance, but he'd assured Paisley he didn't care. That was when he'd been trying to convince her to marry him. It'd worked, much to her everlasting regret.

"You gonna eat that pasta?" Ethan asked as he glanced down at her plate.

She picked up her fork. "Yes. Just thinking."

"Don't think too hard, babe. Eat. Let me worry about it."

She was glad he didn't say Trey's name.

She twisted pasta around the fork and took a bite. "Mmm, this is good. Amazing, even."

He grinned. "Told you Theo made a mean Cajun shrimp pasta."

"You weren't wrong."

They ate their dinner and managed to chat about things that had nothing to do with Trey. Once they were done, Paisley told Violet about going to Rory and Chance's farm with Emma and Blaze. Violet's eyes were wide, and Paisley began to wonder if her child would protest about going without her.

Violet knew that Paisley worked during the day, but at night she was accustomed to having Paisley around. They played games, read together, and Violet had all her attention. Something she hadn't had when Trey was around. He'd insisted on little girls being seen and not heard, and he never wanted to play with her. The times he did, Paisley knew it was so *she'd* be afraid, wondering if he would lose his temper and lash out at Violet.

"Will Merrylegs be there?" Violet asked.

"No, I'm afraid not. Merrylegs lives on a different farm. But there are goats and chickens. And there's a garden where you can help pick vegetables for this restaurant."

Violet's little mouth fell open. "Really?"

"Yes, really."

Emma and Blaze arrived soon after. The men went outside to get Violet's car seat from Paisley's Kia and set it up in Blaze's truck while Emma stayed with Paisley and Violet. When the men returned and the goodbyes were said, Violet skipped out of the Dawg between Emma and Blaze like it was the best day of her life.

"Well, that went a lot better than I thought," Paisley said with a laugh.

Ethan laughed as he sat in his chair. "The kid likes animals."

"All kinds of animals, apparently. I thought Merrylegs was going to be a dealbreaker, but nope."

"Growing up in Brooklyn, we didn't really see goats or chickens or ponies. But there were dogs and cats. And rats. I liked animals. Maybe not the rats, but I wanted a dog. Or a cat. Didn't much care, really."

"Did you ever get one?"

His eyes were shadowed. "No. We didn't really have a place to keep an animal. By the time I was old enough to leave home and join the military, I found out pretty quick that my life wasn't conducive to pets."

Her heart pinched. "You could have one now, couldn't you?"

"Maybe. Except I currently live in the same house as Alex, and I'm not sure he'd go for it."

Amber brought the check and Ethan paid even though Paisley offered to get hers and Violet's.

"Told you I was taking care of you, Payz."

They left the Dawg through the back door. He walked

her to her car and waited for her to get inside, then followed her home. She kept glancing in her rearview mirror, her stomach getting tighter the closer they got to her house. The moment of truth was upon her, and she still didn't know how to do it right. Oh, she was definitely going to do what Emma said and just tell him everything, but was there a way to do it without it hurting so much?

Of course there wasn't. That was the problem. Telling Ethan he might be Violet's father, that she'd slept with Trey so soon after they were together, that she'd been pregnant when she'd married Trey, and that Trey had always known there was a fifty-fifty chance—well, it wasn't going to be easy for either of them.

She waited until Ethan parked and came over to her door to get her, as he'd instructed. She let him disarm the house alarm and unlock the door, glancing around the neighbors' yards while she waited behind him on the porch. It was still light outside, which meant Trey wasn't lurking behind a bush or anything, but she was nervous anyway.

He sometimes bragged about doing things to people that they never saw coming. Ambushing the enemy on missions and dropping them before they knew he was there. It made her shiver.

But the door opened and they were inside, and Paisley felt herself deflating as the stress of thinking about Trey lying in wait eased a fraction. Now that they were here, inside her house alone, she didn't know what to say. She set her purse down and told herself to breathe so she could calm her racing heart.

Ethan came over to her, wrapped his arms around her, and pulled her close. She could feel his heartbeat beneath her ear. It wasn't fast like hers. It was steady, comforting. She closed her eyes and held him. They stood for the longest time, not moving, and the stress in her body ebbed even more.

She realized that he wasn't going to be first to move. He was holding her, comforting her without words, because he knew she needed it. Her body melted even more. He was solid, hard in all the right places, his arms around her a safe haven. She tipped her head back to look up at him.

Their eyes met, tangled, and then he lowered his mouth to hers slowly enough that she could stop him if she wanted.

She did not. Her mouth opened beneath his, and for the first time in nearly five years, a storm of want assailed her. Everything about Ethan had always felt *right*. How had she forgotten it when Trey was comforting her? How had she convinced herself that what she'd felt with Ethan was just chemistry and not destiny?

It was so much more. His tongue tangled with hers and her heartbeat rocketed right back to overdrive again. The kiss was everything she'd been hoping it would be. He nipped and sucked at her lips, his tongue gliding into her mouth again and again. Paisley clung to him, her bones melting until it was only him holding her up.

Her panties were soaked. If he touched her there, she'd come apart immediately. She wasn't embarrassed, because they'd been together before, but she didn't think she'd ever been so wet in her life. So desperate to have him inside her.

His hands slid down to cup her ass. When he pulled her tighter to him, the unmistakable length of his erection made her moan.

"Want you so badly, Payz," he said against her lips, his voice rough like sandpaper. Gently, he set her away from him, putting her at arm's length. "You wanted to talk about something. Think we should do that before we talk about what happens next."

Paisley closed her eyes. Then she moved farther away, wrapping her arms around her body. She'd been so close to heaven and now she had to tell him a hard truth that might make him too angry to ever want to be with her again.

"You should sit," she said.

His forehead wrinkled. "Is it that bad?"

"I-I don't know. Maybe? Depends on you."

He sat on the couch but didn't lean back. He put his hands on his knees and waited. Paisley sank onto a chair, then stood again, her entire body trembling with energy and fear of the unknown. Once she said the words, they were out there.

"Paisley. Look at me."

She dragged her gaze to him. He gave her a soft smile. "Whatever it is, you can tell me."

Her eyes filled with tears. She swiped them away as they spilled over, her chin quivering. He started to rise, but she held a hand out to stop him. He sank back, frowning, and waited.

She loved him so much in that moment. For caring, for worrying, and for giving her the space she requested. Maybe it would all fall apart in a few minutes, or maybe it wouldn't. Either way, she was about to find out.

"You have to understand." She swallowed. "When you left, Trey was there. He was always there, a friend in need. He called me, came to see me, checked on me. He gave me a shoulder to cry on, and he let me vent my heartbreak to him. He also took me drinking."

She swallowed. "It was a week after you'd gone, and I was feeling miserable. He said we'd have fun, that I needed to remember what it was like being young and single, that I had my whole life ahead of me. He picked me up and took me to a club. Somewhere I'd never gone with you. I was careful, but not careful enough, I guess. I don't remember drinking too much, but—"

She dropped her gaze to her feet and pulled in calming breaths.

"Baby, just tell me. It's okay."

"I woke up naked. With Trey."

She watched his Adam's apple move. Saw the hardening of his jaw.

"It was only a week, not enough time to get over you. I should have never—"

"Paisley," he cut in, his voice raw. "You thought I was

gone. That I'd dumped you. If you'd been stone cold sober and slept with him, I couldn't blame you for it. You said you were careful though. Did you ever think he might have spiked your drink?"

Her body was ice. "Oh my God. I never thought…"

But of course he had. Trey had roofied her and slept with her. She hadn't realized it because he'd been soooo very sympathetic the next morning. He hadn't touched her again until after Violet was born. If he hadn't done that, she'd have had no doubts about Violet's father. But he had. Why? He couldn't have known she was pregnant. She hadn't known.

No, he'd done it because he wanted to. Because he could. Probably because it gave him great pleasure to imagine that he'd stolen her from under Ethan's nose. And because he wanted her to think she'd slept with him easily and willingly after a few drinks.

"That bastard," she growled. "That absolute asshole."

Ethan started to rise again and again she put her hand out. "I'm okay. I just need to say this." She dragged in a breath. "I missed my period that month. I thought it was stress. But when I missed it again, and I was so tired in the mornings I could hardly get out of bed, I took a test. It was positive."

He was still frowning. Thinking? Waiting for more?

"I slept with Trey a week after you, Ethan," she said gently, her heart hurting more than ever. "I don't know who Violet's father really is."

26

than stared at her. His entire body was numb. He couldn't feel anything.

And then, like a tidal wave, rage crested inside him, bubbling over the walls he erected to hold it. Spilling over the sides, poisoning everything in its path. He wanted to howl, and he wanted to destroy.

He closed his eyes, folded himself in half, and sucked in air with his head between his knees. He was angrier than he'd ever been. Closer to exploding, too.

Trey McCann had stolen Paisley from him, ruined the beautiful thing they had, and violated her. In the process, he'd stolen Ethan's child. Because there was no doubt in his mind that Violet was his. He'd been thinking about those eyes for days, how similar they were to his own, and he'd been thinking about his mother. She'd been blond while he and his brother were dark-haired.

He'd thought it was a fantasy, the desperate and sad

longings of a man who'd lost the woman he loved and wished her child with another man was theirs instead. He hadn't realized the timing—and hadn't asked either because the situation was fraught—but now that she'd told him?

Fucking now he *knew*. And he wanted to kill Trey with his bare hands.

"I'm sorry." Paisley sounded like she was speaking to him through a body of water, like he was forty feet down and everything was distorted. He clawed for the surface, seeking that voice.

When he straightened again, she was there. Blurred, but there. Still standing across the room with her arms around her body, still looking miserable and sad.

No more. No fucking more. It ended here and now.

Ethan was on his feet and at her side in two seconds. Then he wrapped her in his arms and held on tight.

She was stiff at first, and then she relaxed. Belatedly, he realized she must have expected a different reaction.

"It's not your fault," he said. "Not your fault."

They cried together. Cried for all they'd lost and for all they would never get back. Ethan didn't think he'd ever cried as an adult, even when Eric overdosed for the last time. He'd been numb by then, numb and resigned to losing everyone he'd ever cared about.

Tears slid down his cheeks while he held her, her body shaking against his. He didn't know how long it lasted, but eventually the shaking subsided. He hooked an arm behind her knees and carried her over to the couch, sinking down on it with her in his arms like he had just last night.

They sat together in silence until the shadows creeping across the living room lengthened. It would be dark in another hour, and Violet would be coming home.

His daughter. Even if he was wrong, even if she was biologically Trey's kid, she was his. He was claiming her here and now. Forever.

"I wanted to tell you, and I didn't," Paisley said, her voice cutting into the silence. "How do you tell someone they might have a child, but you don't know for sure? That it's your fault you don't know because you slept with someone else?"

"It's not your fault. Already said that."

Her fingers plucked at his shirt. "You're too good to me, Ethan. I thought you'd be furious I didn't say anything before now, but you're not."

"I'm furious, Payz. Just not with you."

Rage was still a cold inferno deep inside. If Trey was anywhere near here, if he was waiting and watching and planning to make a move, well, it was gonna be his funeral. Because Ethan wasn't taking prisoners. Not this time.

"Emma says we can do a paternity test. I'd want time to explain it to Violet, but if you want to do it, then we will."

"Do you want the answer?"

She tipped her head back to look up at him. "I love Violet no matter who her father is."

"I don't need a test. Not unless it helps you in the divorce somehow."

"I need to ask my attorney. You would do that for me?"

He lifted her hand and kissed her palm. "I would. But listen to me, honey. Violet is mine. You're mine. I don't need a test for that, but if it helps give you ammunition against Trey in the divorce, then I'm for it."

She nibbled her lip. "He's legally her father. But if you're her biological father, then you might have to go to court for an acknowledgement of your rights."

He closed his eyes, jaw grinding. The last thing he could do right now was go to court to fight for parental rights. Ghost would lose his shit.

"We'll worry about that if we need to."

Because no way was he going to tell her he wouldn't fight for Violet. He couldn't explain it to her without divulging secrets he was sworn to protect. *Fuck.*

"Okay," she said, tucking her face against his neck and wrapping her arms around him. "I'm still sorry for everything that happened. I wish it would have been different."

"Me too. But it wasn't, and we're together now. Trey did this to us, Paisley. It's nobody else. Are there things I wish I'd done differently? Hell, yeah. I wish I'd taken time to find you and make you tell me in person that you were done. I wish I hadn't had to leave on that mission in the first place."

"Did you do something important?"

"Yeah." He couldn't divulge everything, even now, but

he could tell her a little. "We were sent to rescue Americans from a terror group that'd taken them hostage. They were threatening to behead them on national television."

"My God."

"We got them out. All of them." It was a high level government official and his team who'd blundered into a place they shouldn't have while on a tour of overseas military sites. HOT was called in. They'd been stretched a little thin at the time, which was why he'd been recalled for the mission.

"Then it's good you went. Those people lived because of you. It might have turned out different if you hadn't been there."

"Maybe. I don't know. Still wish I'd been with you."

"Are you okay, Ethan? I know this is a lot."

He pulled in a breath, let it out. His head churned with thoughts. His heart overflowed with chaotic emotions. He was processing it. Still.

Violet was his daughter, and she'd lived the first four years of her life without him in it. He'd missed everything. First steps, first words, first time she said daddy. He'd missed everything because Trey McCann was a psychotic creep.

"I'm working on it." He shifted her until he could look into her eyes. "I want to be her father. I've wanted it since we started talking that day in the square. Even if she's not biologically mine, which I don't believe is true, I don't care. I still want to be her father. I want her to know what it's like to have a man who loves her, who would do anything to keep her safe and happy. I want her to feel like she can come to me for anything, and trust that I'll be there for her. I never want her to worry that I'd hurt her or you. But I know all of this takes time. I don't expect it right away. I expect it to be work, but I need you to know I'm willing to do that work."

Her eyes brimmed with tears. Her chin wobbled.

"I love you, Payz. Always have. And yeah, I know this is fast and I know there's a lot of water under the bridge, but I want this. I want to see where we go from here. I'm tired of wasting time. We lost five years. I don't want to lose another minute."

"I l-love you, too. I didn't want to, not after it went so wrong before. I'm afraid, Ethan. Afraid he'll come along and smash it all again. I don't want him to ruin this."

His heart soared that she loved him but his gut twisted at her fear. "He's not ruining anything, Paisley. I'm not gonna let him. Not this time."

He'd die to protect her and Violet, and he'd take fucking Trey down with him.

Paisley palmed his cheek tenderly before pulling him down for a kiss. Their tongues met and liquid fire raced through his veins, along his nerve endings, into his cock.

He wanted her. Needed her. It was a primal urge to claim her, make her his again. He couldn't erase the past, but he could make the future what he wanted it to be.

Paisley clung to him like he was her lifeline. He wanted to strip her naked and bury himself in her.

It'd only been last night when he'd told her they needed to go slow. Take their time. Explain to Violet.

Last night might as well be ancient history, though. He'd discovered he had a child with this woman. And he loved her with everything he had. She loved him too. There was no fucking way he was taking his time, not unless she wanted it.

"Payz," he said against her lips between kisses. "Need to know if you want to take this slow. Can't keep kissing you if you do. And honest to God, I don't mind. We're going to rebuild our lives together, I swear to you, and it doesn't have to happen fast—"

She slid her hand beneath the waistband of his jeans and brushed her fingers against his cock. "I don't want to wait. It's been too long, and I want this."

He shuddered as she brushed the sensitive tip, as her finger found the moisture there and rubbed it into his skin. "Condoms," he said hoarsely.

"We don't need them. I have an implant. Unless you want one," she finished, moving her mouth to his neck and nibbling the skin there.

A thrill slid down his spine, arrowing straight for his balls. He stood in one fluid motion, taking her with him, and started toward the main bedroom. The first time he took her, it would be in a bed.

The next time, well, that could be as hot and dirty as she wanted. Or it could be tame and sweet. He didn't care, so long as it made her happy.

That was his primary goal in life now. Make Paisley happy.

He carried her to the bed and set her down, then reached for the hem of her sweet little dress.

When he had it off, when she stood before him in white panties and a white lace bra, emotion punched deep. This woman was his. Always had been.

And he was hers until the day he died.

27

The look in Ethan's eyes made her belly tighten. Paisley stood before him in her underwear and let him look at her. She was still reeling over his declaration of love. It's what she'd always wanted. Ethan Snow in love with her. A future with him.

The love inside her swelled until it hurt. There was fear, because there always was, but that was about losing what she'd only now gained. She could hear Trey's voice chipping away at her confidence years ago, undermining her, emphasizing that Ethan didn't care about her, had only been biding his time, and wasn't ever coming back.

Trey said it and she believed it. Not that she would ever believe his lies again, but she feared he'd do something worse. He wouldn't settle for dividing them with words this time.

Ethan took her hand and tugged her to him, then slid

his fingers down her abdomen. "I wish I'd seen you pregnant with Violet. I wish I'd been there for you."

Tears pressed hard against her eyelids but she wouldn't let them fall. "I wish you had, too."

He dropped to his knees in front of her and pressed his mouth to her belly, his hands shaping her waist before going around to cup her ass. Paisley moaned from all the electric tension zipping through her body. It gathered beneath his mouth when he pressed it to her skin, making her gasp and curl her fingers in his hair.

"I want to go slow, but not sure how that's gonna work," he said before dragging her panties down her hips and pressing his mouth to her mound. When his tongue slid into the seam of her sex, her knees nearly buckled. It was only because of Ethan that she stayed upright.

"Need you on the bed, Payz. Legs spread, ass on the edge."

She did what he said, her heart throbbing with anticipation. If she'd never been with him before, maybe she'd be shy, but this was Ethan.

Ethan.

The man she thought she'd never see again. The man she'd never stopped loving.

"I've dreamed of this," he said, anchoring his arms on the bed and pushing her legs open with them. His gaze fixed on her pussy. When they'd been together before, she'd shaved down there, thinking it sexy and enticing, but these days she was too busy surviving and taking care of her kid to spend time doing anything more than making sure things weren't a jungle.

Ethan lifted his gaze as if he knew what she was thinking about, the heat in his eyes making her heart flip.

"I like what I see, babe." He lowered his head, his eyes never leaving hers, his tongue gliding into her seam and over her clit.

"Oh my God," she gasped.

He spread her with his thumbs and licked her teasingly. "You taste the way I remember. Sweet, salty, and so fucking good."

"Ethan…"

He stopped teasing and attacked, his tongue gliding expertly over the bundle of nerves, down to slide into her, then back again. He built her up with that maddening tongue, knowing just when to glide away and nibble something else—and for how long—before he returned to build the tension again.

When he slid two fingers into her, she moaned and curled toward him to grip his hair. She was a wild woman, chasing her pleasure, rocking her hips to direct the tension where she wanted it, squeezing her inner muscles around his fingers.

She hadn't felt this good in forever. She'd slept with Trey once before they married, and then not again until after Violet was born. She'd cried the first time and he hadn't taken it well. He didn't hit her then, but he said cruel things.

He never made her come. Not once. It was like he didn't care.

But Ethan…. Oh lord, Ethan.

She was so close. She wanted it badly, but she also didn't want it to end. Right now, she could pretend the world didn't exist. But the instant she came and the tension left her body, a different kind of tension would take up residence. The relentless kind that made her stomach knot and fear settle into her soul.

No.

No, she wasn't going to think about that. Life was meant to be lived every moment. It was meant to be lived *right now.* Worrying about the future was normal, but she wasn't going to let it steal her joy in this moment. It was wrong to do so.

Ethan changed the rhythm of his fingers in her body, his tongue circling ever tighter around her clit. She was panting, gasping, making noises she hadn't made in years.

And then he sucked on her clit, hard enough to make her see stars—and her body imploded.

She came with a sob, her legs shaking as she held on to the edge of her pleasure and tried to make it last. When she lay back on the bed, breathing hard and blinking away tears, he started the build again. It didn't take long before she was riding the wave, her body shaking apart as he worked her with this fingers and mouth.

"I-I can't do it again," she cried when she finally made her voice work.

"I think you can, baby," he growled. "Come for me,

Payz. One more time, and then I'm gonna make you do it again with my cock instead of my tongue."

He was relentless, licking and sucking and fucking her with his fingers until her entire body was strung tight like a guitar string. Then it snapped and her orgasm reverberated through her with such power she didn't think she could move for a week.

Ethan stood and dragged off his shirt while she watched. When his arms lifted over his head and the fabric revealed his chest, she cried out.

"You still have it." There was wonder in her voice.

He glanced down at the ink on his chest, and the red heart nestled in its midst. It was the same as the one on the inside of her wrist.

"Of course I have it," he said, his voice raspy and rough.

She got up and went to him, ran her hands over his torso, traced the heart. Then she kissed it, and he groaned.

The fire in her body kindled again. Her pussy was soaked, her nipples tingled, and she needed this man inside her before she died.

But there was something she needed to do first. She unzipped his jeans and pushed them down until he kicked them free and stood completely naked, his body the most beautiful thing she'd ever seen.

Ethan was muscled, golden, with scars and tattoos and a relentless fire in his eyes that said he'd seen much and survived much.

When she dropped to her knees, he made a sound in his throat. She tipped her head back to gaze up at him.

"I want this," she said, wrapping her hands around his cock.

He hissed in a breath as she ran one hand down the length of him and caressed his balls. They tightened as she played with them, but Ethan stood stock still, staring down at her, that fire in his eyes growing hotter by the minute.

When she licked around the head of his cock, his balls responded. And when she slid him into her mouth, his head tipped back, his throat moving as he swallowed.

That was all the encouragement she needed. She took him to the back of her throat, moaning, feeling the vibration ricochet down his shaft and into his balls.

He cupped the back of her head, held her gently while she sucked him, little hisses and gasps issuing from his throat regularly.

She would have taken him over the edge that way, but he stopped her by hooking his hands under her arms and tugging her up. Then he claimed her mouth, gripped her ass in two big hands, and lifted her. She wrapped her legs around his hips and he walked them to the bed, their mouths locked together.

"I've got no finesse left," he said as he tumbled her onto the bed.

"I don't want finesse," she whispered against his lips. "I want you wild."

His cock pressed at her opening. She shifted enough to

let him in—and the world shrank to a pinpoint as he invaded her body.

It was a good invasion. A perfectly pleasure-inducing one. She'd loved sex with Ethan the few times they'd been together. She'd always been somewhat reserved and shy, but never with him. He made her feel like she could ask for what she wanted, like she could be as dirty or as tame as she liked, and he would be right there with her.

In all her daydreams about him lately, she'd thought she would want sweet and hot. But she ached and craved and needed. She wanted him raw and wild, wanted him hard and fast. She wanted to feel pleasure so hot it bordered on hurt. She needed to erase the pain and anger of a life with Trey. Not that one sexual encounter with the love of her life could manage that, but it was a good start.

"Please, Ethan," she begged. "No finesse. I need you. I won't break, and I'm not afraid of you. You would never hurt me."

"Jesus, no," he said, dropping his mouth to hers again. "I love you, Paisley Rose. You're my world."

Joy was a hot, achy thing in her chest. "I love you, too."

He moved slowly at first, testing her limits—and his too, probably—before the restraints fell away and he slammed into her body with all the strength and power of a warrior. She spread her legs wide, her ankles in the air, her body taking everything he had to give and wanting more.

They moved together like a well-oiled machine, bodies

straining, sliding across the bed. The headboard whacked the wall, the bed creaked, and Paisley hooked her ankles around his legs to hold on. Ethan pushed up on his hands and thrust deep, his cock swelling inside her. Her orgasm broke over her, her body shuddering in bliss, his name a sharp cry on her tongue.

She knew the moment he broke, too. Her pulsed inside her, jet after jet of hot semen coating her walls. She was still coming when he bent to kiss her.

"Love you, baby," he whispered.

All she could do was kiss him back. Words were impossible.

28

"How long do we have?" he murmured into her hair.

Ethan lay on his back with his arm around Paisley. She had one leg thrown over his and she lay with her head on the pillow beside him, one arm slung across him, the other curled under her. She kissed his neck and shoulder, sighing.

"Emma said they'd bring her back around nine."

He peered at his phone on the bedside table. "About forty minutes, then."

She traced the heart tattoo. "She'll fall asleep fast," Paisley said. "So we'll have more time together if we want it."

"If? Not a question of if, babe. More like how much energy we have."

She giggled. "That too. If I walk a little bowlegged tomorrow, do you think anybody will know?"

He skimmed his fingers along her spine, over her hip. Touching her was everything. "Mmm, maybe. Or maybe they'll think you've got a backache."

"I'll tell them I did too much gardening."

He chuckled. "That might work."

She was quiet for a moment. "I'm scared of what could happen, Ethan. What he'll do."

He kissed her forehead and squeezed her to him. "I know, Payz. I'm going to take care of you, though. I'm staying with you and Violet every night. We don't have to tell her about us yet. I'll sleep in the living room. But I'm going to be right here. You won't be alone. I know Trey's a scary motherfucker, but so am I. He thinks to get to you, he's gotta go through me. Promise you that's not easy to do."

"I know. B-but I worry about what he might do to you. If he knows we're together. He might target you first."

He heard the fear in her voice. He didn't think anyone had ever been scared *for* him before. He gave her another squeeze. He didn't want her to fear for him, but he wouldn't lie to her about the risk.

"I expect he will. He's not coming for you without reconnoitering the terrain, so he'll know. And I'd rather he targets me than you, if I'm honest. But don't forget, babe—I'm not your only protection. You've got six of us watching your back. Six of us willing to do whatever we have to do to neutralize Trey McCann."

He wasn't sure the others were as willing to kill Trey as he was, but so long as they incapacitated the fucker and made sure he didn't get to Paisley and Violet, that was enough. Not that Ethan thought there was any real danger of Trey taking him out, but he didn't dare assume the man wouldn't try.

Just needed Seth to get a lock on Trey's location. That would help. Trey could be in Destin again, or he could be the man in Paisley's yard last night.

"I know, but you're the one I want. The one I *need*. I can't lose you again, Ethan. Not after everything."

He growled and rolled her beneath him in one move, his hips between her legs, his cock hardening fast. "You aren't losing me, babe. We're never letting that asshole come between us again. I will fucking kill him before it happens."

She shivered beneath him, but he didn't know if it was desire or what he'd said. He wasn't going to play it safe with her, though. Not like that. She needed to know that he wasn't kidding when he said he would do whatever it took to protect her and Violet.

His gut clenched at the thought of the little blond girl. *Mine. Mine, mine, mine.*

It was a litany in his head as he pictured the three of them together.

A family.

Finally, a family.

Paisley reached up and caressed his cheek. He felt the moisture there as soon as she did it. All it took to make him cry was thinking of her and their daughter, of how lucky he was to have them in his life again. To get a second chance to make it right.

"Ethan," she whispered. "I love you. So much."

"You're my world, Payz. You and Violet. That fucking fast. Or maybe not that fast. It's always been this way. I just didn't know about Violet until I met her."

Her hands skimmed his sides, tickling and teasing at the same time. His dick grew painfully hard as she squeezed his ass in both hands. "Need you again. Please."

He bent to suck her tight nipple into his mouth. "Still no finesse, babe. Just raw, animal lust."

"I'm counting on it."

He surged forward, filling her. He held still a moment, taking mental stock of what he needed to do not to come in the next minute, before he started to move. Fast, hard strokes that bounced her tits and slapped their bodies together with grunts and groans and whispered words that escalated to loud ones. Dirty words, sweet words. The kind of words you said in the heat of the moment and the kind you only said to the person you loved most in the world.

They were connected, not just with his cock buried deep in her pussy, but they were connected deep in their souls as well. Connected by love, shared bliss, and a child.

Connected.

That thing he'd been missing his entire life until her. Even without Violet, he was anchored to this woman for all eternity. Part of him had known it from the first moment she'd smiled at him. *Mine.*

He dropped his mouth to hers, tasted her lips, her tongue, the perfection between them as they moved together. Him pounding relentlessly, her opening and giving him more.

"Fuck," he growled as the sensation started gathering at the base of his spine, tingling into his balls. "Gonna come, baby. Need you with me."

He no sooner spoke than her body tightened like a bowstring and snapped free as she choked out a cry. Her pussy gloved him tight. That was all he needed to let go and plant himself deep. He came with a roar that ended only when his body was drained.

He rolled to his back and took her with him until she was sprawled across his damp body. The heat between them was an inferno, but they needed each other too much to separate.

"You've destroyed me," she mumbled. "My pussy will never recover."

He chuckled. "I was thinking you'd destroyed me. My dick's gonna be sore from all the friction."

"Mmm, delicious friction."

"Yeah, it is." He smacked her ass playfully. It was a soft smack, nothing hard. He would never do that to her unless she specifically asked for it. "We need to shower and get presentable, don't you think?"

"Prolly."

"Don't go to sleep on me, Payz. No time for that."

If things were normal, he'd ask Blaze and Emma to keep Violet overnight, give him and Paisley more time alone. But things weren't normal—and he wanted to see his kid. He was scared to see her now that he knew, but he needed it too. He just had to keep it together and not bawl like a fucking baby when she walked in.

"You're right," she sighed. "I just don't want to move."

"Neither do I."

The ceiling fan whirled above them and soft music played from the speaker she had on the beside table. The room smelled like sex and sweat and her perfume. Intoxicating. Comforting.

She eventually pushed herself up and slid to his side so she could look at him, propping herself on an elbow. "We need to talk about Violet."

"I'm listening."

She frowned. "I don't want to confuse her, Ethan. She's not fond of Trey, but she thinks he's her father. I-I need to know you're okay with that right now. If you want to know the truth, we'll get the test. Regardless, we need to take it slow going forward. She likes you, but she doesn't really know you and she's used to Trey being nice to her and then ignoring her. I know you won't do that, but it has to happen slowly."

Anger simmered low in his belly. Not for what she was saying, but the fact Trey treated an innocent little girl that way in the first place. Kids were filled with hope and joy. Why the fuck would anyone want to destroy that?

As if he didn't know. It wasn't always on purpose. Some people were just colossal dicks.

Ethan blew out a breath. Then he pushed himself up

against the headboard until he was sitting. Paisley joined him, sitting cross-legged beside him. He took her hand and held it.

"I need to tell you something. I said I grew up in Brooklyn, and I did. But it wasn't a happy existence in a house with a picket fence. Or even an apartment building. I remember an apartment, or a series of them, all shitty, none lasting for long. My sperm donor was an alcoholic who drank all our rent money away until we ended up on the streets."

Paisley squeezed his hand.

"I lived on the streets for years, in and out of shelters, constantly moving around. The sperm donor—" He couldn't call him a father, not aloud anyway. "—left us, and my mom did her best. She, uh, didn't end up in a good place. Drugs, pimps, the whole thing."

"Oh, Ethan. I'm sorry."

"It's okay. It happened and it's long over. I survived and I'm here. I lost my mom and my little brother to drugs years ago. I joined the Army because I was determined to be somebody. To do something important with my life."

He forced down the knot in his throat. "I'm telling you this not so you feel sorry for me, but so you understand I'm capable of waiting for things to happen. I was always making plans when I was a kid. How to find Mom a job, how to get her off heroin, how to make the first and last month's rent, how we'd live. They were unrealistic plans, I know that now, but it kept me going. I'd even plan which shelter to hit, which bridge to sleep under if the shelter wouldn't take us. I planned everything down to the second. It's what I excelled at in the military, too. Making the plan. So when I tell you I can wait, that I can work on building a relationship with Violet and having her see me as her dad, I'm not telling you what you want to hear. I can do it, Payz, because I love you and I love her and you're both worth that wait to me."

"Ethan." Her voice shook with tears. One slid down her cheek and he caught it, wiped aways the ones that trailed.

"Hush, baby. It's okay. I see everything I want within reach. I'm not going to do a damned thing to ruin it."

"I'm so sorry those things happened to you. No child should live that way."

He lifted her hand and kissed it. "It's in the past, and it made me who I am. Do I wish I'd had a home and parents who were present and involved? Yeah, I do. But I didn't. If anything, it makes me more determined to be a good father to Violet. I want to marry you, Payz. One day, when your divorce is final and you're ready. I'll settle for living together if you don't want to make that commitment again, though. All I need is you and Violet in my life and I'm good. It's enough."

She was crying. "I want that too."

"Don't cry, baby. It's gonna be alright. You and me and Violet. We're gonna be a great team."

"I know that. I just—" She sniffed and wiped her face, then tried to smile. It wavered. "I never expected this. When I saw you again at the Dawg, and the look on your face before you walked out, I was sure you would never speak to me again." She waved a hand around. "And now look at us."

"Yeah, look at us." He waggled his eyebrows to get her to smile. "Naked, sated, but still horny as fuck."

She shook her head and laughed. "Probably. I mean, okay, yes. I'm a little sore, but I'd do it again if I get to feel that way every time."

He hooked a hand behind her head and went in for a kiss. It sparked, because of course it did, but they couldn't indulge it and get ready to greet their daughter soon, too.

"Hold that thought, honey. Once Violet's in bed and we're sure she's sound asleep, I'm planning to eat you until you can't manage even one more orgasm tonight. Then tomorrow, I'm gonna do it all again."

29

"And I got to hunt for eggs!" Violet told them. "Miss Rory said there'd be more in the morning, but there was one and I gots to get it! It was warm and brown."

"Really? How exciting." Paisley stroked her daughter's hair, but Violet was too excited to stand still for it. She ran to where her crayons and paper were laying on the coffee table.

"I hafta draw the chickens. They clucked a lot, and they were scary at first, but Miss Rory held one and let me pet it."

Emma and Blaze were standing in the living room, having delivered Violet, and smiling big as Violet described every moment of her time at the farm. They shared a knowing look as Emma cupped her stomach.

"Do y'all want to sit for a while?" Paisley asked. "Can I

get you something to drink? Wine, beer, sweet tea or water? Lemonade?"

They shared a look again. "Sure, we can stay," Blaze said. "Sassy will be okay for a while yet, but I gotta throw a ball for her before bed or she'll keep us awake half the night."

Emma laughed. "She's still technically a kitten, though she's pretty big now."

Violet perked up. "You have a kitten?"

Emma sank onto the couch near Violet. "Yes, we do. She's not very little anymore."

"I want a kitten," Violet said wistfully. "Mommy says we can't have one."

Paisley's heart twisted. She simply couldn't handle another small creature who needed her right now. "I said we can't have one *now*," Paisley said. "We've only been in this house a month, and we aren't fully settled yet. We can talk about it again in a few months."

"Okay," Violet said, but she didn't sound happy.

Emma patted her shoulder. "It's okay, kiddo. When the time is right, a kitten will find you."

Violet's eyes were big. "It will?"

"Yes, it will."

Paisley shot a look at Ethan. He was quiet, watching Violet, and her heart went out to him. Everything they'd done over the past few hours was seared into her brain, but it was watching his reaction when she told him about Violet that she would never, ever forget. In that moment, she'd thought he would be angry, that she'd lost him again.

She'd been so incredibly wrong that it shamed her she'd ever doubted him. Ethan was strong and honest, the kind of man who would always be there for her. He'd never left her. She'd just thought he had. Pain twisted deep that she'd ever believed Trey's lies for a moment.

His gaze lifted and met hers. The pain in those eyes pierced her. But then he smiled, and she saw nothing but love. She had to tear her gaze away and back to her guests. Emma was smiling. Blaze looked like he was thinking hard about something, but he didn't look upset so that was good.

"Can I get those drinks?" she asked.

"I'll just have water," Emma said. "Babe?"

Blaze seemed to shake himself. "Uh, yeah. I'll have some of that sweet tea. Violet says you make sun tea."

"Yes. And it's not too sweet. I don't like it so sweet it makes your teeth ache."

"Sounds perfect."

"I'll help," Ethan said. They went into the kitchen and got the drinks. Paisley was aware of his presence every second. Her body, so recently sated, wanted more of him. More alone time, more cuddling, and more of those earth-shattering orgasms.

He slid a hand over her ass and squeezed as she took tea from the refrigerator. She bit her lip to stop the moan that wanted to slip out.

"Are you okay?" she asked, turning to him when she'd

poured tea and water from the pitchers she kept in the fridge.

"I'm good, babe. Happy. Still figuring it all out, I admit. Trying not to see myself in her, but seeing it anyway. I know what you said about Trey, but she's mine."

Her heart skipped a beat. "I think so too. But I want it to be true, so maybe I don't see what I think I see."

"Nah, that's my kid out there. Yours and mine. Even if we're wrong, she's still ours."

She liked the way that sounded. Trey had said it didn't matter to him who was Violet's father when he was trying to convince her to marry him, but he'd never talked about *being* a father. And she'd been too naïve—and too heartbroken—to realize the difference.

When they returned to the living room and handed out drinks, Violet's head was drooping onto the table. She clutched her crayon in one hand but it wasn't moving across the paper anymore. She'd played herself out at the farm, apparently.

Paisley leaned over and held out a hand. "Come on, pumpkin. Let's get you to bed before you fall asleep right here."

"Not tired," Violet said stubbornly. But her eyelids didn't agree.

"Okay, so you aren't tired. Let's go get your pajamas on anyway. You can come back and color if you want to."

Paisley knew for a fact her kid was about to go lights out for the night, so she wasn't worried Violet would actually take her up on it. Violet stood and put her hand in Paisley's.

"I'm sorry, y'all, but I'll be back. Ten minutes."

Emma waved a hand. "Take your time."

By the time Paisley got Violet's hands and face washed, put her into her pajamas, and tucked her into bed, fifteen minutes had elapsed. One thing she had never been sorry for was how easily Violet went to sleep when it was time. The kid was like an Energizer Bunny all day and then she simply ran out of steam. Not that Paisley didn't have to fight with her to take baths or go to bed on nights when she was still hopping, but the crash always came at a certain point.

Thank heavens.

Ethan stood the second she walked in. "Everything good? Does she need a bedtime story?"

God, she loved him. "Nope. Passed out cold. All the excitement and fresh air at the farm did her in."

"Ah." He seemed disappointed, and she loved him even more. Adorable man. Big, badass, lethal, adorable man.

He reached for her hand and tugged her down on his lap. "They know, babe. I told them about Violet."

She was surprised at the relief that softened her limbs and made everything less tight inside.

"I'm so damned happy for you both," Blaze said. "And sorry for everything that happened to keep you apart. But you found each other again."

Paisley leaned into Ethan. She really should sit in her

own chair like a lady, but she didn't want to. She wanted to be with him. He had his arms looped around her and he showed no signs of letting go.

"It's a miracle," Ethan said, his voice rough with emotion. "Best thing that's happened to me."

Blaze and Emma twined fingers. "Totally understand that feeling," he said. "Alex will adjust."

Paisley blinked. "Adjust to what?"

"Being the last single guy in the group," Ethan told her. "We started this business as six bachelors, intended to stay that way, yet here we are."

"Last man standing." Blaze chuckled. "He's going to double down on staying single."

Emma shook her head. "You guys. Don't you realize by now that you can't stop fate?"

"You're a doctor," Blaze teased. "You don't do fate. You do science and facts."

Emma didn't hesitate. "The facts are that somewhere out there is a woman who's going to knock Alex Bishop flat on his very fine ass. And he's not going to be able to stop it when it happens. Neither did you, I might add."

"No, and I'm glad about that. But did you just talk about another man's ass to me?"

"Sorry, but it's a fine ass. I'm in love with you, but I'm not dead. Alex is pretty hot. Am I right, Paisley?"

Paisley laughed. "You are correct. He's easy on the eyes, that's for sure. Not my type though. Too intense for me."

Ethan nuzzled her ear. "Thanks, baby."

"You're intense, too, but I like your intensity. I get it. He makes me want to apologize for no reason."

Blaze snorted. "Welcome to the club. That's why he got as far as he did in the military. He commands attention and respect."

"Maybe not from *everyone*," Emma said. "I hear there's a certain woman who pisses him off just by breathing. Wouldn't it be funny if she's the one who ends up knocking him on his very fine rear?"

"I pray you're wrong." Blaze shook his head. "That'd be a match made in hell rather than heaven."

"You never know," Emma said thoughtfully.

They told Paisley about the mystery woman, an FBI agent who came to the range from time to time. Apparently she and Alex were like oil and water. Or fire and ice. Whatever the case, they didn't mix well.

Blaze and Emma stayed for another half hour before they said they needed to get home to Sassy the kitten.

"I really appreciate you taking Violet tonight," Paisley told them.

"She's a good kid," Blaze said. "We'd be happy to take her whenever you need some alone time."

A blush rose on her cheeks. She was positive they knew what she and Ethan had been doing for at least part of that time. "Thank you. I—we—might take you up on that."

Ethan put his arm around her and squeezed. "We might. Appreciate it, brother."

Blaze and Ethan shook hands. "Couldn't be happier

for you, man. I'm just down the street if you need backup at any point. You know that."

"Yep. Know that and grateful for it."

Blaze nodded, Emma hugged her, and then Blaze gave her hand a light squeeze. She stood in the doorway with Ethan and they watched his friends—*their friends*—walk to their truck and get in. With a wave and a promise to get together soon, they were gone.

Paisley went inside, feeling buoyant at the knowledge she not only had Ethan, but she also had friends. It was something after so many years of feeling alone. She and Trey didn't have friends. He entertained business associates, but they were the kind of people who'd always made her feel like she was a goldfish among sharks. Her mother sometimes came to visit between her travels. Trey had always been on his best behavior, but it hadn't been a joyful feeling at all.

Unfortunately, Bree had remained clueless to her daughter's unhappiness and thought Trey was a hero.

Paisley shook off those unhappy thoughts and turned to Ethan. He was still standing in the door, looking up and down the street. Then he stepped inside, shut the door behind him, and twisted the locks. A moment later, he armed the system.

It was a stark reminder that for as much as her life had changed, parts of it hadn't. Trey was still out there. And she was still terrified he was going to ruin everything.

Only this time he'd use far more than lies to divide her from Ethan.

———

Trey watched as Blaze "Shadow" Connolly and a woman got into a truck and drove away. Ethan stood on the porch, looking up and down the street like he owned the place before he went inside and shut the door.

Trey gulped Dr. Pepper and seethed. He could take them out. All three of them. If he rushed in during the night, before Ethan could fully wake up, he could pop him and Paisley in bed. He knew they were sleeping together. He'd watched through the window with binoculars when Paisley sat on Ethan's lap and he'd put his arms around her. No way they weren't banging again if they were that comfortable in front of Shadow and his woman.

Trey knew where the main bedroom was. He could kick the window in, shoot them both, then pop the kid. Or leave without killing the brat. Who the fuck cared what happened to her so long as he eliminated the parents and got the fuck out?

"Not smart, buddy," he muttered. "Not smart at all."

Acting now—kicking in a window and killing his whore of a wife and her lover—was risky.

Too risky. Ethan wasn't some ordinary guy he'd be attacking. Dragon had every bit as much training as he did. He was Hostile Operations Team, but Trey knew those guys were pussies deep down. They choked when the job required decisiveness. They were too focused on the idea of being some kind of hero to do what was required. To root out the enemy without mercy.

Not Trey. He'd built an empire because he wasn't a fucking pussy.

Because he was willing to kill those who pretended they were innocent when what they really wanted was to put a knife in his back the moment it was turned. Or detonate a bomb. He took no chances and left no survivors because it was *smart*.

Because *he* was smart. So much smarter than those HOT motherfuckers. There were six of them in town, running a damned shooting range and training facility. Craziest damned thing, especially when one of them was —or had been—the Deputy Commander of HOT. What the fuck was Colonel Bishop doing in this stupid place anyway?

Trey didn't know, but he had connections. It was strange there were six of them. All HOT, all career men— or so he'd believed. Dragon, Ghost, and Shadow along with Seth "Phantom" King, Kane "Demon" Fox, and Chance "Wraith" Hughes. Why would those six ever chuck it all and move to Bumfuck, Alabama, together?

He leaned back against the seat and dragged in air through his nose before forcing it out his mouth. He needed to be calm, cool, and methodical about this. He'd already deviated from the plan once. He should have returned to Charlotte and boarded the plane to Dubai, but he'd assigned that job to another operator at the last minute.

If he charged into that shitty house and did what he craved because he was pissed, where was the satisfaction? Where was the suffering? The begging? The terror in his target's eyes?

Stick to the plan, McCann.

Head back to Destin. Find out what a HOT team was really doing so close to Huntsville, a city with a high concentration of defense contractors and projects critical to national interests. Couldn't be an accident they were here.

Gather information.

Make a foolproof plan.

Then return and take them all down.

30

Something woke Ethan around dawn. Light filtered in through the blinds, but it wasn't strong light. There'd been a noise, a soft scraping sound...

He turned his head to find Violet standing beside the bed, her eyes wide, holding a stuffed rabbit and blinking at him.

Shit.

He'd meant to go to the living room and get into his sleeping bag after he'd kept his promise to Paisley and made her come until she was boneless. He'd put on the athletic shorts he planned to sleep in and Paisley had dragged on her pajamas, her eyes sleepy, her face soft and smiling.

"Hold me for a few minutes," she'd whispered.

So he had. Unfortunately, he'd also fallen asleep.

"Hi," he said awkwardly, not wanting to make any sudden moves to scare the child. *His child.*

God, she was perfect. He already thought she was a sweet little girl, but there was something about knowing she was half of him that made her the most perfect little being in the world. He tried not to focus on what he'd missed, but the sadness of it was there. Would always be there. He wouldn't let it rule him, though.

"Why are you in Mommy's bed, Mr. Ethan?"

Beside him, Paisley stirred. She'd been dead to the world too, apparently. "Vivi?" she said, propping herself on an elbow. "Did you have a nightmare?"

"Uh-huh."

"Do you want to get in bed with us?"

"Uh-huh."

Ethan threw the covers back and sat up so Violet could crawl in beside Paisley. He thought about leaving, but maybe it was better if he stayed. He wanted to stay. Violet hadn't seemed upset he was there, so maybe he should. He caught Paisley's eye and she nodded so he lay back down and pulled the covers up again.

"Did you have a bad dream, too, Mr. Ethan?" Violet asked.

He turned his head to look at her. She was curled on her side, beside her mother, hugging the rabbit and staring at him. Paisley had an arm over Violet's side, blinking sleepily at him with a tiny smile on her beautiful face.

"Yeah, I kinda did. This is a safe place, right?"

"Uh-huh. Monsters can't get you here."

A sharp pain pierced his chest. So long as he was alive, he intended that to be true. "That so? Well, good thing we're here, right?"

"Yep."

Violet closed her eyes. So did Paisley. He watched them both, his heart suddenly pounding in his chest. He wouldn't lose them again. He couldn't. How the fuck his own father—sperm donor—had let his children suffer the way they did, Ethan would never understand. But he wasn't ever going to be the kind of man who allowed his child to know what that was like. He knew she would experience emotional events as she grew, that she would have loneliness and heartbreak and confusion. It happened to everyone.

That didn't mean he had to let her feel unsafe. Ever.

He fell asleep with those thoughts in his head, then woke sometime later and slipped from the bed to go make breakfast for his family. Violet was on her back, one arm above her head, the other wrapped around her rabbit. Paisley was on her side, breathing softly.

He closed the door and went into the kitchen. The house was small, but it was enough for three. He stopped in the act of putting water in the coffee pot. Was he really thinking of moving in here? Making this a home? He looked out the kitchen window. The yard was huge with mature trees and plants. He could see a pool, not a big one, but something he could erect in a weekend. Something to enjoy when it was hot the way it was now. Maybe they could put something in the ground eventually. Nothing big. A lap pool that Violet and her friends could swim in as they got older.

There was plenty of room to add an addition to the house. Extend the living space to make a new, modern kitchen and a family room. Maybe they could add a new main bedroom suite, give Violet the current one and reserve her room for another kid or two.

The thought staggered him. The water overflowed the pot as he cursed and flipped off the tap.

"Penny for your thoughts."

He whipped around to find Paisley in the entry. Her silky pajamas were short but she had a robe open over the top of them. Her nipples were pebbled against the fabric and his dick responded. He had to forcibly drag his attention away from thoughts of sucking those pretty nipples while she rode his cock. If he didn't, he'd drag her into the nearest closet and fuck her against the wall while praying Violet didn't find them.

"Don't want to scare you, Payz, but I was thinking of where to put another kid, should we be blessed with more."

Her eyebrows rose. Then she laughed. "Oh, is that all? Here I thought you were doing calculus or something."

"Calculating square footage and additions. If your aunt ever agreed to sell the place to us."

Her mouth fell open. "You'd want to stay here?"

He shrugged. Not that long ago, he'd been determined to go back to DC and active ops when this was over. Now?

Now he was thinking of Sutton's Creek for life. And it filled him with the kind of joy he'd never thought to experience. *Belonging. Home. Family.*

The things he'd always wanted and never really had other than with his team.

"This house has good bones. A big yard for adding on but still enough room for kids. And it's classic. Not only that, but we're in the historic district. A short walk to downtown and plenty of kids to play with. But if she doesn't want to sell, that's okay too. We could find something else. Diego's always doing jobs in town, and he knows who's planning to sell soon. Might not be the historic district, but there are nice homes that aren't as old."

She closed the distance between them, then threw her arms around him and stood on tiptoe to drag his mouth to hers and kiss him. His body ignited as if it was made of straw. He gripped her ass and dragged her against him, kissing her with all the fire he had in him. When they separated, they were both panting.

"What was that for?" he asked hoarsely.

"For being you. For being a man who sees the beauty in simple things. For not wanting to impress people, but thinking of your family and what they need."

"I'm not a perfect man, Payz, but when I tell you that you and Violet are my focus, I'm not kidding."

"I know." She squeezed his hand and then dragged in

a breath. "Let's get that coffee made, hmm? I could use some. You wore me out."

Water poured, coffee made, breakfast in progress—fried potatoes with eggs, toast in the toaster—they moved companionably around the kitchen, setting the table, stirring the potatoes, whipping the eggs, getting the bread ready. It was completely domestic and normal. The thing he'd wanted his whole life, if he was honest. Mostly as a child, but having it as an adult wasn't bad either.

"What do you want to tell Violet?" he asked as they waited for the potatoes. "About this morning, I mean."

"Ah. Well, she didn't freak out that you were there. That's a good thing."

"Agreed."

"She doesn't understand, of course. She wasn't allowed to get into the bed when I was with Trey. He didn't like it." Her fingers shook as she reached for her coffee.

He gripped her hand and lifted it to his mouth to kiss her fingers. "Babe. I'm sorry."

"I know. She cried sometimes, and he got mad and yelled. But she didn't have a negative reaction to you this morning, and that's good. She seems able to separate you from Trey, and I am profoundly grateful for that."

He was too, but his gut was ice. "If it's better that I sleep in the living room, I will. We can introduce her to the idea slowly."

Paisley shook her head. "No, she handled it well. I say we don't go backwards here."

He agreed, but he'd been prepared to do whatever made Paisley comfortable. Whatever worked for Violet. He'd bend over backwards for that little girl. He'd cut his arm off for her. If she was ever scared of him, it would kill him. He knew it wasn't realistic to think she'd never react if he raised his voice or had an emotional reaction to anything. But he was fucking determined to be mindful of those things.

"She thought I had a nightmare. Does she have them often?"

"Not very often, but they still happen. I let her come to bed with me because it soothes her. Maybe I shouldn't—"

"No," he said. "She's four, she's been through a lot, and she's scared."

Her smile was wobbly. "You're going to be a great father, Ethan Snow."

Of all the things she could have said to him, that was by far the best. "Gonna do my best," he said roughly.

She slid into his arms and hugged him tight. "I know you are. I'm sorry you got thrown in the middle of the deep end, but thank you."

He squeezed her to him and bent his mouth to her ear. "No apologizing, Payz. I'm right where I want to be."

Ethan was waiting at the kitchen table when Violet trudged in after Paisley went to wake her and get her ready for the day. Paisley came behind her, dressed in another of those beautiful summer dresses she liked to wear. This one was a maxi dress, navy blue, and she wore a cream colored button up sweater over top because it got chilly in the library.

Violet had on pink shorts and a cream top with pink flowers on it. A pink headband held her hair back from her face. She looked pretty and grumpy at the same time. Reminded him of himself as a kid. He'd always been groggy and grumpy when he first woke up. He'd thought it had to do with living on the streets, because he only remembered the time in an apartment as being perfect, but maybe he'd always been grumpy.

No longer, thankfully. He'd grown out of that when the US Army got a hold of him. Oh, and coffee. Coffee helped a lot.

"Morning, sunshine," he said to the little girl. "I saved you some eggs and potatoes."

"Morning, Mr. Ethan," she grumped, plopping down at the table beside him. He took food from the covered dishes on the table and put it in front of her. He'd watched Paisley while dishing it out to make sure he didn't give her too much. When she nodded, he stopped.

Violet stabbed her fork in and ate a bite. Then she started humming. Paisley grinned at him and he grinned back.

A few seconds later, he nearly choked on his coffee.

"Are you going to be my daddy now, Mr. Ethan?"

Paisley's expression reflected shock. Ethan swallowed

the coffee, thankful he hadn't spit it all over the table. "Uh, well…"

"Baby, why would you ask that?" Paisley said, coming to his rescue.

Violet looked between them like it was obvious. "Daddies sleep beside mommies. And they eat breakfast with you. That's what Lily's daddy does."

"Oh, I see. Well, would it bother you if Mr. Ethan stayed with us all the time?"

She cocked her head and gave him a look. Then she shook it so hard her brain must be rattling. "I like him. He doesn't yell and he doesn't make you cry."

There was a knot in his throat. "I like you, too, Miss Violet. And I like your mommy. I don't ever want to make her cry, but sometimes adults cry for reasons other than being scared. What if I made your mommy so happy she cried?"

Violet seemed to think about it. "You mean if you gave her a pony and she cried because it was the best present ever?"

This kid. "Exactly like that."

She pursed her lips in all seriousness. "That's okay then. But not too often. Crying makes your face hurt. And then you can't see."

"That's true," Ethan said because he felt like he should agree. He was at a loss for what to say next. It was up to Paisley to decide when and how they introduced the concept of a new daddy, not him.

"How about we let Mr. Ethan stay with us, then? He'll

be here at night when we go to bed and in the mornings when we wake up. He'll eat with us, and we'll do things together on the weekend. Does that sound nice?"

"Yes." Head nodding this time. Also exaggerated.

"Okay, good." Paisley locked eyes with him. "You can still call him Mr. Ethan if you want to. There's no rush to think of him as your daddy."

"I don't like my daddy. He's mean. Mr. Park is nice. He plays with Lily and tickles her and talks Korean to her."

Jesus.

"I know you don't, baby. But it's not your fault he's mean. He's a mean person because of himself, not you."

Violet played with her potatoes. "He was nice some-times. He gave me toys. But then he yelled and slammed doors and scared me. And he made Mommy cry."

Ethan clenched his hands beneath the table. Paisley's eyes shone with tears.

"I can't promise I'll never be loud," Ethan said, his heart breaking. "I'm a big guy and my voice is big too. But I'm only mean to people who are mean first. Does that make sense?"

"Yes," she said softly. "You would be mean to my daddy if he was mean to mommy."

"That's right."

Her little mouth flattened into a hard line that reminded him of Eric when he was being particularly stubborn about something. "Good."

She went back to humming and eating and Ethan let out a breath. Paisley arched an eyebrow and surreptitiously wiped her eyes. Ethan reached for her hand and squeezed it. She squeezed back, and he knew they'd be okay. Violet was cautious but resilient. Whether it was because Paisley had sheltered her from as much of the bad shit with Trey as possible, or because she was more like Ethan and she made plans for how things would be better from now on, he didn't know. All he knew was he loved her and he intended to do whatever it took to make the transition good for her.

When his phone rang, he picked it up and walked outside so he could talk to Seth alone. "Hey, man."

"Trey walked into McCann Solutions this morning at seven-thirty." Seth didn't waste time and Ethan appreciated that trait more than ever.

"Jesus, how'd you find out?" It was eight-thirty. Almost time for him to go to work and for Paisley to take Violet to her aunt's house since Mrs. Park had to ferry her kids to doctor appointments today.

"Child's play. I broke into his building's server. And then I monitored the cameras inside the building. He entered the building at seven-thirty and fourteen seconds to be precise."

"Huh. Wonder where he was between Charlotte and Destin."

"Still looking for a rental in his name or his company's name, but coming up empty. He was in Charlotte on Friday, supposed to fly on Monday, but he canceled the ticket and showed up in Destin this morning."

Ethan raked a hand over his head. He didn't like it,

but then again Trey was a mercenary now. He ran his own company and did jobs for the people who could pay. There could be a hundred reasons why he'd canceled the Dubai trip and why he'd dropped off the radar before reappearing in Destin this morning.

Fact was, he was in Destin. He was nowhere near Sutton's Creek, which meant Paisley and Violet were safe. At least for now.

"Okay, thanks. You'll keep looking?"

"Yeah, brother, I will. Gotta head out on that consult today with Shadow, but I've got some inquiries out there about McCann. If I find anything, you'll be first to know."

Ethan pocketed the phone and looked at the fence where a person had hopped it two nights ago. It wasn't so much the fact somebody had come over the fence and cut through the yard. It was the way they'd stared at the house before they'd moved again. Was that the behavior of a teen on his way somewhere he shouldn't be? Or was it more likely a man with a grudge against the occupant of the house?

"Everything okay?"

He turned to find Paisley standing on the patio, watching him with apprehension on her face.

"Yeah. That was Seth. Trey's definitely in Destin. He was seen entering his office about an hour ago."

Paisley put a hand to her chest. "Oh thank God."

Ethan went over and wrapped an arm around her, pulled her against his side. She was small and perfect and he loved her like he'd never loved anyone else. Except

Violet. He was finding that his feelings for her were every bit as deep as those for Paisley.

"He doesn't know where I am. We're safe," she whispered.

Ethan kissed the top of her head. "That's right," he said.

But he wasn't sure it was true.

31

aisley felt like she could breathe. Like her life wasn't hanging on the edge of a precipice. For two weeks, she'd slipped deeper into life in Sutton's Creek. Just this past weekend, she and Ethan took Violet to the park to play in the newly opened splash pad. They also went for pizza and strolled around the square to visit the stores together.

Ethan stayed every night. They slept together in her bed, and they worked very hard at staying quiet so they didn't wake Violet. No headboard banging unless Violet wasn't home. The kid slept like a log, but Paisley was pretty sure the noise they sometimes made was enough to wake the dead. That's why they saved it for whenever they had some alone time.

Then they got as loud as they wanted. Paisley blushed to think about all the things she begged Ethan to do to her when he was teasing her mercilessly with his tongue and fingers. Or all the things she did to him when she got the chance.

Life with Ethan was *so* good. She was still scared that Trey would show up to try and ruin her happiness, but the fear receded a bit every day. Maybe he was done with her. Maybe he had better things to do than obsess about punishing her for leaving.

A tiny part of her insisted it wasn't that easy, that Trey wasn't that kind of man—but she continued to cling to hope as the days went on and life stayed quiet and ordinary.

She was happy, Violet was thriving, and Paisley could actually see a life for them now. A good one that held new friends and new experiences. Pre-K was starting soon and Violet would be going. Lily Park was also going, and Violet was excited to start with her best friend. Mrs. Park —she'd told Paisley to call her Eun-Ji—would pick them up on the days when Paisley was still at the library. And sometimes Ethan would do the child collecting.

The past three weekends had been spent going to cookouts with the One Shot gang. To Rory and Chance's place, then to Daphne and Kane's, and once at the range itself. Merrylegs and the deaf goat reappeared on both those occasions when the range property was the destination.

Violet loved riding the pony and the goat made her laugh with its random bleats and spooky eyes. The farmer said the goat didn't have a name. But Violet named it Candy Kane—emphasis on Kane—much to the amusement of Daphne. Paisley still wasn't sure how that'd happened, but everyone seemed to think it was funny. Kane handled it with humor and grace.

She was no longer surprised at how any of the men responded to their women. They laughed and joked and hugged and kissed. They were fiercely protective, too, and she had the impression that any one of them would take a bullet for his woman if necessary.

She certainly hoped it was never necessary, though apparently Blaze and Emma had met when he'd interrupted a robbery at the Gas-n-Go outside of town. There'd been a bullet then, but the gunman was a poor shot and hadn't hit anyone.

Paisley walked out of her office and into the main library. Fern was at the circulation desk. She caught Paisley's eye and looked down again. Paisley wished the woman would lighten up and *try* to be friendly, but it was probably never happening. She did, however, avoid doing anything that might upset Paisley.

And with good reason. Paisley had called Fern into her office, with Megan as a witness, and told her in no uncertain terms that if she *ever* sent an anonymous threatening text again, Paisley was calling the police and handing over the information she had about Fern's burner phone.

Then she told Fern if she thought to buy another one and try again, Paisley would still give everything she had to the police. They would have no trouble getting a search warrant and Paisley would have no trouble pressing charges. She'd added that she also had a record of Fern buying paint at Sherwin Williams for her front door—and that the paint smeared on her own front door had been color-matched to the same shade.

It hadn't, but Fern didn't know that.

The threat had been enough. Since that day Fern had been, if not delightful, at least not a total bitch. She didn't go out of her way to make small talk or join into employee conversations, but she didn't sneer or make passive aggressive comments either. And she signed her suggestions in the suggestion box these days, though she'd gone light on those as well.

Thankfully, Mr. Watson wore less suggestive T-shirts and Fern had nothing to say about them. Paisley's personal favorite was a cinnamon roll with adjectives describing the flavors—delicious, scrumptious, yummy— and a caption that said *Synonym Roll.*

Even when Chance Hughes strolled in wearing a T-shirt with a chicken on it that said *Bawk, Bawk, Motherclucker,* Fern had not uttered a word. Paisley had, though. Lord, that man.

She'd spoken with him while Fern glowered. "Sorry, Paisley," he'd said. "I forgot I was wearing it."

"You didn't. You just wanted to see what she'd do."

He'd grinned. "Got me." Then he lifted the book he'd been carrying. "I'm going. Just returning this for Rory. She said you've got another one on hold for her."

"Yes, we do."

"More wolf shifter porn, I take it?"

Paisley had eyed him. "Are you complaining?"

"Oh hell no. You give her all that wolf porn shit you got. I'm not complaining in the least."

She'd given him a book that was sure to singe his eyebrows if he peeked inside and sent him on his way.

Yes, life was good as a small-town librarian with a hot, beautiful man who loved her and friends she was happy to call her own. Even if she'd gotten them through the beautiful man, they made her feel like she'd always belonged. Like maybe, if she wasn't with Ethan, they'd still like her for herself.

Paisley made her way over to the shelf she wanted and found the book the mayor had called about. She plucked it from the shelf so she could take it to the desk and tell Fern to put a hold on it.

When she turned, Ethan was strolling into the library with a bag from Kiss My Grits. He walked straight toward Fern. Paisley could see her face go pale.

"Hey, Fern," he said as Paisley hurried that way to head off any trouble. "How's it going?"

"Fine. Can I help you?"

Ethan leaned on the counter and smiled like a shark about to swallow something whole. "Nah, just seeing how you're doing. Making sure you're all right and not feeling at all compelled to harass my lady."

"I don't know what you're talking about."

"I know, I know. And that's good, yeah? No texts, no paint, no harassment. Life is good."

"Hi, Ethan," Paisley said.

He turned and held up the bag. "Babe, brought you lunch. Just talking to Miz Fern here for a sec. Making sure we understand each other."

Paisley slid the book across the counter. "Fern, can you put a hold on this for Mayor Green? She'll be by later to pick it up."

"Of course," Fern said, shooting a wild eye at Ethan before attacking her keyboard.

"Great talking to you, Fern. Remember, any hint of trouble, I'm looking at you."

Fern didn't speak as Ethan took Paisley's hand and headed for her office. When they were out of earshot, Paisley said, "You're terrible."

"No, just thorough. Can't have her thinking it's safe to start her shit again. I want her to know she's got no space to breathe in. That I'm watching and I'll know."

Paisley went inside the office first. Ethan shut the door behind him and twisted the lock. She arched an eyebrow.

"What are you doing? I thought we were eating lunch."

"I ate lunch. I'm here for dessert. Brought you lunch, though."

The gleam in his eye made her stomach twist in the best way. Her panties grew instantly wet. Her pussy throbbed.

"What did you have in mind?"

"Bend over that desk and you'll find out."

Oh, God.

"In a minute," she said, launching herself at him and wrapping her arms around his neck. Their mouths met, tongues tangling, bodies tightening. He kissed her until she forgot herself, until her heart threatened to pound right out of her chest. She wanted him so much. But then she pictured everyone outside this door.

"Wait, Ethan. It's not professional. We shouldn't—"

He kissed her again, and her resolve melted. Hands slid along her thighs, pushing her skirt higher. "You sure?"

She wasn't sure of anything.

He nibbled her ear. "You tell me to stop and I will."

She didn't want him to stop and that was the God's honest truth. Her panties dropped to her ankles and then she was on the edge of the desk, her skirt hiked around her hips, and his face between her legs. "Been thinking about this all morning."

"You just did it last night."

"Too long." His tongue swiped right up her middle before circling her clit. He threw her legs over his shoulders and licked her so expertly she came in less than a minute. Didn't hurt that he sucked her clit into his mouth at just the right moment. Her back arched, her legs shook, and she exploded. Quietly. Just in case.

"Damn that's fantastic," he growled. A moment later he was on his feet, his jeans open, stroking himself before gliding his dick to her opening. "You're so fucking wet. I love it, Payz. Love you."

She was a mass of nerve endings waiting for another explosion. "Love you, too, sexy man. Now fuck me hard and make me come again."

He shoved inside to the hilt, dropped his mouth to hers, and took them both to paradise on the express train.

There was nothing better than small town life.

32

than winked at Fern as he left the library. She turned her head. Okay, so maybe he was a bit intimidating, but fuck all if he'd let that evil bitch terrorize Paisley ever again. According to Paisley, Fern hadn't so much as said boo since the first time he'd confronted her.

He'd left Paisley in her office, glowing from three orgasms and stuffed full from a Reuben sandwich with potato chips. Nothing in this world he liked better than taking care of his woman and child.

Violet had never been stand-offish with him, but these days she was so happy to see him—and comfortable being around him—that it almost felt like she'd been a little reserved at first. Even though she hadn't been.

True, she called him Mr. Ethan most of the time, but sometimes she said daddy.

His heart melted when she did that. He never pointed

it out, because he'd read that he shouldn't make a big deal of it, but he didn't discourage her either. She had to say it in her own time, and he had to let her.

The past couple of weeks had been amazing, but he hadn't stopped worrying about Trey. Seth had expanded his surveillance to Trey's executive assistant's computer, so he knew when Trey was scheduled to go out of town. Trey had gone to Washington once, back to Destin, and now he was in London.

He traveled frequently, but so far his travel plans hadn't brought him anywhere near Huntsville. Though he appeared to have a couple of clients in the area, he hadn't had any in-person meetings in several months.

Paisley's attorney called once to tell her there'd likely be a hearing in September that she would need to attend. She'd squeezed his hand when the lawyer said that, her eyes wide and fearful. He'd wrapped his arms around her and whispered that he'd be with her. She wouldn't have to go alone. He'd work it out with Ghost when the time came, but he wasn't letting Paisley go to Destin by herself.

Ethan hopped in his truck, his balls still tingling from having Paisley wrapped around him while he shot a load deep inside her. She made him feel so fucking good. He hadn't intended to eat her pussy on her desk until she'd walked into her office in front of him, hips swaying, and he'd found himself locking the door. He'd only meant to bring her lunch and talk with her while she ate.

But, nope, he'd dived in face first and devoured her sweetness until she'd shattered. Then he'd fucked her like an animal on that desk—but he didn't regret it. She didn't either if the stars in her eyes told him anything.

His girl loved it when he filled her with his cock and made her come. He just hadn't planned on doing it in the library during opening hours.

Ah well, something to check off the bucket list of places he intended to make love to Paisley.

When he got back to the range, Kane met him at the door. "Boss wants us in the SCIF. Daphne's covering the front. There's nobody on the range."

Well, fuck. That couldn't be good. Maybe something had finally cracked open on Brent Gannon. They'd gotten nothing out of the surveillance they'd planted at his work, and Daphne and Kane didn't have anything interesting to report about his time at the brewery. He usually drank a couple of beers, listened to a band, and hit on women. Sometimes he got lucky and went home with one, other times he struck out. Nothing ground breaking yet though they continued to surveil him.

The men filed into the SCIF, which was located behind a closet door and down a short hall in Ghost's office. Looked like storage from the outside, but it was state of the art security inside.

Ghost was already in his chair. Lights flickered on computer equipment, and the overhead screen was currently dark.

"We've got a problem," Ghost said when they were all inside and the door shut behind them. "There's been a breach in Washington. Somebody attempted to access our service records. Not the official ones, but the hidden ones. Nobody seems to know if they actually succeeded or not before they got locked out, but we're operating on the assumption they did."

"You mean our real ones," Blaze said, his voice reflecting the shock Ethan felt. "The ones that were locked down and replaced with that bullshit about being Rangers and retiring."

"That's exactly what I mean."

"Why?" Ethan said, more to himself than anyone else.

"You tell me, Dragon. Why would you break into our records?"

Ethan met Ghost's troubled gaze. "To ascertain if we're on a mission."

"And then?"

"Put together a plan to surveil us, gather information, and stop us from completing that mission. Assuming whoever it was is an enemy of the United States."

They'd been watching Brent Gannon, looking for a connection to The Dashevsky Group, but somebody'd been watching them, too. Putting enough things together to want to know more.

"Bingo. That's what General Mendez thinks. I can't fucking get anything out of POTUS's chief of staff. He's conveniently too busy to return calls, and President Willis is in Europe for a G7 meeting about NATO."

"Somebody talked. Somewhere," Seth growled. "There's no other way. We're six former military men among thousands of former service members. Us being here isn't unusual or suspicious. Not unless we've either been careless and left a trail, or somebody knows we aren't just your typical military guys with typical training."

They looked at each other. They hadn't been careless. They got in and got out and left no trail. Not that they'd had to break into anything lately. Not since Daphne's brother was in town a few weeks ago and they'd crashed that warehouse.

"Your ladies know we've got something happening, some of them more than others," Ghost said. "But I know it's not any of them. They're too fierce and protective of all of you to risk it. It'd take somebody with access and a lot more knowledge about what we really are to go after our records."

"Agent Corbin has access and knowledge. She knows everything about what we're doing. And she was there for the warehouse break-in. Maybe she's pissed we didn't wait for Jackson O'Malley to reveal the buyer for his Stingers."

Ethan wasn't surprised it was Seth speaking. They were probably all thinking it anyway. Diana Corbin was ruthless and cool-headed in pursuit of justice, but that didn't mean she wasn't potentially a traitor. No matter that she'd been the one to tell them about the Dashevsky investigation in the first place.

"Know that, too," Ghost said. "And I'm not saying she's incapable, but I can't see *why* she'd do it. What's there to gain? She already knows our mission. She wouldn't need official HOT records to interfere if that's what she was about. She could just set us up and watch us take the fall. Get us out of the way if that's what she wanted. I don't think she's above throwing us under the bus, but I can't see why she'd do it now."

That was true, too. Why break into their secret records? Unless it was all a bunch of misdirection. A way to get them chasing their tail and not seeing what was happening in front of their eyes. Something Diana Corbin *was* capable of. Though she wasn't the only one. Her uncle knew about them. So did the FBI director. Both of them were career men, but there were others in their organization's hierarchy that were political appointees with agendas of their own. Men who couldn't spell FBI or CIA until the president gave them the job. They had access to things they'd likely never had access to before, and that could be tempting to people who only cared about lining their own pockets.

Ethan shared those thoughts with the group. Ghost frowned and nodded. The other guys had hard looks on their faces, and he knew they agreed.

"We've had a few soft months, not accounting for the O'Malley business and the Griffin Research Labs saboteur," Ghost said. "Think we need to get used to the idea that's about to change. Somebody has an idea about us, and it doesn't matter what set them on the track. We're in the crosshairs now, like it or not. That means, potentially, your women, your children, this range, the town. We have to be more vigilant than we've ever been. The consequences are life and death, gentlemen. For all of us. That's how we have to act, how we have to prepare. Or everything we've done, everything we've gained, will turn to ash—and take us along with it."

Ethan's gut twisted hard. He could tell by the looks on the faces of his teammates they were right there with him. They were in love with women who understood them for the first time in their lives, they'd found a home and a family they'd never envisioned, and they were reaching for a future they desperately desired with people they loved. To lose it all now?

Unthinkable.

Ghost tapped his pen on the desk, his forehead furrowed. "I think it's time we started taking care of business. Stop waiting for orders from Washington and go hard at the problem."

The men exchanged looks. Blaze was the one who spoke. "What did you have in mind?"

Ghost looked up as if he'd forgotten they were all there. "Not sure yet. I'll let you know when I figure it out. All I know is that I'm done sitting around with my head up my ass. Gave up too much to end up being put out to pasture and forgotten about like a broken down nag on its last legs."

He nodded as if deciding something. "You've all given up too much. I'm not letting that sacrifice be for nothing. We stay vigilant, we do our jobs, and we celebrate when Athena goes live and our mission is done. Because it's going to happen. Promise you that."

He stood and they stood too, sensing this was the

colonel in charge rather than the friend. This was the man who'd run secret ops from a residential basement, against orders, to save John "Viper" Mendez when he'd been accused of going rogue. Not only had he saved Mendez, he'd saved the Hostile Operations Team. They were who they were today in part because of Alex Bishop.

When the colonel made up his mind to do something, nothing was going to stop him short of death. An involuntary chill shuddered through Ethan. He'd heard Emma Sutton call that a ghost walking over your grave. He'd thought it quaint at the time. Now he thought it too close for comfort.

"You've got your orders, men. Keep doing what you're doing," Ghost said. "Dismissed."

Nobody said a word as they left the SCIF.

"Not sure I liked that," Chance said quietly when they were in their office and away from the SCIF and Ghost. "What do you think he's planning?"

It took Ethan a moment to realize the question was directed at him. "I have no idea, man. If I was him, I guess I'd be thinking about how to shake the tree and see what falls out. Doesn't have to be anything radical, though."

Blaze scratched his chin. "Hope you're right. I got a baby on the way. So does Chance. You've got a little girl to take care of. I'd really like to be around for it, you know? Ghost gets radical, I'm gonna have to be there to help. And who knows what kind of trouble that'd bring."

They all knew what they'd signed up for. Unofficial. Deniable. They got in trouble, nobody was bailing them out. The president and her team would deny any knowledge. They would be rogue former operators taking matters into their own hands and they'd be prosecuted to the fullest extent of the law.

Ethan sucked in a breath, blew it out again. "Look, we can't worry about this. Ghost is a reasonable man. He's not a criminal and neither are we. So let's get back to work. We've got a self-defense class this afternoon for a church group, and a ladies shooting course at six. We're going to the Dawg later to wait for our ladies because they've got a book club meeting at the library. We're going to drink a beer while we wait for them and laugh about shit, and then we're going to wrap our women in our arms and hold them tight, okay? Day at a time is how we take this."

"Amen, brother," Kane said, looking fierce.

The rest of the Ghost Ops team chimed in. Seth put his hand out. They all joined in, hand on top of hand like they were a football team in a huddle.

"Where None Dare," they chanted as one, repeating the HOT motto before breaking the circle.

It's who they were, what they were. They hadn't uttered it since leaving Washington behind, but they did now. It was brotherhood and community, service and integrity, purpose and belonging.

They were HOT operators. They would fight and win.

No matter the odds.

33

onight was the Bookalicious Besties Book Club night and Paisley was excited for it. They were having it at the library because it was convenient. Central location and a kitchen for the potluck they'd decided to make a part of their routine, plus they could all walk to the Dawg afterward and meet up with the guys.

The library closed at seven and the Besties met at six-thirty, but that was okay because Paisley had the key. Violet was with Aunt Hettie tonight because Ethan was at the range for a ladies shooting class. Paisley had teased him this morning about the reviews that were sure to come and warned him not to flirt too much.

He'd kissed her until she was boneless and told her there was no other woman in the world he'd want but her. Then he'd shown up at lunch today and demonstrated why she didn't need to spare a thought for him flirting with anyone else.

Not that she'd believed she did, but it was fun to tease him about the effect of his hotness on other women. Especially when he used all that hotness on her. She was never going to look at her desk the same way again. Megan had come in earlier to tell her about preparations for the fall festival with the Angels Cove library. Paisley had spent the whole time blushing to her roots because Megan was sitting in the chair Ethan had shoved aside so he could drop to his knees and lick her senseless.

Mercy.

Emma and Rory were the first to arrive, bearing casserole dishes and book bags filled with reading journals—something Callie had gotten them all started on—books, pens, sticky tabs, and things like lotion and chapstick.

"I told Chance not to wear that shirt," Rory said when she walked in. "But he clearly didn't listen."

Paisley laughed. "It's fine. It was a good test for Fern and she passed with flying colors."

"You mean she didn't throw a hissy fit and storm out of the library?" Emma said.

"Nope. Oh, she turned red and glowered, but not a word from her lips. And Chance promised not to do it again."

"Don't listen to him," Rory said. "The devil on his shoulder will get the better of him every time. The man is a walking, talking button pusher. Ask me how I know."

They all laughed. "He's fun, though," Paisley said.

"He is," Rory sighed. "Adorable idiot. Did I tell y'all that he wants to name this kid Albert if it's a boy and Alice if it's a girl?"

"No way. Why?" Emma had her head tilted like a puppy that'd heard a strange noise.

"Big Al," Rory said in explanation. "And his companion Big Alice."

Paisley snickered. "Oh he really doesn't, does he?"

Rory shrugged. "Who the heck knows? He said since I love Alabama football so much, we should name the kid after the mascot. His other choice is Bear."

For Bear Bryant, of course.

"He's ribbing you, Ror," Emma said. "But that's funny. I seriously didn't see the Big Al connection, and I should have."

"That's Chance. A laugh a minute," Rory said, but she was grinning.

Daphne breezed in with Callie following a minute later. They set their dishes on the counter, chattering the whole time.

"Where's Nikki?" Emma said.

Callie waved. "Last minute trip with her trainer to look at horses. Not for her, I might add. But when Lisa goes on a horse buying trip, she takes the girls with her if they can go. Callie hated to miss, but between horses and book discussions, she's going to choose horses every time."

"Oh dear," Paisley said. "I'm afraid this is Violet's

future trajectory if she doesn't stop talking about Merrylegs."

"That's how it starts. But sometimes little girls just like ponies. They don't necessarily want to ride horses all the time. Or compete, which is a whole new level of expenses."

"I should be mad at Ethan for putting the idea in her head, but I can't be," she sighed. "He wants her to be happy."

"Like any good dad should," Daphne said, sounding like she was sad and angry at the same time. Paisley didn't know the full story but she knew Daphne had come from something that wasn't good. She'd found her home and her love in Sutton's Creek, and she wasn't looking back. She waved a hand. "Sorry. It's a compliment for Ethan because he's a sweetie, but also an indictment of my own father, who was a dick. I didn't mean to make it about me."

Everyone reached over to pat her or squeeze a hand or an arm. Daphne nodded and patted back, her eyes suspiciously shiny. "You aren't making it about you," Paisley said. "We're friends and we talk, right?"

"That's right," Emma said. "The Besties discuss books, men, life, and people we'd like to see get hit by the karma bus."

Daphne laughed. "I believe my dad has been run over by that one. Then it backed up and ran him over again. Prison's gonna be hard for a man like him. Now are we talking about this book or what?"

"Yes, let's talk," Callie said. "I want to hear what you thought."

"I like the Fae aspect, and it was a lot hotter than I expected," Rory replied.

Callie groaned. "I know. So embarrassing to read with your baby sister. But she's almost seventeen and she's going to read that stuff. If I suggested a clean"—she finger quoted the word—"romance novel, she'd tell me to stick it up my behind."

"It wasn't that bad," Daphne said. "I've read sexier books."

"It doesn't hurt her to read about sex," Emma said. "Especially when the male main character makes the female main character's pleasure a priority. She needs to know that she has a right to expect that from a man."

"I want to stuff my fingers in my ears and block out thoughts of baby Nikki having sex," Callie said. "But she's not a baby and she'll be in college next year."

"You know, I don't like that word *clean* to describe books," Rory said suddenly. "What are they saying? That sex is dirty? That anything with sex is somehow tainted? I hate that word in relationship to romance. It's ridiculous. How do these people think they got here anyway? Through sex!"

"It's a way of letting people who don't like sexy books know they can safely read a book because it's chaste," Paisley said. It wasn't her favorite either, but as a librarian she tried to understand what kind of terms people used when searching for the books they wanted to read. Not everyone wanted to read descriptions of people getting naked and free flowing bodily fluids happening all over the place.

Rory huffed. "Then call it chaste. Clean implies dirty, and sex isn't dirty. Unless it is, and that's a whole other thing entirely. It's also how I ended up pregnant. I read too many damned reverse harem books. When Chance hit on me, I was primed to say yes." She laughed. "Best damn decision of my life, I might add."

The discussion moved on to the characters and plot of the current book while they filled their plates with appetizers, enchilada casserole, and desserts. There was no wine because two of the women were pregnant, though they'd both insisted they didn't mind if the others drank.

Daphne waved them off. "I can get wine at the Dawg or at home."

"Same," Callie said.

"I'm technically in charge of the library, so I'm on duty," Paisley added.

Daphne snorted. "That is not a thing. Is that a thing?"

Paisley laughed. "Just made it up. Sounded good, right?"

"I believed you," Callie said, swiping a chip through ranch dip. "Did y'all paste the book cover in your journals yet? I brought my mini printer if you need me to print."

"I printed mine," Paisley said. She'd started a notebook after the last meeting. She printed all the covers they'd picked for the year onto one sheet and cut them out, using a glue stick to paste the first two in. She also started pasting in the other books she read. Not that she'd read much lately. She was too busy taking care of Violet and then spending her nights making love with Ethan to read.

"Yep, got it," Rory said. Callie and Emma did also.

"Sorry," Daphne said. "I've been a bit distracted at home. But I'll get it done."

Callie waved a hand. "I got it. Don't worry about it."

She took out her mini printer and turned it on. Paisley ate a stuffed mushroom. She wondered if Fern would bitch about the leftovers this time or if she'd enjoy some for herself. Hard to say, really. And she also didn't care. Fern Carter was a footnote to her new life. Under control, tamed, in her place. If she decided to step up and be a good person, Paisley wouldn't hold a grudge. But she'd never trust her, that's for sure.

She reached for another mushroom but the lights went out before she got there.

"Well, shit," Rory said. "Did somebody forget to pay the light bill?"

"It's probably a rolling blackout," Paisley said. "It's been so hot, and the drain on the grid has been immense. We got notice of rolling blackouts if necessary."

The emergency lights were on in the hallway, illuminating the exits. If the lights didn't come on soon, they could exit the library and lock up.

"Yeah, saw that," Callie said, turning on a tiny flashlight that she pulled from her book bag. "Seth rigged up a generator at the house so we don't have to worry about it."

"No generator here, I'm afraid," Paisley said. "Where did you get that light?"

"Seth bought it. It's a clip on and it's so lightweight you don't even notice it. It's so dark at our place that he got them for me and Nikki for when we check on Charlie in the evenings. It's better than a phone light, and you plug it in to charge."

"Oh, I want one," Rory said. "Can you send a link?"

"Me too," Paisley replied.

"I'll send it to the group. I don't think it was expensive."

There was a pop and a metallic scraping noise in the distance.

"What was that?" Emma said.

"I don't..." Daphne seemed to be listening. "I think it was a door. Like somebody wrenched it open."

Sudden dread flooded Paisley's heart. Had someone broken into the library?

A sound like fabric rustling came from the hallway. And then a man materialized in the door, dressed in an assault suit with night vision goggles, a vest, and a pistol he held casually in one hand.

"Good evening, ladies. Am I interrupting?"

Paisley's blood froze. "Trey? What are you doing here? I have a restraining order."

Of all the stupid things she could have said. He laughed, the sound chilling her. Then he strolled over and backhanded her.

"Yeah, about that," he said. "I don't fucking care."

The other women hadn't moved. It took her a moment to realize why. Three other men had entered the room behind Trey. And they were leveling pistols at her friends.

Trey grabbed her by the front of her dress and dragged her up to kiss her hard. "Hey, sweetie. Missed you. Did you miss me?"

"W-what do you want?" she managed, her lips cold, her heart dead. *Violet*, her mind screamed. Where was Violet? Was she safe?

"To teach you and Snow a lesson, of course. Come on, boys. Let's get these bitches out of here. We've got an appointment to keep."

"No," Paisley said, launching herself at him. He knocked her to the floor and aimed a kick at her ribs while the other women erupted with screams and shouts. They went silent almost immediately and she knew the men must have moved to restrain them.

"Shouldn't have left, Paisley. Shouldn't have humiliated me like that. Told the judge I was abusive? That Violet was next? My own little flesh and blood? Fuckin' bitch."

Paisley whimpered as Trey dragged her up and shoved her toward the door. The other women were on their feet, being marched through the library behind her like prisoners.

"Let them go," she said. "It's me you want."

"Nah, need all of you for what I have in mind."

"Violet," she added. Begged, really. Amazing what you could say with one word.

"Got plans for her, too," Trey said, jabbing his pistol in her ribs. "Plans for all of you. Just wait."

The class ended at seven. Ethan and Kane cleaned up, locked up, and then went to join the others at the Dawg. They rode together since Kane would ride home with Daphne, and they spent the time talking about Ghost and the coldness in his tone earlier. He'd been back to himself when they last saw him at five, and he said he'd be at the Dawg tonight. Normal shit, that. Thankfully.

The guys were all there when Ethan and Kane walked in, sitting around their usual table, eating wings and burgers and laughing about something Rory had said to Chance recently.

"Told me to fucking get off my pity pot," Chance was saying. "And I said what the fuck is a pity pot? Apparently it's where you sit when you're complaining about shit."

Ghost arched an eyebrow as he reached for a wing. "What were you complaining about?"

"Chicken shit. Those fuckers got out of the enclosure and ran riot. Shit on Chuck Two and Clyde, but Clyde's used to it. I threatened to get Liza Jane and take care of all of them. We could have a huge fried chicken dinner if I did."

Seth snorted. "Yeah, she took that well, didn't she?"

"Man, you have no idea. Lucky I still got my balls."

Rory named everything for some reason. If you didn't know the shorthand, you'd be lost. But Ethan knew that Liza Jane was a shotgun, Clyde was Rory's Grandpa's old truck, and Chuck Two was Chuck Norris the Second, the truck Chance bought after Chuck Norris the First got run off the road when RJ Davis attacked Rory.

All of that meant the chickens got loose, shit everywhere, including on the vehicles, and Chance threatened to make dinner out of them.

"You're the one chose a farm girl," Kane pointed out.

Chance's grin was goofy. "Yeah, I know. She makes me laugh and she makes me mad. Then we make up and I want to piss her off again so we can start over with the making up."

"How was class?" Ghost asked.

"Fine. I expect there'll be a few more happy reviews if Daphne has her way," Ethan said. "I might have wiped my forehead with my shirt and exposed my abs as instructed. But only once. She wants more than that, too bad."

Kane laughed. "That's my girl, thinking up ways to keep the money flowing." He looked at his phone. "They should be done soon, right?"

"I haven't heard anything," Seth said. "But Nikki didn't go tonight, so who knows what they'll end up talking about. I think Callie feels less inhibited when Nikki isn't there. The kid's going to college next year but Callie still acts like she's twelve sometimes."

Susan was their waitress tonight. She stopped by for orders and Ethan asked for a beer and a chicken sandwich with potato wedges. The food came and they ate while talking about the record heat and wondering what their first fall in Sutton's Creek would be like.

Colleen Wright appeared out of nowhere, trailing a cloud of patchouli, purple caftan flowing around her ankles. "Good evening, gentlemen."

"Ma'am," they said.

"Reba and I are holding a workshop on crystals and haunted objects this weekend if you're interested. Also, my spirit guide wants me to tell you that everything will work out. Have faith."

She glided away and the six of them looked at each other.

"That's ridiculously spooky," Seth said. "Am I the only one?"

"Nope," Ghost replied. "If I were the kind of man who believed in that nonsense, I'd think she was tapped into something. But since I don't believe, I'm just gonna go with she has an uncanny knack of saying things that apply to whatever you're dealing with at the time."

"Still spooky," Chance said.

"Yep," Kane agreed.

At a quarter after eight, Ethan texted Paisley to ask if he should go pick up Violet and get her home and in bed. He didn't expect a reply to immediately fly back to his phone, but when five minutes passed and his text remained unread, a sense of unease uncurled in his belly.

"Any of you hear from the ladies?" Blaze asked, looking at his phone, obviously thinking the same thing.

"No," Seth said.

"No, but I can see she's in the library," Chance said.

"Same," Seth, Kane, and Blaze added.

Ethan looked at the tracking app on his phone. "Same here, too."

"But none of them are replying. Could be they're so caught up in the discussion they don't hear their phones." Seth frowned.

Ethan's gut twisted. "Paisley wouldn't do that. Not with McCann still loose in the world. You said he was in London, right?"

Seth nodded. "That's what was on his calendar. Left two days ago, due back on Friday. He's not in the country."

Ghost chimed in. "Think it's time to go to the library, don't you?"

They stood as one, tossed money on the table, and filed out of the Dawg. Ghost went, too. They didn't drive. They jogged the couple of blocks, slowing when the library came into view. It was dark inside. Paisley's Kia was in the parking lot. Daphne's car, Rory's new ride, Callie's vehicle. Emma was the only one without a car in the lot, but she would have walked over or ridden with Rory.

The tickle of unease in Ethan's gut turned to cold spikes of fear. "I don't like this," he growled.

"Agreed," Blaze said.

"We need to go in." Chance was already headed toward the doors.

"Wait," Ghost barked and Chance stopped, his eyes as wild as Ethan felt. "Think. Need to do a perimeter search, then breach. You don't want to walk into a trap."

"He's right," Ethan said, though the words were a hard knot in his throat. Where was Paisley? What the fuck was going on?

"Dragon," Ghost said. "The plan."

Ethan forced himself to think, to run the scenarios. He was like a chess master, but with mission planning. That's how he thought of it. The potential moves, the countermoves. Everything remained dark and still in the library.

"We need to check the doors for tripwires. Then we go in, sweep the rooms, but slowly. Have to look for tripwires so don't rush. Whoever did this is counting on us to panic. *If* this is what we think it is, *if* it's McCann, we have to think like he thinks."

"Spread out, three and three," Ghost said. "Sweep around the outside first. Find anything, call."

Ethan, Blaze, and Ghost went left while the other three went right. They searched the perimeter of the building and met at the rear entrance. The door was propped open with a brick. Kane got down on hands and knees to search for any signs of explosives.

"It's clear," he finally said.

They ghosted into the building, pistols at the ready, and swept from room to room. They didn't have their usual gear, but they had training and experience. They split up to check the building, and Ethan could smell the food as he and Kane made their way toward the meeting rooms in the back. The door was open, the food on the counter.

Ethan's marrow froze. Chairs were overturned, and cell phones were tossed on the table, their screens lighting up with unread messages.

"Goddammit," Kane growled. "If the O'Malley family has somehow come after Daphne—"

He choked the words off and worked to get himself under control. Ethan understood where he was coming from. He was having his own hard time right now.

"Violet," he breathed. "I have to check on Violet."

He turned to go, crashing to a halt when his light illuminated a piece of paper stabbed into the wall beside the door with a knife. He moved closer, heart pounding.

Fuck you, asshole. I win.

"What the hell does that mean?" Kane asked, his voice cold and hard like a man who was about to go medieval on some motherfuckers.

"It's McCann. He's not in London."

The others piled into the room then, wild eyes following Ethan and Kane's gazes to the note.

"How do you know it's McCann?" Ghost asked.

"It's a piece of Violet's paper," he said, his heart numb. "I put a V in the bottom corner for her because she asked me to. Like an artist." He pointed. "There."

"Ah, Jesus," Ghost said. "Need to get to Hettie Woods' house, see if Violet and Hettie are there and secure them if so."

"McCann wants something." Ethan's entire body was both numb and screaming with pain at the same time. "That note is meant to goad me, but he's not done yet."

"Then we've got a shot," Seth said.

"Let's roll, goddammit," Chance growled, grabbing Rory's phone from the table. "That's my entire life he's taken. I want her back."

They each snatched their woman's phone and then headed out the door. Ethan was last. He yanked Violet's paper off the wall, folded it, and stuffed it in his jeans pocket.

Trey hadn't won. Not yet.

35

Trey and his men put bags over their heads and shoved them into a van. Paisley didn't know where they were going, but she tried to pay attention to how long it took. Not that she could really know but she had a pretty decent sense of time when she paid attention. It was a skill she'd learned during her years as a waitress. Show up too early, the customers were annoyed. Show up too late and they were mad and unlikely to leave a good tip.

Inane chatter.

Yeah, maybe so, but at least it kept her thinking.

The other women were quiet because the men hunkered over them in the van had told them the consequences of talking would be a fist to the face. After about a half hour, the van slowed and turned. They were on a gravel driveway because Paisley heard the pinging of the gravel against the wheel wells. The driveway hadn't been maintained very well because they bounced in and out of ruts as they drove.

When the van came to a stop, the door screeched open and Paisley was yanked onto the ground. She heard the gasps and groans as everyone else was yanked out too. The bag over her head disappeared and she could suddenly breathe again. She dragged in air, her head turning as she searched out their surroundings.

It was dusk, but the light was failing quickly. It was a new moon, so as soon as the light was gone, everything would be black.

A dilapidated house sat against a backdrop of trees. Fields went in every direction and there were no lights from other houses anywhere along the way. The sky in the far distance glowed brighter than the rest and she knew that was Huntsville and its suburbs. So far away, though.

"Where's Violet?" she asked when Trey appeared.

"Shut the fuck up and get inside."

He jabbed his gun in her side and pushed her toward the house. The other women also trudged inside.

"Sit."

Paisley plopped onto the chair he stabbed his finger at. The other women sat too. The men tied them to the chairs and stepped back.

They were all wearing black greasepaint and she didn't know who they were, but she thought she might be able to identify them if she had to. Maybe. The fact Trey was letting her and the others see their faces didn't bode well for them. She knew that, but she wasn't going to voice it aloud.

She glanced at the others. What she saw shocked her. They should be scared, probably were, but they also looked spitting mad. Rory in particular looked like she'd shank somebody if she had a knife.

Trey hunkered down in front of her and squeezed her face to force her to look at him. His eyes were evil. How had she never realized it before? But something was missing in them. Some piece of humanity that other people seemed to have and he did not.

He was gleeful. Like a child with a new toy.

"You were a good fuck, Paisley. I enjoyed that part of being married to you, at least at first. But you were also so fucking whiny about that kid, and about Ethan Snow. He left you and you still wanted him."

"He didn't leave," she blurted, then cringed inside. What was she doing baiting him?

But he only snorted. "He told you that, huh? Yeah, what the fuck does it matter now? He had to go on a mission, fucking HOT business and shit. He was rubbing it in my face because I'd gotten kicked out of the unit. Because the HOT command were pussies and wouldn't do what it took to keep the soldiers safe. But I did. Got prosecuted and sent away for my trouble. Fucker comes to me and asks me to tell you he had to bug out but he'd be back."

Paisley didn't know what he was talking about or what this hot thing was, but she wasn't going to say anything now. She wanted to hear it all. Wanted to hear it from Trey's mouth that he'd lied.

"But you didn't."

"Nope. He didn't deserve you, Paisley. I would have taken care of you, like I said, but all you did was whine and cry. And then that fucking kid. Jesus, you'd think you were the only woman on planet earth to ever give birth."

Her heart ached. "She could be yours and that's how you feel about her? That she's a fucking kid?"

He pinched her face harder. "She's not mine, you dumb bitch. I had a vasectomy years ago, before I met you." He barked a laugh at the shock in her eyes. "Yeah, that was the best part. Knowing she was Ethan's, taking his kid away from him. Arrogant bastard. But you know what? I got an entire HOT team coming and I'm here to teach them a lesson. Including the deputy commander. That fucker wanted me thrown out of the Army and now he's here in this miserable little town, pretending to be a harmless safety instructor. How the mighty have fallen." He grinned. "Got you to thank for this present, honey."

Paisley was lost, but she wasn't going to convey it to him. And she didn't dare look at the women for support or confirmation. The most important thing he'd said was that Violet wasn't his. Had never been his. Ethan really was Violet's father. It wasn't just a dream or a hope, it was real. She wanted to tell him, and she might never get a chance.

Don't think that way.

"Where is she, Trey? What have you done to her?"

"You don't need to worry about that, babydoll. Your brat and the old lady are already dead."

Her heart cracked in two. A sob bubbled into her chest, her throat.

Violet! Aunt Hettie! No!

Trey looked positively gleeful. "Yeah, that's right. Cry for me, honey. I love the sound of your crying. Makes me hard."

Rage boiled to the surface. She might be tied up, but she wasn't helpless. Paisley reared back and head butted Trey with all her might. Blood burst from his nose as he roared.

She didn't care. She fucking didn't care. She rocked like a mad woman, her chair scooting across the floor, murder seeping from every pore of her body. She would fucking kill him. Even if she had to die herself, she'd do it.

"Fucking bitch," Trey yelled, getting to his feet and holding a hand over his nose. He started for her but one of his guys grabbed his arm.

"We have to go. The plan. Stick to the plan."

"I can fucking kill this bitch and they'll still show up. The rest of the women are waiting for rescue. Snow will find her body, and then they'll all burn. Is it wired?"

"It's wired. Ready to blow. Let's get out of here, stick to the plan."

Trey looked wild. Conflicted. Paisley would have hidden her eyes in the past but now she glared. Daring him. Hating him.

"Mick," the man said. "Let's go. She's gonna die anyway."

Trey still didn't move. Then he wiped his face with his sleeve, smearing blood everywhere, and she knew he'd gotten a handle on himself.

"Yeah, all right. You hear that, Paisley. When your lover comes for you, and he will, this whole building's gonna go up in smoke. Gonna get an entire team and all their bitches this time. You think about that, darlin'."

Trey lifted his weapon—and then smacked her across the face with it, slashing her cheek and knocking teeth loose. At least that's what it felt like.

She fell over, slamming her head to the floor. The room swam for just a moment. Then everything went dark.

36

The team rushed back to the Dawg, piled into vehicles, and raced to Hettie's house. The old Queen Anne stood sentinel beneath tall trees, lights blazing from the windows. Ethan couldn't stop to think about what he might find. Trey had stolen a piece of Violet's paper to write on. The only way he'd gotten that was from Hettie's house. He hadn't been inside the cottage on Chestnut Street because the alarm hadn't been tripped.

Ethan was first out of the vehicle, first to race across the yard. He skidded to a halt at Hettie's door, scanning for anything out of place. Then, because he didn't know what the fuck he would find, he pounded a fist on the door, praying beyond hope that Trey hadn't actually been there. That he'd found a piece of Violet's paper on Paisley's desk or something.

It was possible. Anything was possible.

"Miss Hettie," he called. "Violet. It's Ethan."

The sound of his pounding echoed throughout the house. His team raced onto the porch, eyes wide, faces grave. They were all missing their women, all worried, yet they were here with him. Looking for his little girl. And Miss Hettie.

Just when he was ready to kick the door in, it swung open to reveal a wizened old face. Hettie Woods was stooped with age, but her eyes flashed fire.

"Ethan. There was a man. He came inside but Violet and I hid behind the secret panel." She put a hand to her heart. "Dear Lord, I was afraid to come out until I heard you shouting. Well, Violet heard you if I'm honest, which is why I'm here and she's still in the library."

She turned to yell over her shoulder, but her voice wasn't very loud. "Vivi, honey, come here! It's Mr. Ethan and his friends."

Violet was there a moment later, her little eyes wide, blond hair flying. She ran into his arms and he caught her close, lifting her, dropping his nose to her hair. *Strawberries.*

"It was my daddy," she said. "The mean one. He was here but me and Aunt Hettie hid. He cussed a lot."

Jesus.

Violet reared back to look at him. "I want you to be my daddy, Mr. Ethan. Forever."

He squeezed her, his heart hammering. "I want that, too, honey. I'm proud to be your daddy. Can you tell me if

Trey—that's your mean daddy—said anything? It might help me find him."

Her lower lip jutted out. "Why? He's mean. You don't want to find him."

"I really do, honey. I want to make him pay for being a bad man. Make sure he never scares you again."

She curled her little fists into his shoulders. "He said the house was gonna esspode. When everyone was there. I don't know what that means. Where's Mommy?"

Ethan exchanged a look with his team. Kane's jaw was granite. He was their explosives expert. They all knew Trey was rigging a house to explode based on what Violet said, but Kane would have a better idea than any of them on how he planned to do it. Ethan didn't think it was this house since nothing had happened when Hettie opened the door, but he wasn't taking chances.

"Mommy had to work late, honey." He hated lying, but he wasn't going to tell her that Mommy was in terrible danger. "Miss Hettie, need you to come with us. You and Violet both. Going to take you to the Suttons' house." Blaze nodded when Ethan gave him a look. The Suttons were the safest people he could think of since he didn't want to involve the police yet. "John and Ellen will watch over you both until we can make sure everything's good to return."

He expected a fight, but Miss Hettie gave him a once over and nodded. "Let me get my purse, young man. I've read enough murder mysteries to know what the correct course of action is. You don't have to worry I'm going to be stubborn."

"I really don't think you should go back inside—"

She reached over where he couldn't see what she was doing and returned with a handbag. "I keep it inside the credenza by the door. I'm ready. Vivi, are you ready to go with your daddy?"

"Yes, ma'am. But I want my drawings."

"I'm sure the Suttons have paper, dear. We need to get moving so your daddy can get the bad men before they hurt anyone. Isn't that right, Ethan?"

"Yes, ma'am, it is."

"Precisely." She stepped out of the door and gazed at him expectantly.

"Seth and Blaze will take you, ma'am," Ghost said, stepping in to take control. "We need to look around."

Hettie's eyes sparked. "Ah, of course. Clues. Vivi, say goodnight to your daddy. He has work to do."

Violet hugged his neck tight and then kissed him on the cheek. Ethan's heart was a mess of emotion. Love for his child, love for Paisley, and fear he wouldn't get to her in time.

"Bye, Daddy Ethan. See you and Mommy later. But I'm sleepy so maybe I won't see you until I wake up in the morning."

Ethan kissed her cheek. "It's okay, baby. I'll make waffles for you and Mommy, okay?"

"Okay."

He set her down and she put her hand into Hettie's.

The two of them went down the steps and strolled to the street with Seth and Blaze.

"Demon?" Ghost said to Kane.

"I don't see any wires. I honestly don't think he put charges on this house. The women aren't here."

"Agreed," Ethan said.

"Then let's get inside and see if we find anything that might lead us to McCann."

They searched the downstairs first. When they came up empty-handed, Ethan wanted to scream

He wasn't the only one. The look of pain on his friends' faces tore him in two.

Yeah, he'd had some good news, but it wasn't enough.

He was so damned thankful Violet was alive. He hadn't known what to expect when they'd rolled up to Hettie's house, but he'd tried to prepare for the worst. To have Hettie and Violet alive and well was more than he'd expected—and everything he'd hoped for.

Now he had to rescue Paisley. How would he live without her after they'd just found each other again? And how would his team live without the women they loved and the children on the way?

Jesus.

Ghost was the only one whose heart wasn't compromised on this mission but he was there beside them, going into battle with them. Just like they'd go into battle for him.

Please, Jesus, just let Paisley be alive. Let them all be alive.

But where?

They raced for the range and rushed inside to put on assault suits, paint their faces, and arm themselves to the teeth. They miked up but they didn't have anywhere to go. Not until Trey deigned to tell them. Ethan was banking on the man wanting to gloat, wanting them to suffer, but it was possible Trey would be satisfied by simply taking the women and making them disappear.

He'd clearly wanted Violet, too, but he hadn't found her. Thank God for big, old houses with hidden doors and secret staircases. Hettie had delighted in showing him those features when he'd worked with Diego on a job for her, and he was more thankful now than he'd ever been.

Seth was busy on his laptop, typing things in, searching, asking questions of his contacts. He looked frustrated and angry and Ethan understood. He felt the same things. Along with a despair that said he'd never be happy again.

"Clint Harris!" Seth yelled, startling them all. "Fucking hell."

"Clint Harris? What's that?" Kane snarled.

"Trey Clinton McCann. He grew up on Harris Street in a little town in Idaho, which took me fucking forever to dig up. Clint Harris! He fucking rented a car in Huntsville and then returned it in Destin the same day McCann arrived there a few weeks ago. Then I traced the name back to Charlotte. He boarded a plane to Huntsville from Charlotte the day McCann arrived and checked into the airport Hilton. But Harris never made the return trip to Charlotte, and McCann never went to Dubai."

Ethan stiffened. It was confirmation Trey had been in Sutton's Creek, watching Paisley. He'd probably been the man on the camera that night. But he hadn't done anything then. He'd returned to Destin. To plan. To come back and do whatever he was doing now. To involve all of them, not just Ethan.

"How does that help us now?" Ghost snapped.

"Clint Harris is one of Brent Gannon's contacts. Which means I've got audio of a call they had two days ago when Gannon was in his office at Eagle Defense Systems. It didn't raise any alarm bells at the time, but Harris asked if the property was ready for their hunting trip. It's coyote and feral hog season year round so nothing suspicious there. Gannon said it was. Then he gave an address. Harris thanked him and said he and his friends would be arriving the next day, which was yesterday."

Ethan surged to his feet along with the rest of the team. "What?" Kane barked, hope flaring in his voice. "You have an address?"

Seth closed his laptop and stood, a feral smile on his lips. "Yeah, I do."

"Then let's head out, men," Ghost said.

They piled into Kane's Yukon and Ethan's truck, because they were less suspicious than a van—plus there was room to bring five women home—and headed for the remote property between Sutton's Creek and Triana. They hashed it out over the comms, deciding on their approach. Trey was too unpredictable and too dangerous for them to waltz in like this was an ordinary op. Not that ordinary ops weren't dangerous, but the targets weren't usually people with the same training they had.

When Ethan's phone rang, the caller was unknown. He hit the screen to accept the call, his teeth clenching tight.

"Hello?"

Because he had to play it dumb. Blaze and Ghost were with him but he could only see Ghost's face in the front seat. The man looked angry. And vengeful, like a dark god who'd been tricked somehow.

"Ethan Snow," Trey said, sounding joyful—and slightly nasal. "How's it going, my man?"

"What do you fucking want, Trey?"

"Oh, I think you know. Paisley. I've got her. Got all the bitches. Thinking about killing them if you don't show up. You and the whole team. Wraith, Shadow, Demon, Phantom—and Ghost most especially. Can't wait to see that fucker again."

"What's the plan, Mick?" he said, calling Trey by his call sign. "What happens when we show? You just planning to let them go?"

"Not really, no. Thinking we'll do a trade. The six of you for the five of them. You come here, show good faith, and I'll let them walk. Then it's you six against me and my boys. You might win. You might not. But at least your ladies will be free."

He wondered how to ask for a head count on the 'boys'. That'd be helpful, knowing numbers. "How do I know I can trust you to let them go?"

"My word as an operator. We're a brotherhood, Dragon. We've served. Seen some shit. Done some shit. You show up, and I'll let them walk. Then we'll see who comes out on top."

"Okay," Ethan said. The man was full of shit and they all knew it, but the only option was to bargain with him. Let him think he was getting what he wanted. "When and where?"

"Nope, not telling you that yet. You're gonna need to follow some clues, kinda like one of those mystery games where you gotta solve a puzzle to get a clue."

"You're a fucking bastard, you know that?"

Trey laughed. "Heard it a time or two. But you know what? I'm a rich bastard, and you aren't. You can tell Ghost that for me. I'm fucking rich. People pay me to do the kind of work I did for free in the goddamn Hostile Operations Team. The kind of work he didn't appreciate."

Asshole. "Then why do you want to risk it all by taking us on? You could walk away, enjoy your money, and know we've got nothing like that. That we still have to work a nine to five while you can light your cigars with hundred dollar bills."

He laughed. "Thousand dollar bills, my man. But I like a challenge. Keeps my skills honed."

"Seems like a dumb fucking risk if you ask me. You might lose. Then what?"

"I think you overestimate your ability. But maybe you're right. Still, it's too late now. I've got your lady tied to a chair in a house in the middle of fucking nowhere. There's a bomb under the kitchen table. It's got one hour on it. You follow the clues, get here on time, and I'll stop the countdown. Don't figure it out and boom, bye bye pretty ladies."

"We'll be there."

He laughed. "I'm sure you will. But will it be on time or not? I'll send over the first clue. Finding the rest is up to you. Oh, and don't bother trying to trace this phone. Phantom isn't the only IT guy worth his weight in gold. You'll waste too much time and that's not what you need to be doing right now."

The line went dead. Blaze exploded in a torrent of obscenity and plans for murder. Ethan was right there with him. He gripped the wheel and concentrated on the road in front of him. His phone pinged with a text. Ghost picked it up.

"*I have cities but no houses, forests but no trees, and water but no fish. What am I?*" he read. "For fuck's sake, it's a map. How much of a douche do you have to be for this shit?"

"That's it?" Blaze asked.

"There's more. *Go to the Gas-n-Go. Find the object I've described and look closely. You'll find the next clue there.*"

"He wants us to go to the Gas-n-Go to chase down a map? Is he fucking crazy?" Ethan growled.

"Yeah, well, we aren't doing it. You hear me, fellas?" Ghost said. "He'll send us on a wild goose chase and we won't learn a fucking thing from any of the clues we don't already know."

Kane responded from the other vehicle. "Roger that. No fucking treasure hunt."

"No fucking treasure hunt," Ghost agreed. "We do this the way we planned."

They just had to hope what they planned was enough.

37

aisley's cheek throbbed and her head ached, but she was alive. *Violet. Aunt Hettie.*

Despair flooded her and she wished she could pass out again. But something inside her said she couldn't believe Trey. He wanted her to hurt, but he would say anything to make that happen. There was a chance, a small chance, that Violet and Aunt Hettie were well.

The more she thought about it, the more she believed. Trey would want to hurt her as much as possible. He wouldn't kill Violet and tell her about it. He'd kill Violet in front of her.

She shuddered. She would *not* give up hope. She would fight with everything left in her.

"Paisley," Emma cried as her eyes cracked open. "Honey, say something to me."

The room was illuminated by a single lamp sitting on

a table. The bulb was weak, but there was some comfort in being able to see the other women.

"This sucks," Paisley said, her throat tight.

The women laughed, though the sound wasn't as carefree as it normally was. "No kidding," Rory said. "I'm about tired of this shit. First it was that psycho ex of Emma Grace's, then it was RJ Davis trying to roast me alive, and now it's another psycho ex, though I guess he's a psycho commando ex, who hates our men because they served in something called HOT and his feelings and masculinity are hurt by it."

Paisley lay on her side, tied to the chair, and found herself laughing. Which was crazy, but sometimes you just had to laugh. "I'm sorry," she said. "So sorry. It's all my fault."

"It's not your fault," Daphne said, her voice hard. "Men like your ex are evil and broken and grandiose. He reminds me of my brother. He gets off playing with people's lives. He wants to make a show of the confrontation with the guys, and he wants them to lose. We're collateral damage."

"He said the place is wired to blow. When the men show up, the bomb will go off. I'm thinking there's a trigger mechanism on the doors. Or maybe he's watching from somewhere close and plans to trigger the bomb once they breach the doors." Callie swiveled her head, looking around the room.

"We need to get out of these chairs," Daphne said. "Get out of this house if we can."

"I've been working on that," Rory said. "But so far the zip ties are holding strong. Why couldn't they have just tied our wrists together behind our backs? I know how to get out of that one thanks to Chance's instruction."

Paisley lay there, taking stock of the aches and pains in her body. Things throbbed. Her jaw hurt. She lifted a hand to wipe away a trickle of blood that tickled her cheek.

"Paisley! Your hand's free!"

Paisley stared at the hand in front of her fact. "Oh my God, my hand is free! The zip tie must have broken when the chair fell."

Fresh energy flooded her veins as she twisted herself around. Her hand was free, but her legs were still tied along with her other hand. But if she'd broken one, she could break another.

She groped at her ankles, but the zip ties held tight. And then she discovered that the support bar on the bottom two legs jiggled when she touched it. She grabbed on and jiggled harder.

"Keep going, Paisley," Callie said.

Paisley worked harder—and the bar broke free of the hole it was seated in. She worked the zip tie down her leg until she was no longer tethered to the chair leg. Adrenaline surged as she pushed herself up and grabbed the edge of the kitchen counter that jutted away from the wall and acted as a breakfast bar.

When she managed to stand, the chair hung to one side. She was still tied to it, but only on her left side, which meant she could pivot the chair either direction. She worked to get it where she could stomp the other crossbar. Then she stood on it and pulled with all her might.

If the chair had been vintage, made of good wood, it might not have worked. But it was a cheap chair, made of pine, and the bar snapped. Her other leg was free.

"See if there are any knives in the drawers. Or scissors," Emma said.

"Good idea," Paisley said. "I should have already done that." And not worked so hard to break the other chair leg. Duh.

"I just thought of it," Emma said sheepishly.

The women exchanged a look.

"If we get out of this alive, we'll never speak of how none of us thought to look for knives or scissors until after Paisley got both legs free," Rory said. "The men would never let us live it down."

"In our defense," Callie said. "We aren't trained for this."

"I should have thought of it," Daphne replied. "Considering my family. But I have to admit I've never been in this situation before. I was focused on Paisley getting free."

Paisley dragged the chair around the counter and started opening drawers. "Hey, doesn't matter how it happened. I'm looking now." She yanked open drawers. Butter knives, flatware, a spatula. There wasn't much here, which told her the place was hardly ever used, if at all. Probably not ever considering the layer of dust everywhere.

"Aha!" she cried, coming up with a paring knife. She slid it into the zip tie still holding her wrist to the chair and sawed. It wasn't sharp but it worked and her wrist came free.

The women cheered, though not too loudly in case Trey and his men were close by. Paisley sawed Rory free and then Emma. Emma took the knife and handed it to Rory. "I want to look at you," she said to Paisley. "Sit."

Paisley sat and Emma tilted her head back to study her eyes. "What I'd give for a penlight," she murmured. "You probably have a mild concussion. Are you light-headed or dizzy?"

"I don't think so. Maybe."

"Nausea?"

"No"

"Headache?"

"Definitely that."

"Blurry vision?"

"Not at the moment."

"The cut on your cheek isn't deep. But there's swelling and there will be a bruise. Potentially a small scar." Emma hesitated. "What Trey said about Violet and your aunt..."

"He's lying," Paisley replied. "I don't believe a word of it."

Emma squeezed her shoulder as the other women stood and shook out arms and legs. Maybe Emma thought she was kidding herself, but Paisley knew she was right. Trey had not harmed them. Not yet anyway.

"Maybe there's some ice," Callie said, walking over to the fridge and yanking it open. "No ice, but a cold pack."

She returned with a cold pack wrapped in a towel she'd found in a drawer and handed it to Emma, who put it on Paisley's face. Paisley grimaced.

"Hold it there for twenty minutes. Jeez, listen to me, doctoring like we're in a normal situation. Keep it there for as long as you can tolerate the cold or until we start running across the field."

They didn't have watches or phones because Trey and his men had stripped them of electronics. So they couldn't be traced.

"Does anyone know where we are?" Daphne said.

"I have an idea," Rory replied. "They drove us east. Go far enough east and Redstone Arsenal blocks your path, which means we're between Sutton's Creek and the Arsenal. Triana, maybe? South is the river, north is the airport. East is the Arsenal and west is home."

"So we need to sneak out and head west," Daphne said. "But probably not on the driveway. They could be watching that."

"There are woods to the south. We should go there," Rory said. "Then track west. If I'm right, we'll come out on the highway and we can flag somebody down."

"We have to be careful," Paisley said. "Trey is probably watching the house. He wants the men to try and rescue us so he can blow the house with all of us inside. Which means there's a bomb somewhere."

"Uh, ladies," Callie said. She was standing in the dining area, her hand on the table. "Found the bomb. It's under here, and it's a big one. When it blows, it's taking the house and everything near it."

Paisley shuddered. "Is there a timer? Any wires leading to the doors or windows?"

"No wires I can see. There is no timer. It's rigged to a cell phone."

"Which means he plans to call the phone to trigger the bomb as soon as the men are inside. He's told them where to find us."

"That part's good. But we've got to get out of here," Daphne said.

"Agreed. I say we go out the bedroom window closest to the woods. Trey is arrogant enough to think we're helpless, so I don't think he'll be expecting an escape. He'll be watching for the men to arrive." Paisley stood, her body aching anew. Lord what she wouldn't give for a muscle relaxer and her own bed right now. "I'll go first. No reason for anyone else to risk their lives if I'm wrong about him watching."

"You're hurt," Emma said.

"I'll go," Daphne replied as she walked back in from the room in question. "I'm the tallest, and I can help everyone else down. It's a long drop on that side because there's a drainage ditch. I opened the window and listened. I don't hear anything but frogs and some night birds out there."

Paisley pulled in a fortifying breath. She wanted to insist it was her responsibility to be the first out the window, just in case, but Daphne was right. Paisley needed to trust her friends. She'd been thinking how much she loved being around these women but the truth was she hadn't fully let herself believe they were going to be there for her no matter what. She was used to losing people because of the way she'd been raised, and she'd told herself that so long as she had Violet and Ethan, she'd be okay. She didn't need anyone else.

But these women were a team the same as the men were. They were friends, forged from circumstance, perhaps, but loyal and true and capable of making their own decisions. She needed to trust them. Really trust them.

"Okay, yes," Paisley said. "I don't like it, but you're right it's the best idea. Are we ready to go?"

"Ready," they agreed.

Paisley dropped the cold pack to the kitchen counter and went into the bedroom with her friends.

"Do or die, ladies," Daphne said as she stood by the open window. "I love you all."

Paisley's eyes stung with tears. "Love you too. If anything happens, run. Don't wait for us."

"Nothing's happening," Rory said. "Except we're getting out of this clusterfuck and back to our lives."

"Amen, sister."

Daphne climbed onto the sill and dropped over the side.

38

They parked a mile from the house and piled out of the vehicles, a military team armed to the teeth on a rural Alabama road. Then they fell out, humping through the woods and across fields, making no noise and casting no shadow. It was a dark night, a new moon, which worked best for special operators on missions.

Trey knew it too which was at least part of why he'd chosen tonight. That and the convenience of having all the women in one place where he could grab them together. Seth had found a terrain map and they'd studied it on the drive over. This area was dotted with creeks—tributaries running into the mighty Tennessee River—and it was hilly. Not big rolling hills, but smaller ones. There were fields and woods, and the population was sparse. There were huge tracts of land and one house sitting on each, a mile or more from the next.

The house where Trey had stashed the women was on a twenty-acre tract, surrounded by woods, though the trees didn't appear to go all the way to the house except on the southern side. There were fields on the other three sides, and then the woods that hid the house from the road.

Trey and his men would be there somewhere, watching. But they weren't expecting an incursion a full forty-five minutes before Ethan and his team should arrive if they were chases their asses around Sutton's Creek looking for clues.

The only purpose for that game that Ethan could see was to get inside their heads, rattle them with the ticking clock, and make them careless when they arrived with minutes to spare. Trey was obviously in control of when the bomb went off because he wasn't going to let it happen before they were inside the house with the women.

He'd called again to ask if they were enjoying the clues. Ethan responded that they didn't have time to talk if they were going to make it in time. Trey laughed and hung up.

Sick fuck.

The whole thing was a game, a mindfuck. Because Trey was butthurt he'd been ejected from HOT and butthurt that Paisley fell for Ethan instead of him. He'd had five years to gloat over what he'd taken from Ethan, but that wasn't enough. Now he wanted to make all of them pay.

Ethan gritted his teeth. Joke was going to be on Trey because these HOT operators hadn't come this far to dick around with an arrogant, evil motherfucker who got off on hurting women.

"House on the hill," Blaze said through the comm. "Single light on."

"Where do we think Trey and his men are waiting?" Kane said.

"They aren't expecting us this soon," Ethan said. "One is watching the driveway approach because they expect us to come up the road and drive to the house."

"Agreed," Ghost replied.

"Don't know how many he's got, but Trey can see the house. He won't leave it. He wants us to drive up and breach because time's running out. He expects us to flip the script he's laid out for us."

"We approach through the woods closest to the house," Ghost said. "Give ourselves as much cover as possible. He's got NVGs like we do so the field is a no go, even if it's more direct."

"Hey, there's a tree stand in that copse of trees, about a half mile from the house," Chance said, lowering the high-powered binoculars. "Bet that's where he is."

Ethan's throat squeezed. "That's it, Wraith. That's where he'll be waiting. He can see everything, but he's far enough from the house for safety."

He wanted to charge for that stand, leap up the ladder, and put a bullet in Trey's head before the asshole could blink. But of course that wouldn't work. Trey had night vision goggles and he'd see them coming. He'd open fire and that would be the end of everything. Paisley and the women would die because he'd trigger the bomb.

"Let's move out, men," Ghost said. "We need to get to that house and get the women out. We'll deal with McCann and his mercenaries when we're done."

"Copy that," Blaze said. The others echoed him.

They melted back into the trees, moving as fast as they could through underbrush, over creeks, and downed trees. Leaves crackled as they moved, but they kept their progress as quiet as they could make it. They were deep enough into the woods not to be seen through the trees with night vision.

They just had to hope that none of Trey's mercenaries lay in wait up ahead.

The women made it out the window and started for the tree line. It was a good fifty feet away and they hunkered low to the ground, trying not to make themselves a big target. They didn't know where Trey and his men were, but they had to try to get away.

Freedom was so close. Get to the woods, run like hell south, then make their way west when Rory told them to. The woman seemed to have an internal compass that Paisley did not have. She vowed, if she got out of this situation, to get better at that.

Ethan and the guys taught self-defense so that was

going to be priority one. Take self defense classes. Not that he hadn't taught her some moves because he had, but there had to be more to it.

She also wanted some survival training. How to use a compass, how to live off the land. How to know which damned direction she was facing without her phone to tell her. She didn't like camping because of bugs and wild animals, but damn if she wasn't going to learn to deal with it. And she wanted Violet to know. Very important.

"Hey," someone shouted.

A chill of fear zipped down Paisley's spine. It wasn't Trey, but it was one of his men.

"Run!" Daphne whisper-yelled.

A shot rang out, bark and leaves rained down on Paisley's head, and she passed under the cover of the trees before getting to her feet and stumbling forward. Daphne grabbed her arm and pulled her along. The others seemed to hesitate, waiting for her, but Daphne growled at them to keep going.

"I can't," Paisley panted as they followed the other women. "It hurts."

Her head, her cheek, the joints in her body. When she'd fallen, she'd slammed the floor pretty hard. She'd been running on adrenaline but that adrenaline was fading.

"You can," Daphne grated. "You fucking will."

Behind them, more shouts rang out. Daphne wrapped an arm around her shoulders and propelled her forward even though Paisley was slowing her down.

Paisley wanted to give up, sink to the ground, and fade into nothingness. If she did that, she could save her friends. Ethan would take care of Violet and she would grow up safe, happy, and whole. Ethan would find another woman, someone who would be a mother to Violet, and they would have a great life together.

"You're nothing, Paisley!" a voice shouted behind her. "You won't escape! Violet's dead! Ethan's dead! Nobody's left to save you!"

Trey.

He was coming for her, like he always was, and there was nothing she could do.

"Think of Ethan and Violet," Daphne said. "Picture their faces. You're running toward them. You can do it, Paisley. Run!"

Somehow, Paisley found fresh strength. It swelled in her limbs, her veins, propelling her forward faster than before. They ran through the woods, dodging downed trees, trudging through creeks, their breaths rattling in their chests. Behind them came a rustling wave as the men rushed after them. She knew they had night vision goggles, knew they could see the women when they weren't covered up by trees.

The men were coming, and they would win. There was no stopping them. It was a miracle they hadn't fired yet because they could surely see well enough to do so. If they weren't firing it's because Trey had other plans. He wanted them in that house, wanted them to be there when the bomb blew.

He knew he could catch them, knew it was only a matter of time before they got lost and tired and had to stop.

"No," Paisley growled, surging forward. "No."

She wasn't going to give up. She couldn't. Not now. They might make it. They might stumble onto the road and a passing car might stop and Trey might not shoot.

So many *mights,* but they had to try.

She ran for all she was worth, body aching but feet propelling her onward. Daphne was still beside her, still there to make sure she didn't quit. Ahead of them, one of the women cried out.

A heartbeat later, a group of men in tactical gear surrounded them.

Paisley gasped for air, her head throbbing, fury gathering deep in her soul. *Why?*

Why had they made it so far just to lose now?

She drew in breath to scream her frustration to the universe when the circle broke as the other women threw themselves at the men.

Strong arms wrapped around her. She struggled until the voice penetrated.

"Payz, it's me. It's okay. I've got you."

"Ethan?"

"Yes, baby. It's me."

The shouting and movement in the distance behind them was still happening, but there was laughter as well. Laughter because Trey and his soldiers thought they had the advantage.

"You have to keep going," Ethan said. "The guys and I have a job to finish."

"No, Ethan, please. He said Violet—"

"She's fine. Both of them are. Now go, Payz. Go with the women. If you reach the road, stop and wait for us to catch up."

Daphne grabbed her hand and tugged. "Come on. Let's go."

Once more, they were running for all they were worth.

39

than could breathe again. The women might not be safe, not yet, but now he and his team stood between them and Trey McCann.

The Ghost Ops team melted into the night, using the trees for cover, watching the approaching men. Only four, including Trey. Ethan knew he was there because they'd heard him taunting Paisley. When the shouting first started, his team figured out that the women had gotten out of the house somehow. He didn't know how they'd done it, but he was fucking proud. All the guys were, no doubt about that.

He prayed the women weren't too traumatized by the experience, but no way of knowing until this was over. He gripped his rifle tighter and waited. The men had night vision, but HOT had more discipline. They used the trees to their advantage, each man plastered to a trunk, waiting in silence for Trey and his men to jog into their circle.

"Fucking bitches," Trey said. "The HOT team will be here in twenty minutes, give or take. We gotta get them rounded up and back into that house."

"Go," Ghost said softly through the comm.

Ethan was lucky enough to be on the outside of the circle closest to where Trey and his men entered. He, Kane, Seth, and Chance slid from behind the trees and rushed the four men from behind.

But his foot snapped a twig and slipped out from under him before he connected. The men whirled, guns lifting. Ethan's team managed to take out three of the men, but one was left.

Trey. His rifle barrel landed square on Ethan's chest. He was wearing a vest, but at this range it didn't matter. He had one knee on the ground, the other bent in front of him as he'd tried to regain his footing.

"Back the fuck off," Trey shouted, still in that nasal tone. Like he'd been hit in the face. "Or I'll fucking kill this asshole. Drop the rifle. Hands where I can see 'em, Dragon."

"You're going to do it anyway," Ethan grated, lifting his hands and letting the rifle fall. "You've been jonesing for it since you discovered Paisley was with me again."

Trey shoved the barrel harder into the vest. "You're like a fucking cockroach, you know that? I got rid of you once before, took your woman and kid—oh yeah, I knew from the beginning the brat wasn't mine. Took them. Fucked your woman over and over again. How do you like being with her now, knowing I've been there too? I've had my dick all up in that pussy, man. My fingers, my face. Must kill you to know that."

Trey wanted him pissed and reckless, but he wasn't going to get it. "It doesn't, actually. She's a grown woman and she had a sex life before she met me. Don't see why I'd be upset about you. Other than the fact you didn't deserve her, and you hurt her."

"Bitch needed to be taught a lesson. Thinks she's so fucking smart with that library degree."

Stay cool. Say nothing.

"Let my guys go," Trey ordered.

"Sorry, Mick, not happening." It was Ghost who materialized from the darkness.

"Oh man, the legendary Ghost," Trey said. "Ooooh, I'm honored."

He didn't sound honored, of course. He sounded sarcastic as hell.

"Got a bead on your forehead. Who do you think can pull a trigger faster? And even if you beat me to it and kill Dragon, I'm still taking you down. How's that a win?"

"Thanks, Ghost," Ethan said. "Appreciate the love."

Trey chuckled. "That's the thing about Ghost. He doesn't give two shits about you or me or anybody. He'll fucking sacrifice your ass and sleep like a baby. Still think he might care enough to bargain when he hears what I got to say."

"Wouldn't be too sure about that," Ghost said.

"A fucking HOT team in Alabama. With the deputy in charge. Yeah, I wondered about that. A lot. Rumor is you're on a mission. Something earth-shaking. The kind of thing that keeps men up at night trying to figure out how to get control of it."

Ethan's gut turned to ice. He could feel rather than see his team's reaction.

He inched a hand downward while Trey was distracted.

"I am impressed," Ghost said. "Didn't think you'd have the kind of connections that could break into secret servers."

"Oh yeah, I got 'em. Fucking pussies. Money will buy a lot. Not that you'd know that, broke ass bastards." He snorted as he watched Ghost. "You think I'm a problem? There are powerful people who know your name and want to see you go down. Even if you weasel your way out of this, you've still got trouble coming. But I'll tell you this—if I'm going down, I'm taking this asshole with me."

Boom, boom, boom.

"Jesus fucking Christ, Dragon!" Chance yelled. "How much longer were you going to wait?"

Ethan got to his feet, the pistol in his hand smoking. Trey lay on the ground, eyes staring up at nothing. Ethan shot him point blank in the groin, the bullets traveling up through his heart and emerging somewhere around his shoulders. He'd died instantly, which was entirely too good for him.

"I wanted to hear what he had to say."

Ghost lowered his rifle. "Much as I appreciate

knowing he's the one got to our records, you could have done that sooner."

The three men on their knees with their hands over their heads were wide-eyed. Probably thought they were next.

If Ethan had his way, they would be. But no, they'd be bundled up and sent off to Washington for a little interrogation, HOT style. What happened after that, Ethan didn't much care.

"So what was the plan anyway?" he asked them. "And how did you fuckers get involved?"

"Just do what I'm paid to do," one guy said. "Mick calls with a job, I go. He said you were a rogue spec ops team needed dealt with. Didn't like the women being involved, but it was the only way to get you all in one place. There's a bomb in the house, meant to blow when you went inside for the women."

"Hey," Kane said, voice cold. "We could use this. Let's take these fuckers back there along with McCann's body and send them all sky high."

"I like this idea," Ethan said. "A lot. Can we do it? Pretty please?"

Ghost sighed. "Children, children, what have I said about playing with explosives?"

"Not to get caught?" Chance said.

"Not to blow ourselves up?" Blaze added.

Kane chuckled. Ghost sighed.

"No, we aren't blowing these dickheads to smithereens. More because I'd rather not answer questions about the house blowing up than anything. We're pretty close to the Arsenal, and while a lot of folks might think it's the usual exploding shit going on over there, people will figure it out. Then we'll very likely get a visit from our favorite Feds."

"Fine," Ethan said. "But you never let us have any fun."

"You people are weird," one of the men on his knees grumbled.

"Nah, we just have a code of ethics," Blaze told him. "Which is something I'm going to guess *you* people aren't familiar with."

"Can we fucking go now?" Seth asked. "It's hot, I'm getting swamp ass in this tactical gear, and I need to hold my woman."

"Amen, brother," Ethan said. "I'm so fucking done with this shit."

He needed a shower, Paisley and Violet in his arms— and the rest of his life to recover from the fear Trey had nearly succeeded in taking away everything Ethan loved.

40

One month later...

"Mommy! A spider! Come get it!" Violet screamed.

Paisley looked at Ethan. "Oh hell no," he said, shaking his head. "Not me. She's yelling for you."

Paisley sighed as she got to her feet and went to grab the bug catcher she kept in the pantry. Violet was perched on the toilet lid in the bathroom, staring down at the small spider sitting on the floor. Paisley calmly squeezed the handle on the catcher and scooped up the spider.

"There," she said. "Can you come down now? Finish getting dressed?"

"What are you gonna do with it?"

"I'm going to let it outside."

"Noooo, it might come back!"

"Baby, spiders are good for the environment. He'll eat bugs and mosquitoes. That's a good thing."

Violet looked doubtful but Paisley left her and went to the back door. She stepped onto the porch and opened the catcher, dropping the spider onto the ground where it skittered away. Ethan was waiting in the kitchen when she went back inside.

"Big one?" he asked.

"No, a little one. Honestly, how on earth did you ever get through training to be a special ops soldier in the first place? There had to have been spiders in the great outdoors when you trained."

"There were." He shuddered. "I got through it, but I don't have to when you're here."

"And real world missions?"

"Teammates. Usually." He grinned.

"You and your child. I swear. And the two of you want to go camping." She shook her head, laughing.

Ethan gathered her in his arms after she put the bug catcher away. It'd been a month since Trey had taken her and the ladies from the library. They'd made their way through the woods to the road that night, waiting for the men to come for them. Paisley's face had hurt, her head hurt, and she'd started to grow nauseated.

But the men returned with three others, though not Trey, and they went back to town. Emma had examined her, patched her up, pronounced she had a concussion, and given her meds. It wasn't until a few days later when Ethan told her what happened to Trey.

Dead.

She'd heard the words and gone numb. Then she'd been happy and ashamed of herself for it because what kind of person was happy that somebody died?

But she was, and that was on him. He'd been cruel and he'd wanted to kill her. He would have killed Aunt Hettie and Violet if not for Hettie's big, beautiful old house with the hidden passages and secret doors. They'd hidden and stayed safe, and Trey had to move on and abduct her and the women from the library if he wanted his plan to work.

Thankfully, it had not worked.

"It'll be fine. If there are any spiders, you'll handle them for us."

"You're ridiculous."

He nuzzled her ear. "Yep. I love you, Payz. So thankful you're mine."

"I love you too," she sighed. "I'm safe, Ethan. He didn't hurt me."

"I know. I just need to hold you."

Ethan had always been affectionate, but since that night, he'd seemed to be more so. As if he was afraid it was all a dream. He squeezed her and then started to laugh.

"What?" she asked, pushing back to look up at him.

"Sorry. I was thinking of you head-butting Trey in the face and busting his nose. Wish I'd seen it."

Paisley grinned. It'd been scary at the time, but head-butting Trey was turning into a fond memory. "I wish I'd done it sooner. Five years sooner, if I'm honest."

"I wish a lot of things, baby. But we're together now and that's all I need. You and our daughter."

They'd talked about Trey's confession, wondering if he'd been lying, trying to manipulate them by giving them hope that he wasn't in the running to be Violet's father. But then Ethan came home a few days later and told her it wasn't a lie, that Trey had really had a vasectomy. Alex had gotten his military records to confirm it. Trey had a zero sperm count.

As if Violet wasn't daily becoming more and more Ethan's child. The eyes, the love of pizza, the grumpy morning face—which Ethan was still capable of when he didn't get enough sleep—and now the spiders.

He took her arm and lifted her wrist to his mouth, kissed her tattoo. The twin of his. Fire kindled in her belly, flame licking along her limbs and into her core.

"Ethan," she whispered.

His eyes were fire. "I know. I feel it too." He licked the heart and then stepped away.

She could strangle him. "What the heck?"

"We have to go to Aunt Hettie's for lunch in twenty minutes. Or did you forget?"

Paisley's cheeks heated. "Not completely, no. But in the moment, yes."

"Not like we could do anything anyway. Vivi's coming out any minute."

"True. What is taking that child so long? I better check."

Before she could, Violet skipped into the room, blond hair bouncing, cheeks bright. "I'm ready!"

Violet was wearing her princess dress, the pink one that Paisley had found at the thrift shop last week. She'd intended it for a Halloween costume in another couple of months, but she should have known better. Violet wanted to wear it *now*. In fact, she wanted to wear it every day. Paisley had convinced her it was only for special occasions, which meant it came out a couple of times a week rather than daily.

"Lunch with Aunt Hettie is a special occasion," Ethan whispered.

"I know. Vivi, you look pretty."

"Thank you." She twirled and then went to Ethan and held out her arms. "Carry me, Daddy."

He scooped her up. "Got you, baby. You ready for lunch?"

"Yes!"

They walked to Aunt Hettie's since it was only a couple of streets over. The big house held court on a double lot on the corner with trees and flowers and flowering bushes that bloomed profusely. Aunt Hettie greeted them at the door and led them to the big dining room where she'd laid out her silver and china like she was serving royalty.

Which, apparently, meant Violet today.

After they sat down, Hettie picked up her knife and tapped it on her glass. "I have an announcement to make."

Even Violet went quiet.

"I'm moving."

"What? Where are you going? To Fairhope?"

"No, child. I'm moving to Chestnut Street. The house is small and more suited for me. I'm not getting any younger."

"Oh, of course." Paisley looked at Ethan. He shrugged. It wasn't their house and now it never would be. They'd talked about asking to buy it, but they hadn't done it yet. Too many other things to settle first.

"This house is big. It's made for a family. For children. For someone who will love it and care for it the way Horace and I did."

"It's a lovely house," Paisley said. "Somebody will be so pleased. Do you know when you plan to sell?"

They would have to find a new place to live, but that was okay. It would still be in Sutton's Creek. She knew that her man was doing something important here, even if she didn't know exactly what that important thing was. When she'd told him what Trey said about a HOT team, he'd explained what that was and why it was important she not talk about it to anyone other than their small group of friends.

"As soon as you're ready, dear."

"Oh, well, we'll need to look for a place to live, of course, but we can do that right away."

"Dear child," Aunt Hettie said. "I mean that I'm selling to *you*. You and Ethan will buy my house, and I will move into the Craftsman."

"But Uncle John—"

"Lives in Fairhope with his family. He doesn't want this house, dear. He has plenty of money and a life of his own down there. He doesn't need this house and I'm not going to live in it until I'm dead just so he can sell it after I'm gone. It will go to you and Ethan, for a reasonable price, and I will hold the mortgage. Unless you'd rather not?"

She looked at Ethan. He looked stunned. Then a smile bloomed on his face. He'd been a child without a home, and he was a man who worked on homes in his spare time, but he'd never owned one. He knew this house was special, just like she did.

"I think we would, Aunt Hettie. Wouldn't we?"

Ethan's smile lit her world. "We would. Hettie, thank you so much for trusting her to us."

Hettie smiled. "Yes, you understand. This house is a her, and she has a soul. I knew you were right for her. And don't you think it's time you called me aunt?"

"Yes, ma'am, Aunt Hettie."

"Wonderful. Violet, would you like to live here with your mommy and daddy?"

"Yes, peas!"

"Please," Paisley said.

"Please," Violet repeated. "Mommy?"

"Yes, honey?"

"Can I have a kitten when we live here?"

Paisley laughed. And she was relieved, too. At least the child wasn't asking for a pony. Yet.

"Yes, I think you can have a kitten."

"Awesome! I'm going to name it Ethan."

"It might be a girl. Then what?"

Violet blinked. "Miss Rory."

"Well, of course," Paisley said, catching Ethan's eye. He was grinning big, likely thinking of Rory's reaction to having a kitten named after her. These days she would probably cry and blame it on hormones. Which Paisley understood. Hormones were a bitch.

Hours later, when Violet was asleep in her bed, dreaming of kittens (and probably ponies too), Paisley wrapped her legs around Ethan's hips and welcomed him deep inside. They moved together, slowly, kissing, touching, exploring, until the pressure became too great, until he pounded into her while she caught the wave and leaped over the edge, him right behind her.

"We're so good together," she whispered sometime later.

He kissed her throat, her jaw, then licked a nipple. "We were meant to be, Paisley. From the first moment I saw you, something shifted inside me. It never shifted back, even when I thought you'd dumped me. I just covered it up and kept on living."

"I never stopped loving you. I tried, but I couldn't."

"It's over now. We're together." He wrapped his arms around her and held her close.

"We are," she sighed.

They fell asleep like that, tangled together, happy. The next morning when she woke, he was already up, probably in the kitchen fixing coffee. The buzzing of her phone on the nightstand had her reaching for it.

"Yes," she mumbled, not quite ready to get up.

"Paisley?"

"Yes."

"It's Mae. I've got some news."

She listened to her lawyer in disbelief, then hung up and went to find Ethan.

"What is it, baby?" he asked, concern in his voice.

"I just heard from my attorney. Since Trey was killed on a job—" They both knew what the *job* was and how it'd happened, but that wasn't the official version. "—And he didn't have a will for some stupid reason, I'm the sole beneficiary of his estate. But I don't want it, Ethan. I don't want his blood money. I don't want anything that was his."

He came over and wrapped his arms around her, pressed his lips to the top of her head. "You don't have to take it. Or, you do, but you can give it all away. Start a charity for battered women and children. Give it to an orphanage. Literacy. Hell, start a home for homeless kittens. Use his money in ways that would piss him off if he were still alive. Do good, Payz."

She held him for a long while, thinking. And then she pushed away and gazed up at him. "You're wise, you know that?"

"I try." He grinned.

"We're going to do all that. And we're including home- less children on that list, okay?"

His eyes glistened as he nodded. "Sounds perfect, honey."

"Good. Thank you. I feel better now. Is there coffee?"

"Coming right up. Sit down and I'll get it for you."

Paisley sank onto a chair at the kitchen table and watched the birds outside the window flying to the feeder and away again. Nature was so relentlessly beautiful. It made you realize things about yourself. About life.

She nodded, decision made. They would do good things with the money. Wonderful things. Lives would be changed for the better.

Just like hers had been when she moved to Sutton's Creek. She'd found Ethan again, and she'd found friends. She'd found belonging. She loved her job, and even Fern was tolerable these days.

A world of possibility lay before her. All she had to do was take it.

With Ethan. With Violet.

He brought her cup and sat beside her. Then he reached for her hand and they twined fingers while they drank coffee and talked about everything they planned to do today, tomorrow, and for the rest of their lives.

Thank you for reading Ethan and Paisley's story!

Now it's time to set my sights on the final book of the

series, ALEX! You've been asking for Ghost's book for *years*, and now it can be yours!

ORDER ALEX NOW
at www. lynnrayeharris.com

SIGNED COPIES ARE AVAILABLE
at https://shop.lynnrayeharris.com/.

Keep reading for a sneak peek at Alex's book …

SNEAK PEEK AT ALEX

GHOST OPS, BOOK 6

An enemies to lovers, forced proximity, military protector romance from *New York Times* bestselling author Lynn Raye Harris.

Alex "Ghost" Bishop doesn't let people in. Not after a childhood spent isolated and alone, forced to survive on his own terms. Trust is a weapon that can be turned against you, and love is a distraction he can't afford. His team is everything. Everyone else is a risk.

So when FBI agent Diana Corbin pushes her way into his

operation, he resents every moment of it—even when he can't stop thinking about her.

Diana learned the hard way that trust is dangerous. The people you believe will protect you can destroy you instead. She's built her life on proving herself, on never needing anyone, on keeping the world at a careful distance. She doesn't have time for a man who makes her want things she can't have.

But when they find each other undercover in an operation neither should be running, something shifts. Working together becomes inevitable. The denial becomes harder to maintain. And the pull between them —electric, indisputable, terrifying—won't be ignored.

As the mission spirals into danger and their secrets threaten to unravel everything, Alex and Diana discover that sometimes the only person you can trust is the one person you swore you never would. And that love isn't a weakness—it's the only thing that might save them.

BUY ALEX TODAY
at www.lynnrayeharris.com

SIGNED COPIES ARE AVAILABLE
at https://shop.lynnrayeharris.com/

Present day...

He was going to die.

The cold crept through his limbs, numbing his joints, making his fingers and toes clumsy as he stumbled through the snow.

Everything was white. His breath. The trees and mountains and fields.

Ice as far as he could see. Behind him. Before him.

He'd never make it. He'd been stupid to leave. Stupid to try.

"No," he whispered. *"No."*

He stumbled onward, determined. He had to find a way.

Before the sun dropped behind the mountains. Before the temperature dropped another sixty degrees.

And then the wolf howled.

He stopped, his heart in his throat, his head jerking in every direction as he spun where he stood. Where was the wolf?

Another howl joined the first. A third, fourth, and fifth.

And then so many he couldn't count them anymore.

They were coming closer.

He started to run, his heart hammering, his eyes stinging as the moisture froze in them. His breath razored in and out, his blood beating in his ears.

So loud. Too loud to hear the wolves behind him.

He had to find a tree or a cave, somewhere to shelter. Somewhere to stay until the danger passed.

A branch snapped. He threw a look over his shoulder.

The wolf was big, white, with piercing blue eyes. Blood dripped from its teeth as it closed the distance between them.

"No," he panted, struggling onward, fear a cold thing inside that twisted his guts and made his heart leapt into his throat.

He stumbled on a root, his knees buckling, body sprawling in the snow.

The wolf was on him, jaws snapping. He lifted his arms, tried to fight. But the teeth sank into his tender flesh. There was pain, futility, defeat.

He was going to die—

Ghost snapped awake with a start, bolting out of bed and whirling, his pistol in his hand.

Nothing was there. Nothing at all.

Just him. Sweating, the taste of fear sharp and acidic on his tongue, his body aching from the accumulation of old injuries that wouldn't have bothered him just a few years ago.

"Fuck," he muttered, lowering the pistol to his side, and shoving a hand through his damp hair.

What the hell was happening to him?

The dream wasn't new. It was an old dream that happened sometimes when he least expected it. The feelings of helplessness from that time in his life had never completely gone away, and he hated the reminder of them. Hated the weakness.

He sucked in a breath and stalked to the kitchen for a beer. Maybe not the best way to cope, but it's what he was gonna do. The Ghost Ops mission would be over in the next few months. He had to stay focused. Get the job done, save the world, disappear somewhere. Not permanently.

Just long enough to get his shit sorted, stuff this dream back into the dark chasm it'd crawled out of, and figure out what the hell he planned to do with the rest of his life since his options had changed so dramatically when he agreed to this job.

Nothing he couldn't handle though.

Sure, he'd have to leave his team, the life they'd built in Sutton's Creek, and begin somewhere new. He got a pang at the thought, but it was no different than rotating out of one assignment and into another in the military. It's what you did, what you expected.

He was used to being alone. Used to moving on. He had no roots, no home. No family.

It's why he was here. Why they'd picked him to lead Ghost Ops.

He grabbed the beer, popped the cap, and took a long drink. Then he lifted the lid on the laptop he'd left on the counter and scrolled through the news. Not the most relaxing way to spend the early hours, but he wasn't getting back to sleep anyway. So why not?

President Willis smiled on the screen in one of the articles. That wasn't what caught his attention, though. She was overseas on another state visit and suddenly having to deny rumors of a new weapon the US was developing.

He frowned as he scanned the text. Sighed and rubbed his forehead. Fucking Athena Project. It wasn't a weapon, but it could be wielded as one by essentially giving whoever controlled it the ability to attack other countries without fear of retaliation. Nothing was getting through that shield, and that was a problem for people who were being asked to trust that the president wouldn't order a strike if she got pissed enough.

He understood the fear, but he also knew why the US needed the shield. It was revolutionary and meant to protect the citizens of this nation. And if they didn't develop it first, somebody else would. Then what? Could they trust Russia or China not to launch a strike if they had the technology?

He'd spent too many years in the military, too many

years preparing for war scenarios, to believe they wouldn't. The fact the project was actively being targeted by foreign operatives, resulting in Ghost Ops moving to Alabama to protect it, was proof enough.

Ghost snapped the lid shut and went outside, onto the screened-in porch at the back of the house. It was early September, and still hot as fuck during the day. But nights weren't bad at all. Not cool, but not sweltering either.

He liked the heat. Preferred it.

When he'd been nine, his dad had come home one day and announced they were moving to Alaska. His mom had seemed stunned, but she didn't argue. They'd sold everything, packed up what little they'd kept, and drove from Florida to Alaska over the course of three weeks. Mom had been optimistic and tried to make the trip fun. Dad had been jubilant, certain of their future. Certain that taking his family to Alaska was the right move to protect them from all the chaos he believed was coming.

Ghost sipped his beer as the memories crowded for space in his mind. He'd been a kid, excited about bears and caribou and seals. About the adventure of it all.

If only he'd known how bad it would get. How twisted his dad's mind would become.

He hadn't though. Probably a good thing since he'd been fucking nine and couldn't have done anything about it anyway. Some things were better not knowing.

Thanks to those years, he didn't trust many people.

His team. General John "Viper" Mendez.

That was about it.

If he didn't know he was adopted, he might have worried he could crack the way his father had. His parents had been good people, loving, but Desert Storm had triggered something in Calvin Bishop's psyche that never recovered.

Ghost finished the beer and took a shower, then headed up the driveway on foot. One Shot Tactical, the range and training facility he ran with his team, sat on a small rise about a quarter mile from the houses on the property. It was four in the morning and the moon was sliding across the sky, sinking toward sleep.

Some of the guys would arrive early to workout. Others would stay in bed with their women a while longer. He'd picked this team for their lack of relationships of any kind, and yet every last one of them was shacked up and planning to get married when this job was over.

If anyone had asked him back in December, he'd have said there was no way *any* of them would go against orders to form a relationship, let alone *all* of them.

Then again, it was a stupid fucking order some asswipe in Washington had thought was a good idea. Yeah, getting involved made them vulnerable to manipulation, but it wasn't enough of a reason. They were smart and capable—and special operators got married all the time. It wasn't the priesthood.

Honestly, the best way to blend in was to become part of the community, which is why he hadn't come down too hard on any of them. If the suits in Washington wanted to get pissy about it, Ghost would go toe to toe with them.

And if this operation went tits up and the worst happened, it could be the end for all of them anyway. Might as well enjoy life while they could. Fall in love. Feel those highs. Make plans for the future.

Even if the future didn't come.

He entered the range and locked the door behind him, then went down the hall to his office. Inside, he opened the door to what appeared to be a closet but was really a short hallway leading to the secure part of the facility. The SCIF was hardened, a place where classified information could be shared and discussed. When he was inside, doors locked behind him, he typed in his password and pulled up his encrypted messages.

There was one from Viper.

> **Viper:**
> It's a risk. You know that. But I'm with
> you. Do what needs doing. You were
> sent there to do what it takes, not to sit
> around with your thumb up your ass.

Ghost typed a reply, knowing Viper would get it the next time he logged in.

> **Ghost:**
> I'm not asking you to stick your neck
> out. You've got a family to think about.
> Just wanted you to know, in case it goes
> wrong, that I didn't actually go rogue.

He didn't expect a reply to ping back immediately, but he should have known Viper wasn't asleep. The man was always on alert.

> **Viper:**
> I'd know it even without you saying it.
> Time's running out. We still don't know if
> McCann passed your records to anyone,
> which means you need to be fucking
> careful.

Their official military records were sealed, hidden, and replaced with plain Jane assignments and histories that weren't theirs at all. All evidence of the Hostile Operations Team was gone. They were former Army Rangers. Special Forces, but not the kind of elite operators they really were.

Except that Paisley's ex-husband, Trey McCann, had seen them all in Sutton's Creek when he'd been stalking her. Since he'd been a former HOT operator himself, he'd gotten suspicious about their real purpose. He'd paid hackers to break into their files—but had he sold the information to anyone? Or had he died before he got the chance?

They'd never know because Ethan had shot the bastard before McCann could kill him.

Know that, Ghost typed. *I'll be careful.*

> **Viper:**
> You fucking better. I haven't liked
> anything about how this has gone down
> since you boys left here, but it's not up
> to me. I thought it was important or I
> wouldn't have asked you to go.

Ghost scrubbed a hand over his head. He'd made his choice and he wouldn't allow himself to regret it.

> **Ghost:**
> It is important. I'm not sorry we're here.
> But I wouldn't feel right about taking
> action without telling you.

> **Viper:**
> You've told me. Get the job done. Then
> come to Washington and we'll toast
> your success.

*HUA**, he typed. Once he knew Viper had seen it, he deleted the messages and logged off. Viper was deleting the ones on his end as well. Not even Seth "Phantom" King could retrieve them now.

Ghost took out the file on Viktor Dashevsky. All evidence pointed to Dashevsky being behind the attempts to steal the Athena Project's technology and use it for his own evil purposes. He was a Russian oligarch who ran a humanitarian foundation, but that was just a front for his real activities. He trafficked in weapons and humans,

------

* Heard, Understood, Acknowledged.

according to FBI Special Agent Diana Corbin, and he was amassing his own private army for purposes as yet unknown. But it wasn't good, whatever it was. Nobody formed a private army so they could give away more money than they already did.

To protect his humanitarian efforts in war torn countries? Also not likely since UN peacekeepers and private security often went into those places alongside the workers. So what was his objective?

Ghost continued to study the information on the Dashevsky Group's alleged members in northern Alabama, looking for connections he might have missed. Sometimes information had a way of slotting together suddenly when you looked at it, but no such luck yet. His team had been working hard to compile a dossier, but it was thin. Diana claimed she didn't have any more information than they did, but he didn't know if he believed her.

"Shit," he muttered as Diana's face lingered in his mind. Once she was in, it wasn't easy to push her out again. She was there to stay, in all her irritating glory.

He leaned back in his chair and studied the ceiling, thinking about the next steps he needed to take to move this mission along. It didn't help. She didn't fade.

Her long blond hair and sensible pantsuits—navy blue with white shirts, usually—lingered. He'd seen her in jeans, too. Off duty. She was shapely and beautiful, but icy cool. Like a marble statue.

She'd been a thorn in his side since this operation

began, gliding into his range with her partner, Clay Ackerman, and sticking her nose into Ghost Ops business like she had a right. He'd gotten her dismissed and sent to Kentucky, but she'd boomeranged right back again.

Because Diana Fucking Corbin was an Adler. The Adlers had been a fixture on the Washington scene for generations. Their influence and connections ran deep. She'd used those connections to return to her job at Redstone Arsenal.

And now it was ten times worse because she knew who they were and what their mission was. Knew and inserted herself into it. Pissed him off. Because everything he had, he'd worked his ass off for. He didn't know what it was like to be born with a silver spoon in his mouth, or what it felt like to snap his fingers and have shit happen.

When the Smiths had saved him from the hell his life had become in Alaska, they'd given him direction and encouragement, but the work had been up to him. He'd been incredibly far behind when he'd reentered public school, but he'd been driven. Because of that drive, he'd excelled. So much so that he'd gotten into West Point. If not for that, he wouldn't be where he was now.

All Diana had to do was call Uncle Stephen. Or Uncle Don (he assumed the FBI director was like an uncle to her, though they weren't related). And, boom, she got what she wanted.

He couldn't deny that she'd given his team information they'd been able to use—but she was still fucking infuriating. Her privileged existence annoyed him the hell out of him. The way she'd gotten involved in his mission like it was her right made him want to chew nails.

But the fact she made his balls ache? Now that didn't help his attitude in the least.

He hated that she affected him, but he had to admit she did. A man would have to be dead or gay not to notice how beautiful she was. With great tits and an ass he could hold onto.

Ghost growled as he closed the files. Diana Corbin was a walking, talking danger zone, and he wasn't stupid enough to wander into it.

No matter how fun it might be to peel off one of those staid pantsuits and discover the delights underneath.

He left the SCIF* and headed for the small gym they'd built in one of the bigger rooms. Nothing like a hard workout to purge an inconvenient attraction for a woman who'd slap him in cuffs if she got the chance.

And not the fun kind, either.

Want more?
BUY ALEX NOW
at www.lynnrayeharris.com

SIGNED COPIES ARE AVAILABLE
at https://shop.lynnrayeharris.com/

---

* Sensitive compartmented information facility.

BECOME A VIP READER!

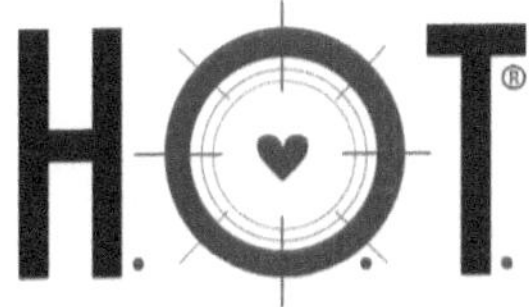

Sign up for Lynn's VIP Reader List at lynnrayeharris.com (or scan the QR code to the right) and never miss a new book or sale and get exclusive content only available to subscribers, including bonus scenes & epilogues!

Lynn sends a weekly email (usually) with fun character take-overs, interviews, or scenes, plus other content, you might enjoy.

SIGN UP TODAY at

https://lynnrayeharris.com/newsletter/

BECOME A HOTTIE!

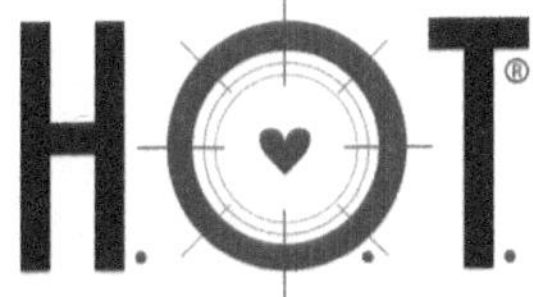

If you love HOT — if you can't wait for the next Special Operator to get his own book — Lynn's Facebook group is the place to be! Discuss all things HOT with fellow readers and fans as well as the author herself.

JOIN TODAY at
https://www.facebook.com/
groups/HOTReadersAndFans/

WHO'S HOT?

HOSTILE OPERATIONS TEAM®
★ STRIKE TEAM 1 ★

Matt "Richie Rich" Girard *(Reckless Heat & HOT Pursuit)*

Sam "Knight Rider" McKnight *(HOT Mess)*

Kev "Big Mac" MacDonald *(Dangerously HOT)*

Billy "the Kid" Blake *(HOT Package)*

Jack "Hawk" Hunter *(HOT Shot)*

Nick "Brandy" Brandon *(HOT Rebel)*

Garrett "Iceman" Spencer *(HOT Ice)*

Ryan "Flash" Gordon *(HOT & Bothered)*

Chase "Fiddler" Daniels *(HOT Protector)*

Dex "Double Dee" Davidson *(HOT Addiction)*

Commander

John "Viper" Mendez *(HOT Valor & A HOT Christmas Miracle)*

Deputy Commander

Alex "Ghost" Bishop (see Ghost Ops, *ALEX*)

Freelance Contractors

Lucinda "Lucky" San Ramos, now MacDonald *(Dangerously HOT)*

Victoria "Vee" Royal, now Brandon *(HOT Rebel)*

Emily Royal, now Gordon *(HOT & Bothered)*

HOSTILE OPERATIONS TEAM®
★ STRIKE TEAM 2 ★

Jake "Harley" Ryan *(HOT Witness)*

Cade "Saint" Rodgers *(HOT Angel)*

Sky "Hacker" Kelley *(HOT Secrets)*

Dean "Wolf" Garner *(HOT Justice)*

Malcom "Mal" McCoy *(HOT Storm)*

Noah "Easy" Cross *(HOT Courage)*

Jax "Gem" Stone *(HOT Shadows)*

Ryder "Muffin" Hanson *(HOT Limit)*

Zane "Zany" Scott *(HOT Honor)*

Freelance Contractor

Bliss Bennett *(HOT Secrets)*

THE HOT SEAL TEAM

Dane "Viking" Erikson *(HOT SEAL)*

Remy "Cage" Marchand *(HOT SEAL Lover)*

Cody "Cowboy" McCormick *(HOT SEAL Rescue)*

Cash "Money" McQuaid *(HOT SEAL Bride)*

Alexei "Camel" Kamarov *(HOT SEAL Redemption)*

Adam "Blade" Garrison *(HOT SEAL Target)*

Ryan "Dirty Harry" Callahan *(HOT SEAL Hero)*

Zach "Neo" Anderson *(HOT SEAL Devotion)*

Corey "Shade" Vance

Freelance Contractor

Miranda Lockwood, now McCormick *(HOT SEAL Rescue)*

BLACK'S BANDITS
HOT HEROES FOR HIRE:
MERCENARIES

Jace Kaiser *(Black List)*

Brett Wheeler *(Black Tie)*

Colton Duchaine *(Black Out)*

Jared Fraser *(Black Knight)*

Ian Black *(Black Heart)*

Tyler Scott *(Black Mail)*

Dax Freed *(Black Velvet)*

Thomas "Rascal" Bradley

Jamie Hayes

Finn McDermot

Roman Rostov

Mandy Parker (Airborne Ops)

Melanie (Reception)

Freelance Contractor

Angelica "Angie" Turner *(Black Out)*

GHOST OPS

Blaze "Shadow" Connolly *(BLAZE)*

Chance "Wraith" Hughes *(CHANCE)*

Seth "Phantom" King *(SETH)*

Kane "Demon" Fox *(KANE)*

Ethan "Dragon" Snow *(ETHAN)*

Alex "Ghost" Bishop *(ALEX)*

ABOUT THE AUTHOR

Lynn Raye Harris is a Southern girl, military wife, wannabe cat lady, and horse lover. She's also the *New York Times* and *USA Today* bestselling author of the HOSTILE OPERATIONS TEAM® Series of military romances, and 20 books about sexy billionaires for Harlequin.

A former finalist for the Romance Writers of America ® 's Golden Heart Award and the National Readers' Choice Award, Lynn lives in Alabama with her handsome former-military husband, one fluffy princess of a cat, and a very spoiled American Saddlebred horse who enjoys bucking at random in order to keep Lynn on her toes.

Lynn's books have been called "exceptional and emotional," "intense," and "sizzling" — and have sold in excess of 4.5 million copies worldwide.

Connect with Lynn Raye Harris online!

lynnrayeharris.com & hostileoperationsteam.com

facebook.com/AuthorLynnRayeHarris

instagram.com/lynnrayeharris

tiktok.com/@lynnrayeharrisauthor

goodreads.com/lynnrayeharris

bookbub.com/authors/lynn-raye-harris

9 798891 170995